Phoenix Rising Temptation

The Trybrid Chronicles, Volume 2

Rebecca A. Nagy

Published by Rebecca A. Nagy, 2025.

Copyright

Author's notes

Phoenix Rising: Temptation continues the exploration of science fiction, metaphysics, fantasy, and romance while weaving together imaginary and real-life experiences with teachings from the Ancient Wisdom tradition, which may also be referred to as the Ageless Wisdom Teachings or the Wisdom Teachings. While this narrative further develops scenarios, spiritual teachers, historical figures, prophecies, and organizations that may be inspired by or based on actual people, events, or entities, readers should approach the story through the lens of artistic expression within its genre.

The interpretations and viewpoints presented remain solely those of the author and should not be taken to represent the positions of any referenced person or organization.

As with the first book, readers are invited to engage with this continuation as a fictional journey examining universal themes of spirituality and eternal love, appreciating how the interplay of fact and fantasy enriches the storytelling. Those drawn to explore the underlying concepts more deeply are encouraged to consult authoritative sources and pursue personal investigation—many resources for which can be found on the author's website.

The terms "white" and "black" refer to energetic qualities of purity and spiritual integrity rather than race or cultural identity.

The White Circle is a group of elite celestials, human, and devic beings who have dedicated themselves to the spiritual advancement of Earth and those who are native to Earth. This group is derived specifically from my own mystical experiences with an entity that introduced himself as "Master of the White Circle."

The Masters of Wisdom are synonymous with what Alice Bailey calls "The Hierarchy" or "The Great White Brotherhood." They are highly evolved humans who work behind the scenes to guide planetary evolution.

The Dark Brotherhood is synonymous with evil and the left-hand path.

The Shift of the Ages is a transitional period between astrological ages. Earth is currently in the shift from the Age of Pisces to the Age of Aquarius, which in esoteric astrology occurs approximately every 26,000 years. This shift represents a movement from the Piscean qualities of belief, spirituality, and hierarchical authority to the Aquarian values of humanitarian concerns, innovation, and collective consciousness. The transition marks not just a change in celestial positioning but also a profound transformation in human consciousness and societal structures.

For more information about the Ageless Wisdom and Rebecca's spiritual teachings,
please visit: rebeccanagyauthor.com[1]

---

1. https://www.rebeccanagyauthor.com

Acknowledgments

This second book of the Trybrid Chronicles is inspired by my dreams, inner plane experiences, and past-life work since beginning my own spiritual quest for truth. While partly a work of fiction, the past-life scenes are meticulously researched for historical accuracy.

Many of the ideas in this narrative stem from discussions I've had over the past two decades with my spiritual students and colleagues about the illusions perpetuated through social media and online conspiracy theories that often defy logic. This book is my attempt to explore those themes through the lens of Ageless Wisdom from both Eastern and Western traditions.

Additionally, a real-life prophecy shared with me by my former astrologer, Steve Nelson (1947–2014), speaks of a ley line connecting Charlotte, North Carolina, to the United States Capitol—one with the potential to change the world. You can read more about him and his work in an article from 2010 on my author's website.

I continue to owe a deep debt of gratitude to my parents, Richard and Rita Nagy, who nurtured a creative child who lived in a fantasy world and spoke to the entities that inhabited it.

I would also like to recognize my spiritual mentors and teachers: Reverend Ellen Resch, Reverend Dr. Joseph Vaughn, Reverend Dr. Carol Parrish-Harra, and my advisors at Sancta Sophia Seminary, Reverend Katie Anne Yarborough, Reverend Marjorie Stuth, and Reverend Sarah Brown. They taught me that true spiritual growth demands tough love, and their guidance helped shape my path.

My editor, Melisa Graham, truly took me to the next level as an author in challenging me to ensure accuracy in my use of metaphysical and esoteric concepts, while introducing me to the *Chicago Manual of Style*.

My sincere appreciation to Brad Swift, a fellow visionary fiction author, mentor, and writing coach, whose support and encouragement have deepened my purpose as an author.

A warm thanks to my circle of spiritual sisters, Karmic Astrologer Susan Reynolds, Reverend Constance Baldwin, Diana Mahaffey, Uni Smith, and Heather Scovel, who have put up with me having mostly two topics of conversation for the past three years: "my book" and "my book." Their steadfast encouragement was instrumental in convincing me to soldier on, even as I struggled with impostor syndrome while writing this second book.

Gratitude is also extended to my beta readers, Patrick Mullin, Laura Sutherland, Diana Mahaffey and Steve Long who also challenged me to rethink and reconsider those places that needed clarification and/or improvement.

Lastly, my deepest gratitude goes to my longtime spiritual sister, Glenda Bradshaw. Our shared journey, which began years ago in New York City, has taken us on extraordinary adventures—from exploring the crystal mines of Arkansas and experiencing "first contact" to visiting the sacred caves of Boynton Canyon in Sedona, Arizona. Together, we have wandered through countless metaphysical bookstores, both in the United States and abroad, where books seemed to leap from the shelves, and Native American shamans appeared in the most unexpected places. And still, the journey continues. Thank you, my dear friend, for walking this remarkable path with me.

Part I: Time and Time Again

Life is designed to knock you down. It will knock you down time and time again, but it doesn't matter how many times you fall—it matters how many times you get back up.
Lilly Singh

Prologue: What Has Gone Before

Beneath the incandescent curtain of stars stretched across the Aquarian sky, Ayesha (now reborn as Cassandra Oberon, or simply Cassie to friends) found herself amidst a communion of beings that represented celestial, devic, and human lineage. Her eyes, a blend of ancient wisdom and youthful curiosity, scanned the six figures beside her. Each one was a facet of divinity, a unique representation of virtues sculpted by the cosmic architect. They were souls with destinies entangled by an unseen hand; each had answered the heavens' clarion call to converge at this momentous juncture: the advent of the Aquarian Era.

Cassandra's fingers synchronized with her thoughts, creating an aethereal keyboard that shaped the fabric of reality, a holographic tableau in the astral night. Her motions were fluid and swift, the tactile echo of her terrestrial skills as a computer master. The spectral screen flickered to life, manifesting symbols of the light, representative of her trybrid heritage.

A shudder radiated through the cosmos, as if reality itself quivered in anticipation. Across the astral panorama, the Dark Brotherhood, ever vigilant in its quest to enshroud the world in chaos, had discovered Cassandra's earthly location. The brotherhood's malicious tendrils sought to tighten around her newly awakened soul, endeavoring to crush her like a nascent star before it could fully ignite.

For Cassandra, the challenges ahead would be a labyrinth, one she would navigate not just as an Aquarian Avatar, but also as a symbol of the new evolutionary frontier. She embodied both the ancient karma of Ayesha and the emerging potential of a celestial-human-fae amalgam, not just *a* trybrid but *the* Trybrid. Her life had become the crucible where prophecy, destiny, and free will would clash and coalesce.

Karim, the warrior beside her, met her gaze, his eyes alight with profound understanding, as if peering into the depths of her soul. In that fleeting moment of connection, he summoned his armor and sword, encasing Cassandra in intangible yet powerful shields of protection.

Next to the warrior, the healer's aura thrummed with life in perfect synchronization. Seraphina unleashed undulating currents of restorative energy, creating a resonant web that flowed seamlessly through the unseen spiritual dimensions.

Together, warrior and healer formed an imposing nexus of defense and healing, each amplifying the other's abilities in a display of synchronous might and compassion.

The other avatars—Marcus, the seer; Yirribindi, the sage; An-Mei, the mystic; and Teodor, the bard—each revealed their unique gifts in an unfolding tapestry of talents. They were the chosen, the seven prophesied in ancient scrolls that would lead humanity through the challenges ahead to emerge triumphantly into the Age of Aquarius, a time of unprecedented peace.

They stood as an indomitable force, etching their will upon the cosmos.

For Cassandra, the transformation was complete. She was ready to face the looming threats, armed with newfound strength and a resolve born from lifetimes of sacrifice and learning.

Thus, the seven avatars were now primed to break the fetters of darkness and guide humanity through the turning tides of fate. They were the living symbols of an age-old prophecy now revealed, a celestial decree awaiting its moment of cosmic vindication.

As they dispersed back into their earthly roles, Cassandra felt a newfound weight upon her shoulders, yet also an ineffable lightness. She was both Ayesha, burdened with the karma of past deeds, and Cassandra, the beacon of humanity's next evolutionary leap.

But the Dark Brotherhood had other plans and had resurrected the ancient evil embodied in the form of one of their most powerful dark lords, who was determined to have Cassandra by his side for his own evil designs. His lust for her and for her power had dogged her soul lifetime after lifetime, for he had loved her from the start, if love it could be called. Now the stakes were at their highest, as the cosmic crescendo began to play, and the final days began to loom. So he had taken her by force to his undersea fortress to begin his conquest of the Earth. She would be by his side, or she would be destroyed.

However, fate was fluid, molded in a trial of choices, sacrifices, and indomitable will. Her true soulmate would move both the heavens and the earth to free her from this ancient evil. United, they would join with the Aquarian Avatars and the intergalactic forces to push back the darkness so that humanity would not just survive but thrive.

With the intricate tapestry of their united destinies now illuminated against the backdrop of the stars, they were ready for the Shift of the Ages—the transition from the Age of Pisces to the Age of Aquarius. Even in the darkest hour, on the brink of chaos, the ultimate evolution of Scorpio energy would rise. This was not just about power; it was about transformation—the death of the old and the birth of the new. Just as the Phoenix must burn to be reborn, so too must the world endure its own crucible of change, from the mystic heart of the South to the nation's crown. None of them could have imagined just how literal that transformation would be.

Chapter 1: Underwater Enclave

The grip on her throat tightened, cutting off her breath.

Cassie gasped, her hands clawing at the invisible force crushing her windpipe. The world spun in a sickening blur—a vortex of cold saltwater and flickering lights—pulling her down, down, down. Her gut clenched, warning her of the ominous journey ahead. She tried to maintain her composure as they plummeted, but all she perceived was a nightmare-like drop into a bottomless abyss.

She kicked wildly, her body twisting in the suffocating grip of an unseen force. Somewhere above—miles above now—her life still existed. Her home in Charlotte. Her mission. Her fellow avatars. The World Peace Meditation. All of it was slipping away like sand through her fingers.

A voice, deep and dark as the ocean itself, curled into her mind. *Fighting is pointless, my love.*

She knew that voice.

She had heard it across lifetimes.

She desperately wanted to take a deep breath, but the icy hand against her neck trapped her. His other arm around her waist further constrained her movements. His overpowering desire for her was evident, and she struggled to suppress disgust.

Sirkan.

In that nightmarish moment, the weight of cosmic destiny bore down on Cassie. It felt as though the universe itself conspired against her, and a sense of doom threatened to consume her. She knew she had to fight back, to break free from his hateful hold and reclaim control over her own fate. With every ounce of strength, she mustered the will to resist, seeking the slightest opportunity to overturn their roles and reclaim her own power and purpose.

"It's no use struggling, girl." Sirkan's voice dripped with sadistic triumph. "Your powers will be useless where I am taking you. I have waited millennia for this. Nothing and no one will stop us now. You are mine and will always be mine."

"Hell no, you bastard," she spat, her voice barely escaping her lips as she teetered on the edge of his deadly embrace.

He jerked her head back even farther, cutting off her ability to speak. She couldn't breathe. Couldn't focus. *Get a grip, girl*, she thought. *You know what to do.*

Then, suddenly, it was over.

She slammed into a solid floor. Cold metal. The dizzying effects of the abyss had vanished, but the impact jarred her bones like a marionette cut from its strings.

She was no longer falling.

She was somewhere else.

The *absence* of motion sent terror coursing through her veins. Her knees wobbled, but the suffocating grip around her throat refused her even the luxury of collapsing.

Her resistance waned, and she allowed herself to go limp, a calculated move she had employed before when he had first taken her after the fall of Atlantis. Memories of their dark past, of power and submission, flashed through Cassie's mind. This dance had played out across countless lifetimes. *But not in this life! By the Radiant One, not in this one!*

Her karmic journey on Earth was nearing its end, and she refused to let him drag her back onto the left-hand path. Amidst the chaos of the moment, she fought to regain her composure, searching for clarity amidst the turmoil. Months of training and discipline had prepared her for this very test. She closed her eyes, blocking out the whirlwind of energy that still engulfed their descent. She needed to think, to find that inner calm that would fortify her against his wicked schemes. *Breathe.*

Slowly, she opened her eyes, and a gasp escaped her lips involuntarily. The sight before her was straight from the pages of Jules Verne's wildest imagination. Damp air swirled around her, filling her nostrils with a peculiar combination of sea air and a faintly antiseptic scent as she took in the surreal scene.

They were on the bridge of a submerged ship of obvious celestial design. Its somehow familiar structure and ornate metalwork-framed portals revealed a mesmerizing seascape beyond. Aethereal lights, in shades of green and blue, danced in the water, creating an otherworldly ambiance. Her eyes glimpsed graceful sea creatures among the aquatic wonders, making the scene even more otherworldly. It felt familiar in some way. Her eyes widened as she absorbed the cold, hard reality of her captivity. The underwater chamber was a sanctuary of darkness, devoid of warmth, devoid of hope. The type of sanctuary that Sirkan relished.

"Welcome home, my love," Sirkan purred, his warm breath brushing against her ear. His grip around her waist remained firm, but he removed his hand from her neck, much to her relief. Finally letting her go, he paced the chamber, tracing his fingers across the sharp runes that adorned the walls. "You will fulfill your true purpose now, free of those imbeciles of the White Circle. You are my true queen, my consort. We will realize once more our complete dominance over this world."

Cassie glared at him. "I'm not your consort, and I'm not your pawn. Not anymore."

Sirkan paused, studying her. "Ah, but you were, Cassandra. And the memories linger within you. You can't deny it."

Her eyes narrowed. "I've moved on."

He smirked, activating a holographic interface that projected vivid images around them.

Cassie found herself enveloped in a desert landscape, the pyramids serving as sentinels against the horizon. She was dressed as an Egyptian high priestess, her garments embroidered with occult symbols that resonated with potent energies. Beside her stood Sirkan, dressed as a high priest of dark arts.

"Do you remember, Cassandra? The power we wielded. The love we shared." Sirkan's voice whispered in her ear, even as his past incarnation stood beside her in the memory. The power they'd wielded was immense, intoxicating. "We were gods."

Her pulse thundered. The memory called to her, seductive and terrible. The flashback disintegrated, and they were back in the undersea chamber, but the weight of the past hung heavy.

"I remember the tyranny. The suffering we caused," she spat back, clenching her fists.

"But you cannot deny the exhilaration, the control. You were a dark priestess, second only to me. And still, you resist my offer to share power once again. It is … disappointing."

Cassie's eyes locked onto his. "I also remember breaking free from you, escaping your poisonous influence. Finding a new path."

He grinned menacingly. "And yet here you are, back in my grasp. Fate is a relentless hunter, my love."

"Deep down, you know you loved the power, the dominion," Sirkan taunted, his feline eyes gleaming like shards of citrine.

"Power is just a tool, Sirkan," Cassie retorted. "It's how you use it that defines you. And I've found a new way." The room darkened, as if to challenge her, yet her voice remained steady. "I'm no longer that naive little girl you tried to manipulate at my Aunt Isla's Unseelie Court. My power comes from a source that you'll never understand, one that's grounded in wisdom and compassion."

He snarled, his composure cracking for the first time. "You reject your destiny, Cassandra, reject *us*! Our power could have transcended worlds, epochs! We were gods!"

"We were tyrants," she countered, her voice unwavering. "And I've learned that true power is used in service to others, not to dominate them."

Sirkan stared at her, his gaze piercing. "You may deny your past, Cassandra, but you can't escape it. It's part of who you are."

"And that's why I must stop you, Sirkan," Cassie said. "Because I've seen the darkness, and I know how to fight it. I won't let you drag the world down the path we once walked. Never again."

Sirkan's eyes narrowed. "Then you'll die a fool's death."

"Better a fool fighting for what's right than a queen ruling over a world of wrongs," she countered.

The tension was electric, the room pulsing with energies both dark and light, each vying for dominance.

Cassie straightened, lifting her chin. "I don't belong to you, Sirkan. I never did. And I sure as hell won't start now."

As Sirkan left the chamber in a fury, Cassie whispered to herself, reaffirming her newfound purpose. "I will defeat you once and for all."

Chapter 2: Chaos in Charlotte

"Get the mundanes away!" someone shouted, their voice strained over the deafening roar of the wind. By *mundanes* they meant the unfortunate humans with no magical abilities and no defenses against the dark power whirling around them.

Marcus Castoldi, one of the seven Aquarian Avatars, scanned the chaos for the voice's source as he rushed toward Raziel, Cassandra Oberon's angelic guardian.

Raziel turned sharply, his ice-blue eyes narrowing at Marcus. "You do not want to be here."

Stunned, Marcus froze. *I do believe you're right,* he thought, realizing he had fulfilled his purpose. His work was done. With a swift motion, he opened a portal, abandoning the guise of "Marcus the avatar," and retreated into the darkness, disappearing from the scene.

The World Peace Meditation at the intersection of Trade and Tryon Streets in Charlotte, North Carolina, had descended into utter chaos. Just moments earlier, the participants had been seated in orderly concentric circles at the city's busiest crossroads. Now, their peaceful intentions were replaced by panic as they scrambled to escape the madness.

The event had been planned for months. It was more than just a symbolic meditation; it was a coordinated spiritual effort meant to unite diverse belief systems and shift the energy of the powerful ley line running between Charlotte and the United States Capitol. The gathering was the brainchild of Cassandra Oberon, the seventh Aquarian Avatar, working under the cover of an ordinary college student at Queens University. She had developed a meditation practice to be released worldwide, designed to raise humanity's consciousness and shield people from subliminal programming spreading across social media and gaming platforms.

They had chosen this specific date—the full moon of Aries, a time of esoteric significance marking the true start of the New Year—to harness the moon's energy in their effort to foster peace on a national scale.

Organizing such a massive event in the heart of Charlotte's bustling uptown was no small feat. The city had rerouted traffic for the day, barricading the intersection and filling it with volunteers in white armbands. Banners promoting peace fluttered in the breeze, hanging from nearby office buildings. The crowd was as diverse as the city itself: Elderly women in saris sat next to tattooed millennials; monks from the local Buddhist center meditated beside small business owners, college students, and professors; and clergy from multiple faiths circled the perimeter, chanting quietly.

For a time, the energy of the gathering felt almost alive—a charged stillness settling over the crowd, as if the entire city held its breath. The distant murmur of traffic faded, replaced by an eerie quiet, thick with anticipation. A pulse of raw power shimmered through the air, thrumming in their bones like a plucked string, resonating with the ley line beneath them.

Then the world ruptured.

A deafening crack split the silence, and the very fabric of reality seemed to twist. The air convulsed. A force unseen but unmistakable tore through the intersection with merciless hunger. A shockwave slammed into the gathered hundreds, sending bodies staggering, shrieks rising as people clutched at each other for balance. Papers, debris, and loose fabric were yanked skyward, spiraling into a furious current. The atmosphere itself had turned predatory.

The howling winds escalated into a monstrous force, pulling at hair, at clothing, at breath. Some tried to run, but the unseen force dragged them back, relentless, insatiable. Streetlights flickered and groaned. Glass shattered. The crossroads, once a place of unity, had become a battleground between forces beyond human comprehension.

Only then did someone shout the word—*Vortex!*—naming the nightmare as it raged, swallowing the light.

Amid the turmoil, the remaining five avatars moved swiftly to shepherd the crowd away from the vortex, preventing a stampede. Across the street, members of the White Circle worked frantically, casting cloaking spells to obscure the true nature of the event from the mundane onlookers. The lingering crowd, dazed and bewildered, began to lose clarity of what they had just witnessed. The magic seeped into their minds, blurring memories, reducing what should have been an extraordinary event into the memory of a bizarre, inexplicable weather phenomenon and nothing more.

But those attuned to the deeper forces at play felt the sharp disruption in the energy of the ley line, the vibrations still humming ominously through the bones of the city. Members of the White Circle exchanged worried glances, sensing the ripple effects of the vortex. The absence of Cassandra Oberon, the Trybrid avatar, was unmistakable.

As sirens wailed in the distance, growing louder by the second, Artemus, the leader of the White Circle, remained silent. His amber eyes stayed fixed on the spot where the vortex had opened and was threatening to expand. His gaze shifted to the remaining Aquarian Avatars, who were now adding their energies to guiding the terrified crowd away from the chaos. They moved with practiced precision, their magics subtly calming the masses. But fear clung to the air, replacing the peace that had once saturated the intersection. The other members of the White Circle in attendance, along with white witches and celestials, had formed an energetic perimeter around the intersection.

The meditators, their hopes of peace now a distant memory, were driven by sheer survival instinct as they fled the scene. Their dream of using the ley line to create a web of peace across key power points in the nation had been utterly shattered. The vortex's destructive hunger had consumed everything they had intended to channel.

The Dark Brotherhood had succeeded. Its mission wasn't just to disrupt the meditation; it was to break the energetic link of peace and capture its key player, Cassandra Oberon.

But even in the wake of this destruction, one question hung like a bitter aftertaste: *Who had taken her?*

SIOBHAN SINCLAIR AND Master Elena, two powerful figures from different realms, stood side by side at the center of the crossroads, united in purpose. "We need to close this vortex," Siobhan said, her voice steady yet tinged with urgency. "It looks like it may lead to some kind of dimensional rift, and we could very well be pulled into its depths."

"And the whole city along with us," Elena agreed. "It is spinning faster and expanding rapidly. We need to pull out all stops and bring in reinforcements from the Devic Kingdom. I believe Earth's elementals will serve well here."

Siobhan nodded.

Elena, her expression determined said. "Their power is unparalleled, and this vortex is unlike anything we've encountered. We need their ancient wisdom and strength."

Siobhan Sinclair, the "Lady of the Glen," was a white witch from the Devic Kingdom and a member of the White Circle. She used her expertise in the natural and magical realms and conjured a protective dome of mystical energy around the area. Standing alongside her was Master Elena, a founder of the White Circle and one of the original celestials who had come to the planet millennia ago to aid in teaching an awakening humanity. Elena was from the Sirius star system and was revered as the Wisdom Keeper, a guardian of ancient and powerful knowledge. Siobhan nodded, fully grasping the gravity of the situation. She closed her eyes, concentrating her thoughts and energy. "I will contact the elemental lords of the four directions. Their control over earth, air, fire, and water will stabilize the vortex."

They stood in silence for a moment, gathering their strength for the task ahead. Then they each began their invocations.

Siobhan pointed her hands towards the earth, releasing energy through her palms. Her voice rose in a chant, melodic and powerful, calling forth the elemental lords:

Ancient devas, spirits of grace,

Join us now in this chaotic space.
With your elemental might combined,
Help us heal the rifts that bind.
In the name of the Glen, I call thee near.
In unity, we face what we most fear.
Lend us your power. Let your presence be shown.
In this crucial hour, let our victory be known.
Lords of the Devic Kingdom, hear my call,
Elemental powers, great and small.
From the Glen's heart, I summon thee.
Lend your strength to set this realm free.

Elena then raised her hands toward the heavens. Her words, ancient and lilting, reached out to the distant stars, seeking the wisdom of the Sirius elders:

O star elders, blessed triad, ancient and wise,
Hear my call through the cosmic skies.
From Sirius' radiant, shimmering light,
Lend us your power and wisdom on this fraught night.
Through the void, let your energies cascade.
With your cosmic might, come to our aid.
Seal this rift, this chaotic breach.
Restore the balance, we beseech.
Triad elders, in you our trust we place.
Illuminate us with your ancient grace.
In unity, our voices we raise.
Guide us through this transformative maze.

Their voices melded in the aethereal incantation, celestial syllables and earthy chants weaving an intricate tapestry of sound that filled the air. Each word was a prayer, drawing forth the potent magic inherent in their unique heritages.

The surrounding air began to shimmer with energy, the ground vibrated, and a gentle breeze stirred. A sense of ancient power started to build. The elemental lords and the triad of celestial elders—one from Sirius, one from the Pleiades, and one from Arcturus—merged their energies into those of Master Elena and Siobhan, creating a luminous web of light that stretched across the intersection like a protective dome. It pulsed with a cosmic frequency, vibrating with the knowledge of eons, as if the very stars had descended to shield the city from the encroaching darkness.

The barrier stretched out and enveloped the ever-growing funnel cloud of destruction. The ominous vortex began to writhe and contort as if in agony when touched by the magic-infused light. But the funnel cloud of black energy was pushing them back, slowly but surely, the tendrils of chaos and darkness gaining momentum.

Seraphina, the Aquarian Avatar from Ireland, joined them. "We need Tatiana!" she shouted. The air crackled, and Tatiana, the white witch from London, stepped out of a portal onto Tryon Street right beside Siobhan. "Did you think you could have a cosmic gathering without inviting me?" she quipped, blending humor with urgency.

With Ian MacGregor, Siobhan's cousin, leading the way, members of Tatiana's coven emerged. They formed a circle around the perimeter of the intersection, their energies resonating in the air. Their hands, each acting as a conduit of power, connected the circle's points like links in an unbreakable chain. Streams of luminous energy from the triad and elemental lords joined them in an energetic sequence of power as they pushed back the darkness with coordinated gestures. Auras merged, and powers mingled. Strength coalesced.

For a moment, the darkness wavered uncertainly.

But it was far from defeated. A cataclysmic roar shattered the air, as if the sky itself were violently cleaved by an unseen, colossal force. Violent flares of electromagnetic energy erupted from the vortex's core. Three searing tendrils lanced out, striking three of Tatiana's coven members. They screamed, buckling under the sudden onslaught.

The darkness did not back down. Flashes of sizzling energy erupted from the core of the vortex, striking two more of Tatiana's coven. With a roar of defiance, she redoubled her efforts, and searing lightning flashed into the black energy. The stench intensified in the surrounding air, causing the forces of light to choke and gag.

But they persevered.

Then a battle cry resounded around them as Master Artemus flashed into their midst, shoulder to shoulder with the warrior priest of Sirius, Manu Abulafia. The infusion of their power intensified the circle, and they all leaned into the cosmic struggle, a unified front against the relentless dark.

A sonic boom. Then an eerie silence.

The battle ceased.

Siobhan and Elena lowered their arms. The celestial triad and the elemental lords withdrew, their energies fading like the last traces of twilight. As they ascended back to their respective realms, the air grew lighter, the weight of their presence gently lifting from the Earth. A quiet reverence filled the space they left behind, a reminder of the delicate balance they had restored. Elena and Siobhan, still connected to the lingering threads of cosmic power, exchanged a look of weary gratitude, knowing the battle was not yet over, but this victory, however fleeting, had bought them precious time. Yet, as the triad's light fully dissipated and the elemental lords returned to their ancient slumbers, the sense of foreboding lingered.

Joyful whoops echoed through the circle while dazed faces absorbed the magnitude of the victory. And then reality crashed into them, like a freight train.

Cassandra was gone.

Manu stood bereft at the center of Trade and Tryon, holding out his hands, palms down, searching for an energetic clue as to who—or what—had caused this disaster. "I can't sense Cassandra at all. There is only a dark, cloying energy here. It is unfamiliar to me."

Tatiana and Master Elena joined him, each using their hands as they would dowsing rods. Several minutes went by as they circled the area.

"Nothing," they said.

"It must have been a dimensional rift, and she is no longer on the earthly plane," said Manu. "I'll talk to Artemus. We will begin searching with the *Eridu*, my mother ship. We *will* find her!"

"In the meantime, damage control," said Master Elena. "We need a cover story for the mundanes as to what happened here."

Siobhan said, "I will visit with the grand master of the Masonic Lodge. He has a long reach into the media. Perhaps a little tornado touched down?"

"Perfect," nodded Master Elena.

Chapter 3: Dark Messiah

Seated behind the Resolute desk, President Conroe Soter wore a self-satisfied grin as he studied the wall of screens. The montage displayed dozens of live feeds: college students hunched over gaming consoles, their pupils dilating rhythmically as hidden code pulsed beneath vibrant graphics; office workers scrolling mindlessly through social media feeds, unknowingly absorbing the fractal patterns embedded in seemingly innocent memes; families gathered around smart televisions, their expressions blank as neural-triggering sequences flashed imperceptibly between frames of popular streaming shows. On several monitors, real-time data streamed in—brain wave patterns synchronizing across disparate populations, behavioral modification metrics climbing steadily upward, and countdown timers for the next phase of mass deployment.

"Your results have outstripped even my wildest expectations," he said. "The subliminal prompts we've laced into the visual feeds at the rallies and across digital platforms have woven their spell."

Dhawan returned the smile with a sly smirk and a reverent bow. "Under the guidance of the Technomancer, and soon with the addition of the Trybrid to our ranks, we will become an invincible force." He studied Soter, who had taken to dressing in all black, looking every inch the "dark messiah" he purported to be.

"Yeah, I want to know more about that. In the meantime," Soter turned to his chief of staff, Katherine "Kate" Mendez, who hovered by the door leading into the hallway, "ask the others to join us."

Kate quickly opened the door and ushered in the president's cabinet. The sixteen members, led in by Vice President Jessica Stewart, gathered around Soter.

Soter stood, his imposing height of six-foot-four towering above the gathered assembly, his charcoal eyes reflecting a fire fueled by a vision only he could see. Around him, the select group of advisors waited in silence, their expressions a mixture of awe and apprehension. They had seen that the world outside was a maelstrom of information, misinformation, and digital skirmishes, all hidden beneath the veneer of everyday life.

"Ladies and gentlemen," Soter began, his voice resonating with a chilling calm that belied the chaos he was orchestrating, "we stand at the dawn of a new era of warfare. We do not fight it with guns and bombs, but with information and emotion." He paused for dramatic effect.

"The strategy is simple yet powerful. By controlling the digital sphere, we incite outrage; we provoke division; we harvest the raw energy of mundane humans' anger," Soter continued, a shadow of a smile playing on his lips. "Every click, every share, every heated comment fuels our cause and fills our coffers."

He motioned to Dhawan. "Dhawan is the envoy of our newest ally. I will let him explain."

"Our Technomancer has mastered the art of rage farming, a digital alchemy turning raw human emotion into a new kind of power," Dhawan began. "This rage is a valuable treasure, more potent than oil and more abundant than uranium. We have mined it, refined it, and now we wield it. A populace divided is easier to control, easier to direct. With each scandal, each controversial decree, we stoke the fires of public outrage, creating a smoke screen for our true intentions."

Soter nodded appreciatively, watching as an algorithm categorized millions of comments into emotional vectors, harvesting and redirecting the most volatile responses through their network of bots and compromised influencer accounts. The viral spread of engineered outrage followed predictable patterns, each eruption of public fury precisely timed to coincide with another phase of their subliminal programming.

"The beauty of it," Dhawan added, "is that they willingly expose themselves to our influence. Every indignant share, every furious comment, every minute spent doom-scrolling—they're simply opening themselves wider to our embedded triggers. Their righteous anger blinds them to the real manipulation occurring beneath the surface."

"What is a *technomancer*?" The question came from Secretary of State Oliver Mitchell.

Like he was speaking to a toddler, Dhawan explained. "Imagine a wizard, but instead of a magic wand, he uses technology. Our wizard, the Technomancer, has special powers that let him talk to and control all kinds of gadgets and computers through special implants in his body and brain. This, combined with his arcane magical abilities, allows him to infiltrate computer systems with no one being the wiser. In essence, he can embed spells into digital code in any program or app that's connected to the Aethernet. He can send out messages and stories that make people feel really, *really* angry."

Soter interrupted, "This is where the rage farming comes in. The Technomancer uses his control over technology to find out what makes people angry and then creates more of those messages. It's like he's planting seeds of anger in people's minds, and then he watches them grow and spread. He collects all of this anger, like a farmer harvests crops, and uses it to make people do what he wants … or what I want," he smirked. "While they're planning bombings and riots, they aren't paying attention to what I am doing right under their noses."

An uncomfortable silence blanketed the room, thick with tension and unspoken thoughts. Around the table, the members sat like statues, each absorbed in their own reactions to this information. In the far corner, Secretary Jenkins shifted uncomfortably in her chair, her eyes darting from one face to another, reflecting a mix of skepticism and disbelief. She leaned back, arms crossed, her furrowed brow showing her doubt about the feasibility of the Technomancer's powers.

Beside her, Secretary Mitchell's hands trembled slightly, visibly shaken. Every so often, he cast a nervous glance toward his phone, as though expecting it to spring to life with the Technomancer's manipulations.

Unlike her colleagues, the vice president's expression was harder to read. Something flickered behind her eyes as she studied Dhawan, her posture suggesting neither approval nor dismissal.

Soter looked pointedly at his chief of staff.

Katherine cleared her throat in preparation for winding up the info dump. "This information does not leave this room. Do not speak about it. Do not share it except if you are in the Oval with either me or President Soter. You most likely have always believed that the word *magic* was just a concept in a fantasy book. Well, it's not. We are incredibly privileged to be working for our president, who has untold depths of knowledge and connections. If you do not want to be a part of this team, let me know, and we will discuss alternatives." She met each cabinet member's eyes, one by one. "Any questions?"

With her own enhanced abilities, Kate knew exactly who was going to be a problem, who would simply go along, and who would be the president's strongest allies. When no one spoke up, Soter waved an imperious hand in dismissal.

The cabinet of the United States of America shuffled out, the door thudding behind them.

"Well?" said Soter.

"The vice president is intrigued, but I get neither a positive nor negative read from her. I'm sure she will be with us." Kate shared her insights into each of the cabinet members and then paused as she got to the secretary of state. "Mitchell is our biggest problem. He still has enough remnants of morality that he could do something stupid. At least none of them know about the White Circle. He'll probably go running to his church and light a thousand candles or something. He's a devout Catholic, so he may even go to confession."

Soter looked pointedly at Dhawan, who nodded.

The next morning, headlines across the globe blared, "United States Secretary of State Oliver Mitchell dies in tragic car crash."

SOTER WASN'T SATISFIED. His foot tapped impatiently under his desk. "What about The White Circle?" he asked. "They're hot on the heels of recovering the Trybrid, that Cassandra Oberon, aren't they?" his eyes narrowed as he pondered his enemies' activities. "Don't we need to take them out next?"

Dhawan's eyes darkened, and his voice took on a cautionary tone. "All in good time. The White Circle will be dealt with when my master sees fit. What I need to focus on are the six avatars that remain a threat."

"Six? I thought there were five now that, uh, 'what's his name' was no more."

Dhawan shrugged. "When I vacated *Marcus Castoldi's* body, I presumed that his life would end. However resilient the human body is, it should not have survived. But since he is not only an avatar but also a human/devic hybrid, his body is unusually resilient. And then there's the natural order of the universe: there is no such thing as an empty vessel. A living body instinctively seeks to reunite with its consciousness. So as soon as I left his body, Marcus's consciousness found its way back to its physical vessel, although I'm quite sure his memories will be more than a little foggy, fragmented, or completely erased. In particular, he won't have any recollection of my identity or the fact that I had inhabited his body for the past three years." *I hope,* he thought.

Soter wasn't convinced. "I'd be more confident in this whole thing if the boy were dead. Need I remind you that the division of labor was clear when we shook hands on this pact," Soter said, elongating each word for emphasis. "You, Dhawan, were to deal with these so-called supernatural avatars, these abominations that could disrupt our plans. On my end, I've been diligently steering the unknowing multitudes down the path we've set for them. With the prophesied 'Shift of the Ages' looming ever closer, I fully intend to take my rightful place as world leader."

As if Sirkan would ever let that happen, you moron. Dhawan suppressed a smirk, pasted on a composed face, and said, "Rest assured, Mr. President, the grand designs laid out by my master remain unaltered."

With a flourish of his hand, a swirling vortex appeared beside Dhawan. Stepping into it, he vanished, the portal contracting behind him, leaving only a flicker of ghostly light as it disappeared.

Soter gazed at the space where the portal had vanished, his brows knitting together. *What master? I thought Sirkan was dead.* "Intriguing, the way they manipulate those gateways between realms," he mused aloud. "Maybe it's high time I enlisted my own team of mystical experts. After all, knowledge is power, and I intend to have both."

He clicked the hidden knob on the right leg of the Resolute desk, and a spirit screen slid silently into view over the curtained windows behind him. A dark-hooded form shimmered into view.

"I need you in my private quarters. Ten minutes."

Chapter 4: Settling In

Sirkan extended a hand toward two small, blue-skinned beings. Their appearance was like a page torn from Cassie's childhood storybook of aliens, their heads too large for their slender necks and large almond-shaped black eyes. Their gaze held an age-old sagacity, reminiscent of entities that might have witnessed the formation of galaxies and stars igniting from cosmic dust.

One of the beings, its gaze locked with Cassie's, tilted its head slightly. It was a small gesture, but one that seemed to carry a familiar acknowledgment. Cassie could almost feel a wave of profound understanding washing over her. Around these creatures, fear seemed an unknown concept, replaced by a warmth that tingled in her veins, a sense of empathy she couldn't quite grasp.

Sirkan's voice broke the spell. "You know what to do," he instructed the blue-skinned beings. He aimed for a tone of gentle authority, like a kind uncle, but the words came out stiffer, less natural. "Make sure my lady is comfortable within the secure confines of her chambers."

Cassie pivoted to face him, only to find herself transfixed. She'd been so preoccupied with trying to access her powers that she hadn't really looked at him until now.

Catching her startled gaze, a smug smile danced across Sirkan's flawless face. He caressed his face that once bore a ragged scar from temple to jawbone, relishing the feel of his own immaculate skin. "Ah, yes, rebirth has its benefits. My ... faithful servant has rare gifts."

"A necromancer?" Cassie spat.

"Far from it," Sirkan said. "The universe holds more mysteries than you know, Cassandra. I look forward to showing you its many wonders."

He released her into the hands of the two beings. They quietly led her out into the hall.

Cassie became a little more relaxed and continued to observe her surroundings. She could feel Sirkan's gaze upon her retreating form but refused to turn around. Instead, she focused on memorizing their steps. No time like the present to plan her escape.

She found herself lost in an endless maze of passageways. Other-worldly beings and droids would pass them from time to time, studiously averting their gaze. The vessel seemed to be composed of a crew from the far reaches of the universe. Determined not to be distracted by the diverse array of species, she focused instead on the sharp turns that opened into long hallways. Mysterious carvings adorned the walls, shining in the dim, silvery light. Winding staircases she assumed must lead to the living quarters spiraled upward in an organic, fluid design. Assumption confirmed, they came upon a door at the top of an especially beautiful staircase, its iridescent metallic surface shimmering with an otherworldly sheen.

"These are the quarters we prepared for you, my lady," one announced, shattering the silence like a pebble on a still lake. The other waved their hand, and the hatch door slid open without a sound.

The suite was a symphony of opulence, with spaces and arches bending and twisting to an unseen celestial rhythm. Walls made of a translucent substance glowed with a bioluminescent light. Frescoes of silver and hues of blue showed an undulating seascape, like a living mural. Alien furniture, resembling a fusion of solid and liquid, flawlessly integrated with the suite, each piece appearing as much a part of the room as of the sea beyond.

Stepping into a sleeping chamber, she gasped when she saw the immense bed shaped like a seashell. It gave the impression of floating on a platform of rippling water. But after examining it carefully, she realized the "water" was another mural.

Then, to her delight, she saw another space off from the bathing area. It functioned as a gym of sorts. She could keep up with her training! Oh, thank the Radiant One!

Her excitement quickly faded. In another situation, she would have enjoyed this place. But it was a prison, one she wasn't sure she could escape.

Cassie tried once more to access her powers that had manifested during her training as an Aquarian Avatar ... nothing. She closed her eyes and focused next on her third eye, calling her psychic awareness forward. Again, nothing. She stomped a foot in frustration. Something was blocking her. *Well, yeah. Sirkan!*

Cassie went back into what she would call a living room. She turned around and around taking in exquisite furnishings and amazing colors. At the far end of the room, a panoramic portal framed a seascape in constant motion. The room and the world outside of it seemed to meld in a symbiosis of form and function. *At least my prison is beautiful,* she thought.

One being pointed to a wardrobe, revealing a stunning collection of aethereal garments. Intricate gowns made of shimmering silks and satins were displayed alongside form-fitting unisuits resembling opalescent seashells. Fabrics in hues of ocean blue, coral pink, and sea-foam green glimmered softly, as if imbued with the very essence of the underwater world.

Accessories filled drawers carved into the lower third of the armoire: belts made of woven strands of pearls, intricately carved combs made from coral, and delicate circlets crafted from what looked like seaweed woven into titanium and imbued with a phosphorescent glow.

A far cry from the typical wardrobe of a junior in college. Cassie looked down at the torn jeans and rumpled white blouse she had worn to the World Peace Meditation in Charlotte. *Was it just hours ago?* She shrugged in resignation. She was determined, however, not to wear one of those freaking gowns!

"Mistress." Startled by a sudden break in the silence, Cassie's body jolted as the word reverberated through the air. "I am called Vega, and this is my twin sister, Nova. We are Arcturians and here to serve you. Lord Sirkan ..." she hesitated. "He enslaved us when our scout ship crashed after the sinking of Atlantis. Our mother ship had sent us out to investigate the disturbance in the intergalactic energy signature of Earth. We were caught in a vortex that pulled us out of our orbit and sucked our ship into the fire and the destruction of the sinking continent. Upon impact, we lost consciousness. The next thing we knew, we were aboard this craft and in chains." Vega hung her head, unable to go on.

Cassie reached out to her, putting a hand on her delicate shoulder. She felt so small and frail. "I'm so sorry to hear …" Her thought trailed off as she realized why they'd seemed familiar. "You have taken care of me before."

Nova came forward and put her hand on Cassie's. "Yes, lady. We have served you throughout time whenever you were with Lord Sirkan. We serve you, not him."

Vega continued. "We have learned much about subterfuge and shielding thoughts. He has no idea our loyalties lie elsewhere."

Cassie looked at them both. "He is not to be underestimated. This is the second time, in this lifetime alone, he's bypassed safeguards to capture me."

"But, lady, you are a different being in this life walk. As of yet, your powers are untested."

Untested.

The word hung in a long silence.

Cassie put her hand to the torc resting at her collarbone. Its normal tingle was a pale echo of what it had been.

"I can't even contact my basic abilities here. It feels like I am encased in amber."

The Arcturian pointed toward the alien symbols that adorned every wall of the chamber. "Given time, you can neutralize them."

Cassie had a sudden realization. "Those are celestial wards, aren't they? They are blocking my powers."

The twins nodded in ascent. "But they are neither Sirian nor Atlantean. Lord Sirkan came to this planet from Lyra. That is why the sigils can dampen even your powers."

The next communication came telepathically.

We will continue to aid in any way we can. You can communicate this way?

Cassie responded in kind. *Yes.*

Their eyes met in a silent acknowledgement.

"Then let us help you settle in, lady."

THE TWINS WERE TRUE to their word. They prepared a luxurious bath that did a lot to soothe and calm Cassie down. No use wasting time being upset or frustrated; that just sapped energy. Then she chose a simple turquoise tunic and matching flowy pants. The fabric was shimmering and soft, but unlike anything she had ever seen. She stared at herself in the large mirror that dominated one wall of the sitting room. It resembled the spirit screens she had seen before, but she couldn't get it to activate. Well, maybe it was just a mirror after all.

Cassie paced.

"What a mess," she mused. "I can't access my abilities. My magic is non-existent and ..."

Paxton's voice echoed in her memory: "There will be times when you can't use your magic. Training with third-dimensional weapons is essential. You can imbue them with magic, but you need to learn how to use them first."

Her eyes welled up as she remembered her first love, struck down during the battle in Sirkan's tower in her Aunt Isla's Unseelie Court. *No, don't go there. Honor his memory by using what he taught you.*

Cassie scanned the room to see if there was anything she could make into a weapon. After meticulously searching the chest of drawers in the bedroom, she moved to the armoire and ended at the desk in the main room. Not even a pen. Cassie dropped into the chaise lounge by the portal window, letting out a sigh.

Again, her hands reached for the torc around her neck. The sigils etched into the metal held her fae magical lineage. It was ancient magic. The magic of the fae who had dwelled on this planet since the dawn of time, long before humans had gained consciousness. Why would celestial wards affect it even if they were Lyran glyphs?

Her father's lessons drifted back to her: "This torc will help you embrace your lineage as a member of the fae royals."

When her father had placed the torc at her collarbone, a kaleidoscope of vivid images flooded Cassie's mind. She saw countless fae women adorned in royal attire from bygone eras. The vision culminated with her fae grandmother, who had infused fae magic into the amethyst crystal her mother had given her. This ritual had activated Cassie's full powers, marking her as the first trybrid.

Could these Lyran hieroglyphs truly have the power to strip her of her abilities? Or had she allowed Sirkan's mind games to disempower her?

Cassie jumped up and ran to the little room equipped like a gym. A mat, a barre for stretching, some of those stretchy bands, a few hand weights, nothing fancy, but she could do her yoga asanas and Krav Maga formations. She turned to go back to the wardrobe to change when she heard the swish of the door. One of the twins wheeled in a trolley with domed plates and a pitcher of wine-like liquid. Cassie suddenly realized how hungry she was as the aroma of the meal wafted toward her.

She went over to the small table where the platters were being laid out, then recoiled as she saw that plates and goblets were placed at either end of the table. Noticing her dismay, the Arcturian said, "Lord Sirkan will be joining you shortly. He specifically ordered that an assortment of light meats and vegetables be prepared, along with his special spiced wine from his own vineyards on the mainland."

As though magically summoned, Sirkan materialized beside Cassandra, eliciting a startled gasp and a hesitant step away from him. He motioned her to take a seat. "We will be sharing our evening meals when I am aboard," he announced. She remained standing, then thought better of it as she saw his eyes narrow. Best to go along with the small stuff. And she was hungry. She sat down reluctantly.

"You may serve us," Sirkan commanded the twins. The air filled with the enticing scents of rosemary and garlic.

"I recall your fondness for lamb prepared this way," Sirkan reminisced, attending to the crystal goblets, "accompanied by roasted vegetables and fruit salads you always seemed to enjoy."

He poured the wine and raised his glass. "To the future."

Even through her dampened senses, she felt a pang of warning and paused. Noticing her hesitation, Sirkan met her eyes and drank from his goblet, as though showing that the beverage was safe to drink.

"I prefer water," Cassandra declared, setting her goblet down.

An eyebrow raised in amusement, Sirkan conjured a glass of water with a flick of his wrist.

"Water it is," he said nonchalantly. "I had no intention of poisoning you. The wine was a simple toast to the future. It's your choice."

Oh, he's good, she thought, *but I'm not buying it.*

The meal proceeded in an awkward silence, Cassie eating mechanically, more for sustenance than pleasure, aware of the need to stay strong for what may come.

"Tomorrow, I will show you to your new workstation, equipped with the latest technology to aid your research," Sirkan revealed, outlining plans for their collaboration. "Then we will discuss other more ... personal ... matters."

Cassie, keeping her composure, simply arched an eyebrow in response, her gaze steady and unyielding.

SIRKAN HAD THOUGHT long and hard about this next step. Cassie had proven more difficult than expected, even after he had dampened her powers. The sigils and spells engraved throughout the ship had only strengthened her resolve to resist him at every turn.

Now he stood beside the Technomancer, Danax, in the ship's command center. Danax was a canvas of technology and arcane power, his cybernetic augmentations pulsing with electromagnetic energy. Fiber-optic veins glowed beneath his skin, and his metallic eyes interfaced with streams of data flowing around him like a river of stars.

"With this virus, we will steer the minds of anyone who plays the game with the embedded subliminals. Their thoughts will no longer be their own. They will be ours," the Technomancer had said.

Sirkan was more than pleased with the virtual reality game the Technomancer had created: *Battle for Infinity*. The game had taken the world by storm, capturing the imagination of youths and adults alike. The game's theme centered around futuristic space battles and the quest to save the universe.

How close to the truth that is! Sirkan thought. The game would be the ultimate instrument of mind control.

"The game is designed to be played on a quantum-enhanced virtual reality, or VR, system," Danax had explained to Sirkan when they first had come up with the plan. "This system does not merely create visually immersive environments but also integrates with the neural processors of the player. The haptic function built into the requisite game gauntlets will add another level of reality. When the player reaches out to grab a virtual control or weapon, the gauntlets will give them tactile feedback, so it feels like they're actually touching something. Their body becomes part of the game. It's a tool we can use when we take the Aethernet war to the next level to annihilate our enemies."

"As players engage with the game, the VR system subtly alters their brainwave patterns, making the subconscious mind more receptive to the encoded messages," Danax continued. "This method ensures that the subliminal control can occur without the player's conscious awareness, blending the boundaries between the game's virtual world and the player's perception of reality.

Sirkan's thoughts snapped back to the present as Danax spoke, his voice charged with anticipation.

"And now we are ready to deliver the Mindscape Manipulator virus through the players' Aethernet connection. Once it's unleashed, it will spread exponentially with every click of a mouse or tap on a holographic screen."

Together, they gazed into the heart of a digital vortex, ready to unleash the powerful virus.

"At your command," the Technomancer said.

"Make it so."

Around them, holographic displays pulsed with eldritch coding languages and arcane symbols, each a demonstration of the Technomancer's mastery over the confluence of magic and machine. With a flourish of his hand, Danax summoned the virus. It slithered through the digital aether, finding the heart of the game with unerring precision.

While the virus took root in the digital domain, Sirkan watched its progress. Code streamed at lightning speed, setting into motion a future where the lines between technology and sorcery, freedom and control, were inexorably blurred.

Chapter 5: Possessed

His eyes flew open, startled by the surge of energy coursing up his spine. The sudden jolt ripped him out of his meditative state, leaving him disoriented and on edge. Confusion and fear lingered in his wide chestnut eyes as he fumbled for his journal, desperate to capture the vivid vision that had just consumed him.

Marcus's mind raced as he scribbled furiously in his journal, his handwriting barely legible in his urgency. "This can't be mere coincidence," he muttered, his eyes still wide with the remnants of the vision. The image of the girl with her penetrating gaze remained vivid in his mind, almost as if she had been right there with him. "Why her? Why now?" he questioned quietly. Each encounter with her in his dreams left him with a sense of profound significance, a puzzle piece he had yet to place.

He closed his journal and ran his fingers over the cover, feeling its texture under his fingertips. "She's trying to tell me something," he whispered, his voice laced with awe and apprehension. Deep down, he sensed a connection between these visions and the enigmatic seventh avatar, a missing piece that the Sirian oracles had recently identified.

This connection to the seventh avatar wasn't clear yet, but his gut screamed that it was pivotal. He had learned to trust his intuition, a silent guide that had never led him astray. "I need to discuss this with Cecilia," he said, determination firming his voice. He carefully tucked the notebook into his backpack. It was time to seek guidance.

Making his way to the tower where the trainers all had their quarters, he sighed as he looked up at the winding stone staircase. Why did Cecilia have to be at the very top level? Rolling his shoulders, he began his ascent, counting each step out of habit. He stopped abruptly when he realized there were far more than the usual fifty. Finally, at the one hundred eleventh step, he arrived at the landing, faced a carved doorway, and traced the requisite magical symbol in the air before the barred door, silently seeking permission to enter.

"Come," a melodic voice beckoned from within. He pushed open the door, stepped into the room, and drew up short at the scene before him. His trainer was not alone. Without turning from her desk, she motioned for him to enter. "You are just in time, Marcus," she said, her pristine white robes billowing as she moved. She turned then, revealing the imposing figure seated behind the desk. Recognizing the golden breastplate that adorned the guest's white robes, Marcus bowed deeply before the commanding figure of the warrior priest, adhering to protocol that the master of the White Circle must acknowledge him before Marcus could meet the master's eyes.

"Master Artemus, this is Marcus Castoldi, from Florence. He was the first identified avatar novitiate," his trainer's voice was unwavering in the introduction.

"Marcus, please relax," Artemus said as he came around to him and put his hands on the boy's shoulders. The master of the White Circle, Artemus, had been one of the leaders of the expedition that came to Earth from Sirius millennia ago. Their mission had been to guide humanity in each step of their evolutionary journey and give them spiritual understanding of the Radiant One.

Marcus raised his chestnut eyes to the master's steel blue, relieved to see them filled with warmth, a slight smile on his face.

"I sense that you are not here by accident. Why have you sought out your trainer?" Artemus asked, his voice steady and composed.

Marcus swallowed hard, his mouth suddenly dry.

"Come, we have no secrets here," Cecilia encouraged, motioning Marcus to one of the chairs in front of the desk. Artemus returned to his throne-like seat behind it, his expression unreadable. Marcus noticed that the usual small chair for Cecilia had been replaced by a much larger one, accommodating the considerable size of the master of the White Circle, who stood all of seven feet tall.

He took the leather-bound journal out of his backpack and opened it to a dog-eared page, although the contents were imprinted in his memory. His voice was steady yet tinged with urgency.

"About three years ago, as I neared the end of my first year of training, I had a dream. I saw a young girl with violet eyes and white-blonde hair, about my age. In the dream, she was crying and desperately calling for her mother. Her accent suggested she was American, possibly from the Southern region. That was all I saw in the initial dream, but as time passed, she began appearing in fleeting visions during my meditations too. Sometimes she seemed joyous, working on a computer. Other times, she sat alone in a garden gazebo, consumed by the absence of her mother.

"At first, I thought maybe her mother had passed away, but her desperate pleas for her mother's whereabouts made me realize she must be missing. The visions subsided for a while, but recently, they have resurfaced with greater intensity and clarity. A few weeks ago, I saw her at a sprawling university campus, lush with greenery and red brick buildings. She laughed with other girls in what appeared to be a cafeteria, but then a dark mist enshrouded the scene, and I felt her fear. In today's vision I saw a massive, winged figure whisking her away through a portal, filling her with sheer terror. The emotional intensity shattered my meditation. I knew I needed to share these experiences with Master Cecilia immediately."

Artemus watched him, his face expressionless. "This is the first time you have chosen to share these visions with your trainer. Why now?" he inquired, his tone measured.

Marcus swallowed again, his nerves tightening. "Until today, I didn't feel the urgency. Previously, I carefully recorded each vision in my journals, hoping that eventually, they would weave together, revealing the message carried by the girl. But now, I sense a deeper connection between us. I believe she may be the missing seventh avatar."

Artemus pushed himself up from the desk, his movements unhurried, and slowly walked to the leaded windows lining the east wall, his hands interlocked behind his back. Taking a deep breath, he directed his gaze out into the vast expanse of clouds. The room was engulfed in his contemplative silence as he weighed and processed the information he had just received.

Artemus, his voice soft, broke the prevailing silence. "Thank you for sharing this. Rest assured, I will summon you to my tower once I've had time to meditate on what you've revealed. In the meantime, continue your training. Take comfort in the knowledge that you have done the right thing."

Cecilia made a subtle gesture, signaling that it was time for Marcus to leave. He brought his palms together, offering a respectful bow, and uttered a quiet "namaste" before stepping out of her tower.

The door closed behind Marcus, and Artemus turned his attention to Cecilia. "Well, this is an interesting turn. It seems that he has no memory of the past two years, nor of his quickening at his initiation. It's almost as though he is a different person." He leaned forward, his face tightened with intensity. "Before I make any decisions, I value your opinion on the matter. You have guided him since he came into the Praxis Institute in Milan."

Cecilia hesitated, her thoughts measured and deliberate. "Yes, he seems to have lost the events of the past two years." She bit her lower lip in consternation. "Now I feel his energy signature is totally different from what it was last week at the World Peace Meditation."

Tension gripped Artemus, and his eyes turned icy, emitting sparks of frustration. "It's almost as if he had been possessed." With a forceful thud, he slammed his palms on the desk. Cecilia jumped at the sound reverberating in the room. "How in the hells did we not see this—did *you* not see this?"

"When Marcus was brought to me, he was a shadow of his potential, burdened by deep emotional scars," began Cecilia, her gaze locking with his. "His early years in Florence were darkened by a tumultuous home life. He grew up in an abusive household, where his father's alcoholism cast a long, oppressive shadow. The fear of eternal damnation was a constant terror, a remnant of his family's strict religious beliefs. To survive, Marcus turned to thievery, compelled by his father to steal in order to feed their large, impoverished family of eight. Fate intervened, and Marcus's life took a pivotal turn when he was caught stealing. They took him before the Polizia di Stato and then before the *Giudice*, the judge. One of the Polizia who was familiar with Marcus's situation suggested, since the boy was barely eight, that he be granted asylum with the Ruggiero family, known for their philanthropy. Salvatore Ruggiero, the patriarch, is one of our esteemed initiates. The Ruggiero family didn't just offer Marcus shelter; they adopted him, providing a nurturing environment where his latent talents could flourish. They recognized his unique gifts and decided to bring him to our Milanese institute for evaluation. There, Master Elena took him under her wing. She conducted a thorough assessment, including running his astrological chart. The results were undeniable: Marcus possessed the rare markers of being one of the seven."

Artemus listened attentively, his expression inscrutable.

"Upon introducing him to the Milanese institute for advanced training, he found his calling in both computer skills and intuition." After a pause for reflection, she continued, "However, since about six months before initiation, his demeanor became surly and secretive. He retained his sensitivity and enthusiasm, leading me to think his change in behavior was due to nervousness about becoming one of the seven." Regret colored her tone. "I now realize I was wrong."

Artemus nodded, his expression reflecting a mix of concern and realization. "True. It seems we were all mistaken. Our attention has been so singularly focused on Cassandra Oberon that the Dark Brotherhood managed to slip into our midst unnoticed. It seems that this Marcus is changed from the Marcus that has been wreaking havoc since initiation. I will speak with Master Elena."

THE NEXT MORNING, CECILIA knocked on his door at dawn. "Marcus, get up. We don't want to be late." He stumbled up and padded toward the bathroom. "I will wait for you in the hallway," said Cecilia through the door.

Hurriedly, he splashed water on his face, pulled on freshly laundered pants and shirt, and put on his battered leather jacket. Grabbing his backpack, he shot out of the door.

Cecilia led Marcus into an unfamiliar room in the Milanese institute. Standing outside of a massive carved door, Marcus inhaled deeply, sensing something amiss but unable to pinpoint it. He felt as if a shadowy barrier trapped part of his mind, concealing something just out of reach. Exhaling, he rolled his shoulders when he heard the directive, "Come."

Two masters stood to greet them. Marcus struggled to conceal his awe at the sight of the circular room lined with three levels of ancient books interspersed with glowing crystals of various shapes, sizes, and colors that seemed to magnetically draw him in.

Elena watched Marcus gravitate toward the fragments of the ancient record-keeping crystals. They contained teachings collected by celestials from across the galaxy. She exchanged a meaningful glance with Artemus. Their choice to meet in this room was intentional. They needed to learn the true identity of Marcus and decide if he was the one behind the treasonous acts of the past year or if he had been compromised by the Dark Brotherhood in some way.

Cecilia bowed to the masters, "Adonai in the name of the Radiant One." The Masters Artemus and Elena responded in turn. "Adonai." Marcus mirrored their greeting, barely able to whisper the words. He felt bound in an endless pause.

Elena motioned for Marcus to sit in one of the ornate chairs that formed a sitting room of sorts to the left of her desk. Relief washed over Marcus. Informal then. Panic soon followed, however, when a buzzing in his forehead started, then escalated into a painful shockwave that bounced between his ears like an electric charge. He gasped in pain and slumped into the proffered chair.

Elena looked at Marcus, her topaz eyes narrowing with a mix of concern and suspicion. "Are you all right?" she asked. She moved a hand over a set of crystal orbs on her desk. Each orb emitted a soft glow designed to balance the energies of the room. Marcus grimaced, gripping the arms of the chair. And then the pain subsided. "I don't know. It felt like an electric charge running through my head."

Elena raised an eyebrow, intrigued. "Ah, the vibrational shift. You're more sensitive than I thought. This room is protected by various spells and wards. Normally, they keep the energies pure, but for those who are not used to it, the shift can be ... jarring."

Marcus looked up, puzzled and a little unsettled. "A protected space?"

"Yes," Elena nodded. "There are energies and entities that we do not see but can deeply affect us, even at Praxis. This room is guarded from such influences."

Marcus sighed, a realization gradually dawning upon him. "So, ... this isn't just a casual discussion then?"

Elena smiled enigmatically. "In our line of work, nothing is ever 'just casual.' We're dealing with matters that transcend time and space, Marcus. Knowledge that can unlock new dimensions or bind dark entities."

A silence stretched between them, heavy with the weight of unsaid secrets and unasked questions.

Finally, Elena broke it. "Shall we begin?" Marcus tried not to slump in his chair. "Let's talk about your dreams, Marcus. How do you feel when you get up in the morning?"

He hesitated, not sure how to answer. "Well, I think maybe I haven't really been dreaming. I get these visions only when I'm meditating. They feel so real, like memories ..." His voice trailed off, his eyes reflecting a mixture of confusion and curiosity. "I also had these feelings of being watched, as if something, or someone, lingers at the edge of my consciousness."

Elena leaned forward, her gaze intense. "Dreams, or the lack of them, can be messages from the deeper realms of one's psyche, sometimes even from other planes of consciousness." She paused, allowing the weight of her words to sink in. "This feeling of being watched ... when did it start?"

"Within the past month or so."

Elena turned to the array of shelves, searching. "Tell me, Marcus, have you ever heard of the Akashic records?"

Marcus nodded slowly, his interest piqued. "Sure, in my studies. They're said to be a compendium of all human knowledge and experience, accessible through certain states of consciousness."

"Partly," Elena replied, her smile widening. "What if I told you that your feeling of being watched may be an indication that you had been overshadowed by another entity?"

He jumped. "Well, that's kinda creepy. You mean, like, being possessed?"

"These visions may be a sign that your subconscious is trying to connect you to some hidden truth within the far reaches of your mind," said Elena. "Ultimately, our journeys in a physical form are not just about understanding the outer universe but also the inner cosmos. There is a way to ferret this out."

Marcus's mind raced with possibilities. The idea that he could access such profound knowledge was both exhilarating and daunting. "But how? How do I tap into that?"

Elena stood up and moved toward a bookshelf crammed with esoteric tomes and ancient artifacts. She selected a small, intricately carved soapstone box and placed it on the table between them.

"Inside this box lies an ancient medallion, linked to the wisdom of the great Egyptian mystic Thothmes the Seer. Thothmes had the power to decipher the Akashic records, revealing past, present, and future events encoded in the energetic field of the Earth. With this, we can begin your training to access the Akashic records and unlock the mysteries of your soul." She put it around his neck.

A sense of destiny enveloped him. He realized that this moment was a turning point, not just in his understanding of the universe, but in his personal quest for enlightenment and his mission as an Aquarian Avatar.

Elena motioned Cecilia forward. "You know the process. Work with Marcus first thing in the morning to access his Akashic records. Be sure and have a recorder turned on to capture the sessions. Report back here, together, after the next full moon."

"Marcus, continue to record any insights, dreams, or visions you have in your journal. We will review them when you return."

She turned to Artemus after they left. "I agree with your assessment. The boy's detachment from his body and mind suggests possession. The medallion will prevent future intrusions but can't restore his memories. The possession was thorough and complete, likely orchestrated by a high-ranking member of the Dark Brotherhood."

Elena paused a beat. "If he is able to access his Akashic records, it may help in restoring his memory."

"We will affirm that," Artemus inhaled deeply. "The timing, coinciding with Cassandra's recent abduction, is no accident. I'll inform the other trainers to increase vigilance around the avatars. We must be prepared; this won't be the last attempt to sever bonds."

Chapter 6: Eristides

A brilliant explosion of light pierced through the thick clouds, showering the backyard of Cassie's childhood home with its radiance. Her mother, Rebekah, had been spending more time at their Charlotte home since her rescue from the Unseelie Court the year before. It gave her a sense of security and a sense of being close to her missing daughter. Cassie's father, Ayden, bolted outside, frantically calling, "Rebekah! Come away!"

Rebekah staggered backward. Her voice caught in her throat, unable to utter a single word. Ayden rushed to pull her away from the glowing beam emanating from a giant orb hovering over their house. In a fleeting moment, the intense light vanished, leaving behind the spectral form of a man.

Standing before them was an imposing figure, easily seven feet tall, adorned in a shimmering silver jumpsuit, a majestic deep-purple cape flowing from his broad shoulders. Tousled platinum hair framed his chiseled face where a gentle smile was accentuated by the captivating brilliance of his topaz eyes.

The celestial took three steps forward and extended his arms in a tender, welcoming gesture. Rebekah's heart pounded in her chest as she dared to speak, her voice barely a whisper, "Father?"

Without hesitation, she rushed into his arms, tears streaming down her cheeks. He enfolded her, holding her close in a long-awaited embrace of reunion.

"Oh, my dear, how I have missed you," Eristides St. Claire murmured, his voice tinged with emotion. He tenderly held her at arm's length, studying her face, savoring every detail as he cradled her cheeks with his hands.

Three more figures rushed out of the house, their eyes widened with alarm. Raziel, Cassandra's angelic guardian, skidded to a halt and stood rooted to the ground, awe-struck. Beside him was Azazel, a former dark Watcher and now chief advisor to the fae king. The third figure, cheeks still flushed from cooking over a hot stove, couldn't contain her incredulity. "By the Radiant One!" she exclaimed.

Ayden, quick to react, rushed to Rebekah's side. He attempted to draw her away, but Rebekah whispered reassuring words, "It's all right, my love. This is my father. He's returned!"

The celestial standing before them appeared no older than forty, defying the aging process experienced by third-dimensional beings. Ayden knew that celestials aged differently due to their time spent in higher dimensions, which acted much like a rejuvenating chamber. The vehicle he had arrived in, obviously a mother ship, confirmed his celestial rank. Clearing his throat, Ayden extended his hand politely, introducing himself. "Nice to meet you, sir. I am your daughter's husband, Ayden."

Eristides stepped forward, warmly grasping Ayden's hand with both of his own. "The pleasure is entirely mine," he replied graciously. "I am Eristides St. Claire, commander of the Pleiadean Central Command assigned to this sector." His attention turned back to Rebekah, drawing her into his embrace once more. "It seems I have a granddaughter! I intercepted an interstellar transmission while I was returning from my last command in the Andromeda system. It was an intergalactic alert about one of the seven Aquarian Avatars being taken. I immediately contacted Artemus, and he filled me in. After I got over the shock, I quickly made arrangements to come join in the mission. I am here now. All is well."

"Oh, Father," Rebekah sobbed, "we have no idea where she is now." She paused for a heartbeat, looking at her husband, and voiced her deepest fear. "Somehow, I feel that Sirkan has her. Somehow …" she repeated, trailing off.

"Sirkan." The commander's voice was full of revulsion as his mouth twisted. "That monster has been the bane of humanity's existence since he came to the planet during the first wave of celestial mother ships. Little did those originals know that his allegiance lay with the Dark Brotherhood." He paused. "Wasn't he eliminated by one of his own creations when you were rescued from him, my dear?"

"Yes, Ayden saw it with his own eyes. Sirkan was nothing but ash after the creature incinerated him. But I thought I sensed his energy signature for just a moment when the vortex opened at the World Peace Meditation."

Eristides closed his eyes and took a breath. "I will go to that place to see if I can pick up on any residual energy with my own equipment. Something might have been missed."

Rebekah nodded. "Oh, that would be so wonderful! I would like Manu to join us as well, if that is all right with you?"

The general hesitated, but then nodded in turn. "I will meet with him first. We have other things to discuss." He met Ayden's eyes.

He put an arm around his daughter, "Now, I need you to fill me in on the last twenty years or so." A rueful smile touched his lips. "Time behaves differently when we're away from this dimension. For me, only two years have passed. Your mother's loss is still fresh in my heart." His voice grew determined, steely. "We must honor her now and get her granddaughter back!"

He turned, his eyes examining Ayden, then glanced over his shoulder at Raziel and Brigida, an intrigued expression crossing his face. "It seems we are quite the interspecies group," he remarked, a note of curiosity and approval in his tone.

Rebekah beckoned Brigida forward, "Father, this is Brigida. She came here to help take care of Cassie. Brigida was Ayden's nurse, governess, and then his ... oh, I have so much to tell you!"

Brigida made a curtsy to the commander. "Come in the lot of you. I will whip up some refreshments." Food was Brigida's solution to everything.

Commander Eristides took her hands into his, "A nice glass of wine would be greatly appreciated, dear lady."

Blushing, Brigida bobbed her head. "But of course, Commander. His majesty keeps a well-stocked wine cellar here." With that she turned and led the way into the house.

Raziel fell in step with Eristides. "Commander, I am keen on working alongside you in this endeavor. As Cassandra's guardian, I believe I can be of much help."

Eristides slapped the angel on the shoulder, almost making Raziel wince with its force. "Indeed, Raziel, that would be appreciated."

Bringing up the rear, Rebekah and Ayden looked at one another, hope shining once more in their eyes.

"Things will be better now. Father will make it so."

Ayden nodded.

"WE WILL NEED TO ELICIT aid from the other realms," said Eristides.

"Yes, I will reach out to the rest of the Devic Kingdom," said Ayden. "However, I am reluctant to bring in the humans. This battle will be fought on levels invisible to them, and I don't want to endanger them in any way."

Eristides arched an eyebrow. "They are already in danger from the actions I have perceived in the Aethernet. They are being influenced in ways beyond their ability to fight."

"My point exactly. They are too vulnerable and ill-equipped to be pulled into this battle now. The magics of the fae and the mental abilities of the celestials will be needed to protect and guide them," said Ayden. "Their physical strength is no match for the forces we are dealing with. We must rely on the wisdom and power of the mind. Only by tapping into the deeper realms of consciousness and harnessing the latent psychic abilities within us can we hope to counter the malevolent energies at play."

Eristides, his gaze distant as if peering into unseen worlds, continued. "The Aethernet is being manipulated. Our foes are using it to sow discord and confusion, clouding the minds of those who are uninitiated in the mysteries of the Ageless Wisdom. We must act, not only to shield the innocent but also to restore balance to the Aethernet itself."

"Cassie had started a world-wide meditation training so that we could reinforce human's minds," said Ayden, "an integral ability to guard against the subliminal programming the Dark Brotherhood has been proliferating. But critical mass has not been reached. The six remaining avatars are continuing the program, but it is far from complete."

Raziel had been silent, but he could no longer stay that way. "I have been monitoring their progress, per instructions from Master Elena." The Dark Brotherhood has been attacking the monthly meditation gatherings and corrupting the meditation programs. Our Praxis institutes are doing the best they can, but the viruses that have been embedded into the programs are causing a fair amount of brain damage. Our healers are doing all they can, but the humans who have been accepted into the training programs have become fearful. They still aren't aware that the avatars are anything more than human, and Master Elena wants to keep it that way. But we cannot continue to put them in harm's way."

Rebekah said, "We cannot win this battle *for* humanity. We are here to teach and train, to guide. The final battle for this planet must be won by the entirety of the human kingdom, hybrid and mundane alike."

Raziel nodded in agreement, his expression grave. "Yes, and we must empower them. The meditation training Cassandra initiated can be fortified. By building a stronger psychic shield, we can potentially thwart the Dark Brotherhood's harmful mind manipulations."

Rebekah's eyes sparked. "I will meet with Master Elena. She will gather all the best minds from Praxis, not just the avatars. We'll collaborate to augment the meditations and work on generating a psychic resonance capable of warding off the Dark Brotherhood's negative energies."

Azazel stood up, his wings billowing around him. "I will confer with Metatron. Perhaps hidden scrolls and forgotten spells might aid us in this endeavor. The wisdom of our ancestors could be the key to safeguarding the mundanes."

With a renewed sense of purpose, Azazel and Rebekah prepared to embark on their respective missions.

Chapter 7: The Golden Temple

Master Elena stood in front of the Golden Temple doors. She had asked the heads of each institute to amp up the meditation training programs to include intuitive development exercises. Developing intuition required opening the next level of mental acuity. This sixth sense would be a crucial tool in resisting the subliminal manipulation bombarding the Aethernet via social media and VR games.

Elena thought about the last time she had been here, right before the avatars' initiation. It seemed like eons ago, yet it had only been three years. She knew this time of testing was not without precedent. She had seen it many times before. But that didn't make it any easier. After her meeting with Rebekah, she knew she had to elicit the archangels' aid.

The doors swung open. The great Metatron, guardian of the Wisdom Teachings and second to the Radiant One, stood in his shining robes, his golden wings unfurled. Silently, he beckoned Elena into the temple.

Elena always felt small and insignificant in the presence of this great angelic being. Metatron had ordained her as a Wisdom Keeper when she had first come to this planet. She was still in awe of the great responsibility.

Metatron smiled at Elena, "your thoughts are still the same. Do I need to have you write five thousand times, 'I *am* worthy'"?

Elena almost blushed in embarrassment. Shaking her head, she said, "No, Metatron. I know that you and the Radiant One would not have given me the role of Wisdom Keeper for this planet if he did not think me worthy. But at times like this, the weight of the mantle is heavy."

They entered the great hall of the temple, where scores of angelic scholars sat busily recording their respective insights of the Ageless Wisdom Teachings. These insights shifted as each soul in each realm made choices and set consequences into action, the law of cause and effect, or karma. The vast chamber was lined with towering shelves holding ancient tomes and scrolls that illuminated the eternal truths underlying all creation. These, in turn, would be integrated into each soul's book of life in the Akashic records. A deep aura of reverence and learning permeated the hall as the angelic beings worked tirelessly to expand the boundaries of spiritual understanding across multiple dimensions.

Metatron proceeded through the hall and into a private space. It was comfortably appointed as a large sitting room. Overstuffed chairs, luxurious rugs and a faint undertone of incense permeated the space.

"I had an interesting meeting with Azazel," began Metatron, "as you are aware. I have meditated on his ideas and have found them worthy of consideration."

Knowing how enigmatic Metatron could be, Elena simply waited for more explanation. Metatron was, quite literally, the head of the angelic kingdom, and she knew his words would set events into motion and could direct any of the angelic hosts.

"I have deemed it necessary to call in Mikha'El. He has developed a close relationship with humanity over the millennia, and his power is immense when it comes to protecting their minds. The other archangels are preparing their armies for the final battles with the Dark Brotherhood, and I would keep them in place."

Elena was surprised that such a formidable angel would be assigned to this mission. Picking up on her thoughts, Metatron continued. "Yes, he is the most powerful of the angels, which is why I have assigned him thus. Humanity is on the threshold of taking its next step on their evolutionary path, an initiation of their own. This next step will allow the more advanced humans to gain the ability to think in abstract and universal terms. They will be able to penetrate the essence of the world around them through the power of pure reason and intuitive perception. They will also increase their ability to manifest on the physical plane exponentially to their levels of heart-mind power. Manifestation cannot occur without the heart working in concert with the mind. Meditation is the foundation of these abilities and a necessary tool, even a weapon, against the influence of dark forces."

Elena nodded in assent. "This is why Cassandra is such a pivotal player in the next step in their evolution. Her amplified mental abilities are the blueprint."

"Yes, our Trybrid must be allowed to continue her work." Metatron said.

A golden light suddenly filled the room.

Archangel Mikha'El stepped forward. He spoke in a voice that seemed to reverberate through every cell of Elena's being.

"Greetings in the name of the Radiant One." He bowed first to Metatron, then to Elena. She had not been in his presence for quite some time, and it was almost overwhelming.

"I understand the time has come to lend my powers to assist humanity's coming challenges on the higher mental plane. I hope our Trybrid will take over this important task soon. The Radiant One ordained that she would carry this new ability to the mundanes. In the meantime, I am more than willing to pick up the slack, as it were."

Elena waited for a beat and responded. "Shall I gather the remaining six to convene at the Citadel?"

"No," said Metatron. "The Citadel was a good starting point, since its vibratory frequency is higher than the Earth's, but I would have them trained here in the temple."

Elena was surprised but said nothing.

Mikha'El continued, "Under my guidance, the Aquarian Avatars shall become vessels to amplify these teachings to all who are ready. First, I will strengthen the avatars' own meditation practices, taking them to heights they have not yet achieved. This will align their energic bodies and expand their consciousness to cosmic levels. Once anchored in this state, I shall impart the keys to tap the vast reserves of the heart and mind connection, the powers that lie dormant within all humans. Visualization, compassion, concentration, and single-pointed focus ... when mastered, these can turn thought into reality."

Elena nodded, "Yes, each of the six avatars can take a method suited to their talents and abilities in order to magnetize those most in alignment with them. Some humans will be drawn to the contemplative silence of Yirribindi. Others to the fierce intensity of An-Mei's marshal art methods. Seraphina shall attune them to the rhythms of nature, while Karim's connection to sacred geometry shall link mathematical precision. Marcus's path merges science with spirituality, as Teodor's creative passion inspires through sacred music and art."

As she finished, she felt Mikha'El's penetrating gaze on her. "And you, Wisdom Keeper, will monitor the groups to identify those who are ready for the next neophyte training classes. In this way, humanity shall break free from the fetters of the lower mind, and gain the ability to access the fifth dimension: pure thought."

The angel's radiance intensified as he declared with finality, "The Dark Brotherhood shall be powerless against the impenetrable force-field of consciousness we shall raise around this planet. Their lies and deceptions cannot sway those who have glimpsed the ineffable truth. We shall succeed in this vital campaign to secure Earth's trajectory into the light."

Metatron summoned his staff from the aetheric plane and struck the ground with it three times. "Let it be so, and so it is."

Chapter 8: Are They Really Worth Saving?

The hairs on the back of her neck rose moments before the door to her chamber slid silently open. *Sirkan.*

Cassie stood with her back to him, continuing to look out the portal window at the seascape beyond. Silence hung in the air. She refused to be the first one to break it.

Exasperated, Sirkan strode up to her, grabbed her by the shoulders and spun her around.

"Cassandra, it's time we had a serious talk. I have given you enough time to consider—"

"There's nothing to consider," Cassie interrupted. "Even with your 'new' appearance, you are still the face of evil incarnate. The workstation you installed in that command center is impressive. But the dampening spells you have scattered around every room I'm in prevent me from accessing those all-important powers you want me to use. You can't have it both ways. And you are hell bent on the destruction, or enslavement, of humanity. I will do everything in my power to stop you."

Sirkan sneered, his citrine eyes narrowing as he manifested a golden goblet in his right hand. He lifted it to his lips, the familiar rich red liquid inside shimmering in the dim light.

He always did like his damn wine! thought Cassie.

Sirkan took a slow sip, as if savoring the baseness of humanity in each drop. Setting the goblet down with a disdainful thud, he let out a scoffing, guttural noise that sounded much like "Bah!"

He grabbed her by the arms and pulled her to him. He bent down, his hot breath an unwelcome caress against her right ear.

"Observe them, shall we? The race of men," he began, gesturing dramatically toward the intricate mirror across the room.

Guess it is a spirit screen then.

She tried to pull away, but he held her to him, forcing her to look at the screen. The surface flickered, revealing an ancient spirit screen, much like the one she had seen in Master Elena's office at Praxis in New York. The screen displayed a dizzying kaleidoscope of transient scenes: humans engaging in various acts of indulgence, eating decadently, dancing sensually, having sex, and clenching money in their fists, followed by brutal scenes of rampage, war, and destruction, each more harrowing than the last. The images shifted rapidly, a chaotic whirlwind of human vice and violence, as if the screen were not merely showing events but peering into the collective subconscious of humanity, a reflection of its darkest impulses and desires.

"See how they scuttle after fleeting pleasure? Like rats in a maze, their noses twitching, their mouths watering. Each one a slave to their senses," he continued, his voice dripping with contempt. His fingers closed into a tight fist as if he could physically grasp the frailty of mankind. "Instant gratification: That's their mantra!"

Suddenly, the screen stilled on a single scene, stark in its simplicity yet profound in its meaning. It was an image of a child standing alone in the ruins of a city, her eyes wide with both fear and a haunting understanding far beyond her years. Her small hands were empty, yet they seemed to be reaching out for something, someone, perhaps for a hope that had long since vanished.

"This is the true cost of their actions, the wars they wage, the indulgences they chase. They're not just fleeting moments. They ripple outward, affecting the most innocent among them."

Sirkan swung her around to face him. He flicked a wrist, and a parchment manifested. "This is an ancient scroll describing the 'seven deadly sins,' written by some sanctimonious monk or priest at the inception of the Christian religion." He unrolled it dramatically. "Gluttony, greed, lust ... they're not just words, you know. They're shackles. The pious may catalogue them, give them names, but they are mere symptoms of a deeper malaise. Man is hopelessly ensnared by his own baseness."

His gaze returned to the spirit screen, his lips curled in a victorious smile, certain that humanity's vices were the keys to his own ascension. "Their blood lust knows no bounds, especially when they perceive their toys will be taken away from them, or better yet, if someone's belief system is different from their own. How many 'holy' wars have been fought in the name of a god or a religion? They are fools and need to be enslaved or obliterated."

Horrific scenes of wars throughout time continued to flash over the screen in a nauseating sequence. Bile rose in Cassie's throat as the assault on her senses hit home. She raised her hands to cover her eyes, but Sirkan ripped them down, gripping her wrists.

"No! You must realize that what you are fighting for is an illusion, a phantasmic lie. There is no redemption for the race of men. They made that decision when they dropped the first atomic bomb." He cupped her chin, steering her gaze back to the screen. Images of mushroom clouds billowing over Nagasaki and Hiroshima appeared, the grim ruins and ashen silhouettes of the victims suspended in an eternal moment. Then darkness swallowed the screen. "Are they really worth saving?" he asked softly.

Tears spilled down Cassie's cheeks, each drop a shattered piece of hope. Her breath came out in fractured, uneven gasps. "I refuse to accept it," she choked out. "Hope exists. Redemption exists. And good ... good will triumph over evil. Always."

Sirkan crushed the parchment between his palms. His eyes blazed with triumph. "There is nothing you can do to save them. They are already mine."

Sirkan pushed her away in disgust. She stumbled, unable to catch herself, and fell to the floor. "I'll leave you to your hope and redemption then. I have other things to attend to. But know this. You will help me in time. You will have no choice."

She stared after him, wiping her eyes with the back of her sleeve. Pulling herself up, she went to the door of her training room.

Time to up the game.

Chapter 9: Actions and Consequences

"Enter."

Dhawan strode into his dark lord's chamber full of bravado—and stopped. Sirkan did not look happy. Aware of the wisdom of doing so, he refrained from speaking until Sirkan was ready. He hadn't seen Sirkan in person since his resurrection, except through a spirit screen or telepathically through the ruby ring all of Sirkan's lieutenants wore. He unconsciously twisted his ring while he waited.

Sirkan's citrine eyes bore into his. The man always reminded him of a python. A shiver ran down Dhwan's spine.

"Marcus Castoldi still lives."

"We never intended to terminate him, master," Dhawan protested. "These past three years were for me to infiltrate the ranks of the avatars, feed you information on their plans, and then deliver Cassandra Oberon to you or end her."

"End her? *End her?* I never gave you those orders! You were to help bring her to me."

"But, my lord, we thought you were dead. At that point—"

Sirkan lunged. "I gave you the ruby ring for a reason, you imbecile. There were contingency plans in place." Sirkan reached for Dhawan's left hand, then drew a dagger from its sheath at his hip.

Too late, Dhawan realized what was about to happen. His eyes widened in fear. "No, please, my lord—"

The ruby ring clattered to the floor along with the middle finger that held it.

"You're lucky I didn't take your entire hand. Unfortunately, I still need you and your technological skills now that Natesh has turned traitor." He waved his hand in dismissal. "Go to the healer and get that mess taken care of. You will report to the command center first thing in the morning."

Sirkan then picked up the ring, sans finger, and stomped out of the room. It was time to get those contingency plans into motion. He still had *one* resource that he could count on.

ARION STOOD IN FRONT of the barred windows, arms crossed over his chest. The flickering flames of wall sconces danced across the intricate gold embroidery that adorned his obsidian tunic, casting an aethereal glow that seemed to writhe with life. His silver hair, flawlessly slicked back, framed a visage so symmetrical it appeared sculpted from cold marble. His impressive height was matched by his powerful physique, tapering from broad shoulders to a slender waist. While his silver-gray eyes probed the shadows with laser-like intensity, his lips parted in a sneer.

Morgandrian found him breathtaking, yet his beauty unsettled her.

He adopted a pose of casual authority, arms crossed while he studied her. His eyes ensnared Morgandrian in a palpable psychic grasp. She tried to divert her gaze but found herself held captive by the enigmatic allure radiating from him.

"So," Arion intoned, each word melting into the silence like butter on a hot griddle, "you're the agent of chaos I've heard so much about."

Rooted in place, Morgandrian allowed her eyes to betray her pounding heart but did not reply. She could only stare at him.

"I'm impressed," he said. "You've managed to stay one step ahead of us for quite some time. Seems your luck finally ran out."

Morgandrian retreated, a mirror of his advance. "I have no intention of going with you," she declared, her voice a fragile blend of defiance and fear. She knew her cell was somewhere in the depths of the Citadel, the fortress out of time and space that the Masters of Wisdom and the members of the White Circle used as their way station between dimensions. She had been imprisoned there since they had rescued Cassandra Oberon from the clutches of Cassandra's aunt, Isla, queen of the Unseelie Court, and Sirkan, Isla's former consort. Now, all that was left of Sirkan was ash, and Isla was being held in some other prison.

Arion's lips stretched into a smile devoid of warmth, as chilling as the touch of winter frost. "Now that Sirkan is no more, and Natesh is ... how do I put this? Persona non grata? You really have no one to turn to for your rescue. But I digress. I have an offer for you that you will find difficult to refuse. I have something or rather *someone* you cherish."

Her brows furrowed in confusion. "What are you talking about?"

"The one you've been so concerned about leaving behind."

She felt her heart stutter. *Her daughter.* "What have you done?"

"Actions await your decision," he replied. "Compliance ensures safety."

The man was beginning to piss her off. He was as hard to follow as the damn fae.

Her breaths now heavy, Morgandrian said, "What do you want?"

"Come with me," he ordered, "and share with the White Circle what you know about the Dark Brotherhood." His gaze swept across the confines of her cell, a space less damp than most but a stark contrast to the grandeur she once knew as the former high priestess of a dark coven.

"I can't betray them," she refused, her voice laced with finality. "Sirkan was not the only dark lord on this planet."

His eyes locked onto hers, an unspoken challenge lingering in the air. "I'll offer you one opportunity to reconsider. Choose wrongly, and you forfeit any hope of being reunited with your progeny."

He took yet another step, narrowing the space even more. Her back met cold, unyielding stone. Trapped. Cornered.

"I'm not afraid of you."

Laughter, dark as a moonless night, spilled from his lips. "Ah, but you should be, Morgandrian. For I am the herald of your undoing."

Yes, she would do anything to keep her child safe. But betray the Dark Brotherhood? There would be no safe haven for her, nor for her daughter.

"If I tell you anything, they will find out. My death would result in Devika's death as well. They will find us both."

Arion sighed. "Ye of little faith. There is no way the Dark Brotherhood can infiltrate the Citadel." He stopped, unwilling to give up any more intel about their location. She had been freed once before. Albeit from a third-dimensional prison. He resolutely held the silence.

"I was the go-between for Sirkan and President Soter. Soter is at the center of the worldwide manipulation of the Aethernet. He means to control the world through mind manipulation." She shuddered, unable to continue.

Picking up her thought process, Arion's glacial eyes bore into hers. "Are you willing to play double agent?"

Morgandrian closed her eyes and took a deep breath. "Yes, if it means I can keep my daughter safe."

"And how do you plan on explaining how you escaped from the Citadel's inescapable prison to His Darkness?"

"I believe you and the powers that be can help concoct that scenario."

"I'm sure we can."

And then he vanished.

TRUE TO HIS WORD, ARION had come up with a cover story as to how Morgandrian had escaped the Citadel's "inescapable" interdimensional prison. It helped that Eristides's mother ship was in the vicinity and was able to arrange a significant disturbance that reverberated into the aether. Every non-human being was aware that an energy surge that mimicked dark energy had disrupted the electromagnetic grid. The alarm went out that Morgandrian had escaped with the aid of an unknown player of the Dark Brotherhood.

For the ruse to work, Arion had to ensure that the White Circle truly believed Morgandrian had escaped. Artemus was the only one who knew the truth. Arion possessed extraordinary glamouring abilities, and his flawless imitation of a dark lord was truly impressive. His ability to manipulate the aura of shadows and darkness had convincingly mimicked the signature energy of the Dark Brotherhood.

Once free of the Citadel, Morgandrian ported to her throne room. Arion stood leaning against the archway. "Looks pretty damn empty, my dear."

Morgandrian's lips thinned. "No thanks to you and the White Circle. That turn coat Adrianna has decimated my coven. Her and her little girlfriend Glenda. Hundreds of years of growth and planning gone in an instant. I've managed to rally a handful, but they are wary of coming back into the fold."

"It doesn't really matter now, does it?" Arion sighed. "Your only mission is to keep your end of our bargain and report back to me on Soter's and the Dark Brotherhood's plans. Once your mission is done, you will be taken to a safe place and can raise your daughter as you see fit, except as a dark witch."

"So ... what? I'm supposed to become a white witch? I'm sure Master Elena and Siohban Sinclair will allow *that* to happen!"

"You will need to do penance for your sins, my dear. Magic won't enter into it. Your powers will be nullified. You may just have to live like a human."

Morgandrian literally shuddered. "You would condemn me to live as a mundane without any powers? That's a death sentence!"

"You'd be surprised how a simple life can be balm to the soul. You can start by ferreting out the latest plans of your dark messiah."

Chapter 10: Perchance to Dream

Cassie pulled up from the floor, rubbing her right elbow. Sirkan had really hurt her—*the jerk!* Yes, her abilities were weakened, but that didn't mean her body should be. Back to her training tomorrow.

The encounter with Sirkan had shaken her. She truly did believe in her mission and the innate goodness of humanity. The horrific scenes Sirkan had shown her, although ripped from history, did not represent all of humanity. They only focused on the evil, not the good.

Her inability to meditate deeply and connect with her inner guides and teachers had begun to take its toll. She felt empty and disconnected. Most of her dreams were mere flashes, a series of disjointed scenes that made no sense. Those damnable wards!

What was it that Manu had said? *The brain is the muscle of the mind.* She knew from her studies with him and Master Elena that "meditator's mind" was one of the most powerful weapons that could be used against subliminal programming or negativity. So, her mind needed more exercise sessions as well. She had to saturate her consciousness with visions of a positive future.

She also desperately needed to dream walk.

Dream walking wasn't just a choice for her; it was a necessity. The fragmented visions that had been haunting her sleep needed more context. The crumbling temple under a starless sky, its ancient stones whispering of lost knowledge, the shadowy figure, its face obscured, reaching out to her across the chasm of time and space were so disjointed, she had no idea what messages they held. She needed answers, answers that only the dream world could provide.

Her thoughts then drifted to Manu. Ayesha's soul mate. *Her* soulmate. She still could not fully embrace the idea that *she* was Ayesha. She was Cassandra Oberon and had accepted a destiny in *this* lifetime as one of the seven Aquarian Avatars. She had memories of other lifetimes and fully accepted the whole reincarnation thing. But she just couldn't fully embrace that she and Manu were meant to be together as lovers and mates in this lifetime.

She sighed. "Let it go. Stay in the present moment." She would not give up. She *could not* give up. She had other tools that would give her access to all those past lives.

Cassie's grandmother had crossed over into the spirit realm but could still be reached through dream walking. The beautiful fae queen, her father's mother, had helped her to return to the land of the living all those months ago when she had almost died after a malicious computer virus attacked her mind. She remembered her grandmother's words: "You are surrounded in all realms by guides and teachers. All you need do is call, and we will all be here for you."

OK, so let's give this another try.

She started her deep breathing ritual to still her mind. She called on her guides and teachers using the mantra she had composed with Master Elena during their training sessions.

"I am a being beyond physical matter. I have the ability to sense and understand realities that extend beyond the visible world. Therefore, I desire to grow and explore; to gain knowledge and comprehension; to master and use such higher forces and systems of energy that would be advantageous and constructive for myself and those who work with me. Thus, I call upon my guides and teachers on the inner planes, the saints and sages who are sent by the Radiant One."

Excruciating pain shot between her temples as if a steel band were tightening around her head, squeezing the breath from her lungs and blurring her vision. Cassie screamed in agony, clutching her head. She was vaguely aware that the twins rushed in. Nova sprinted to the bathing chamber to get a cool washcloth while Vega put her healing hands on either side of Cassie's head, intuitively knowing what to do. Cassie felt like a fish out of water, her mouth opening and closing to gulp in air.

Nova wiped away the sweat and tears that were pouring down Cassie's face and then reached for a glass of cool water tinted with green. "Mistress, take a sip. This tincture will help relax you and ease the pain." Cassie opened her mouth enough to take a small sip of the brew. She shook her head and tried to push it away. The taste was god-awful. "No, my dear one, take some more. I know it tastes foul, but it will help you."

Dutifully, Cassie swallowed some more. Her head stopped throbbing. Another sip and she fell back onto her pillow with a sigh of relief.

Vega's brows furrowed in concern, gently dabbing Cassie's forehead with the cool cloth. "What happened?" she inquired, her voice a blend of worry and curiosity.

The discomfort began to subside, but as Cassie tried to speak, she faltered. "I was practicing my dream walking mantra, but I couldn't finish it," she managed to say, her voice cracking. "When I mentioned the Radiant One—"

A surge of pain even more intense than before cut her off abruptly. In a flurry of motion, Nova leapt to her feet and dashed out of the room. The sound of Cassie's groans echoed throughout the chamber.

When Nova returned, she held another tincture in her hands. Gently yet firmly, she propped Cassie up, carefully administering the healing draft, swallow after painstaking swallow.

Cassie's pained gasps subsided, and Vega's expression hardened, her voice taking on a grave tone. "Dark energy engulfs this place," she said. "You must not invoke that name, not even in your thoughts."

Cassie closed her eyes in frustration. "Then I need to get out from under the influence of these walls. This is getting ridiculous." She looked at the Arcturian twins. "You have been here since Ayesha was taken by Sirkan. Surely there are ways to escape the ship?"

They hesitated. Then, telepathically, Cassie heard, *We cannot speak out loud. The very walls have ears, especially when Sirkan is not in residence. There is a way to leave the ship, but you will then be in the sunken city of Poseidia. It lies outside of this dimensional rift. There are groups within the city aligned with a powerful white witch who works with the human kingdom against the Dark Brotherhood. They are able to travel between the dimensions. We may be able to elicit their help.*

Nova concurred. *I am due to leave for provisions in two days' time. I will see what I can do.*

Cassie looked at her wide-eyed. She had no idea there was a whole city outside of the ship. Picking up on her questioning eyes, Vega nodded. *Yes, this mother ship is in a dimensional rift but is connected to Poseidia on the other side of the ship by a tunnel.*

Cassie furrowed her brow. *A dimensional rift?*

Nova turned to her. *A dimensional rift is a tear in the fabric of space,* she explained. *A liminal pocket between realities where time and physics twist in ways the human mind can barely comprehend. This mother ship exists within this anomaly, hidden from ordinary perception, yet tethered to Poseidia through a passage that defies conventional laws of the universe.*

Is Poseidia also in the dimensional rift? Cassie asked.

No, it dwells within the third dimension, but at a depth that no human can reach. It was established after the sinking of Atlantis under the protection of the god Poseidon.

Tamping down her excitement, Cassie held out both of her hands to the twins and squeezed them in solidarity. *We will all escape!*

Chapter 11: Silver Cords

In a dimly lit chamber of the Milanese branch of Praxis, Cecilia sat across from Marcus, her chestnut eyes reflecting the flickering candlelight. The walls, adorned with ancient symbols and scrolls, seemed to hum with an unseen energy. This would be their fourth journey into the Akashic library.

Marcus, his heart pounding with a mix of anticipation and trepidation, focused on Cecilia's serene face.

"Shall we begin again?"

Marcus nodded, taking a deep breath to steady his nerves. Cecilia began to softly chant an ancient incantation that was different from the one she had used before. The walls around them vibrated with a resonance that he could feel in every cell of his body.

The chant continued. Marcus slipped into a trance. Mind awake, body asleep. The room and its physical boundaries began to blur, giving way to a vast, star-filled expanse. He felt as if he were floating, weightless, in an endless sea of cosmic energy.

"Now visualize that you are standing once more in the foyer of a great mansion. You see the spiral staircase that stretches endlessly upward, each turn revealing new landings adorned with doorways. Each of these doorways are portals to your past lives. But you want to go to the very top of the spiral to the final landing. There, you will find the doorway that will lead you to the Akashic records. I will wait while you do this."

Marcus murmured, "I'm there."

"Good. Now open that door and ask your guide to show you the Hall of Records. Once you are there, you will see countless rows of books. These are the books of life for every soul that resides or has resided upon this planet. You can call your book to you once you sit at the large marble table in the middle of the hall as you enter."

The door whispered open, and he stepped inside and found a single table. He sent out a searchlight from his third eye, willing it to find his book. He had found it easily before, but now it was not forthcoming. He imagined himself a lighthouse, looking for a lost vessel. Searching ... searching ... then his searchlight illuminated an ancient tome. The cover shimmered with a pearlescent blue light, pulsating in rhythm with his heartbeat. It, too, was different from the book he had connected with before. Larger. He picked it up and took it to a nearby table.

"Focus on your current life walk, the life of Marcus Castoldi, the Aquarian Avatar," Cecilia instructed. Her ability to establish an aetheric link with his mind permitted her to be in the Akashic library with him. This, in turn, allowed her to easily guide him. "Ask to gain understanding about the time that your body was inhabited by another soul."

He opened the book. The pages flipped rapidly before halting at a chapter that emitted an ominous, red glow.

"That's it, Marcus. Confront it. Do not fear it," Cecilia's voice resonated firmly around him. This was the part of his journey that had eluded him in their earlier visits into the Akashic library.

The words on the pages transformed into a holographic image that projected around him. From the shadows, a grotesque figure appeared, unmistakably a minion of Sirkan, a being of pure malevolence. The being's hair, as dull as over-brewed tea, draped limply around its pallid, pinched face, while its beady black eyes sparkled with malevolent intent.

Sirkan, acting like a sinister puppeteer, directed the vile creature to infiltrate Marcus's mind, effectively pushing his consciousness to the edges of the Shadow Realm. The minion's presence was overwhelming, serving as a channel for Sirkan's evil to flow through.

Marcus, now merely an observer, was engulfed by a profound sense of helplessness as he watched the unfolding scene. The process of possession had been meticulous and insidious. It had begun like a mere whisper, a subtle intrusion into his thoughts, which gradually escalated into an overpowering roar that drowned out his sense of self. Marcus saw his past self valiantly fighting against the intrusion. Nonetheless, the strength of Sirkan, channeled through his minion, proved too overwhelming. Witnessing his own body being controlled by another was a torment unlike any other.

In the midst of this horrific memory, a soothing presence emerged. Cecilia.

Her words were a balm to his tormented mind. "Understand, Marcus, this was not your doing. You were a pawn in a larger game."

The scene dissolved, and Marcus found himself enveloped in a comforting warmth, a stark contrast to the cold, oppressive atmosphere of the possession memory. He was ready to leave the Akashic library, to step back into the reality he knew. But something held him back.

Drawn by an invisible force, Marcus found himself in front of another row of tomes, far more ancient than the shelves where his record had been kept. A thick leather-bound tome the color of honey acted like a magnet, beckoning him. He reached out to touch it. He felt a connection to something profound and timeless, yet personal and familiar.

The name on the spine of the book was "Ayesha."

He drew back his hand as if bitten by a viper. Then he saw it: a fine thread of silver light connecting Ayesha's book to his own. As Marcus's gaze traced the path of the glowing tether, a realization dawned upon him. This was no ordinary link; it was a bond forged by destiny, signifying a shared mission or purpose that transcended their individual selves.

In that moment, fragments of forgotten knowledge began to surface in Marcus's mind. He understood that his and Ayesha's destinies were intricately woven into the fabric of a larger cosmic plan, a plan that was crucial to the balance and harmony of the universe. They were not just two souls journeying separately; they were a part of a soul mission that was pivotal to the unfolding of cosmic events. They had agreed lifetimes ago to take on the mantles of Aquarian Avatars.

With a mixture of awe and a newfound sense of responsibility, Marcus reached out once more and gently touched the spine of Ayesha's book. The instant his skin made contact, a surge of energy coursed through him. Visions flashed before his eyes: scenes of ancient battles, moments of profound wisdom, and glimpses of a future that was not yet written. He saw himself, Cassandra, and six others in different forms and lifetimes working together, their efforts seamlessly aligned toward a common goal.

These visions were more than just echoes from the past. They were confirmation that he, Cassandra, and the other avatars had all been together over the ages, preparing for this moment in time. When the visions subsided, Marcus felt a sense of clarity and purpose. He realized that locating Cassie and comprehending their joint purpose was vital for the greater good, not just their personal journeys.

The thread of light between the books glowed brighter, as if affirming his realization. Marcus closed his eyes and took a deep breath, feeling both the weight and the privilege of the path that lay ahead. When he opened his eyes again, the Akashic library seemed different, like it had acknowledged his acceptance of the mission.

With a newfound determination, Marcus stepped back from the ancient tomes, the knowledge of his connection with Ayesha and the others etched into his being. He felt Cecilia's hand on his shoulder, grounding him. The library faded, and he returned to the present time.

"You have faced a hard truth today, Marcus. But in facing it, you have reclaimed a part of yourself," Cecilia said softly, her eyes kind.

Marcus sat, tears glistening on his face, not of sorrow but of release. "I still can't fully remember all of the time that filth possessed me, but at least I know about it now." He turned and met Cecilia's eyes. "You saw the thread between my book and Ayesha's?"

"Yes, and the maze of threads throughout the Akashic library connecting all of us. But the fact that you were guided specifically to hers tells me that you may have a major role in finding out where she is. There is a connection there that we need to activate." She got up and offered him her hand. "And there were six other avatars beside you and Cassandra. That is perplexing. Come, we need to see Master Elena immediately."

Chapter 12: The Chalice of Persuasion

Sirkan gritted his teeth as he put the Chalice of Persuasion his overlord had given him on the table. Every time he had been resurrected with the goblet, Sirkan had accomplished his assigned mission without many problems, ensuring his continued existence. This time, however, presented more challenges. The crucial factor was Cassandra's definitive shift to the left-hand path. This was the lifetime when she finally had balanced her karmic debt. And damn it, she was at the height of her power. He only needed to unleash it and take it for his own.

She looked more like Ayesha than ever before, a fact that made his blood boil and his lust insatiable. He must have her: body, mind, and soul. He gloated to himself that at least he had taken her from right under the nose of that sanctimonious bastard, Manu. The battle for Ayesha ended in this lifetime.

His musings were interrupted when the door to his private quarters whooshed open.

He whirled around and stepped back in surprise. Standing before him was Ninhursag, one of the ancient Anunnaki who had taught him genetic manipulation. She had established herself as a Sumerian goddess when he'd first met her, long after the final sinking of Atlantis, during the Early Dynastic Period of the Sumerian Civilization, nearly four thousand years ago. Her beauty had captivated him, and he had eagerly learned from her, both as a student and a lover. She had left the planet when the last Shift of the Ages had occurred with the birth of the Piscean avatar, Jeshua ben Joseph, to lead another exploratory mission to galaxies unknown with a promise to return "when the time was right."

I guess the time is now, he thought.

"So, I see that the current planetary alignment has brought you back to this planet. Or have you been here for a while and only now are gracing me with your presence?"

"My dear, now that you have been reborn, how could I stay away any longer?" She said, skirting a direct answer as usual. Looking him up and down, she came closer and took his face in her hands. "Even more handsome than when last we were together." She reached for his left hand. "No ruby ring I see. So ..." she trailed off as she spotted the golden goblet sitting on the table in front of him. "It's the infamous Chalice of Persuasion this time around. I see your overlord is still up to his old tricks. Or shall I say *his old controls?* I take it you are once more in thrall with a reincarnation of the ever-reticent Ayesha? What is the ultimatum *this* time?"

Sirkan reached for the cup once more. He had to drink the elixir it produced in order to maintain his rebirth. "I have until the next fall equinox to turn her to the service of the Dark Brotherhood. Otherwise, this is my final resurrection."

Her eyes widened. "You can't be serious? He would destroy his most powerful asset after all these millennia?"

As she spoke, he had to fight the urge to roll his eyes. "Of course, he would. Remember who he is. He is what the mundanes refer to as 'the devil.' Whatever ... I seem to recall that your own leader, An, had his dark opposite in Lilitu who governed forbidden knowledge or the darker aspects of magic. The god Seth came from that line. You had left the planet by then for your little galactic excursion, so you missed witnessing the evolution of Seth's cult. Then I found Ayesha reborn as a young priestess, Menhit. I was able to turn her, and she became one of my most powerful consorts."

"That must have set her karmic debt back a few hundred lifetimes."

A muscle pulsed in Sirkan's jaw. "Indeed. I was not able to find her for several hundred years after that lifetime ended. The stakes are much higher now. Once I turn her, she will be lost to the light once and for all. This is the point of no return now that she has been initiated as one of the Aquarian Avatars."

"Then failure is not an option. How may I help?"

He looked at her over the goblet, taking another gulp. "Let me throw that back to you. How *can* you help?"

Ninhursag pursed her lips. "Let me observe her. Get to know her. Then I will come up with a plan."

Her eyes remained neutral while Sirkan's gleamed with anticipation.

After she left, Sirkan knew he could not trust her alone. It was time to make his resurrection known to his one of his last remaining lieutenants—Morgandrian.

He moved to the far side of the chamber, where the shadows thickened beyond the sconces' flickering reach. She must still have her ruby ring. He no longer had his, but he had the one he had cut from Dhawan's finger.

At his private console, he pressed a hidden spring, revealing a compartment of carefully guarded artifacts. Among them lay the ring—its crimson gem dulled but still potent.

Holding it in his left hand, he drew a rune-etched dagger from his belt and dragged the tip across his palm. Blood welled, dark and viscous, smearing the stone as he pressed his wound to the ring.

The gem pulsed.

If Morgandrian still followed the old ways, she would feel it—a summons in her marrow, a message without words but as clear as a blade at the throat: *Sirkan lives.*

Now, it was only a matter of time.

NOVA AND VEGA, ENTERING earlier than usual, said "Lord Sirkan has asked that you join him in the main dining quarters for the evening meal."

Cassie furrowed her brows. "Join him? That sounds formal. What's going on?"

The twins hesitated, an underlying fear reflecting in their large black eyes.

Nova mustered her courage. "A very powerful friend and ally has arrived. It is my understanding from my lord's servants that he wants you to meet her."

Vega rummaged through the wardrobe, finally settling on a diaphanous, blue-green concoction made from layers of chiffon sprinkled with miniscule abalone pearls. Cassie heard Nova preparing a bath and sighed in resignation. If she resisted Sirkan's dinner plans, the twins would feel the fangs of his anger, not her.

Elaborate preparations completed, Cassie examined the results in the full-length mirror. Vega had topped off the high-waisted seafoam green gown with long strands of freshwater pearls cascading to her thighs. She had twisted Cassie's long locks into a loose braid down her back, woven with the same pearls.

She caught her breath. "All I need is a crown."

"That can be arranged," a male voice said from the entrance of her dressing room.

Sirkan waved a hand, and a delicate filigreed circlet, composed of titanium braided with scattered pearls and iridescent crystals, materialized on the dressing table.

He came behind her and placed it upon her head, its large, center crystal nestled at her forehead. Cassie met his citrine eyes in the mirror.

"Now you look like the queen you are."

He took her by the shoulders and turned her around, looking her up and down. "Perfect." She recoiled as he leaned in to kiss her.

Narrowing his eyes, Sirkan grabbed her face and claimed her lips in a hard, greedy kiss of possession. "You will not pull away from me, girl. You are mine and will remain so until I deem otherwise." He tucked her arm into the crook of his elbow and practically dragged her out of her apartment and down the winding corridors.

When they stepped into the luxurious dining room, a tall woman with blue-black hair coiled in an intricate pattern that wrapped around her head like a regal crown dominated the scene. Her back served as a momentary shield to her identity.

The lavish décor dimmed beside her graceful pivot, which released a wave of magnetic energy so tangible that the air shimmered with its vibrant force, infusing the entire room.

The torc that rested on Cassie's collarbone pulsated subtly, resonating with the charged atmosphere. Heat spread into her fingertips. In that moment, Cassie felt a surge of her dormant abilities reigniting, flowing through her with renewed vigor. She tamped down the desire to place her hands to her ancestral torc. Sirkan would surely question the move.

"My dearest Cassandra, may I introduce my long-time friend and ally, the Lady Ninhursag from the planet Nibiru."

Ninhursag inclined her head royally, "It is my pleasure to finally meet you. I have heard so very much about you."

Many things seemed left unsaid, hovering between each syllable. Cassie managed a slight nod. Something about this woman was familiar.

Sirkan took his place at the head of the table and placed Cassie in the seat to his right. She tried to recall all the protocols her Aunt Isla had drilled into her while she had been in the Unseelie Court. She knew a lot of significance lay in where they all sat at a formal dinner such as this. Ninhursag took the seat at the other end, signifying her status as Sirkan's equal. Obviously, the woman was showing her dominance, which didn't bother Cassie in the least.

Servants began to bring in platters of food. Heaps of Sirkan's usual fare of meats and exotic vegetables prepared in spiced sauces and glazes were offered to each of them. To cater to her taste for lighter options, a variety of fish and chicken dishes were also served, accompanied by steamed vegetables, which his guest appeared to favor as well. Baskets of fresh flat breads, warm from the oven, and crocks of creamy butter were carefully placed at each place setting.

Cassie found that she was suddenly famished. *Perhaps because my powers are coming back,* she thought.

Ninhursag watched with amusement while Cassie dug into her full plate with relish. She motioned to the wine decanter in front of her. "Cassandra, you must share this special wine I brought back from my recent travels. It is an exquisite blend of light red wines and spices. It is quite addicting."

The servant placed the faceted crystal wine glass to Cassie's right. She put it up to her nose, sniffed, and took a tentative sip. It was delicious. She took a swallow, then another. Yeah, she could get used to this one, unlike the heavier wines Sirkan kept trying to ply her with. But she wasn't a big drinker, so she put the glass down and buttered a roll. No way she was going to get tipsy in front of this formidable woman.

Feeling Ninhursag's gray-blue eyes on her, Cassie decided to engage her in conversation. She had no idea about that planet Sirkan had mentioned.

Using a ploy she had learned from Master Elena, she said, "So, Lady Ninhursag, tell me about *you*."

Chapter 13: Holographic Dojo

Cassie was deeply unsettled after her encounter with Ninhursag. She knew the woman was hiding something but couldn't figure out her end game. One thing was clear. Cassie needed to up her training and strengthen her body. Her powers, though still subdued, were noticeably more potent than mere days ago, possibly due to Ninhursag's influence. But why? Was it a calculated move? Cassie felt that she needed to be wary of her, but a small part of her couldn't shake the feeling that Ninhursag might not be completely aligned with Sirkan's agenda.

She went into the practice gym on the far side of her apartment and over to the console that housed a remarkable piece of technology. She had jimmied it open three days ago and was at first dismayed to find what looked like a jumble of alien tech. Her goal had been to reprogram the console, originally designed for holographic projection, for a purpose more aligned with her needs. It was no small task, considering the console's alien origins. The technology operated on principles that were not just foreign but practically unfathomable to her human understanding. Time to give it another try. After all, she had celestial DNA that was most likely responsible for her knowledge of advanced computer science.

Mind over matter, she thought as she exhaled, steadying her neural patterns and engaging the mental frameworks ingrained by years of meditation training. Cybernetic systems, like minds, could be hacked—not just by code, but by will. Softening her focus, she let the electromagnetic signatures of the wiring shimmer into view. The machine had a pulse, and she spoke its language fluently.

Her palms hovered over the console, heat building at her fingertips—an interface where high magic met quantum logic. Her celestial blood processed the machine's rigid intelligence while her fae heritage infused high magic with the computer's mind, thereby interfacing her aetheric body to the computer's. Her fingers flew through the wires, weaving through encryption and security glyphs that would have stopped any ordinary hacker. But she was not ordinary.

The system resisted, counter-intrusion algorithms flaring like an immune response. Sparks snapped against her skin. She adjusted, threading a strand of celestial harmonic resonance through its pathways. AI recognized logic. Magic recognized intent. She fused both into a seamless override command.

One final keystroke—not with her fingers, but with her mind.

The console flickered, firewalls collapsing. The system yielded. She hadn't just cracked it. *She had rewritten it.* A beam of light shot out.

An expansive virtual dojo materialized on the floor-to-ceiling display panels, its wooden floors polished to a high gloss. Cassie quickly changed into a sports bra and yoga pants. "Dang, no Everlast," she muttered, realizing she had no hand wraps. Improvising, she grabbed some hand towels from her bathing chamber, tore them into three-inch strips, and wrapped her hands like a boxer. Back in front of the console, she waved her right hand over the newly programmed dojo.

"Select training scenario," a terse computer voice said. "Hand-to-hand," Cassie said and got into a fighting stance. Her holographic opponents shimmered to life dressed in battle gear from across the galaxy. The computerized referee counted down, "Three ... two ... one ... begin!"

Cassie sprang forward and unleashed a torrent of strikes against her foes. She drove a spear hand toward one's throat, flowed into a reverse punch targeted at its solar plexus, then initiated an outside crescent kick toward another's head in a smooth offensive. Her holographic enemies effortlessly blocked each attack before counterattacking with blinding speed. A heel stomp cracked into her foot, and then a vicious elbow slammed into her ribs and drove the air from her lungs. Cassie rolled with the impacts to dissipate the damage and narrowly blocked an attempted throat jab with her forearm as she fought to regain her footing.

She took a step back and circled, catching her breath. Her holographic opponents mirrored their stance to match her skill level. Cassie debated her next move, thinking, *They're adapting too quickly.* She feigned another kick, testing their reactions. They effortlessly perceived her actual wind-up for a reverse hook punch. One red-skinned alien intercepted her fist and smoothly transitioned into a brutal shoulder throw, attempting to lay her flat on her back. Cassie managed to twist mid-air, breaking the fall with her hands, and sprang quickly back to her feet. Pain lanced through her limbs, slower and already fatigued from the ruthless onslaught. She needed to end this and fast.

Cassie charged forward to meet another hologram head-on. The final clash was furious as they traded lightning-fast blows. Her spinning backfist met blocking forearm, and a lunging sidekick caught only empty air as she dove under the attack into its guard. She grappled its torso and hooked its leg, grinding it to the floor. A brutal elbow to its jugular as she straddled its chest left it twitching and damaged, hissing static through a speaker as the simulator powered down. Victorious but exhausted, Cassie got to her feet as the life-like hologram faded away.

"Well, it's a start."

She went into the main room of her suite and poured a tall glass of the juice that Nova always left for her. She really missed coffee. Maybe the twins could figure out how to get some for her on their next supply run. Jumping into the shower for a quick cool down, she dressed in a tunic and tights and decided to see if she could unlock more of the alien tech.

"And see if I can get outta here."

She went back into the training room. "OK, let's see what we can do with some of that soul DNA, Ayesha." Cassie smiled and went over to the padded wrestling mat. This would do nicely as a meditation area.

She sat in a lotus position and began her meditation routine. But she needed something more. She needed to go back in time to that first lifetime when Ayesha had been on this very ship after the fall of Atlantis, a self-guided past-life regression.

Thus, she set her intention: "I am ready to connect with the wisdom of my past. I call on my guides and teachers on the inner planes to guide me to the time when my soul lived on this ship as the high priestess Ayesha. With an open heart and a clear mind, I welcome the memories and lessons of a life once lived. I trust in the journey of my soul, knowing that each step taken in the past has shaped who I am today. I am safe, grounded, and surrounded by light as I explore these deep waters of my eternal self. In this regression, I seek understanding, healing, and growth. I ask that I be allowed to connect with myself as Ayesha in such a way as to understand the technology of this ship. With each breath, I draw closer to the truths hidden within my soul, ready to embrace the insights and revelations of my past life."

She closed her eyes, her breathing slowed to the gentle rhythm of her heart. The world outside faded away as she focused inward, her body becoming a distant thought. She envisioned each muscle, each fiber, relaxing and releasing the grip of the physical world. In her mind's eye, a grand, spiraling staircase materialized, descending into the depths of her subconscious. With each step, she dug deeper, and the external world melted away, replaced by a serene sense of detachment.

At the foot of the staircase, a glowing portal shimmered with pulsing light. Cassie stepped through, her heart leaping as she crossed the threshold into the unknown.

Images flickered before her, like the fragments of a long-forgotten dream. She was in another time, another place, the details hazy yet imbued with a profound sense of familiarity. Emotions washed over her in waves—joy, sorrow, love, loss—each a vibrant thread in the fabric of her being.

Gazing down, she noticed she wore jeweled sandals peeking from under flowing, sheer white robes. Her surroundings mirrored her current life, yet she was acutely aware of her past identity. Approaching the spirit screen, she studied her reflection. Amethyst eyes so similar to her own gazed back at her. They were framed by long blonde hair veiled in gauze and crowned with a silver circlet. A crystal pendant on her forehead marked her as a high priestess.

She searched her reflection's eyes, pondering her past existence, the lessons learned, and their echoes in her present life. Seeking answers, she communicated through images rather than words, conjuring visions of a ship's control room, its motherboard and crystals, mingled with the warding sigils of her current confinement. She formulated her questions about overcoming Lyran wards and interfacing with the ship's technology.

A myriad of images coalesced into a beam of white light. Within this light, a speck of color expanded into a double-terminated crystal, rich with occlusions and etched triangles. Ayesha's voice spoke in her mind: *This crystal is a portal and a guide, attuned to our vibrations. It is an Atlantean record keeper. Seek this crystal within the throne. Once held, it will allow you to bypass any magical or celestial wards. We receive guidance and power from it.* A vision of a throne-like chair appeared. It had a Star of David made of semi-precious stones set into the back of the chair. The record keeper was at the center of the design.

The image began to dissolve, and Cassie found herself gently pulled back, ascending the staircase that symbolized her return to the present. The portal's light dimmed, and she crossed back into the realm of the now.

Her eyes fluttered open.

Now, to find that throne.

Chapter 14: Guardian's Fire

In the stillness of the ancient temple, Dhawan's heart hammered in his chest, the sound almost deafening in the eerie silence. He advanced, his eyes scanning his surroundings, acutely aware of the labyrinth of knowledge that sprawled around him. The shelves towered, stretching endlessly, filled with scrolls and tomes bearing secrets of the cosmos, their covers aglow with a faint, mystical luminescence.

His thoughts wandered to the esoteric wisdom these walls safeguarded, the mystical teachings from the stars that had guided civilizations. He thought of the Sirian oracles, beings of immense knowledge and wisdom, who had watched over these teachings for eons. Their presence was palpable, a silent yet formidable force that seemed to scrutinize every intruder's intention. He navigated through the maze-like structure, his steps echoing softly on the ancient stone floor. The air was thick with the scent of aged parchment and incense. He passed a series of intricate murals depicting celestial events and the interstellar journeys of the ancients, their vibrant colors glowing softly in the dim light.

A sly grin crept onto Dhawan's face as he moved stealthily through the temple, his black cloak blending him into the shadows. He was on a quest to find a specific scroll hidden in the ancient library within an expansive archive, safeguarded inside an interdimensional chamber in the south paw of the Sphinx. This hidden trove held not only the Ageless Wisdom Teachings but also crucial information about the history of Atlantis, the origins of human civilization, and untold spiritual knowledge.

It was also rumored that rescued scrolls from the Library of Alexandria were protected in another section of this hidden chamber. Those were of no great importance to him. The scroll he sought contained the complete prophecy about the seven Aquarian Avatars and something called the Avatar of Synthesis.

Guarded by vigilant temple priests and priestesses over millennia, no one had ever been granted access to the library other than a member of the White Circle or a Sirian oracle. However, Dhawan was well trained in the art of picking even the most mystical of locks, and that wasn't his biggest concern. The issue was that the scroll was written in an obscure language, and he would need to acquire the codex, a cryptographic key held by the high priest, Artemus, which was needed to decipher the scroll. His mission was complex, a game of wits and secrecy with zero room for failure. Determined to prove his worth once more and get back into Sirkan's good graces, he would present him with this elusive prize.

He shook off his wandering thoughts and focused on his prize, moving deeper into the labyrinthine library. The library was a tribute to the ancients who had traveled through the interstellar light streams from Sirius millennia before. This elaborate structure bore their stamp, a magnificent repository of wisdom. Now that the time of the Aquarian Avatars had arrived, more of the teachings would be released to humanity.

The Dark Brotherhood, intent on suffocating any emerging wisdom, had tried time and time again to infiltrate the library, to no avail. Thanks to his time spent as Marcus, Dhawan had discovered the location of the trove. He felt his heart drum with excitement. He would seize the scroll and then use his restored position as Sirkan's acolyte to unveil and corrupt the teachings before they could see the light of day.

Reality snapped Dhawan back from his reverie when a subtle shift in the ambient energy tingled through his senses. The interdimensional portal he sought loomed near, according to his intel. His hand instinctively sought the reassurance of his ruby ring, only to brush against the raw reminder of his lost finger. He comforted himself by conjuring a mental image of Sirkan promising redemption and restoration.

The air grew cooler as Dhawan ventured farther into the heart of the library. Dim, aethereal lights flickered on the walls, casting shadows that seemed to whisper ancient secrets. Shelves upon shelves of scrolls and manuscripts towered around him, each one potentially holding knowledge that could reshape the world. He knew the risks he was taking; the priests and priestesses were known for their unwavering vigilance and supernatural abilities to sense intrusions.

Dhawan moved with calculated precision, his fingers deftly navigating the complex magics of the lock mechanisms that barred his way. As he approached the inner sanctum where the codex was kept, he could feel the weight of history pressing down on him. Every step brought him closer to the codex and closer to the danger of being discovered. The silence was palpable, broken only by the faint hum of energy that seemed to permeate the walls.

Finally, he reached the ornate door behind which the codex was rumored to be stored. He recognized the ancient glyphs that adorned its surface, intended to protect the precious wisdom within. Dhawan took a deep breath and steadied his nerves. He pulled his wand from his jacket, and with a few swift movements, he bypassed the final lock and slipped inside.

The room was bathed in a soft, otherworldly glow. At its center stood a pedestal, and upon it lay the codex. The cryptographic key was a beautifully crafted artifact covered in glimmering gemstones and runes. Dhawan slowly reached toward it, sure that it was covered in traps designed to prohibit unsanctified hands from touching it. There was a brief sizzle and spark, but his hands went right through some sort of force field with no problem. He carefully retrieved the codex, feeling a surge of triumph. Yet he knew his task was far from over. Escaping undetected would be the true test of his skill and resolve.

With the codex in hand, Dhawan backed out of the room carefully until his heel felt the threshold of the door. He retraced his steps through the library's maze-like corridors. Each turn brought new fears that he would be discovered, but he remained focused, driven by the desire to fulfill his mission and reclaim his place in Sirkan's favor.

So far so good, he thought.

As he neared the exit, he released the breath he had been holding in relief.

Then, amidst the silence, the faintest whisper of a flutter reached his ears, akin to curtains dancing in a storm's gust. It was closely followed by a primal growl and the muted thuds of padded steps. With trepidation, he raised his witchlight torch, its beam slicing through the darkness to reveal the source of the sounds. He barely suppressed a scream at the sight before him.

The creature's wings, vast and ominous, unfurled with a rustle that echoed eerily through the cavernous expanse. Before Dhawan stood a nightmarish fusion of beasts: lion's paws, powerfully muscled, met the ground with a quiet, predatory assurance, while the sinuous form of its dragon-like body weaved a scene of terror. The creature shifted. Dhawan's spine tingled with primal fear.

A voice, resonant and commanding, permeated the chamber. "Who are you?" it boomed.

Dhawan's attempt to respond resulted in nothing more than a strangled croak.

Undeterred, the voice swelled in volume, demanded once more, "Who are you and why do you stand in these hallowed halls?"

The codex suddenly flew out of his hands and disappeared into the dark recesses of the chamber. He fell to his knees as waves of pain surged up and down his spinal cord. A single, despairing thought flashed through Dhawan's mind: *I am so screwed.*

In that fatal moment, the creature exhaled a torrent of fire. A blazing inferno enveloped Dhawan, swiftly reducing him to nothing more than a pile of ash.

An ancient Sirian oracle, keeper of the Hall of Records, stepped in front of the creature and shook her head. "They never learn."

She patted the newest guardian of the Wisdom Teachings. "My friend, I sense you will be needed on a special mission very soon. It is time for you to go back to the third dimension."

Chapter 15: Akashic Revelations

Master Elena opened the door, Cecilia's hand in mid-knock. "Ah, there you are. I had a feeling you would be coming today. How are your visits to the Akashic library?"

Cecilia took the proffered seat in front of Elena's desk and directed Marcus to the one next to it. "Go ahead, Marcus, tell Master Elena about your experiences."

Marcus took a deep breath, his voice trembling slightly as he recounted his vision. "In the Akashic library, I saw ... I saw a light, Master Elena. A thread connecting my soul's records to Ayesha's. It was as if our destinies were woven together, transcending time."

Cecilia nodded in agreement, her eyes reflecting the flickering light of the chamber. "It was unlike anything I've seen before. The light ... it seemed alive, full of emotions and memories."

Elena's brows furrowed slightly, her topaz eyes searching Marcus's for answers. "How does this vision shape the connection you've forged over centuries? What path does it guide you toward?" she asked, her voice tinged with curiosity.

Marcus looked blank for a moment, then said, "It means that the Dark Brotherhood, or more specifically Sirkan, knew I had been a part of Cassandra's soul journey for quite some time. We had a bond as a soul family, and I had a soul contract with her that would culminate in this lifetime when we took on the roles of Aquarian Avatars."

Elena nodded and urged him to continue.

He closed his eyes and focused on following the thread that had begun to lead him to more answers from the mists of time. Haltingly he began, "We all have been together countless times, preparing for the coming Shift of the Ages. Through countless lifetimes, we, the Aquarian Avatars, have perfected our talents and balanced our karma. This lifetime we have agreed to lead humanity through the final battle between the darkness and the light."

Elena nodded. "Do you understand now why you were chosen as the target to be possessed by Sirkan's acolyte? It was not because you were weak. You were targeted because you are so closely connected to the Trybrid, to Cassandra."

"Now it's important for me to follow that thread of light that connects our Akashic records and find her," he said.

"Yes," said Elena. "No matter what dimension she is being held in, that bond transcends time and space. I believe you will need to be physically closer to access that connection, however."

She turned to Cecilia. "Ian MacGregor, as you know, is a powerful white witch and an expert on navigating rifts. A reconnaissance mission will be sent out soon. I want you both to be a part of it. Manu is even now researching some leads with Artemus and Commander Eristides. Once they return to the Citadel, I will reach out to you both to come and meet with them as well."

Elena turned to her spirit screen after the pair left. Artemus's face filled the screen.

"Hello, Elena. We were just talking about you." He stepped aside as he motioned to Manu and Eristides. "I believe we have pinpointed three viable locations to begin the reconnaissance mission."

Manu stepped forward. "I have also had a missive from Natesh. He wants to meet with us about this latest situation with Cassandra. Ian and I will be seeing him tomorrow here at the Citadel."

SERAPHINA STARED INTENTLY at her ruined experiment, now a steaming mess of blackish greenish bluish slime.

"Geeze, Sera! It's burning a hole in the table!" yelled Yirribindi, sending streams of freezing energy from the palms of their hands. The ooze solidified into a frozen mess.

Karim ran into the lab. "What the hell is going on? The stench is circulating through the vents." He slid to a halt, retching.

"I ... I was trying a new universal healing salve to take with us on the mission to the rift."

"Yeah, that worked out really well," drawled Karim, "I won't be able to eat for a friggin' week."

Tatiana flashed into the room, "In all that is holy, what is going on here?" Her hazel eyes raked over the three avatars. "Seraphina?'

Yeah, of course she knew it was me.

Seraphina sighed, "I was experimenting with some ideas for healing balms and potions to take on our mission." She held up her hands. "They backfired."

Tatiana shook her head and went over to the frozen ooze and scanned it with her hands. "The next time you decide to try your hand at potions that involve dragonsbane and mandrake resin, I suggest you come to me." With a shake of her head and a quick flick of her wrist, she effortlessly made the mess vanish.

"OK, teaching moment," said Tatiana. "Fetch the gryphon claw. It's on the highest shelf on the left side of the room. It's a concentrated powder and bestows heightened endurance and recovery."

"Here, I can get it," said Yirribindi and levitated to the shelf. "Anything else up here?"

"Yes, get the marble urn marked 'dittany.' It's a restorative herb that can rapidly heal wounds and can be safely mixed with Athelas leaves. They can revive the injured or ill when crushed."

She turned to Seraphina. "What spell did you craft for the salve?"

"Sana vulnera dire, putredine purgata. Restitue membra viva. Dolor hic demigratus. Ancestralis magicae per me effluxit ars. Curat iam haec pyxis vetus damna nova."

"Translate please."

"Heal dire wounds, purged of rot and decay. Restore living limbs. Banish all pain away. Through me flows the ancestral magic art. This ancient unguent now mends new hurts."

"Ah, I see where the issue was. You used *dire*. That implies fear. Use *gravis* instead. The English *serious* does not invoke the same emotional charge."

The ingredients assembled, Tatiana took out a large mortar and pestle. The three gathered around. "Seraphina, take just a pinch of the gryphon claw and grind three Athelas leaves into it and begin the spell."

Seraphina began the chanted spell in her soft, melodious voice.

"Now take the dittany and crush that in. Say the spell two more times."

A pungent smell began to emanate from the concoction. It smelled faintly of fallen leaves.

"One last ingredient to bind: mandrake resin. It can restore vitality to the near dead. Use no more than two tablespoons."

The salve began to coalesce into an ointment-like paste.

"Now do your blessing over the salve and ask for right action."

While Seraphina completed the spell, Yirribindi went to the supply cupboard and took out a handful of small tins. Seraphina had enough of the concoction to fill three of them.

Tatiana nodded her approval. "This can only be made in small batches like this. Do not attempt to make them larger, and do not make more than two batches a day. It will deplete your magic. Something we cannot risk right now."

Elena walked in, waving a hand in front of her nose. She looked pointedly at Seraphina and smiled. "Well, it looks like salves and potions training has reached new heights. It is time to do the same with your meditation. Archangel Mikha'El will be here in about an hour. Clean up and meet him in the meditation chamber.

THE SIX AQUARIAN AVATARS sat in a circle in the Citadel's serene inner meditation chamber. Their eyes closed, they began their preparatory breathing. Archangel Mikha'El stood in the center, his luminous presence filling the room with an otherworldly glow.

"Avatars," Mikha'El spoke, his voice resonating through every cell in their bodies, "today, we shall delve into the depths of consciousness. Are you ready to ... how shall I say it? Up your game?"

The avatars nodded in unison, their faces reflecting a mix of anticipation and reverence. Mikha'El smiled, sensing their eagerness. "Let us begin with an advanced seed-thought meditation. Close your eyes and imagine your awareness expanding beyond the confines of your physical body. Feel your consciousness merging with the infinite intelligence of the universe."

They followed Mikha'El's guidance as he walked around the circle to monitor their auric fields. He nodded in satisfaction when he felt their profound sense of connection to the Radiant One.

Seraphina gasped as she experienced a glimpse of the unity underlying all creation.

"This is incredible," she whispered, her voice filled with awe.

"Now use this seed: *Stillness reveals the gateway to the cosmic mind.*" Mikha'El paused and then continued, "You know the process: focus your mind intently on the seed thought. Repeat it mentally, allowing its meaning to permeate your being. Dwell upon its significance, letting it become the center of your awareness."

He waited for several minutes, allowing himself to align with each of them. Then he continued, "Reflect deeply on the implications of this seed thought. Contemplate its profound truths and allow your understanding to expand beyond the boundaries of your current perception. Let the seed thought take root in your consciousness, guiding you toward greater insight and wisdom."

Five minutes of silence, then: "Now, enter a state of quiet receptivity. Release any mental chatter or distractions and become attuned to the deeper meaning of the seed thought. Allow it to integrate into your thoughts, transforming your consciousness from within."

The great archangel could see into the mental levels where the avatars minds were connected with cosmic consciousness. Their combined power on the mental plane could raise the vibratory frequency to such a level that they would be able to penetrate the dense layers of negative thought forms and limiting beliefs that had long plagued humanity.

A brilliant, pulsating light began to emanate from their collective aura, filling the temple with its radiance.

"And now, in the final stage of contemplation, surrender yourself completely to the spiritual truth embodied by the seed thought. Transcend intellectual understanding and open yourself to a direct, intuitive realization of its essence. Experience unity with the cosmic principles it represents. Allow your individual consciousness to merge with the infinite expanse of cosmic consciousness."

Mikha'El paused in his guidance for a full eight minutes. Then he began to guide them back to full waking consciousness. "Feel your body within its space. Take three deep breaths. Allow your awareness to come back into the room. Wiggle your toes and your fingers. Put your hands over your eyes. And slowly, slowly, open your eyes. And when you're ready, lower your hands and connect with one another by looking into one another's eyes. End your meditation time with your hands palm to palm and the salutation *shanti, shanti, shanti,* which means 'peace, peace, peace.'"

The avatars slowly returned to physical awareness, their eyes shining with the light of newfound wisdom and purpose. They exchanged glances, each one feeling the sense of connection and unity that now bound them together even more closely.

"And now," said Mikha'El, "share your insights on the concept behind the seed thought."

An-Mei was the first to respond. "The esoteric truth behind the seed thought, stillness reveals the gateway to cosmic mind, is rooted in the understanding that within the depths of inner silence, one can access the infinite wisdom and intelligence of the universe."

Marcus proffered, "Stillness is not merely the absence of noise or movement, but a profound state of inner tranquility and quiet. It is a space where the chattering of the mundane mind stops." He paused, trying to give voice to the vision. "And the soul can begin to attune itself to the subtle whispers of the cosmic consciousness."

Mikha'El nodded. "Yes, you have penetrated the seed thought well. I want you to continue to meditate on that exact seed thought for the next month and record your insights in your meditation journals. You will continue to receive 'downloads,'" he said with air quotes, "sometimes out of the blue, during meditation, or even in dreams."

He looked at each of them in turn. "Be aware that you have set in motion a transformative wave that has the potential to change the course of human history. Your work on the mental plane can ignite a global awakening. This is why it is so imperative that you continue working with the human kingdom and teaching as many as possible to meditate. The progress of your individual efforts will keep developing in the days, months, and years ahead. Remember, you are not alone on this journey. You have the support of the entire spiritual hierarchy, as well as the love and guidance of the Radiant One."

"And we need Cassie more than ever," whispered Seraphina.

Mikha'El looked at her meaningfully. "Do not focus on absolutes. No one person is more or less important to the success of this mission. Your roles may be different, but all are equal."

Suitably admonished, Seraphina bowed her head in acknowledgment and thought ruefully, *I do believe I will practice silence for the rest of the day.*

Chapter 16: Echoes of the Past

Cassie rubbed her tired eyes, her sleep yet again riddled with disjointed dreams. Absorbing the cold, hard reality of her captivity, she clenched her teeth. It had been months since the travesty at Trade and Tryon, months since Sirkan had taken her.

Since making the pact with the twins, she eagerly awaited news of progress during their weekly trips to Poseidia for provisions. Preparing for an escape, she had redoubled her training, a routine honed from her time with Paxton in the Unseelie Court and Master Artemus at the Citadel. She vowed she would damn well be ready when the opportunity to escape presented itself.

She sprang to her feet, remembering the coffee that the twins had gotten for her on their last trip to Poseidia. She programmed the nutrichef that Vega had arranged to be installed in the living room. It was quite the device, stocking preprogramed meals, snacks, and, thank the Radiant One, coffee! Inhaling the life-giving scent of real coffee, she took a large sip of the liquid gold. Eyeing the preprogrammed breakfast menu, she ordered up scrambled eggs (she could only imagine what kind of eggs), rolls, and berries. It tasted pretty good, although she knew some of it had to be synthetic. Nova and Vega did their best to get as much fresh food as possible, but she also knew they had to supplement it with synthesized ingredients. Synthesized food notwithstanding, she finished every bite. She needed her strength. Today, she was determined to work on accessing her power to connect her mind with the ship's technology and to find the Atlantean record keeper crystal.

Changing into one of the unisuits that populated her wardrobe, she rummaged through the rows of footwear. She found jade-colored boots that laced up to her knee. Glancing in the mirror, she chuckled at her space girl appearance, a moment of levity in her grim reality.

OK, let's see if I can manage to get out of this place, she thought. *First things first: I need to connect with the ship's computer.*

Turning toward the door that served as her only route to the ship's passageways, she rubbed her hands together to ignite her clairsentience, then began her deep breathing, in through the nose for six seconds, hold for six, and a slow exhale for six. Splaying her hands against the surface of the door, her fingertips skated along its cold, metallic edges, scouring every inch for a concealed latch or button. Each exploration met with disappointment. The door was immovable, and the countless sigils etched into the walls of her apartment only reinforced the web of her captivity.

OK, maybe if I visualize the crystal ...

She went back to the image that Ayesha had sent her and began to build it in her mind's eye.

Damnit! It just won't coalesce!

About to give up, a subtle tingle rippled from her forehead to her fingertips. The outline of the crystal began to form in her mind's eye. The sensation pulsed like a heartbeat. Her mental synapses connected with the physical realm in that moment, like two cogwheels locking into place. She pulled energy from the now fully formed image of the crystal.

Guided by this intuitive link, she visualized a button under her right hand. With a satisfying click, the door slid open when she pressed her fingers on the imagined spot.

A wry smile spread across Cassie's face as she congratulated herself. *Not so much of a captive now, am I?* she thought, savoring the victory. *All of those hours fusing tech with my own mind weren't for nothing. That lock didn't stand a chance.*

She mentally thanked Ayesha. She still couldn't totally connect with the fact that they were one and the same, but still.

Cassie's toes made tentative contact with the floor as she escaped her apartment. She swept her eyes over the hallway. It lay vacant, like it was holding its breath along with her. Exhaling softly, she began to navigate the narrow corridor, her feet barely making a sound. A fork in the hallway beckoned her to the right. That's where she had seen an iridescent hatch; its unique energy signature etched into her memory when Vega and Nova had escorted her to her apartment on that first day on the ship. Could it be a portal to access Poseidia?

In that moment, she yearned for Gabriel, her feline familiar whose shape-shifting abilities would have been invaluable for reconnaissance. She really missed that ball of fur. *Make do with what you have,* she admonished herself.

Time stretched slowly as she crept closer to the fork. Each passing second on the verge of discovery felt like an eternity. What if Sirkan returned to find her missing? A shudder rolled through her at the thought. But then again, what could Sirkan do? Kill her? The thought barely grazed her; the man already had her in chains, so to speak. Slap her around, perhaps? It wouldn't be the first time he resorted to such measures. She shook her head and focused instead on the iridescent glint that marked her potential escape, edging ever closer to the hope of freedom.

With her palm flush against the iridescent hatch, Cassie began the process she had created to sync her mind with the technology of the door. Concentration furrowed her brow as she sought to decipher the more complex mechanism of this door. Each second stretched interminably, tormenting her with its crawl through time. Her heart pounded in her chest, its staccato rhythm echoing so loudly in her ears that she feared it would serve as an alarm, broadcasting her covert efforts.

Keep calm, she silently entreated herself, acutely aware that any emotional fluctuation, be it fear, anxiety, or anger, would disrupt the delicate energetic connection she was striving to establish. Her mental faculties needed to be at their peak. So, she took a deep breath and quieted her mind. But her powers were still a faint echo. She stopped and reached with both hands to the torc at her collarbone, the link to her ancestral fae magic.

It began to hum in solidarity with her avatar senses. She could feel the spark of power begin to flow between her consciousness and the door's hidden locking mechanism. Quelling the storm of emotions, she kept her left hand of receiving on the torc and raised her right hand of sending energy back through the hatch. She thought she heard the sonorous clacking of a metronome mocking her attempts. *Tempus fugit. Come on!*

She began to move her hand across the doorway. Maybe a different place? Still nothing. The longer it took, the more determined she was that this door *had* to be opened. She looked nervously around and pulled herself back once again. She focused her attention on her third eye in the middle of her forehead and shifted her attention to connecting with the energy of the locking mechanism. Tick ... tick ... tok! *Finally.* Success!

The hatch slid open just enough for her to squeeze through.

And slammed behind her.

CASSIE STEPPED INTO the chamber. Her breath hitched when her eyes flickered over rows of sarcophagi that hummed with the resonance of stasis machinery. The room seemed a haunted echo of the spectral tomb where her mother, Rebekah, had once been imprisoned in the dungeons of her aunt's Unseelie Court. She moved through the labyrinthine aisles. Her skin tingled, the fine hairs on her arms standing on end.

The dimness of the chamber strained Cassie's eyes. She inched closer, her gaze flitting over the figures encased within. The dresses and robes on these silent figures spanned centuries, a tapestry of time woven into their fabric. Each sarcophagus was an eerie testament to the historical expanse these women had traversed.

It was the plaques, however, that drew her in, an unsettling revelation at the base of each sarcophagus. The hieroglyph for "Ayesha" was unmistakable, followed by inscriptions in a babel of languages. The realization dawned on her with creeping horror. These were not just any women; they were all Ayesha in different incarnations.

A shiver ran down her spine as Sirkan's haunting words resurfaced, a smoky echo in the crypt-like chamber. "Think of it as Ayesha 2.0," he had said, a twisted promise that now found its embodiment in this grotesque gallery. The memory of Sirkan guiding her into a past-life regression in order to take her to a dark past flooded back. Her sacrifice of Oleander, her loyal servant under Sirkan's influence, was a stark reminder of the path she had once trodden.

The chamber itself seemed to defy the laws of space and time. It stretched endlessly yet felt oppressively confined. Each sarcophagus stood like a grave marker of her past selves, turning the chamber into a surreal blend of factory and graveyard. It was a mirror maze of her darkest selves, a maze with no clear exit. Each sarcophagus housed not a corpse but a perfect replica of one of her dark lifetimes, each clone suspended in an eternal moment when her power had blazed brightest. They were scientific marvels, flesh-and-blood photographs capturing the apex of each lifetime. Some bore the flush of victory, others the serene calm of absolute control, all preserved at the height of her beauty and power.

Bile rose in her throat. Cassie turned on her heels and began making her way back to the arch and into the chamber of her past-life shells. She gripped the edges of the sarcophagi so she wouldn't fall to her knees. Her fingers started to tingle when they skimmed one halfway through the room. She stopped abruptly at the sarcophagus that revealed a familiar face from her past-life regressions with Sirkan.

Her hand trembled as she ran her fingers over the icy surface of the glass. She recoiled at a sharp pain, like it had bitten her. She looked at the drop of blood on her finger. It *had* bitten her! She sucked at the oozing blood and then looked into the face of an "Ayesha" that wore the garb of an Egyptian high priestess. *Menhit.*

Her reflection stared back in horror as it overlaid the café au lait face, an eerie blend of past and present.

Turning, Cassie ran to the hatch, her hands trembling in horror as she accessed the opening mechanism once more. She felt she was no longer in her body, her head misty.

I have to get out of here.

The hatch swung open effortlessly. Not caring if anyone heard her, she sprinted down the hallway to her apartment and stumbled inside.

Cassie's fingers tightened once more around the torc encircling her neck, willing it to ignite those ancient fae powers from her father's lineage. Her eyes shimmered. In a pulsating moment, a tiny flicker danced along the intricate metalwork.

A spark!

Then a fizzle.

Damn it to hell. All that training, all that knowledge, useless!

Frustration smoldered in her eyes like a volcano ready to erupt. She cast her gaze toward the damnable alien symbols that snaked their way along the intricate patterns of the room's architecture. The walls, the floor, and the ceiling seemed to writhe with the essence of dark magic, the same dark magic she recognized from her unsettling time in Aunt Isla's court. Those twisted memories flooded back: Sirkan and her gullible aunt weaving spells and past-life memories into her awareness, aiming to sway her toward the left-hand path.

A shiver of resentment coursed through her. Why was she being tested yet again? She had accepted her role as an Aquarian Avatar. She had trained in the Ageless Wisdom Teachings, in the techniques of the light warriors, and in white magic. Hell! She had trained countless *lifetimes!* Her work in developing AI programs in advanced meditation techniques had been coming along beautifully. Her first international peace meditation had gone off without a hitch. Until ...

Not allowing herself to lose control, Cassie went to the bathing chamber and washed the wound on her finger. *Hello, Sleeping Beauty,* she thought. With a suppressed laugh, she decided she needed a nice, warm bath to soothe her frazzled nerves. The tub miraculously began to fill with steaming water. Just as magically, Nova appeared at her door, her forehead creased with worry.

"Here, my lady, let me help you." Nova helped her undress. As Cassie stepped into the scented water, the Arcturian grabbed her hand. The pricked finger had spread into a spider web of red and purple veins, spilling into her palm. Her eyes widened. "My lady! How did you get this wound?"

Unwilling to lie to one of her two allies on the ship, Cassie shared a shortened version of how she left her room and had discovered the chamber of horrors.

Nova shook her head. "You see, we told you that you would be able to access your powers given time." She took Cassie's hand in hers. "But I am concerned about this wound. It seems that it is not merely a prick. There may be some sort of poison now in your blood."

Cassie shrugged. "I'm fine. I'll just drink more water and do some Reiki healing." Then she froze. Even those abilities were muted with the warding sigils that Sirkan had imposed on her and her quarters. She kept attempting to access them, but it was useless.

She would not let fear paralyze her. She sunk deeper into the soothing warmth of the water. "How about one of those healing tinctures?" she asked Nova.

The Arcturian nodded and scurried out of the room.

The spider veins of the wound seemed to have stopped spreading, but her hand throbbed like a bitch. Cassie knew the twins would weave the same magic they had the week before, when she had the incident with her mantra.

Nova and Vega both bustled into the room. Nova had some sort of bath salt concoction she poured into the steaming water. Vega handed her a vial filled with the familiar healing tincture. Cassie sunk deeper into the tub while sipping the noxious potion. "Geeze, why can't healing tinctures *taste* good?" She fell into a lightly altered state of consciousness as she allowed the toxin to be sucked out of her system.

Then there was an urgent knock on the door.

Chapter 17: New Best Friend

Ninhursag had smiled in satisfaction as she'd watched Cassie through her spirit screen. The serum she'd distilled from Sirkan's supply of Ayesha's DNA mixed with sacrificial blood should be surging into the girl's bloodstream. Ninhursag had made sure that the serum was strategically placed on spring needles on top of all the sarcophagi in the first chamber. That way, no matter which sarcophagus the girl pricked her finger on, she would have enough dark energy infused into her blood to begin the turning process. Finding Sirkan's version of Madame Tussauds filled with Ayesha's past-life effigies had been invaluable.

It was time to make her move.

She tapped lightly on Cassandra's door. No answer. Ninhursag sighed and knocked again. "Hellooo! Cassandra?"

A muffled response. *Well, damn,* she thought, *I'll just have to take matters into my own hands.* Fortunately, one of the Arcturian twins threw open the door.

"I was coming down the corridor, and I saw that poor young girl running down the hall and into this chamber. She seemed very upset. Please, allow me to help."

Nova's eyes widened in alarm, but she had no choice but to obey. Ninhursag was an immensely powerful Anunnaki and not to be ignored. The Arcturian bowed deeply and stepped aside. Ninhursag glided into the chamber and waved Nova inside. "Come with me."

Cassie was standing at the far side of the sitting room, palms held up to the glass of the panoramic window, tears streaming down her face. She whirled around as she saw Ninhursag's reflection in the glass.

"Who ... who are you?" she sputtered.

"My dear, I am Lady Ninhursag. Remember? We met at dinner?"

Cassie furrowed her brows as she tried to understand the words coming from the woman's mouth. It sounded like English but heavily accented. The woman's features resembled someone who had stepped out of an Egyptian relief. She had pale skin with elongated oval eyes the same color as the kohl that outlined them. She wore a pleated linen tunic that flowed to her knees and modern, flowing pants. Her hair was styled every bit like an Egyptian queen, long beaded braids with heavy bangs. She was quite striking.

Something was pulling at the back of Cassie's memory, but she couldn't get a handle on it. Cassie sighed, figuring it might be a past-life recognition.

Ninhursag inched forward as if approaching a feral cat. She tentatively reached out a hand. "I was walking back to my chamber and saw you running down the hallway, obviously upset. Since I recognized you as Sirkan's new guest from Earth, of course I wanted to offer you what aid I could."

Cassie still couldn't manage to put a coherent thought together, much less speak intelligibly. Her hand was throbbing.

Then she noticed Nova and reached out to her.

Nova rushed to her side and put her arm around the girl's shoulders. "There, my lady. You need to rest a bit."

Cassie noticeably slumped against Nova and nodded. She then turned to her guest. "Thank you, Miss Nin ...?"

"Ninhursag. But please, call me Nin. Of course, my dear. I will summon my handmaid to fetch some healing herbs that I have in my stores and make a tincture for you." She looked pointedly at Nova, daring her to say anything.

An hour later, Cassie was sipping the tea that Ninhursag had concocted. Nova had left to get her a light supper.

"You are feeling better then?" asked Ninhursag.

Cassie took a deep breath and nodded.

"Perhaps you would like to share with me what upset you so much? You can trust me. I have been a part of this community for, well, a very long time."

And that's exactly why I shouldn't trust you, thought Cassie. Anyone on this ship was sure to be part of the Dark Brotherhood. Except, oh yeah, the twins. But there was no way in hell she was just going to trust this woman who looked like someone out of Sirkan's lust-filled past lives.

Cassie took another sip of the soothing tea. It reminded her of rosehips with honey. Not bad. She was definitely beginning to feel more relaxed, but she knew she could never speak about the horrific room filled with her past-life clones.

The door finally slid open, and both Nova and Vega came in with dinner for two. The delicious smell of chicken soup and freshly baked bread made Cassie's mouth water. She suddenly realized she was famished and applied herself to the simple meal with relish.

"There are many secrets aboard this ship," Ninhursag said. "I know about Sirkan's work and his eternal quest for Ayesha over the millennia."

Cassie's head shot up. "Excuse me?"

"My dear, let us be frank. In many ways, I'm as much of a prisoner here as you. My people came here during Sumerian times and established a dynasty that later evolved into a branch of the royal houses of ancient Egypt." *Speak enough truth to get her to trust you,* Nin thought.

"You do look like someone out of ancient Egypt," said Cassie.

The woman threw back her head in a genuine laugh. "You are a delight. So refreshingly honest. I like you."

Cassie shrugged. Mutual trust needed to be earned.

"Sirkan is off the ship for some time, I believe. Let's the two of us get to know one another. There are many places of wonder on this ship. I will show them to you. The hydroponic gardens are a marvel. And the swimming grotto is my absolute favorite place to relax. Why, we could even go for an evening swim tonight if you are up to it."

"No, I just want to go to bed and block out this day as much as I can. Maybe tomorrow."

"It's a date. I will swing around with a special morning meal. How is that?"

Cassie shrugged. "Sure, it's not like I have anything pressing to do." *Except escape,* she added silently.

"Marvelous. Sleep well then." And she was gone.

Cassie turned to the twins when they began to clear away the dishes. She had a thousand questions but decided to keep her own counsel for now. She prepared to send a telepathic message to the twins when she noticed that the torc around her neck seemed to be humming again, like it was coming back in sync with her energy. *Oh my god.* It felt like she was coming out of that dampening fog. She jumped up and ran energy down her arms and into her fingers. Her fingertips sparked!

Vega noticed and grabbed her hands. "My lady, your powers?"

"Yes, *yes!* I feel like they are coming back." Then she figured she'd really go for it and said, "By the Radiant One."

Zap.

Well, that's not going to work ... yet, she thought.

After the pain subsided, Cassie continued to channel energy through her hands. It remained faint, but it was undeniably there.

Nova reached out to her, "My lady, I suggest you not overdo it. You have been a long time without being able to access your powers. You don't want to deplete them or exhaust yourself. Why not get some sleep and see if you can access your dream walking?"

Cassie hugged the diminutive alien. "You are absolutely right, Nova! Do you have the makings of the amazing hot chocolate you made for me before?"

Nodding, the Arcturian left the room.

Ninhursag watched through the spirit screen. It was time to put the next part of her plan into action with Manu.

CASSIE AWOKE IN HER bed four hours later, the two Arcturians by her side. She smiled wanly. "I'm OK. Really. You don't have to hover."

Vega took the wounded hand in hers. "It still looks raw, my lady. We will continue to look for healing options. We don't know what Lord Sirkan injected into the needle that you pricked your finger on. The sarcophagus that you indicated must be self-sterilizing, as when we went to examine it, it was clean. It will be best for you to rest for a time. He left for the surface yesterday, and we do not know when he will return."

With a sigh of relief, Cassie got up to prepare for her breakfast "date" with the mysterious Anunnaki woman. She couldn't remember her name. Her powers seemed to be coming back little by little, but her mind was fuzzy whenever she thought about the woman.

As if on cue, the door to the outer room chimed, and Nova went to open it.

Ninhursag waved in two of her own attendants who rolled a cart loaded with domed plates and platters. "I have brought our morning repast, some of my favorites that I want to share with you." The two small, dark figures silently laid out the food on the table in the main room, then silently stood awaiting orders from their lady.

Ninhursag lifted the domed plates. "I believe this would be called 'ancient grain' bread, which I've had toasted and topped with a butter made of dates and almonds, blended with a hint of cinnamon and vanilla." She put a slice on her plate and offered another one to Cassie.

The Anunnaki then pointed to a steaming platter of unfamiliar meat. It had an unappetizing, blue-tinged color, but the spicey smells wafting from it were tempting. Ninhursag noticed her interest and scooped some onto another plate, along with what looked like a potato of some kind.

"This is a rare bird I brought back from one of my sojourns in the Tiamat Nebula. I was able to introduce it into ancient Mesopotamia's animal husbandry system, and now it thrives in the gardens here on the ship. I promised you I would show you the hydroponic gardens. Let's do that after our meal, shall we?"

Still wary, Cassie watched Ninhursag nibble at the food on her plate. *OK, it looks safe.* Cassie took a few bites. "Oh my, this is amazing."

Ninhursag took a pitcher of fruit juice and poured out two glasses. As she offered a glass, her voice, smooth and reassuring, hinted at the special concoction's benefits. "This should be quite refreshing," she said, a subtle smile playing on her lips. "I've blended ginseng and holy basil into this juice. It will help you feel better than ever."

What she didn't tell Cassie was the liquid contained not only several more drops of sacrificial blood but also a few drops of Cassie's blood collected from the sarcophagus needle that had pricked her, a silent witness to her unintended offering.

Chapter 18: The Sleeping Prophet

Natesh hated the water. But he was convinced that Cassandra was trapped in an interdimensional realm below the Bimini Islands. A sunken city had been foretold by the "sleeping prophet," Edgar Cayce. Years ago, Natesh had sought out the seer for insight and guidance.

The year was 1932, and the world was on the brink of a major war. Natesh planned to capitalize on the unfolding global conflict. In the waning light of a cold November evening, Natesh strode through the shadowed streets of New Orleans, his mind a whirlwind of memories and thwarted ambitions. The recent election of Franklin D. Roosevelt as president of the United States had stirred the political waters, but Natesh's focus lay on a more sinister tide sweeping across the globe.

He had journeyed from France to America, not in pursuit of its promises, but to expand Europe's burgeoning fascism. Intent on becoming the foremost vampire lord in the Americas, he sought to spread this malevolent influence. However, he encountered an unexpected obstacle. Choosing New Orleans for its diverse cultures and mystical energies as the base for his clan, his plans were thwarted when a coven of white witches arrived, challenging his efforts.

At the forefront of this resistance was Desiree, a young Creole witch whose spirit burned with a purpose that rivaled his own. Her arrival in New Orleans had started as a quest of the heart. She sought her fiancé, a wealthy merchant believed lost at sea, his fate a mystery that tethered her to this new land.

Their first encounter had been under a moonlit sky, where Natesh had felt the pulse of her formidable power. Desiree stood blocking his way, hands fisted on her hips. Her honey-hued eyes had been filled with rebellion, her softly accented voice unwavering when she confronted him.

"You will not bring your darkness here," she said, her words cutting through the humid air. She was petite and dark, her face tanned by the sun, emphasizing her heavily kohled, toasted-almond eyes. The white witch stood firmly, an aura of determination radiating around her. Her hands glowed with a soft, aethereal light, contrasting sharply with the ominous shadows that seemed to cling to the vampire lord.

His black eyes flared as they met hers. He sneered, his face twisting in contempt. "Your feeble light is powerless against the darkness I possess," he replied, his voice a chilling whisper that seemed to freeze the surrounding air. "Run back to your coven and impotent spells before I ensure you no longer breathe on this earth."

The night was alight with the eerie glow of ancient magic and the gleam of fangs. The streets, usually brimming with the soulful melodies of jazz and the laughter of revelers, began to empty. The humans seemed to sense something bad was about to happen.

His clan gathered behind him, many of them newborns, their blood lust barely contained. Their eyes, a vivid crimson, scanned the surroundings with an animalistic keenness, each movement filled with a restless energy. These fledglings, recently turned and still adapting to their newfound vampiric nature, were a volatile mix of human emotion and inhuman desire.

The witches came out from their encampment, their clothing shimmering with enchantments. Gathered around Desiree, they stood their ground in Jackson Square. Their eyes, aglow with the power of their ancient lineage, focused on Natesh. With chants that weaved through the humid night air, they summoned the forces of nature: fierce winds and crackling lightning. The very earth seemed to rise at their command.

Natesh had underestimated her, dismissing her as a mere stumbling block. Yet as their eyes met, he saw not just defiance but also a depth of conviction that gave him pause. This was not merely a clash of powers. There was something more.

He couldn't shake the feeling that he had known her before. Only one woman had affected him along the same lines. Giselle.

With an exasperated gesture, Natesh retreated into his shadow form and signaled his first lieutenant, Mia, to shepherd the clan back to their lair in an abandoned house in the Garden District. The image of Giselle lingered in his mind as he made his escape, her soul essence shining like a beacon in his dark world. The thought that Desiree could be the reincarnation of his long-lost love stirred something within him, a flicker of humanity he thought had been extinguished long ago.

Striding into his private quarters, he contemplated this revelation. The idea that this witch might hold the essence of his past love complicated his plans. Her presence in the city radiated purity and light. This was not only a challenge to his reign but also a haunting reminder. It evoked memories of a life he once knew, filled with love and passion instead of darkness and lust.

The moon cast its silver light over the rooftops, and he found himself torn between his age-old quest for power and the unexpected resurgence of old affections. The vampire lord, once unshakable in his pursuits, now faced an inner turmoil that threatened to unravel the very fabric of his being. He needed answers and he needed them fast.

Since losing Giselle during the French Revolution, he had been to every seer and witch that deigned to work with him to determine if she had been reborn. Lifetime after lifetime, he had searched. Now, for the first time, he felt sure it was her.

Ever since coming to New Orleans, he had been hearing about Edgar Cayce the "sleeping prophet," so called because he did his work in a state of apparent slumber. Perhaps it was time Natesh checked him out.

Cayce had established the Association for Research and Enlightenment in Virginia Beach, Virginia. It was world-renowned for giving powerful insights into a person's past lives, their illnesses, and even their soul missions. Natesh wanted to know why he had such conflicting emotions about Desiree. Was she truly the reincarnation of Giselle?

He hesitated to go to this man, however. Cayce was reportedly a man of the Christian faith and could very well seek to destroy Natesh. Nonetheless, Natesh, driven by an insatiable thirst for understanding, sought out Cayce. Much to the vampire's relief, Cayce's wife allowed him entrée after a generous donation to Cayce's association. He found the prophet in a quaint reading room, where Cayce's serene presence sharply contrasted with Natesh's brooding aura.

"I seek insights into a past life," Natesh began, his voice laced with an undertone of urgency. "A turbulent era during the French Revolution where I lost my love, Giselle."

In his trance, Cayce's words wove a tale both haunting and illuminating. "In that life, you were of noble birth, blinded by power yet profoundly in love with Giselle. Her loss was your heart's greatest tragedy. Giselle is reborn again. Your destinies are entwined, but not as you would wish."

Natesh felt a surge of emotions. "When will we be together again?"

Cayce's eyes opened and held Natesh's gaze. "Your souls are destined to cross paths, to teach and to heal each other. Yet her journey is in a different direction. You walk a path of darkness, but it is not the only path available to you." Cayce's voice was steady and knowing. "Each lifetime you have met this soul, you had to choose between light and darkness. This is one such time."

"But I have not found Giselle since the French Revolution," said Natesh. "How do I know that this Desiree is my beloved reborn?"

"You know this within yourself. Remember that her soul is immortal. Her body is not, but it will be. This one's soul incarnates to seek balance for a karmic debt incurred before you knew her. She has a great destiny. You could be integral in aiding her in her quest."

Natesh left the prophet's presence with a sense of disquiet. Cayce's words echoed in his mind, a reminder that the future was not set in stone, that choices made could lead down unforeseen roads. Actions had consequences, even for a vampire.

That night, Natesh found himself at a crossroads. He walked the streets of Virginia Beach until he gathered his wits about him enough to head back to New Orleans and the French Quarter.

The bright lights of a jazz club spilled onto the street, a stark contrast to the darkness within him. He could continue this battle against Desiree and her coven, pushing forward his agenda. Or he could ponder Cayce's words, consider the paths not yet taken.

In the shadows of New Orleans, a city of magic and mystery, Natesh's next move remained uncertain, a chess piece hovering over a board of infinite possibilities. He needed to decide whether or not to confront Desiree.

He had not chosen wisely back then. He needed to choose wisely now.

DESIREE WATCHED THE vampire lord wander the streets of the French Quarter through her crystal globe. She had felt conflicted about him since their first encounter. Her task was to defeat him as a harbinger of the Dark Brotherhood. Natesh Nandwani's reputation as the most brutal and salacious of all the vampire lords on the continent had preceded him. Now that he was in America, it was her duty to stop him at all costs.

Yet she felt empathy toward him. Vampires were made mostly against their wills. She knew he had been sired by the infamous vampire Philinnion during the time of the French Revolution. Now he was here in modern-day America, a testament to his cunning and resilience. He would be a formidable opponent. She reached out to the head of her coven, who resided in the fae realm. Siobhan Sinclair responded instantaneously to the spirit screen call.

"Desiree! How goes your mission in the new world?"

Desiree smiled inwardly. Siobhan still referred to the United States as the "new world" even though she had been very active during the establishment of the colonies, the American Revolution, and the founding of the United States. "I need some advice and possibly some additional help here," Desiree said. "I have encountered the vampire, Natesh."

Siobhan cursed. "What in all that is unholy is he doing there?"

"Trying to spread the doctrine of fascism from here in New Orleans. This place is a cesspool of dark energy, and he is tapping into it with total aplomb. The youth of the city are enthralled with his good looks and charisma. The hint of war and his promise of immortality are too potent for many of them to resist." She paused. "I feel totally out of my depth."

Siobhan sighed, "Do not try to take him on alone. I will send Ian. He has met Natesh before and survived the encounter. There is a way to neutralize him."

NATESH KNEW HE HAD to leave New Orleans. He would not take the chance of taking Desiree's life and thus pushing away any chance of ever being with her again. The newborns would have to be left to his lieutenants with strict orders not to touch a hair on Desiree's head. But he needed to see her one last time.

He stood at the edge of the forest surrounding the bayou on the west side of New Orleans. The witches had glamoured their coven headquarters as a Romani encampment. He cursed when he saw Ian MacGregor step out of a portal.

"Damn it! Why is he here?" Of course, he knew why. Siohban Sinclair must be the head of the coven. Of all the luck!

Desiree walked over to greet Ian. Natesh felt a wave of emotion as he sensed her energy. Yes, it was Giselle reborn. He also knew that no reconciliation would occur in this lifetime. He needed to disappear and leave her to her own path. He could feel his heart crack with the realization. So be it.

Desiree's eyes widened as she turned and looked in his direction. She could feel him as much as he could feel her. Further confirmation.

He was about to shift into bat form when a blast of energy threw him into a snare, binding him with luminous strands that seemed made of pure light. Ian emerged from the shadows, his expression grim yet determined. In his hand, he held an ancient artifact pulsating with an aethereal glow. The artifact, combined with his own considerable mystical knowledge, had created a trap that even Natesh could not escape.

Natesh struggled against the bindings; his vampiric strength futile against the mystical restraints. Ian approached cautiously, aware of the vampire's cunning. "You've preyed on humanity for too long, Natesh," Ian said firmly. "Your reign of terror ends tonight."

A maelstrom of energy burst through the forest. Morgandrian and her dark coven emerged, their presence a stark contrast to the light that bound Natesh. The air crackled with their malevolent power, sending tremors through the clearing. Morgandrian stepped forward with sinister grace.

"I don't think so," she said, her voice resonating with an ominous tone that seemed to warp the very air around her. Her eyes, ablaze with fury, locked onto Ian and the white witches, a clear challenge in her gaze.

Ian and the white witches readied themselves, their own powers surging in response to the threat. A standoff ensued, the air thick with the tension of opposing forces. The white witches began chanting, their voices weaving a protective spell around them, while Ian focused his energies, preparing for a fight.

Morgandrian raised her hand, and shadows swirled around her fingers, coalescing into a dark, pulsating orb. With a swift motion, she hurled it toward the bindings that held Natesh. The orb collided with the light, causing an explosion of energy that reverberated through the forest. The mystical restraints shattered under the impact.

In the chaos, Morgandrian seized the opportunity. She chanted in a language forgotten by time, and a portal of swirling darkness opened behind her. Natesh, weakened but still standing, lunged toward the portal, closely followed by Morgandrian and her coven. She turned and met Ian's eyes for a heartbeat, and then her dark form disappeared into the void, the portal snapping shut with a final, echoing clap.

Ian and the white witches were left in the aftermath, the forest eerily silent. They had been outmaneuvered, their enemy slipping through their grasp. Ian's expression was one of frustration and loss, though he knew the skirmish was merely another chapter in an ongoing struggle. The white witches gathered around him, their determination unwavering. They would regroup, plan, and continue their fight against the darkness that threatened the world.

Chapter 19: Of Mers and Magic

Elena sat with Artemus and Manu in the Citadel's command center pouring over a series of ancient maps.

"Here." Manu pointed to a large expanse of water with scattered islands off the coast of south Florida. He traced a triangle in the Atlantic Ocean that went from Miami through the Bimini Islands to the Bahamas and Puerto Rico, up to Bermuda and back to Miami. "This is where the third and final sinking of the continent took place."

Elena nodded, "The Bermuda Triangle."

Manu mirrored her nod. "We know the crystals that powered Atlantis could not be destroyed. I want to mount an exploratory mission to determine how much the dimensional rift is growing. Who among your acolytes and the avatars would be of most use in such a mission?"

"Marcus needs to be part of the team. He and Cecelia discovered that he has a strong soul link with Cassandra, and his computer skills will be of great help. He can hack into almost any program. Then there's Yirribindi with their Aboriginal connections to the earth; their intuitive abilities would be an asset." She paused, weighing her choices. "I would also feel better if you had Seraphina along as healer."

"Yes, they would be vital assets in a mission such as this," said Artemus. "Of course, Ian MacGregor will help to lead the team. He has been studying dimensional rifts for centuries. His considerable abilities as a white witch would be invaluable. I will reach out to him."

Manu concurred. "I agree. We don't want an army; we need a laser-focused squad. I would like to leave within the week." He turned to Artemus and Elena. "Is that doable?"

Both nodded.

"And Natesh?" asked Elena.

"Ian has met with him. Natesh had some good intel to share from a seer named Cayce about Bimini. He will meet us there.

FIVE DAYS LATER, THE group met at the rendezvous point in Bermuda. They cloaked the ship from mundane eyes, as well the submersible that would take them to the ocean's depths. Manu had a strong feeling that an interdimensional portal and an underwater city was there. Aquaman's mythology came from somewhere.

Ian pulled out a rucksack and unbuckled the top. He pulled out a bag of multicolored, rough-hewn stones the size of marbles. Light emanated from within them. "These fragments are pieces of Atlantean crystals that I discovered during my exploration of this area." He reached into the bag and took out a handful. "Master Elena has engraved them with Atlantean magical symbols. They have the ability to unlock ancient Atlantean technology and protect against mystical threats. The last time I was here, I was thrown back by a powerful force field that shattered almost every bone in my body. It took close to a year for the healers to put me back together. I won't let that happen to you under my watch." He gave each one in the group a stone. "You too, Manu."

The high priest arched his eyebrow, then shrugged and palmed the proffered stone.

"Put them as close to your hearts as you can; the inner pocket in your unisuits will do nicely." Ian said. "We will need to swim from the submersible to the crystal cave entrance where the interdimensional portal is. That is where our newest ally will come in."

On cue, a tall figure with blue-green luminescent skin entered the room. He was so tall that he had to stoop to come through the doorway. His hair, a waterfall of silver and blue, cascaded to his shoulders, giving him a regal yet untamed look. His eyes were like twin pools of clear ocean water. Around his neck he wore a pendant made of Atlantean crystal that pulsed with soft iridescent light, a fragment of his lost kingdom.

"May I introduce King Caelum Marex, the sovereign of Poseidia."

Manu went to the king and embraced him. "It's good to see you again, brother. It looks like taking to the seas has agreed with you!"

Caelum returned the embrace with gusto, his booming voice reverberating throughout the chamber. "Manu! You scoundrel. You still live?"

The two celestials then slipped into an animated conversation in an ancient language, words unintelligible to the rest of the group, but they all could guess the content.

With a final slap on Manu's back, Caelum turned to the group with a wide grin. "Have any of you heard of the merfolk?"

The avatars' eyes bugged out of their heads.

"You mean, like, *mermaids*?" asked Karim.

"The very same. Though the proper term is *merfolk*," Caelum began, a glimmer of amusement in his eyes. "But before I explain, you'll need a bit of history for context.

"When Atlantis faced its final hours, those of us who were immortal had a choice. We could escape aboard celestial ships and take to the skies, we could follow the human survivors across the seas to rebuild, or we could surrender ourselves to the ocean, adapting to a new way of life beneath the waves. I chose the sea. But we could not survive such a transformation on our own—we needed power, and so I sought the aid of a being revered in Atlantean culture.

"You know him as Poseidon, god of the sea, but the truth is more complex. Poseidon was no deity—at least, not in the way mortals understand gods. He was an ancient earth elemental, a force of nature given form, whose power shaped land and sea alike. His magic was vast, strong enough to raise islands or pull them beneath the waves. To the early civilizations, he was divine, and so they worshipped him. In truth, he was simply older, stronger, and more attuned to the elements than any mortal could comprehend.

"In exchange for our loyalty and our vow to safeguard the ocean, Poseidon did more than grant us access to his seas—he remade us. As Atlantis crumbled, his power surged through us like a tidal wave. Our bodies shifted, changed, becoming something new, something fit for the depths—and the first merfolk had been born.

"And so, we built a kingdom where Atlantis once stood, adapting our heritage to this new realm beneath the waves. Over time, our legend spread, evolving into myths, stories, even movies." He grinned, his eyes gleaming with amusement. "Though, I have to say, Hollywood gets a lot of details wrong."

Manu huffed, "You haven't changed in all these millennia, my brother. Still as cheeky as ever."

Caelum smiled, "We can also come ashore when we need to." He looked around the group. "Ever heard of the Little Mermaid? Mythology, fairy tales, and reality ... all the same. It's only our point of reference that changes when we succumb to a limited point of view."

Ian was practically dancing with impatience. "All right then. Let us be about the mission."

Caelum nodded. "Yes, Manu has filled me in on the situation. I will tell you that I know of a mother ship that has been in the dimensional rift under Bimini for millennia. It has access to our city of Poseidia through a tunnel that traverses between dimensions. We trade with them through two Arcturians who bring us rare jewels and crystals in exchange for various food supplies. My steward informed me that about a year ago their supply requests changed to include more third-dimensional foodstuffs like American coffee, fae spices, and flesh foods. I know the vessel is protected by a powerful celestial force field. I have explored the perimeter of the ship with some of my warriors, but we have not been able to get within a league of it."

"Did you have interface with the inhabitants of the ship before that?" asked Artemus.

"Yes. It has been sporadic, but the ship has been kept alive in the rift since the final sinking of Atlantis. It has remained static, only coming to life every few centuries and then only for short bursts of time. I do know that it is a Lyran mother ship."

Manu whirled around. "Lyran? Then it must be Sirkan's ship."

Caelum agreed and elaborated further. "Indeed, there is more to the story. It is thought that when the ship initially arrived at that location, it carried a king and a queen. These two royals were believed to have founded a significant dynasty, which later laid the foundation for the earliest ruling bloodlines of Egypt. The queen was known by the name Ayesha."

Manu growled.

Nonplussed, Caelum continued. "Sirkan was able to give her a very long life, but she was not immortal. She gave birth to many children who went on to be some of the most powerful demigods in the ancient world. Since the ship was in a dimensional rift, the queen had to go back and forth between the ship and their palaces on land. The high vibrational frequency of the ship was how she was kept alive for so long. It acted as a kind of rejuvenation chamber. I sent delegations to them, but either there was no response, or the delegation never returned."

Caelum paused for a beat before continuing. "There was talk about the Anunnaki having something to do with them, but again, I don't have direct knowledge of this. Queen Ayesha was reported to have great magical powers that were bestowed upon her by a great being from the stars. I always thought it was the great Anunnaki, Ninhursag, who had given her those powers."

Manu searched his memories for what he knew of those chaotic years after he had left Ayesha behind. He had never been able to track her until lifetimes later. It was beyond his ability to grasp that she would have ended up with Sirkan of all people. How in the hell could that have happened?

Picking up his thoughts, Elena said, "Manu, you know that Ayesha had to be under much duress to have succumbed to Sirkan."

Manu's cerulean eyes hardened. "I do not believe that she would have gone with him willingly. I do know that, while she was with him in Isla's court, Sirkan took Cassandra back to some dark lifetimes via past-life regressions, attempting to turn her. She never shared the particulars, and I never pressed."

With that he turned on his heel and strode from the room.

Artemus looked after him, concerned. He turned back to Caelum. "We need more intel. Who are these Arcturians? Can you reach them?"

"Yes. My steward deals with them when they come into the city. I will advise him of the situation and make sure that the merchants they normally deal with are alerted."

"This puts a different focus on our expedition," said Artemus. "If the ship is in a dimensional rift, then we will need some additional members to the team. Has anyone spoken to General Eristides lately?"

"I believe Rebekah was the last one to speak with him. From what I know, he was preparing to reach out to Ashtar."

The Ashtar Command was a diverse coalition of extraterrestrial civilizations and cosmic entities. They were under the leadership of Ashtar Sheran, a highly evolved celestial dedicated to protecting Earth.

Elena turned to the three avatars, who had been uncharacteristically quiet during the discussion. "You three remain in prep mode with Ian. This would also be a perfect time for you to brush up on ancient history and find out as much as you can about the founding of the first dynasties of ancient Egypt."

"On it," said Marcus. He motioned to Seraphina and Yirribindi and opened a portal back to the New York institute.

"Marcus is back in the fold then?" asked Ian.

"Yes, his lost memories are slowly coming back to him. He was most definitely possessed by one of Sirkan's dark acolytes."

Ian rubbed his chin. "I wonder if he can access anything else about that dark acolyte. Perhaps ferret out information about the ship and how to breach it. I will ask Cecilia to meet me at Praxis. Since she was successful in guiding Marcus through the Akashic library, perhaps we can go a little deeper."

"A solid plan," said Elena.

A whoosh of energy announced the arrival of Natesh just before Ian departed. "Sorry I'm late. I had a bit of an issue with one of my lieutenants. Ian, did you give my information to the team about Bimini?"

Ian nodded, "Yes, it was highly beneficial. Your information tracks with our intel about a rift beneath the Bimini Islands. You just missed our deep-sea ally, the king of the merfolk, Caelum Marex. He confirmed the presence of a mother ship beneath Bimini that may well have caused the phenomenon of the Bermuda Triangle, just as your sleeping prophet told you."

"That is good news." Natesh said, then glanced at Elena. "If I may, I need to speak to you privately."

Elena motioned him into the deeper recesses of the cave. "I'm listening."

Taking a deep breath, Natesh began his narrative about his meeting with Cayce and how he had been advised to release his obsession with Desiree so that her soul could complete its mission unhindered. Elena could feel his pain.

"We have both will and fixed design on our path toward enlightenment, Natesh. It looks like you will have to make a very painful decision in this current timeline. Are you prepared to do it?"

"I don't know that I can, but I am prepared to help rescue her and do whatever I can to help her complete her mission. What's the saying? 'The road to hell is paved with good intentions.' I am in hell and have been masking it for close to two hundred years by being the best dark vampire lord I can be." He turned and beat a fist into his palm. "I just don't know that I can let her go. She was and still is the love of my life. Through loving her, I might yet find salvation."

Elena's heart went out to him, but she wouldn't grant him quarter, "Only you can ascertain what is more important in the long run. I pray you will come to the right decision and find peace."

With that, she left him to his own tortured thoughts.

Chapter 20: The Geneva Deception

"It's about damn time you made an appearance!" President Soter shouted. "Things are going to shit here. Where have you been?"

"You sweet talker you," purred Morgandrian. "That is the sort of greeting that will get you … nowhere. You are not the only human on this planet who demands my attention."

"I damn well better be. This is the most powerful country in the world, and I'm its leader. I have been doing my best to up the game with the mind control programs, but it seems Dhawan is now missing in action. Now I need that Technomancer to up *his* game!"

"You mean you don't know how to contact him without Dhawan?

Soter bit back his urge to say *duh*. "Obviously not," he said instead.

Morgandrian sighed. "All right then. Let me see what I can do. I will reach out to you via my spirit screen when I make contact with him. In the meantime, I highly recommend that you gather your little cabinet and start some world leader assassinations and riots in the streets. Or at least, plan economic mayhem with your wealthiest allies. I understand you have an excellent hacker for the financial sector. Use them!"

"I'm planning on doing that and more. I am addressing the Global Moral Coalition in Geneva next week. I plan on planting more seeds of unrest. The Technomancer needs to ensure that the subliminals are in place before I take the podium."

ARION MET MORGANDRIAN back in her throne room.

"The Technomancer and subliminals. How banal. No matter, I will make sure the damage is minimal."

"How?" asked Morgandrian.

His handsome face broke into a wide grin, a twinkle of amusement in his eyes. "You expect me to tell *you* my plans? Really? Just keep doing what you're doing."

Morgandrian stomped her foot as the portal swallowed him. *So fucking frustrating.*

At least she knew Sirkan had risen once more.

She twisted the ruby ring on her finger, smirking. Unexpectedly, it had reactivated a few days ago. That bastard had pulled off another resurrection.

Well, she *was* playing both sides...

And if all else failed, there was always the Technomancer.

IN THE STATELY HALL of the Palais de Nations in Geneva, the flags of countless nations surrounded President Conroe Soter of the United States of America. Under the watchful eyes of the world, he ascended the podium as the teleprompter fired up. The assembled delegates, representatives of global powers and smaller states alike, turned their attention toward him, intrigued by the reputation that preceded him. The room, usually buzzing with whispered negotiations and diplomatic exchanges, fell silent, the air charged with expectation.

Soter studied the assembled dignitaries from all over the world. There wasn't an empty seat in the amphitheater. This speech would be a turning point. Catching the go ahead from his event coordinator, he cleared his throat to begin. The Technomancer had come through. The visuals were coded with the subliminals he had approved just days before. They would be subtle implants that would blossom over the next few weeks after the delegates had returned to their respective countries to begin wreaking havoc. Soter wanted to rub his hands with glee.

Clearing his throat, he began, "Ladies and gentlemen, esteemed delegates," his voice infused with a grave sincerity, "we stand at a pivotal moment in history, confronted by a maelstrom of chaos that threatens to engulf our civilizations. A chaos not born of natural disorder, but of evil design."

He walked slowly across the stage, making deliberate eye contact with various delegates, seeking to engage them directly. "Our world is plagued by misinformation and propaganda, tools wielded by shadow entities with the intent to divide us, to dilute the strength found in our unity."

A wave of murmurs swept through the room while Soter outlined a global conspiracy of economic sabotage. "Our markets are manipulated, creating economic instability that undermines our societies from within. These are not random fluctuations, but targeted attacks by those who fear our collective potential."

Soter's gaze swept the room, capturing the audience with his intensity. "Consider the environmental disasters we face: unprecedented climate catastrophes and dwindling resources. These are exacerbated, if not directly caused by, groups opposed to our progress, ideologues who would rather see us regress into turmoil than advance together toward a sustainable and enlightened future," Soter continued, his voice rising in fervor.

He leaned forward, his voice dropping to a more intimate tone, as if sharing a confidential truth. "And what of the ceaseless international conflicts, the health crises sweeping across our borders? They are not merely challenges to be overcome but are orchestrated crises by those who would destabilize our nations, who envy and oppose the prosperity and peace we strive to build."

Soter paused, allowing his accusations to resonate, painting a world besieged by orchestrated threats, a narrative of global conspiracy. "These saboteurs, hidden within our midst, exploit our freedoms and our openness against us. Their goal is to fragment our global society, to undermine the very pillars upon which our international order stands."

As he reached the climax of his speech, Soter's voice thundered through the hall. "The time for action is now. We must unite to root out these miscreants, to safeguard our future against those who seek to destroy it. Only together, by identifying and eliminating these threats, can we preserve the stability and prosperity of our world."

The applause that followed was not just a courtesy but a resonant endorsement of Soter's call to arms. In that moment, President Conroe Soter had not only redirected the blame for the world's chaos onto invisible enemies but also positioned himself as the leader in the global fight against those supposed adversaries. His message was clear: In the face of such orchestrated threats, only decisive action and unity under *his* guidance could save the world from imminent collapse.

Part II: Something Wicked

BY THE PRICKING OF my thumbs, something wicked this way comes. The sleep of reason breeds monsters. There are times when we must grasp the dagger and advance into the darkness.
Ray Bradbury, *Something Wicked This Way Comes*

Chapter 21: Back to the Beginning

She was standing in the middle of a circular room on a mother ship. Turning around, the high priestess could see a console that held multicolored crystals pulsating with a rhythm that seemed to echo the heartbeat of the cosmos. These crystals, she knew, were guiding and fueling the ship, their multifaceted surfaces casting a kaleidoscope of colors across the sleek metallic surfaces.

Holographic star maps floated along another console, displaying constellations and celestial bodies. The maps were meticulously operated by a uniformed cadet whose elongated, pale-blue fingers danced across the holograms with graceful precision. This being was humanoid, but distinctly not Sirian, with luminescent eyes that seemed to hold galaxies within them and skin that shimmered like a starlit night.

Ayesha looked around the command center of the ship. The room was bustling with the activities of at least four different species, each contributing to the harmony of this interstellar vessel. Small, slender figures with silver skin and flowing robes that defied gravity moved with an air of authority, their telepathic communications creating a symphony of silent whispers. These were the Arcturians, known for their wisdom and advanced psychic abilities.

Nearby, a group of Pleiadeans worked intently. Their features were strikingly beautiful, almost aethereal, with hair that ranged from platinum blonde to deep blue, cascading down their backs like liquid light. Their expressions were kind and their movements full of grace, embodying a profound sense of peace and serenity.

In stark contrast, a robust and rugged species known as the Andromedans huddled around a technical panel. Their muscular forms were encased in armor that was both organic and metallic, a fusion of biology and technology. Their faces were stern, etched with lines of determination and strength, and their eyes glowed with fierce intelligence.

Lastly, hovering above the ground was a Zeta Reticulin, its small gray form almost childlike in appearance but exuding an aura of ancient knowledge. Large almond-shaped black eyes observed everything with an intense curiosity, and its slender hands manipulated a three-dimensional model of a galaxy, rearranging stars and planets with a mere gesture.

Looking up, she saw the vast expanse of space through the panoramic windows of the command deck, stars twinkling like distant fireflies. In this moment, amidst these diverse beings, she felt a profound sense of unity, a shared purpose that transcended the boundaries of worlds and species. It was a realization that in the grand tapestry of the cosmos, each thread, no matter how different, was essential in weaving the story of the universe.

She was on the bottom tier of a three-tiered room laid out in concentric circles. Her eyes focused on the second tier as a swishing noise heralded a hatchway opening. A large man stood silhouetted against a backdrop of intense white light and paused for a moment. The light beamed around him like a celestial halo. Then he descended some steps and strode over to her, taking her hands into his. She knew this man. Cerulean-blue eyes. Silken ebony hair just brushing his shoulders. The sculpted mouth of an angel. Manu.

"My love, what are you doing on the command deck? I thought you were in your study preparing for our landing. We will be on Earth in a matter of days."

She gazed at him intently, absorbing his every feature. His discomfort grew under her steady stare, prompting him to grasp her hands gently. "Are you unwell? You look pale."

Shaking her head slowly, her eyes never left his. "I'm ... not certain. It's as though I'm not fully here. There's a vision of an underwater ship ..." Her voice faded, her gaze drifting, bewildered by the bustling activity around them.

Manu, sensing her distress, tapped his earpiece. "Send Priestess Ayesha's handmaiden to the command deck. She is unwell."

She grabbed at him. "No, don't let me go. I don't want to be separated from you!" His eyes widened. "My love, I'm not going anywhere. We will always be together. You are the love of my life, and I will never let anything change that."

The scene dissolved into a fine mist as she continued to reach for him. "No, don't leave me ... don't leave ..."

CASSIE WOKE CLUTCHING at the bedcovers and with tears streaming down her face. Her heart felt like it had been ripped apart. Then the crystal cave where she had met Manu in an inner-plane vision flashed in her mind's eye. It had been almost three years ago, before her initiation as one of the seven Aquarian Avatars. That vision had ignited her memory of him and the immortal love they had for one another. But she had chosen to reject it. She was Cassandra Oberon in this lifetime, not Ayesha or any of her other past incarnations.

The love of her life had been Paxton Larnach, and at the time, she couldn't imagine spending her life with anyone but her childhood hero and then boyfriend. Then Paxton had been killed, caught in the crossfire between Sirkan and Manu three years ago. She put her face in her hands as she relived that horrendous moment when she held him in her arms, willing him to come back to her. Taking a breath, she tucked the agonizing memory away. She couldn't succumb to that pain. It was in the past and would not define her present.

But her heart was aching. Could she accept Manu's eternal love? Could she trust it? Every time she ventured down that emotional path, she couldn't acknowledge it. Yet there was always that pull, that recognition. But when she was in his presence she balked. Why was that? She tried to get to her feelings. Why did she keep pushing him away? She closed her eyes and tried to visualize Manu just before Sirkan had pulled her away from the World Peace Meditation. He had reached for her, his eyes filled with fear. Then Sirkan had swept her into the vortex at the corner of Trade and Tryon in uptown Charlotte. It happened so fast.

She pressed her hands against her heart, overcome by a deep sense of longing. She had suppressed these feelings, fearing that indulging them would somehow betray Paxton's memory.

Yet, she questioned, would it truly be a dishonor to him? In a different reality, if offered the opportunity, she would wholeheartedly embrace the eternal love she shared with Manu. *If given another chance,* she thought, contemplating the possibility.

"If given another chance," she repeated with a whisper.

Chapter 22: Holonote

He had been haunted for months wondering if Cassandra was once again in Sirkan's clutches. Now, thanks to Caelum, he knew beyond all doubt that Sirkan had been resurrected and Cassandra was on his mother ship. But how to find it? Dimensional rifts were tricky realms. One slip through the wrong portal, and he could be wandering dimensions for eternity.

Manu lay still in his bed, the dawn light casting a soft glow through the curtains of his apartment at the Citadel. His mind, a whirlpool of thoughts, fixated on one of the lifetimes he had found Ayesha in ancient Egypt.

He scrubbed his face with his hands. A vivid detail from that lifetime leaped into his mind, so very similar to this one, when Ayesha's soul had been at a crossroads between light and dark.

In that long ago life, he had been in deep meditation within the well-established Temple of Hathor, the ancient Egyptian goddess of love, beauty, music, and motherhood. The high priestess, Khetara, who could see through the veils of time and physical appearances into the true nature of a person's soul journey, was also an immortal.

The two were in the inner sanctum of the temple, which was filled with the scent of incense and the soft glow of oil lamps. Khetara gazed into a small flame, her voice aethereal: "Ah, Manu, seeker of truths hidden by time. What shadows of the past do you chase in the light of Hathor?"

"I seek knowledge of a soul lost through the ages. Can your sight reveal the path of Ayesha's spirit?"

Her eyes flickered with ancient knowledge when she saw Manu's growing frustration. "Your bond with Ayesha is deep yet also a beacon to those who seek to manipulate her destiny. Sirkan is adept at exploiting such connections."

Manu paced the chamber, his mind racing. "I must reach her before Sirkan does. I cannot allow him to corrupt her path once again."

"You must be swift and wise," said Khetara. "Sirkan's influence grows stronger in the shadows. Ayesha's soul lives in this life as the priestess Menhit. She is torn between the light of Hathor and the dark whispers of Seth."

Manu stopped, turning to face the high priestess. "Khetara, can you guide me to her? Can your visions show me the way?"

The high priestess closed her eyes once more, her lips moving in silent invocation. After a moment, she opened her eyes, offering Manu a small, intricately carved moldavite scarab that she manifested from thin air with her ability to manipulate matter. In Egyptian lore, the scarab symbolized transformation and renewal. "She is still within the walls of the Temple of Seth, dark god of magic. This will lead you to her. But remember that the journey will test not only your courage but also the purity of your heart."

Taking the scarab, Manu felt a surge of determination. "I am ready for whatever trials await. For Ayesha, for the balance of light and shadow, I will end Sirkan once and for all."

Khetara grabbed his arm. "Manu, be careful. Your anger and jealousy will betray you. You must not let emotion or vengeance rule your actions."

With a nod of understanding, Manu went to the temple gardens, the scarab pulsing in his palm. The cool night air was a stark contrast to the charged atmosphere of the temple's sanctuary. In lieu of venturing out himself, Manu summoned two of his most trusted acolytes. The task at hand required a blend of stealth and cunning, especially to liberate his soulmate from the dark priest's grasp. Sirkan, with his keen senses, would instantly detect Manu's unique energy signature if he neared Seth's temple. So Manu decided to send his acolytes as proxies, trusting them to navigate the perilous mission.

He finally reached the secluded corner of the temple garden, under the shade of date palms. His two acolytes stepped out from the shadows.

"You both must infiltrate the Temple of Seth. I have it on good authority that Sirkan will attempt to take the priestess Menhit to the temple and turn her to the left-hand path."

He imbued the scarab with a tracking spell and handed it to Kasmut. "Seek out the young priestess Menhit. Be cautious. The temple holds more secrets than it reveals. When you have located her, all you need do is hold this scarab within her auric field, and it will imprint her energy signature. Then come back to me. Do not attempt anything on your own. I will take care of the rest."

"We will not fail you, Master."

"Remember that time is of the essence," said Manu. "We must act before the next full moon graces the skies. That is the time of the blood ritual."

They nodded, turning to blend into the twilight shadows, embarking on their clandestine mission.

It did not go as planned.

The two acolytes had managed to blend seamlessly into the temple's daily life but soon found themselves ensnared in a web of deceit and sacrificial rites. Sirkan, ever cunning and ruthless, had orchestrated a series of blood rituals leading up to the final night of the full moon. The two acolytes were unknowingly marked as offerings to appease the deity Seth's insatiable thirst for blood. These rituals were intricately designed, serving as a conduit for Sirkan's grand scheme: the conversion of Menhit into a vessel of untold power and darkness, forever altering the spiritual landscape of ancient Egypt.

The room suddenly filled with shadows, snapping him out of his reverie. A spectral figure materialized in the middle of the room, holding out a cryptic, glowing artifact. It spoke in a haunting voice, "The key to the Lyran mother ship lies within the forgotten tomb of Ayesha."

The figure vanished as suddenly as it appeared. A holographic note lay gleaming on the floor with a moldavite scarab. The beetle's carved form sparked a rush of memories. He palmed it and found it was warm to his touch. Could it be the very same artifact he had held long ago in his attempt to save Menhit? Did his musings manifest this?

The holonote flickered to life. Its projection showed a woman, her face shrouded in veils, her message enigmatic yet compelling. "Meet me in Giza, at the Coffee Bean and Tea Leaf café. I can lead you to the hidden tomb of Ayesha. There you will be able to obtain the coordinates to the realm where she now dwells."

A trap? Remembering the rage and hopelessness he had felt when he had been too late to rescue Menhit, he knew he had to pursue this lead. Trap or not, it was not going to happen again!

Chapter 23: Marielle

Cassie was restless. She splayed her palms on the cool expanse of the glass portal in her sitting room and gazed out. Her hand was still throbbing with pain.

The good news was that her powers seemed to be coming back little by little. Was it because Sirkan was away? She sighed and put her forehead against the glass, or whatever the window was made of. She felt feverish on top of everything else.

She turned and started toward her bed chamber, thinking maybe she should just lay down.

But something pricked at the edge of her mind. A thought? A vibration? A tinge of ... curiosity? She pivoted on her toes and scanned the room.

No, she was alone. Then her gaze landed back on the colossal window that served as her only view to the outside world, the underwater expanse she had come to both marvel at and dread. Her eyes widened. What could only be called a mermaid hovered in the aquatic vista, as if suspended in a dream.

Heart pounding, Cassie darted toward the glass, her fingers splaying across the cold surface. The mermaid responded, her own hands pressing into the pane from the other side. They locked eyes: Cassie's weary but hopeful, the mermaid's as deep and enigmatic as the ocean itself. Her hair danced and swayed around her like a blue and green halo.

You are the Trybrid.

A statement, not a question.

"Yes!" Cassie gasped and then responded accordingly to the telepathic query. *Yes! You can hear my thoughts?*

Indeed. We have been searching for you these many months in union with our star brothers and sisters. I am called Marielle. I am—we are the remnants of those who fled Atlantis and took to the seas. We are soul sisters with the one called Ayesha, and now you."

Cassie sagged against the portal in relief. *We?*

We reside in Poseidia and the surrounding sea caves. We are many and yet one. Mariel paused, furrowing her brows. *We are curious as to why you allow yourself to be trapped by the evil lord yet again. You have unlimited powers.*

Cassie's back stiffened in defense. *Sirkan put ancient sigils throughout my chambers and onto my garments to dampen my abilities. I don't know how to overcome them.*

The mermaid's eyes dimmed with dismay. *You are deceived by your insecurities. You can leave whenever you want.*

Cassie stared at her in disbelief. *I've tried countless times, but I can't push past his dark magic.*

Another form burst into view beside Marielle. A well-muscled merman with a powerful torso that ended in an iridescent tail, his shoulder-length hair also a mixture of blues and greens. He looked deep into Cassie's eyes. *We have been searching for you.* He put his hand to the glass as well, and Cassie moved hers, so they were palm to palm. Cassie could feel a mind probe and opened to his examination.

A look of disgust rippled upon his face. His expression hardened to granite. *Look at yourself,* he spat, *hiding behind that glass like a frightened child. The power you seek isn't lost. You've simply stopped fighting for it!* His eyes flashed like lightning in deep waters. *Until you remember your own strength, you are useless to us.* In a violent swirl of currents, he grabbed Marielle and disappeared.

A flush crept up Cassie's cheeks. The disappointment stung like a volley of arrows, each dipped in a poison of doubt. Her head dropped, her forehead resting once more against the cool glass. She instinctively grasped the torc at her neck. The faint pulse thrummed at her fingertips, but it was nothing like the surge she'd felt when her father gave it to her. It was a shadow of the power she had barely learned to wield.

MARIELLE PULLED AWAY from her father. "Why did you do that? She is very confused and afraid. Somehow Sirkan has convinced her that she is trapped within the ship and cannot—"

He stopped her with a look. "She needed to be shocked out of her self-pity."

Caelum's eyes, as deep and mysterious as the ocean they ruled, held Marielle's gaze with an intensity that seemed to pierce her very soul.

"Marielle," he began, his voice a mix of frustration and concern, "you know as well as I that Cassandra's strength lies in her spirit, not her powers. Sirkan's manipulations are powerful, and they prey on fear and uncertainty."

Marielle's tail flicked anxiously in the water, her eyes reflecting the turmoil within. "But, Father, my king, she is still young, even if she is one of the seven. How then can she break free from Sirkan's grasp? His magic is so strong."

Caelum moved closer, his presence both commanding and comforting. "That is exactly why I reacted as I did. If we coddle her, if we treat her as a helpless victim, we only reinforce Sirkan's hold over her mind. She must find the courage within herself to resist, to see through his deceptions."

"But what if she can't?" Marielle's voice was a mere whisper, her fear for her long-lost soul sister evident.

The king's expression softened. "Then we will be there to guide her, to support her. But the first step must come from her. We cannot win this battle for her; she must fight it herself."

Marielle nodded slowly, understanding dawning in her eyes. "So your frustration was a way to awaken her fighting spirit?"

"Hopefully," Caelum replied, a hint of a smile playing on his lips. "Sometimes, a shock to the system is what's needed to break free from a powerful illusion. Now, we must be patient and trust in Cassie's strength."

Marielle nodded and swam back to her favorite crystal cave, which would be the rendezvous point for their united forces, per Caelum's instructions. Her thoughts drifted back to the first time she had met the lost queen, Ayesha. At the time, that's how Marielle thought of her: the lost queen.

When the Lyran mother ship had first landed in the ocean's depths, it had already been many years since the sinking of Atlantis. King Caelum had established Poseidia, and those who had followed him into the seas had adapted well to their new existence. They were twice blessed to live freely within the ocean depths, far away from the evil that ran rampant on the surface, yet they could walk upon the land when needed.

Marielle loved to read and explore teachings of all kinds. With the ocean as her vehicle, she'd zipped around to the seaports of newly established temples of wisdom the Atlantean survivors had established. On one such visit, the high priestess, who was a keeper of the Ageless Wisdom Teachings, appointed her as her acolyte. She had been in heaven. The only issue Marielle could see was that the scrolls were so fragile. Perhaps if she memorized the teachings, she could eventually be a part of the sages who passed the teachings to the next generation of priestesses.

She remembered the day that an expeditionary group of divers who were testing some new submersible craft off the coast of Poseidia came ashore carrying large woven baskets full of stones in various shapes and sizes. The stones glowed from within and reminded her of the power crystals of the great temples across Atlantis but were many times smaller.

"What are those?" she asked one of the divers as they carried the baskets into the temple.

"We're not sure. That's why we are bringing them to Master Elena."

Marielle was compelled to reach out to touch the crystals. When she did, a pleasant jolt of energy traveled up her arm. She felt like the stone had spoken to her.

When she looked up, she saw a striking woman dressed in a blue sari edged in gold coming toward her. Although they had never actually met, she knew it had to be Master Elena. Marielle quickly withdrew her hand in embarrassment and started to back away.

"No, no, stay, my dear. Let's see what this is about, shall we?"

Elena listened intently to the head diver about finding the crystal cave. "It seemed to call to us. I can't explain it, but we had no choice but to disembark from our ship and swim into the cave. The cave was full of colored lights, which we discovered came from the crystals themselves. I decided to touch one, and it practically jumped into my hands, whole and perfect with no appearance of having been harvested, like magic. So, we proceeded to gather several of each shape and color. I knew we needed to bring them back to you, Master Elena."

Elena went to the three baskets full of crystals and ran her hands over them, picked some up, and studied others. "You did well. It seems that Earth has bestowed a great gift upon us. These are very similar to our Sirian wisdom crystals. I will study them."

She directed them to take the crystals to her office and then motioned to Marielle. "Your name, my dear?

"Marielle, my lady."

"Ah, you are King Caelum's daughter then? Come. You're with me."

They spent the day and well into the night at the great temple high in the surrounding hills, sorting out the stones and organizing them on long trestle tables by size and color. They were all elongated shapes ranging in size from an inch to over a foot long. The circumference also varied, with the largest crystal, a smoky quartz, measuring well over seven inches. Marielle thought they looked like smaller versions of the wands that the mages and witches used.

Dawn approached, and Elena, noticing the girl's drooping eyes, said, "Go to sleep, Marielle. And report back here tomorrow after your morning repast. Nothing more can be accomplished now."

That night, Marielle had a dream and was shown how to energetically imprint knowledge into crystals, knowledge that could only then be extracted by those trained in advanced, seed-thought meditation techniques. The process was a mental exercise of holding a scroll's teachings in her mind and then beaming the information through her third eye into a crystal cradled in the palms of her hands. She woke up with the space between her brows throbbing.

After her daily meditation and morning meal, she practically ran to Master Elena's office. The master was there with a high priest Marielle had never seen before. He had the physique of a warrior, unlike most of the priests Marielle had seen from afar during the high holy days, and an aura of power and authority. Still, his presence was calming.

"Ah, this is the young priestess I was telling you about." She held her hand out to Marielle. "Marielle, this is Master Artemus, high priest of the White Circle."

Marielle tried not to gasp. This was the warrior priest of legend. It was rumored that when the current leader of the White Circle ascended, Artemus would assume that role. Meanwhile, he had been leading intergalactic forces on missions across the galaxy to prevent the Dark Brotherhood from infiltrating Earth. The ancients had prophesied that this planet would be the ultimate battleground between the forces of light and dark during the celestial transition from the Ages of Pisces to Aquarius. These prophecies were written into the codex and foretold humanity's ascension into beings of pure creative energy, capable of shaping reality through thought alone. Transcending the boundaries of physical form, this new humanity would become the guardians of universal harmony, their consciousness expanding into realms beyond this planet, and would shape evolution for eons to come.

Unlike other worlds in the vast cosmos, Earth sat at the nexus of ancient ley lines that spanned entire galaxies. These cosmic currents made the planet not just a crossroads, but a wellspring of energy that could either nurture life throughout the universe or, in the wrong hands, corrupt it entirely. It was this very energy that would fuel humanity's metamorphosis, transforming them into beings of light who could shape reality with the power of their enlightened minds.

Marielle bowed to this great priest, hands palm to palm in the celestial greeting, "Adonai, Master."

Artemus mirrored her greeting and studied her through intense amber eyes that she swore could look into her very soul. "Master Elena tells me you have a special gift with Terran crystals. This will be extremely beneficial in protecting our spiritual legacy for generations to come."

Marielle felt the blood rise in her face. "Thank you, Master. I am at your service." *Could he read her mind?*

Elena picked up the thread. "I had a vision last night of how these crystals could be used as repositories of the Wisdom Teachings."

"Yes!" said Marielle. "I had a dream last night about how I could imbue them with the teachings found in the temple scrolls, but ..." She hesitated. "But I have not been trained in that many of the teachings yet. How could I do that?"

"I believe Master Elena can teach you special mental techniques to work that out."

Elena nodded, "Yes, this will require advanced training. We will begin this very day. I will speak with your temple trainer to release your education to me now. You will be my new acolyte."

Marielle tried not to gawk. This was a gift beyond anything she could have wished for.

Elena continued, "The advanced meditation techniques require not just mental readiness but also physical and energetic preparation."

Marielle listened intently, hanging on every word, her heart filled with a mixture of excitement and insecurity.

"Advanced meditation is not merely an act of sitting in silence," Master Elena said. "It is an engagement with the deepest layers of consciousness, an exploration into the very essence of existence. To embark on this journey, one's energy must be clear, free from the disturbances that can arise from our daily habits, especially our eating patterns."

The new acolyte nodded, understanding the gravity of what was being shared, recognizing the holistic approach to spiritual practices.

"This is why," the master went on, "I recommend light fasting before delving into these advanced practices. Fasting, when approached with reverence and understanding, purifies the body and clears the energy pathways, making it easier for you to connect with higher states of consciousness. It's not about deprivation but about creating an internal environment where your spiritual practice can flourish."

Marielle felt an epiphany. The advice resonated deeply as she became aware of the interconnectedness of body, mind, and spirit.

"Remember, though," Master Elena added with a smile, "the journey is unique to each individual. Light fasting should be approached mindfully, respecting your body's needs and limits. It's a practice of loving kindness toward oneself, preparing you to receive the profound wisdom that advanced meditation can offer. We will begin tomorrow at dawn. You may prepare yourself with cleansing rituals for today, and plenty of rest. I will send two temple handmaids to help you prepare."

Being thus dismissed, Marielle went back to her room to prepare for her life's work.

Chapter 24: The Road to Atlantis

Natesh's feet sank into the soft sand as he gazed at the massive rock formation stretching three hundred feet into the ocean, a path sometimes called the "Road to Atlantis." The sound of crashing waves filled his ears, and the salty breeze whipped through his hair. He clenched his fists and furrowed his brow in frustration. Faint energy signatures that unmistakably belonged to Sirkan had led Natesh to this windswept place.

How has the bastard returned? A shiver crawled down Natesh's spine as his mind reeled with questions. He had personally handed Sirkan's ashes and ring to Artemus; they couldn't have been used to resurrect his former lord. He would not rest until he unraveled this enigma.

"Master?"

Natesh turned, his face a scowl. "What do you want, Mia? I told you I would call you when I needed you."

The young vampire lifted her chin. "You also told me to inform you immediately if I detected any action in Morgandrian's coven. I believe there is a problem."

"Of course, there is," he sighed. "Report."

"It seems that Adrianna is recruiting Morgandrian's coven to be deprogrammed and join Master Elena's group. Those who don't want to do so are starting to raise, um, 'holy hell,'" she made air quotes, "all over North Carolina, New York, and Boston. Morgandrian's coven splintered into several factions after her capture, with some members going into hiding while others actively sought new leadership."

"Like I fucking don't have anything better to do!" He pinched the bridge of his nose and closed his eyes. "I really can't seem to care right now. I am on the track of something a little more important than worrying about how many dark versus white witches are in the mundane world."

Mia protested, "But the balance—"

"The balance between the Masters of Wisdom and the Dark Brotherhood is always in flux. Just keep an eye on things for now."

Natesh turned back to the ocean. He stood silhouetted against the waning light, retreating into his own thoughts.

Mia watched him intently, feeling a mix of emotions churn within her. The sight of him in such deep concentration brought back memories of the Natesh who had embodied strength and dark passions. They had ventured together through a world filled with danger and excitement, equally matched in their desire for total gratification of every pleasure the world had to offer.

Until the night Paxton, their angelic adversary, had claimed the life of Natesh's favorite bat boy, Samuel, marking a pivotal shift in Natesh's focus. Mia vividly recalled stepping into the void left by the fallen lieutenant, aligning herself with Natesh's quest for vengeance. Their partnership had deepened, bound by a shared mission and dark pursuits.

But a change had come over Natesh that somehow connected to the seventh Aquarian Avatar. Mia had initially believed Natesh's actions were part of Sirkan's grand scheme. After Sirkan's demise, however, Natesh's path became enigmatic. Freed from Sirkan's influence, Mia anticipated Natesh's ascension as the new dark overlord, yet he remained strangely passive, his focus inexplicably fixed on Cassandra Oberon.

Mia's frustration mounted while she pondered Natesh's motivations. His obsession with Cassandra was confusing. She yearned for the return of the Natesh she knew: the dangerously charming and seductively malevolent force. His current demeanor felt like a betrayal of their shared pasts and ambitions.

With a mix of anger and disappointment, Mia stomped away and transformed into her bat form to return to their lair. She could almost hear Natesh's voice chiding her for her irritation, but it did little to quell her growing discontent. She was more than annoyed; she was pissed.

Mia had been in love with Natesh since he had turned her during the Roaring Twenties in New Orleans. She had grown to depend on him, as her sire, for both sustenance and guidance. She often found him staring at her as though he were looking for something. He was a beautiful man. His exotic features and intense tourmaline eyes made her quake to her very core.

Natesh's appetite for their coupling was once outpaced only by his bloodlust. Mia would do anything to ensure their future together.

NATESH TURNED IN FRUSTRATION from his second. He knew what she wanted and was *not* about to give it to her. That part of their relationship had been over since he discovered that Cassandra Oberon was Giselle's incarnation. His love for her transcended the physical, just as it had all those years ago in New Orleans when he'd met Desiree.

Mia's obsession concerned him. Would she attempt to sabotage this mission because of jealousy? Could he trust her? He would hate to end her, but he wouldn't allow his mission to be compromised. He'd have to worry about it when and if the occasion arose. In the meantime, he knew that Sirkan, somehow, was back. Perhaps he was hiding among the dimensional rifts scattered across this part of the world. He had no aptitude in identifying them, but he knew someone who could.

Chapter 25: We, the Arcturians

Nova and Vega wore talismans that allowed them access to the interdimensional passageway connecting Sirkan's ship with Poseidia. The underwater city was in a unique position as a nexus between worlds, cultures, and dimensions. Encased in a shimmering atmospheric bubble, the city was a hidden gem, invisible to the mundane eyes of the third-dimensional world. The bubble, a marvel of celestial technology, not only protected the city from unwanted intruders but also created an aethereal, otherworldly glow that illuminated the oceanic depths.

They entered the city and wound their way through the narrow maze of streets until they found themselves in a bustling bazaar. A kaleidoscope of colors and sounds filled the air as merchants from different species and worlds hawked their exotic wares, each in their own language. The market was a delicate balance between the familiar and the foreign, comforting yet filled with the thrill of discovery.

Intoxicating aromas beckoned the twins deeper into the heart of the marketplace and to the exclusive stalls that held the rarest of items and magical wares. The twins moved through the crowd with intent, even while their senses relished the sheer diversity and vibrancy of life around them.

Nova always relished these trips to the bazaar, especially to the stalls full of luminous crystals from distant galaxies, intricate metalworks emitting soft, harmonic tones, and fabrics that could change color with the wearer's mood.

Amidst this sensory overload, they spotted their contact, a merchant known for his ties to the leader of a highly advanced sect of white witches and a known expert on rifts, Ian MacGregor. The merchant, a tall being with skin that glowed like moonlight, stood behind a stall adorned with artifacts from all over the known universe.

"Welcome, travelers," the merchant greeted them, his voice a melodious blend of mystery and warmth. "What brings you to my humble shop?"

Nova stepped forward; her eyes locked with the merchant's. "I'm searching for a rare blend of human coffee called Highlander's Roast."

The merchant's luminous eyes flickered. Then he inclined his head and motioned them to a door to the right of the stall. "Ah, that is kept inside with the exotic teas and spices. It will cost you. Let me see your coin."

Nova took out a pouch from inside her cloak and tossed it up and down. The coins within made soft, clinking sounds.

"Come along then," he said and let them into the dimly lit shop.

The merchant, whom they only knew as Bray, put a finger to his nose and led them deeper into the shop. Each wall held bags of various shapes and sizes that emitted a plethora of scents, herbal, floral, and medicinal, as well as the earthy aroma of coffee. He clambered up a three-tier wooden ladder and pulled down a heavy jute bag labeled "Highlander," the code name of Ian MacGregor.

He poured the coffee beans into a smaller bag, his sleight of hand dropping a micro transponder into the contents. "This should suffice for now. Remember that it needs a special brewing device to obtain maximum strength." He led them back to the booth. The scents of spicy alien cuisine, the warm, inviting aroma of freshly baked goods, and the subtle, mysterious fragrances of unknown incenses and oils assailed their senses. "But mind you, this blend needs to be used within the week. It's highly perishable."

Vega nodded, "Yes, we are aware. We have a special method of distilling this for our master, Sirkan." She purposefully uttered his name, deterring anyone watching or listening from interfering.

Nova then picked up several bags of various spices, put them into a mesh bag with the coffee, and then passed a handful of coins to Bray. He nodded and turned to the next customer.

Vega and Nova continued through the bazaar, selecting exotic fruits, fresh fish, and other staples, taking their time to ensure they were seen by the two men who had been shadowing them since entering the city. Completing their shopping expedition, they turned to retrace their steps back to the port.

Chapter 26: Symphony of Chaos

"Enter." President Conroe Soter sat behind the Resolute Desk in the Oval Office. Sirkan and Morgandrian, glamoured to look like mundane oligarchs, swept in.

Soter motioned to his chief of staff. "Kate, please make sure I am not disturbed until I buzz you."

She hesitated, "Do you want me to come back in?"

Sirkan answered before Soter had a chance, "No, this is a private meeting."

The president hesitated. He hated to allow anyone to take control. But the stakes were high. Besides, he had an agreement in place already, and Kate was not a part of it.

"No, just make sure we are not disturbed. I will fill you in later."

Sirkan said, "It's time we upped the stakes with the Technomancer's viruses by implanting more lethal subliminals, not only into the VR games but also into the global online financial markets and military training programs. This will give us the access we need to control the money and the military of every country."

Soter narrowed his eyes. He was no fool. "Yeah, about the Technomancer. Now that we will be taking our controls into the worldwide arena, I want to know how I can contact him directly. I am done with having to say, 'Sirkan, may I?' And what about my role as world leader? I want a world left to lead."

Morgandrian, ever the diplomat, stepped in. "My dear Conroe, this is a virtual war we are waging, for now. Once we have reached a critical mass of mind control and manipulation, we can gradually bring the virtual reality into this third-dimensional reality. Then you will be able to work with Danax, the Technomancer, and direct just how you want to rule, and where."

"Well, I want to see exactly what this Danax is doing then. And make it so that I understand, and it's not just gobbledygook technobabble."

Sirkan arched an eyebrow but nodded. *This man is truly an idiot.* "Pull up your spirit screen, and let's get started."

Morgandrian went to the screen, waved her hand to activate it, and then performed a rapid, complicated series of hand gestures. Danax's hooded form appeared, his pale, almost translucent face an amalgam of flesh and machine. Glowing circuitry traced his cheekbones and jawline. But his eyes were his most striking feature. Rings of advanced optics, which enhanced his vision beyond the spectrum of normal sight, encircled his fiery, metallic gold irises.

His voice, a fusion of organic and synthetic tones, crackled over the spirit screen. "My lord, I have created the next level of mind control for our VR games. I have named it Ludovirus. It is far more lethal than the Mindscape Manipulator virus. It will gradually seep into the brains of whomever is playing the game and—"

Sirkan cut him off, "Yes, yes. No need to explain. Just do it."

Danax's fingers danced across an aethereal keyboard, weaving an intricate web of psychological manipulation into the fabric of his virtual realm. With surgical precision, he spliced the virus into subliminal messages and triggers throughout the massive Aethernet's VR community and targeted training programs, each set of code carefully crafted to exploit the deepest fears, prejudices, and desires lurking within the human psyche.

These hidden manipulations took many forms: flickering images flashing just below the threshold of conscious perception, subtle audio cues layered beneath the game's soundtrack, and/or training instructions. Each element was meticulously designed to bypass the players' rational minds and speak directly to their subconscious minds, slowly reshaping their thoughts and behaviors.

"What about the players who make 'good' choices in the game, or those who see themselves as agents of good in the military training?" asked Soter.

Danax said, "For those who make moral choices, the programs will subtly reshape themselves, presenting increasingly difficult ethical dilemmas that challenge their convictions. The subliminal messages will be stepped up, urging them to abandon their principles in favor of more selfish or ruthless actions. For example, were you, as president, to tell your military generals to go against their moral codes, they would be unable to disobey you. Gradually, even the most righteous will find themselves slipping down a dark path, their once-unshakable morals eroded by the game's insidious influence."

Soter rubbed his hands together in glee.

"In contrast," Danax continued, "players who embraced selfish or evil decisions from the outset will be rewarded with power and success within the virtual world. The game will actively encourage their malevolent behavior, providing them with opportunities to engage in ever-greater acts of cruelty and destruction. The subliminal messages will fuel their darkest impulses, stoking the flames of their egos and ambitions until they become utterly consumed by their own depravity."

Sirkan said, "Regardless of the players' initial inclinations, the ultimate outcome is always the same: a descent into chaos and madness. The Technomancer's manipulations ensure that every path, every choice, leads inexorably toward unfathomable disorder and devastation, and under our total control."

"This is beyond what I ever could have imagined," said Soter.

"There's more," Danax said. "As the players become increasingly absorbed in the game, their real-world behaviors will begin to reflect the changes upon their minds. Those who were subtly encouraged to abandon their morals will find themselves lashing out at loved ones, engaging in uncharacteristic acts of betrayal and violence. The ones who were rewarded for their malevolence will become increasingly brutal and sadistic, their actions in the real world mirroring the atrocities they commit within the virtual realm."

His mission accomplished, Danax retreated into the Aethernet's shadows, leaving Soter and Sirkan to revel in their sinister victory. As the virtual world burned, the cries of the afflicted filled the digital void.

Chapter 27: Menhit

Cassie leaned back against the wall of her bedchamber, a cell in all but name. In the dim light, streams of energy emanated from the engraved sigils that bordered each wall. Since her encounter with the merfolk, she was determined to dismantle the magical force. So far, she had only succeeded in depleting her dwindling reserves of power.

She had, however, been diligent in her physical training schedule. Every morning, she programmed the holographic dojo and went through her warrior training exercises. She had gotten up to fifty sun salutations, then flowed into tai chi, and ended with Krav Maga. The ritual helped keep up not only her physical strength but also her mental acuity. But she still struggled to hold meditations for any length of time. She had to find the throne Ayesha had shown her!

Then there was her maybe friend and ally, Ninhursag. The woman certainly seemed to be forthcoming about Sirkan and his plans to turn her. Cassie kept reliving the horrific discovery of the sarcophagi and then becoming so ill. She still wasn't feeling like herself. Had something entered her bloodstream when she'd pricked her finger on the sarcophagus, or was it something else?

Just in case, she refused to eat during Nova and Vega's visit to Poseidia, fearing Sirkan might spike her food with sacrificial blood, which she knew from past experience would begin to turn her to the left-hand path. She wouldn't risk repeating her dark past life as his consort.

As if summoned by her thoughts, the chamber door slid open, admitting Sirkan. Flanking him, Vega carried a tray of food. Cassie almost sighed with relief to see the diminutive Arcturian.

"Cassandra, enough of this nonsense. Eat," Sirkan barked, gesturing to Vega to lay the tray on the table. Aromatic spices wafted up from a hearty fish stew accompanied by crusty rolls and fresh fruit.

Cassie's gaze remained unwavering as she looked at him.

Vega, picking up her concerns telepathically, stooped and whispered, "The food is untainted, lady. I swear. Please eat. You need your strength."

A spark of mutual understanding flashed between them, allies in reluctant captivity. Gingerly, she sampled the proffered stew. It was delicious.

"Thank you, Vega. It's wonderful." She finished the meal in silence, attempting to ignore Sirkan's presence.

As soon as her last spoonful was taken, Sirkan smiled and rose from his chair. He held a goblet in his left hand, his eyes roaming over her with approval. She stiffened. He sighed, grasped her arm, and pulled her toward the door. Once in the hallway, he stopped and whirled her around to face him.

"I am giving you an ultimatum, my love. You are a being with unknown and potentially unlimited abilities. You now know that I can dampen those abilities. You can either join me, and I will gradually allow you access to those abilities. Or I will shackle you and allow you to slowly wither and die in the confines of my deepest dungeon. But before I make that determination, I have some ... what shall I call them? ... *tests* for you to run through."

Dread washed over Cassie like an icy avalanche, the sheer enormity of his threat crashing down on her. The room seemed to spin and darken at the edges.

He twisted her right arm behind her back and shoved her down the hallway.

"You will quite enjoy this little exercise, I think." His breath was hot on her neck, and she could feel the pressure of his body against hers as he pushed her down endless corridors. The pain felt like a hot poker embedded in her arm, and it was becoming unbearable. She couldn't help but cry out, "Stop! You're hurting me!"

Just as quickly as he grabbed her, he let her go. Turning her around and taking her face between his hands, he brutalized her mouth with his.

Finally releasing her lips, he growled, "There is a fine line between love and hate, Cassandra. You are about to cross it."

Then taking her arm once more in his vice-like grip, he guided her toward a shimmering metal door. The door opened and then closed noiselessly behind them once he pushed her inside.

Cassie stared at the holographic displays on the wall. Full comprehension took her a nanosecond. She whipped around, her fingers aching to break into the code streaming across the screens mounted around the command center. But she couldn't find a way in. Her energy was totally blocked. It looked like the bastard was planning on some type of attack on the Aethernet!

Frustrated, she said, "You can't keep me here, Sirkan. The other avatars and the White Circle will find a way to stop your twisted Aethernet schemes."

Sirkan, relishing his role as the lord of dark code, chuckled while he manipulated a hologram of the human brain. "Ah, Cassandra, you underestimate the power of suggestion. My AI doesn't just hack machines; it hacks minds."

Yeah, I got that. She wanted to scream as streams of malevolent code snaked through neural networks, infiltrating the collective unconscious of mankind.

"You still don't comprehend it, do you?" Sirkan leaned in, his eyes glowing in the dim chamber. "I have state-of-the art technology connected to the most popular social media outlets, constantly streaming subliminal messages across the globe. Thanks to my Technomancer, I have control over one of the most powerful human presidents of all time, Conroe Soter. I don't need to break firewalls or encryption keys. I'm hacking humanity's most primitive instincts: fear, greed, hatred. Now all I need to do is amplify them until society implodes. You will help me do that."

"Like hell I will!" Cassie looked at him, raising her chin in defiance. "You underestimate the resilience of the human spirit, the power of unity, and love."

With a sneer, Sirkan sauntered over to an ornate counter. He caressed a crystal decanter filled with a vivid red liquid. Filling two goblets, he extended one toward her. "Drink," he said, taking a slow, deliberate sip from his own goblet. "Things will go a lot smoother if you begin to embrace who you are at your core."

She was tempted to throw it at him but knew it would do no good.

Think, Cassie, she said to herself. *So, this madman wants world domination and believes you're his greatest weapon in achieving it. What if you take in just a little of the dark magic, just enough to turn the tables on him? Surely, you can stop yourself before it becomes permanent. You are beginning to get your powers back after all. You've had so much training in white magic, you know you can fight off the dark.*

For a heartbeat, she sensed Sirkan's frustration, like a storm gathering on the horizon. Anger flared in his eyes before he visibly reined it in and took a deep breath like he inhaled patience itself. The icy edge in his voice melted into deceitful warmth. "Come. Embrace your true self. Your powers, the influence you can have on the world, will be unparalleled."

Sirkan strode to a console at the far end of the room and waved his hand over a crystal orb. It lit from within, emitting a low hum. He gestured to the screen nearest Cassie. "Perhaps you need a bit more motivation."

The faint glimmer within the orb grew, resolving into a vivid image: the Alpha Omega house in Charlotte, alive with movement. Girls flitted across the lawn, ascending and descending the grand veranda steps. Amid the blur of faces, two stood out sharply: Glenda and Adrianna.

Sirkan leaned closer, his eyes narrowing as he studied the pair. "Ah, those two are still on my kill list," he said, his voice dripping with venom. He turned to Cassie, hissing, "I think it's time to end this charade and obliterate them and their fledgling neophytes." His tone carried a twisted blend of a dare and an invitation.

He exhaled deeply, his sigh heavy with darkness. "Oh, the temptation! Their demise would leave a void for you, wouldn't it? And a gaping black hole in that quaint little corner of your dear Charlotte."

For a moment, his gaze grew distant, as though savoring the destruction he could unleash. Then, snapping out of his reverie, he locked eyes with her. "The choice is yours, my dear. Wield the power you hold; join me or annihilate them." His voice dipped into a soft, mocking purr, but the triumph in his tone was unmistakable.

Cassie froze, the weight of his words crushing her like a vice. The room seemed to close in around her as her mind churned through impossible choices. The burden of her decision loomed like an iron pendulum, swinging lower and lower; no matter how she moved, it would cut her to pieces.

If she refused, thousands would die, innocent people she had fought to protect. Worst of all, her best friend, the one person who had always believed in her, would perish. The thought twisted in her chest like a knife.

But if she yielded … her mind conjured a vision of the city, and then the world, unraveling like a fragile tapestry, every thread torn apart by her surrender. And Sirkan, always watching, was ready to seize the broken strands and weave them into something monstrous.

Her breath hitched as another image flashed unbidden: herself standing beside Sirkan, his dark power coiling around her like chains. The disgust churned in her gut, sharp and cold. What kind of person would that make her? What kind of monster?

Her hands trembled at her sides, and she balled them into fists, digging her nails into her palms until the pain sharpened her focus. Her pulse thundered in her ears, drowning out his voice, his gaze, his presence. Her heart felt split in two, half pleading for her to fight, half urging her to surrender. The weight of lifetimes hung heavy on her chest, as if she were balancing on the edge of a knife.

With one shaky breath, she forced herself to meet his eyes—and she saw it—he was waiting for her to break. To beg. To surrender.

Her fingers twitched at her sides.

Her voice, when it came, was barely above a whisper. "Give me a minute." She wasn't buying time to think; she already knew there were no good choices. She was buying time to steady her resolve.

He knew he had won. "Now, drink."

Slowly, deliberately, she reached for the goblet. Not in defeat—but in deliberation.

She lifted it to her lips and took a slow sip.

The moment the liquid touched her tongue, heat surged through her veins, electric and searing. She barely noticed Sirkan's reaction, his sudden intake of breath as his gaze flickered to the still-festering wound on her finger.

"Where did you get that wound?" He lunged toward her, but it was too late.

She shrugged, her face a mask of disdain. What she failed to realize was that the hatred fueling her actions had woven its own dark magic, leading her further down a path she never intended to walk. Suddenly, her thirst became unquenchable. The single sip only left her wanting more. She ravenously drank the liquid in the goblet, draining it to the last drop.

She threw the goblet at him and clenched her fists. The pricked finger was throbbing with a fiery pain that began to crawl up her arm. Each inch the pain expanded coincided with increased levels of frustration and anger. Cassie grabbed her arm, then her pounding head, willing the thrumming to stop and the pain to subside.

"I'm fed up with being powerless and tired of this abduction bullshit," she screamed. "I've walked the straight and narrow through countless lifetimes, followed every fucking rule, every code, because I was told I'm meant to be more: a teacher, a healer, and then the Trybrid, a beacon for humanity. What's the use? What's the point?"

Her rant escalated. Each outburst hitting octaves that set her cells vibrating. She felt her body threaten to disintegrate under the weight of her existential questions and rising anger.

Sirkan grabbed her by the shoulders, shaking her. "Cassandra, stop! Control your emotions! You're hurting yourself." He took her wounded hand into his, rubbing his thumb over the spreading wound. He paled. He knew that energy signature.

Cassie's eyes rolled back, and the room dissolved into a pitch-black mist that wove around her like a protective cocoon and threw Sirkan back.

He bellowed Cassie's name, reaching for her. The black cocoon pulsated around her, and dark light began to shine at its center. He saw Cassie's silhouette and lunged into the darkness, grabbing her shoulders. A low keening sound emitted from her as her body morphed, taking on an ancient persona. Power surged within her, exhilarating, liberating, and unlimited.

Then the cocoon dissipated.

The woman Sirkan held no longer bore Cassandra's face or shape. The air around her shimmered like a mirage.

"Menhit," Sirkan said, a blend of awe and recognition flooding his eyes. His former consort, the high priestess of Seth, was once more in his arms.

Chapter 28: The Lost Queen

The desert night was cool, the stars overhead a tapestry of ancient lights. Manu stoked the fire he had made in his small encampment. He was glad of Siobhan's company. And, bonus, she was a great cook. But then, what witch wouldn't be? He smiled to himself.

"What is so amusing then?" Siobhan's Gaelic lilt came through his reverie.

"I was being a typical man: grateful that you are such a good cook."

She threw back her head and laughed. "Well, what witch wouldn't be?"

"That's cheating. You read my mind."

"Aye, and it's so very easy to read. C'mon then, here's your stew."

They sat and ate in silence for a while, the flatbread warm and the stew savory.

"Tell me about that scarab. I understand this is not the first time it's been in your possession?"

Manu told her about the lifetime where he had failed in his attempt to keep Menhit from turning to the left-hand path. Siobhan's eyes glistened when he had finished the tale. "The scarab made its way back to me that very night. I knew then that my efforts had been for naught."

"I remember when Tatiana was training me; she used your love story as an example of unconditional love. And now I am living the quest of reuniting you with her once and for all. It's surreal. You were my hero."

Manu snorted. "Yeah, I'm a real hero. Sometimes I wish I had never left her behind. True, I would have lost my immortality, but we would have been together."

"You can't do that to yourself, Manu. You did what you felt was right at the time. The mission was paramount. Just as today's mission, ensuring the Aquarian Avatars complete their mission, is our first priority. Never look back with regret. You know that."

He took a deep breath. "Yes, I do. But it doesn't negate my sense of failure. This time will be different."

After cleaning up the meal, they settled into their sleeping bags.

"We're meeting the Mesopotamian scholar tomorrow at Giza. She says she knows about the legend of the lost queen of Egypt. I hope she's legit."

"The mundanes have a saying: You have a good bullshit detector. I'm counting on that."

Another snort. "Get some sleep. We'll head out before dawn and the blazing sun."

THEY ARRIVED AT THE rendezvous point at 7:00 a.m. It was already sweltering. The café was typical of the region with views of the iconic pyramids offering a breathtaking backdrop. The exterior was nondescript, the customers a mix of locals and tourists.

Both Manu and Siobhan dressed like modern tourists, in jeans and T-shirts with bandanas knotted around their necks and wide-rimmed fedoras. They both sported aviator sunglasses. They wanted to blend in as much as possible.

A lone figure, heavily veiled, sat at the back of the café, her back against the wall. That had to be their contact.

Manu approached with the code word "scarab." Innocuous enough.

The woman bowed her head and motioned for them to sit. A waiter came over to them with a carafe of rich, dark Egyptian coffee and an assortment of dried fruits, nuts, cheese, ful medames (a traditional fava bean dish), and flatbread.

Manu spoke first. "I am Manu, and this is my companion, Siobhan. You are?"

A soft, melodious voice answered, "You can call me Nin."

"OK, Nin. You have some information for us concerning—"

She cut him off. "Let us eat, shall we? Then we can continue to the camel pens. I have reserved four for us. We won't need a guide."

Trying to hide his impatience, Manu scarfed down his food along with several coffees and paid the bill.

Nin led them outside and down a maze of side streets until they came upon a well-tended stable. Three prime camels were harnessed and ready, a fourth laden with what looked like supplies.

"We are preparing for a long trip?" Siobhan asked hesitatingly.

"Not too long. I believe in being prepared."

Leading them into the desert west of the main city, they went past the great pyramids and into a much less populated area of the desert.

After two hours, Manu called a halt. "All right, before going any further, I want some answers."

Nin nodded. "Come. There is a small oasis ahead."

True to her words, the oasis wasn't far. After dismounting the camels, they led them to a small spring. Nin took out a basket from the fourth camel and laid down a blanket and handed them wooden cups to gather water for themselves. Settled in, she unwrapped the veil.

She was breathtakingly beautiful with an otherworldly face reminiscent of ancient Egyptian frescoes. Nin began to recount her tale, her voice weaving through the morning air like a sacred melody.

"Many lifetimes ago, during the reign of Queen Ayesha, I walked the halls of her palace, not as a mere visitor, but as a confidante and advisor," she began, her eyes reflecting the prismatic reflections of the water. "Our paths crossed under the auspices of destiny. She, a queen of unparalleled wisdom; I, a guardian of the earth's secrets."

Manu, his expression a mix of skepticism and curiosity, watched her closely. "So ... you are an immortal?"

"I am from the stars, yes. My origins are not important. My relationship with Ayesha is. We shared a bond that transcended the usual ties of queen and court. We were both seekers of knowledge, delving into the mystical arts that governed the very fabric of our world," she continued, her hands gesturing gracefully, as if she were painting the past in the air before them.

Siobhan, her eyes wide with wonder, asked, "What sort of knowledge did you share?"

With a smile that exuded centuries of wisdom, Nin arched her brow. "We explored the mysteries of life and death, the secrets of the stars, and the forgotten languages of Gaia, whose living being is the very planet we cohabit. Our conversations would last through the night,"

"How did you come to be the guardian of her tomb?" Manu inquired, his voice tinged with suspicion.

Nin's expression turned solemn. "It was in the twilight of Ayesha's reign, as her life began to ebb like the waning moon. She summoned me to her side, her once vibrant eyes dimmed by the shadows of mortality. 'Nin,' she said to me, 'my time in this world draws to a close, but the secrets I have amassed, the artifacts of power I have collected, they must be safeguarded until the world is ready for them.'"

She paused, her gaze lost in the flickering sunlight. "Her dying wish was for me to stand guard over her tomb's location, to protect it from those who would plunder its riches for ignoble ends. It was a vow I accepted without hesitation. She foresaw a time when the truths hidden within her tomb would be vital to the world."

Manu exchanged a look with Siobhan.

"And so, for centuries, I have been the silent sentinel, the keeper of Ayesha's final resting place. The time of revelation draws near, and you are the key to unlocking the ancient wisdom she so fiercely protected."

There was something nagging at Manu. "You know who we are then?"

Nin inclined her head, "I do indeed. You are Manu, the great high priest and Ayesha's soul mate. Only to you may I reveal the location of her tomb. Only to you will its secrets be revealed." She pointed to the scarab around his neck. "That scarab was crafted by the gods themselves. Priestess Khetara pulled it from an interdimensional portal to act as a talisman to connect you to Ayesha, no matter what lifetime she was experiencing. No one else can use it unless you specifically give it to them to use on your behalf."

Manu nodded and stood up. "Let's get on with this. How far is the tomb?"

"Actually, just footsteps away."

Siobhan looked around. "All I see is endless desert."

Amusement sparked Nin's eyes as she fastened her headdress and veil. "Physical sight can be misleading, especially in the desert."

They mounted their camels, and she led the way west once more.

The sand began to shift beneath the camels' hooves. They stopped and refused to go farther.

"We need to dismount and go on foot now. Be sure to bring the canteens and backpacks I prepared for you."

The location was indeed footsteps away. The sand began to give way even more until a step appeared, then another leading downward into what looked like a sand pit.

Siobhan balked. "This does not look safe."

Nin put up her arm to stop her descent. "It will not be if you hold any negativity. This is a sacred space and well protected from the Dark Brotherhood. Take a moment and get centered in your heart."

Siobhan narrowed her eyes at the woman. "Really, Nin, all this bullshitty cloak and dagger stuff is beginning to piss me off," spat Siobhan.

Nin just smiled serenely. "I am standing here with an immortal from Sirius and a witch from the Devic Kingdom: bullshitty indeed. Now let us get down to business and get centered. This tomb has layers of safeguards, both magical and cryptic. It's gone undiscovered all these millennia by design."

They descended the steps, each one revealing itself slowly and deliberately. The steps seemed to need coaxing to allow them to step down and around, a spiraling decent into darkness.

Nin pulled a witchlight from her backpack. "You each have one as well. We will need these in a moment." They suddenly hit an invisible barrier. "Ah, here we are. Siobhan, this is where your magics will be needed."

A door materialized out of nowhere. It was emblazoned with hieroglyphs that looked vaguely Egyptian. Light seeped from around the door's outline.

"I have no idea what these symbols are," protested Siobhan.

"Knowledge has nothing to do with them. It is a riddle: 'I am the keeper of histories untold. In my heart, the sun's journey unfolds. I rise in the east, but in the west, I am found, guarding the queen in her burial mound. I am the child of earth and the sky's embrace, witness to pharaohs and time's endless chase. Yet I am not flesh, nor bone, nor tree. Answer my riddle, and the path shall be free.'"

Siobhan rolled her eyes. "Easy enough, for fuck's sake: It's the sphinx. No magic needed."

Manu blinked at her. "Well, I wouldn't have figured it out that quickly." He turned to Nin, but before he could say anything, the door swung open, revealing a narrow passageway ahead.

Nin continued to lead the way. The passageway kept spiraling downward, the walls depicting the story of Ayesha, from the lift off during the fall of Atlantis to her ascent to the Egyptian throne, along with her consort, to the birth of her children and the dynasty that would give rise to the pharaohs of Egypt.

Manu was so absorbed in reading her story that he was brought up short when the passageway ended abruptly. There, in a rotunda lit with aethereal light, stood a stone sarcophagus, the top carved in effigy of Ayesha. Manu stumbled and fell to his knees, tears trickling down his face as he traced her face with his fingers.

At his touch, the top of the tomb slid open.

It was empty.

Manu's hands clenched into tight fists. His eyes, wide with surprise and anger, fixed on the barren depths of the tomb. "What manner of treachery is this!" he exclaimed, his voice echoing off the cold, stone walls.

Siobhan, ever vigilant and prepared, drew her athame from its sheath, the blade gleaming dimly in the tomb's muted light.

"There is no treachery here," Nin spoke calmly, her voice betraying no hint of deception. "Did you really believe that sacred artifacts of such importance would be plainly visible to mundane sight? Not even the most hidden tombs have escaped the greedy hands of thieves."

As she spoke, she seized a gleaming athame and drew it across the flesh of her left palm. The blade kissed her skin like a viper's fang, leaving behind a crimson slash that welled with her blood. Without hesitation, she reached for Manu's hand and did the same. "Now," she commanded, "let our blood mingle and let it fall as one into the heart of the tomb."

Together, their lifeblood dripped into the center, each drop landing with a sound too heavy for its size, as though the stone itself drank greedily. Her right hand began to move, weaving through the air in deliberate, serpentine strokes. The symbols she traced were invisible, save for the faint shimmer they left behind, like heat rippling off sun-scorched stone. Her lips moved in perfect harmony with her hands, whispering an incantation in a language older than the sands of time, each word a key turning in the lock of an unseen door.

Manu tilted his head, a mixture of curiosity and caution evident in his stance. This language was unfamiliar to him. However, amidst the flow of strange syllables, one name stood out, a name that resonated with a history both deep and mysterious: *Enki.*

A curse slipped from Manu's lips, a realization dawning upon him. Nin was no ordinary celestial; she was Anunnaki, a member of the ancient and powerful race from Nibiru. His mind reeled at the implications of this revelation.

Nonplused, Nin continued her chant with unwavering focus. The energy within the tomb started to stir, responding to her incantations. A subtle vibration filled the air, hinting at the awakening of something ancient and powerful, something that had lain dormant for eons within the cryptic confines of the tomb.

Manu stared in disbelief as a silhouette began to materialize from the shadowy confines of the ancient tomb. Like a whisper turning into a voice, the shape grew more defined, ascending from the crypt's depths until it stood fully before him. The figure was that of an old woman, yet the years had not dimmed the vibrant soul that shone from within. Her violet eyes, deep and knowing, pierced through the dimness, reaching out to him across the sands of time.

Ayesha!

Manu felt an inexplicable tightness in his chest at the sight of her, like his heart had momentarily ceased to beat. There she stood, at the threshold of the eternal, her smile bridging the gap between past and present.

Silently, Ayesha extended her arm, offering him a medallion that glinted with golden light. Its heavy chain, meticulously crafted with engraved links of gold and burnished metals, seemed to blur the lines between earthly and aethereal. His eyes widened. It looked like a pendant that he had given her as a gift when they were still on their home planet. Manu reached out to accept it. The moment his fingers closed around it, a jolt of energy surged through him, igniting every nerve with a power that felt both ancient and utterly new.

Nin interjected, "I imbued the metal with a golden helix that will allow you to feel one another's presence in the third dimension. Ayesha, well, Cassandra, has the same helix implanted within a twin medallion that is hidden within a throne she once possessed. Only she knows where it is located. It has yet to be activated, but it will be ..." She hesitated, then waved her hand as though swatting at a gnat. "No matter, you can feel the power for yourself. Put it around your neck."

He hesitated, then did so. A kaleidoscope of scenes whirled into his mind. Lifetime upon lifetime of searching and finding, or not finding, Ayesha, flashed before his eyes. His emotions roiled. Then he had a vision of a beautiful young woman who resembled Cassandra but was not Cassandra. He grasped the medallion in his hands, willing his emotions to settle. "I see her. She is changed!"

"Yes, that is not too far in the future. She has not changed quite yet, but she will. Cassandra has a test to walk through. I have no doubt that she will do so with flying colors, as only she can. You, however, must be ready and find her. Let the medallion lead the way."

Then she vanished.

He turned to Siobhan. "I hate cryptic messages."

Then his head started to spin. Siobhan reached out and barely caught him as he crumbled.

"Well, fuck," she said as she settled his unconscious form on the floor of the tomb.

Chapter 29: Past Is Prologue

"So ... you are awake," Sirkan said, caressing Menhit's cheek with his fingers.

Her eyes, so dark they were almost black, met his in silent amusement. "I feel more awake than I have ever been." Her fingers absently traced ancient protection symbols on the sheets while her gaze drifted to the ceremonial dagger mounted on the wall, its obsidian blade still holding the same dark energy she remembered from centuries past. Oh, the power was beyond intoxicating. It was who she was.

Menhit tried to raise herself to a sitting position, then fell back, using the moment to survey the room.

Sirkan took her into his arms and covered her face with soft kisses. "Rest. You have been through an ordeal ordained by Seth himself. You have passed his tests with great success. We are bonded for eternity and will soon realize our fullest power and potential, as it was destined."

His high priestess rested her head upon his shoulder, her expression soft and yearning while her mind cataloged the magical energies flowing through him. His power had grown in this timeline, yet she could sense gaps in his defenses, places where his energy ebbed and flickered.

"I feel like I have been separated from you for so long," she murmured, studying his face with calculated intensity, memorizing every subtle change in this version of him. "Yet it seems that only yesterday we were consummating our union, our power ..." She grabbed him in a passionate embrace, suddenly yearning for his body next to hers.

Sirkan closed his eyes in ecstasy, hardly believing that he was reunited with one of Ayesha's most powerful dark incarnations.

He pulled back to drink in the full length of her. His hands roamed over her curves like a desert wanderer seeking out a hidden oasis, tracing the sigils etched upon her flesh through her filmy robe. They were relics of ancient passion and forbidden magic. The glinting blue ink seemed to pulse with an inner light, guiding his fingertips to the swell of her breasts, the curve of her hips, and the heat between her thighs. Patience spent, he tore the filmy cloth down the middle and tossed it away. Her breath came hot and heavy as his fingers danced along bare flesh like tendrils of flame, threatening to consume them both. She clawed at his robe in frustration. He rose above her enough so that, together, they were able to remove the last remnants of clothing that separated them. Then they lunged.

They kissed like drowning lovers, desperate for air, their lips bruising and tongues dueling for dominance. Their bodies slid together, slick with sweat and need, writhing as if possessed by some ancient force that demanded satisfaction.

She thrashed beneath him, and he smiled in satisfaction, feeling her frustration rising with her passion.

"Now! Come to me now!" she begged.

She grabbed for him, but he pushed her hand away and captured one of her wrists above her head, pinning it firm while his other hand delved between them, seeking her core with unerring accuracy. Her hips bucked against his touch as he found her entrance, already wet and eager for his possession. He teased her slowly with his expert fingers at first, drawing out sweet cries of pleasure and frustration before plunging into her. The heat between them threatened to become a conflagration that would consume them both, but neither had any intention of escaping.

Their coupling was frenzied and primal. His hips pistoned between her thighs as he filled her completely, each thrust eliciting a gasp or moan from her lips. Sweat dripped from their bodies, mingling on the sheets beneath them as their pace quickened and urgency built. She writhed beneath him, nails raking down his back in a desperate attempt to pull him closer still.

Her release came suddenly, shuddering through her body like an earthquake, leaving her spent and gasping for breath in its aftermath. But the ancient force within him still needed to be quenched. With a roar, he drove into her faster and faster, pushing them both to the brink of pleasure and pain. Her back arched off the bed as she met him thrust for thrust, begging for more even as her body threatened to shatter under the strain.

At last, with a final surge of power and passion, he emptied himself into her depths. They lay tangled together in the aftermath, hearts pounding and lungs heaving as they struggled to regain control of their bodies and minds. Time seemed to lose all meaning as they remained locked together, basking in the warmth of their connection, a bond forged through eons of longing and desire.

Later, Menhit buried her face into his shoulder. "My love."

No words had ever sounded sweeter. Sirkan held her close, pressing her head to his shoulder with one hand while stroking her back with the other. "We will never be parted. Never."

She pulled back, her expression quizzical. "Of course not, my lord. Why would you ever think that?"

He smiled faintly and kissed her.

Menhit returned the smile, lazy and self-satisfied as power surged through her. It was unlike anything she had ever experienced. She could feel Cassandra's psychic and cybernetic abilities fusing with her own mind, their consciousnesses blending together like rivers converging into a single unstoppable current. Her DNA spiraled and reformed, adapting to accommodate this new state.

Her eyes flickered as she accessed previously unimaginable dimensions of awareness. The air around her vibrated as her enhanced nervous system began processing multiple layers of reality simultaneously. Through Cassandra's evolved mental capabilities, she felt her reach extend beyond the confines of time and space. The sensation was intoxicating. Oh, she would never give up this body!

Yet the process was not complete. Menhit knew she had only partially overtaken the girl's consciousness, even as she had transmuted her physical form. Cassandra was still fighting, clinging to the edges of her own mind like a drowning swimmer refusing to let go.

Stubborn girl, Menhit thought with a smirk. *But soon it will not matter.*

Her smile grew wider as she taunted Cassie internally, testing for cracks in her resistance. Cassie's presence within their shared mindscape was still tangible, a flicker of defiance that Menhit could feel pressing against the edges of her control. But it was fleeting, fragile. All Menhit needed was time. With every passing moment, she pushed Cassie deeper into the void, into a cold, suffocating oblivion.

Once the girl's consciousness was fully extinguished, Menhit would claim everything. The powers of Cassandra Oberon would be hers in their entirety, fully integrated into this new and perfected form that Sirkan had crafted for her. *A high form of magic indeed,* she thought, marveling at the precision and brilliance of his work. And when the final thread of Cassandra unraveled, Menhit would have it all, far more than Cassandra or even her original self, Ayesha, could have ever imagined.

The thought made her shiver with pleasure. Dark power radiated from her core. Soon, she would no longer be bound by limitations, neither by her past nor by Cassandra's.

For now, though, she could afford to be patient. Cassandra's struggle was futile. Menhit was in control, and soon, she would have everything.

NOVA STARED DOWN AT the sarcophagus, her breath catching as quantum resonance emanated from within. Inside lay a body resembling Cassandra's, suspended in a quantum-coherent state. The nameplate read "Menhit," Ayesha's dark priestess incarnation. But this was Cassandra! Nova detected overlapping quantum wave functions, as if two consciousness patterns were locked in superposition, warring for dominance.

Her fingers brushed the crystal surface, and a jolt of recognition hit her. The entanglement between the two neural states was unmistakable. This wasn't a clone. Cassandra's quantum signature was present but phase-shifted, battling against Menhit's ancient consciousness pattern, which was bound to collapse the current timeline.

The implications hit her hard: If Cassandra's body was in Menhit's sarcophagus, then Menhit's consciousness must have quantum-tunneled into the clone vessel that had inhabited this sarcophagus. Cassandra's triple-helix DNA had acted as a quantum channel, allowing Menhit's essence to suppress her current consciousness to ride the energy of both Cassandra's celestial and devic bloodlines.

Nova sent an urgent telepathic message to her twin as she fled the chamber.

Vega intercepted her moments later, coming from the direction of Cassie's quarters. "Where is she?"

"It's worse than we thought," Nova said, her voice tight. "Cassandra's body is in Menhit's sarcophagus. I detected a quantum superposition—her present consciousness is entangled with Menhit's temporal echo."

Vega's expression was horrified. "This isn't just consciousness transfer. This is quantum temporal displacement."

Nova nodded grimly. "The needle in the sarcophagus—it must have injected Menhit's preserved DNA. Her quantum-encoded consciousness must have been stored within the genetic material."

"So, this wasn't just a past-life connection," Vega said, her voice low. "It was quantum genetic transfer?"

"Exactly," Nova replied. "The needle must have carried Menhit's quantum-preserved DNA signature. It established a channel, allowing her essence to tunnel into Cassandra's body through their entangled states."

Vega's eyes widened. "And if Cassandra were to drink sacrificial blood …"

"Menhit's quantum state would fully collapse into this timeline," Nova finished breathlessly. "Her essence would overwhelm Cassandra's consciousness pattern completely. But Cassandra's quantum signature is still there, fighting the collapse.

Vega's voice shook. "If Menhit succeeds, she'll gain access to all of Cassandra's memories, skills, and modern knowledge through their entangled neural states."

Nova's expression hardened. "We need someone who understands quantum genetics and thaumaturgical manipulation. The only one who fits that description is Sirkan, and he won't help us. Menhit was his most powerful priestess."

"Then we need to act now," Vega said. "If Menhit fully integrates, who knows what she'll do? Her ancient consciousness could wreak havoc with Cassandra's knowledge of our timeline."

As they hurried down the corridor, Nova couldn't shake the quantum readings she had detected. Cassandra's body housed two superposed versions of the same soul, but her present consciousness was losing coherence by the minute, overwhelmed by the quantum echo of who she had been.

If Menhit succeeded in collapsing their shared quantum state, she would command modern knowledge and abilities to fuel her dark ambitions. And somewhere nearby, walking in a vessel that should have been lost to time, was Menhit's essence, anchored to this reality through quantum entanglement.

CASSIE DESPERATELY needed to erase the memory of the intimate scene with Sirkan. She shuddered mentally, thankful that she was not fully, consciously present in Menhit's body. The sensation of displacement grew stronger as she found herself thrust into an unfamiliar vessel: the magical sarcophagus that had previously preserved Menhit's essence.

The construct that was Menhit, the clone, felt both foreign and familiar: an ancient form preserved at the peak of its beauty and power. She mentally pounded against the magical barriers holding her consciousness captive. "Let me out!" Cassie demanded, her psyche desperately trying to break free.

Cassie realized the gravity of her situation. "Menhit's going to try to get rid of me completely," she thought, fear gripping her. "Will I die, or will I be trapped in this magical prison forever?"

Cassie's thoughts turned to her own responsibility in the situation. "I was too confident. I thought I could control the blood magic while my powers returned. How could I have been so stupid?"

Menhit's voice interrupted Cassie's thoughts, speaking through Cassie's stolen mind. "Shut up! I can't stand your whining in my head. I swear I will come and destroy that vessel where you're trapped."

Cassie retorted defiantly, "You can't destroy my present-day body, you stupid bitch. If you do, you will die too. My physical form is the tether that holds your soul, my soul, *Ayesha*, to the earthly plane."

Sirkan broke into the telepathic dialogue, "My love, I want to try an experiment. I want to see if you can access Cassandra's technological skills and her avatar abilities."

Menhit shuddered, saying, "Accessing her skills will be challenging around the constant barrage of her voice in my mind."

Sirkan replied, "I will call the Technomancer. He is ... one of *my* most powerful creations, technology and the most ancient magics intertwined into a human body."

They proceeded to a room filled with computers and holograms. Danax stood before a bank of holographic screens, monitoring the Aethernet.

Menhit, seeing the screens and devices as magical tools, asked, "These are tools for scrying?"

Sirkan chuckled. "No, love, these are called computers." He thought for a moment. "Imagine a chamber filled with countless scrolls, each inscribed with the knowledge of the ages. Now, envision that you could access any scroll instantaneously, merely by willing it. Computers are like magical repositories of knowledge, constructed from materials born from the earth itself—silicon from sand, metals from stone—designed to serve as our obedient, tireless servants and oracles, communicating through the language of light. Here, let me show you."

He directed Menhit to sit in a throne-like chair in the center of the room. As she sat down, Sirkan said, "These colored stones on the arms connect you to different streams of information and knowledge simply by pressing them." He took her right hand and placed it over the largest of the crystals. "Once you fully integrate Cassandra's abilities, you will be able to connect with these magical computers simply by thinking about what you want. Press the larger gemstone here on the arm of the throne and allow it to connect with your mind." He paused and observed her. "See, my love? The limitations you once felt in a mortal body, the doubts that clouded your mind as you aged, they are now mere illusions. Embrace this power. Embrace your true nature."

Cassie's consciousness, almost totally merged with Menhit's, felt a surge of exhilaration as dormant knowledge and power awakened within her. Menhit remembered the throne-like chair built for her when she was Ayesha with the record keeper crystals Marielle had created.

"You were always meant for greatness," Sirkan continued. "This power ... it's not just about manipulating machines or bending the physical world to your will. It's about wielding the deeper truths, the hidden knowledge."

"The patterns, the connections ... I can see them clearly," Menhit's voice carried a sense of awe as the combined essence of Cassandra's technical acumen and Ayesha's ancient wisdom coalesced in her consciousness.

Sirkan smiled. "Yes, my love. You are seeing the world as it truly is, not as the weak-minded perceive it. You are beyond them now."

Menhit affirmed, "I am beyond them. I am no longer bound by the shackles of limited understanding, neither Ayesha's nor Cassandra's."

Sirkan leaned closer, his voice a whisper yet carrying the weight of authority. "Together, we will reshape this world. Your gifts, combined with the knowledge of the dark arts, are unstoppable. *We* are unstoppable."

Menhit looked at Sirkan, her eyes ablaze with power and dark purpose. "Yes, I am unstoppable. With this power, I will change everything. I will create a new reality."

At first disconcerted by Menhit's use of *I*, he mentally shrugged. He would rectify that shortly. He placed his hands on Menhit's temples. "Let me attune with you so that I can see what you see and guide you from within."

Cassie's consciousness again tried to resist, but the surge of dark energy from Sirkan's hands amplified Menhit's power over hers.

"Feel the power that lives within you, Habibi," Sirkan commanded. "All of your talents and abilities from every life your soul experienced are ready for the taking to be integrated into this vessel. Release your memories to me."

Menhit groaned under the pressure of the unfamiliar information pouring into her. Sirkan comforted her, "It will be all right, pet. Take a deep breath and surrender your mind to me as you surrender your body. Let me do the work."

Menhit delved into Cassie's subconscious, assimilating her technological abilities. Then she discovered the meditation program Cassie had created.

"Yes!" Sirkan said, seeing through Menhit's mind. "That program is invaluable. We will turn it into a viable weapon by weaving subliminal programming under the music," Sirkan said. "Then we blast it into the minds of the humans who are being groomed by the White Circle as neophytes."

Menhit just shook her head back and forth, the data coming too fast, the information too foreign.

Sensing he was losing her to possible madness, Sirkan motioned to the Technomancer. "Slow the downloads. She is having trouble integrating so much information."

Danax put Menhit's other hand over the keypad embedded on the opposite arm of the chair and pressed her index finger over a red crystal. He turned to watch the screens that were rapidly downloading Cassie's thoughts into lines of code.

"Breathe," Sirkan directed Menhit. "It will help slow things down, and you will not feel so much anxiety." He knew that she would need more time to understand modern language.

Menhit's breathing began to even out. "There, my love. That is better." He looked over at the computer screens. The streams of code had slowed down.

Sirkan began to chant an ancient incantation designed to anchor consciousness into a physical form, a rite he had performed countless times over the millennia as part of his creation spells, a rite he had learned from Ninhursag and had added his own "special" touches.

The spell reached its climax, having melded the essence of Ayesha's past life as Menhit with Cassie's current life's technological abilities into both the dark priestess's mind and Sirkan's computer. As their shared mind vibrated with increasing intensity, reality itself seemed to shudder around them. Cassie's consciousness began to withdraw, not by choice but by necessity, like two notes of the same frequency falling out of phase. The universe itself seemed to recognize the danger of maintaining two expressions of the same soul in full awareness within a single timeline. The withdrawal felt less like an ending and more like a harmonious resolution, her consciousness receding to prevent both destructive soul interference and a temporal paradox that could unravel their shared existence. Menhit, meanwhile, became overwhelmed with trying to assimilate the modern programming, her mind struggling to process the rush of unfamiliar knowledge while reality stabilized around her singular soul presence. She began to lose consciousness and crumpled to the floor.

With a smile, Sirkan carried Menhit back to his suite, knowing that this was the beginning of a new form of power. The Trybrid's capabilities and knowledge were now the heart of his empire where the boundaries between the physical, technology, and ancient magic dissolved into a sea of endless potentials.

Chapter 30: Grandame

Manu stood in a primordial forest, the verdant green foliage surrounding him like a living emerald tapestry. Beams of sunlight filtered through the dense canopy overhead, dappling the mossy forest floor. He breathed in deeply, savoring the earthy, loamy scent of damp soil and growing things. The forest seemed familiar, but he could not yet place the memory.

Taking a step forward, his leather boots sank slightly into the moist soil. The forest felt alive, as if each tree and each drop of dew held secrets of the past, whispering tales of glory and despair to any who would listen. The sounds of the forest coalesced into a melody, a song of the earth that seemed to guide his steps deeper into the green wilderness.

Manu made his way along a narrow deer trail, winding between massive, gnarled trunks of oak and ash trees. Suddenly, a clearing appeared before him as if conjured by the forest itself. In its center stood a grand oak. Beneath the oak's expansive canopy, a cloaked figure was seated. Her cloak seemed to shimmer with the hues of the forest. As Manu approached, the figure lifted her head, revealing features that struck a chord deep within his soul.

"Ayesha," he whispered, recognition dawning. Now he remembered where, or rather when, he was. Long ago in his ancient existence, he'd found her there, his eternal soul mate, the one he sought in each of her incarnations across the vast expanse of time. He had felt her presence, as if their souls had called out to each other. The forest had seemed to guide his steps, leading him to their preordained meeting place.

As he emerged into the clearing, he saw the towering menhirs, the ancient standing stones erected by the ancient Beakers. He had helped erect these stones during one of Ayesha's previous lifetimes as a place of ceremony and communion with the old gods. Ayesha's current incarnation stood in the center, auburn hair flowing over the green cloak and white robe she wore. Their eyes met, and Manu felt the ground beneath them hum with energy, acknowledging the reunion of two souls long separated by the veils of time.

"There you are," Manu said softly.

She smiled, her eyes sparkling with profound affection and memories of countless past lives spent together. "Yes, we always seem to find our way back to each other, lifetime after lifetime. The universe conspires to reunite us."

Manu took her hands in his, marveled at the softness of her skin, the delicate lines of blue veins under the translucent surface. Even after eons, her touch still sent a thrill through him.

"How are you called in this life walk, my love?" he said.

"Danae. Danae Solas."

"You wear the robes of a druid priestess."

"Yes," said Danae. "I was given into training with the sisters of the Misty Isle at birth. My mother was a priestess, and I was conceived on the night of the great hunt. Of course, no one knows who my father was, but my star chart shows he was a mage of great power. And thus, it was ordained that I be prepared for this time of the battle between light and dark."

Manu nodded. "The tribes are fractured, divided. There is a new darkness that is trying to keep the people from knowing the light and love of the Radiant One."

Danae nodded. She knew their purpose on the earthly plane was to be champions and spiritual shepherds for the people. "Together we will show them the ways of the ancients, the ways we brought with us from the stars."

They walked through the forest, and Manu's mind drifted back to the sacred rituals they had performed together, time and time again. Now, he and Danae would lead the Celtic people in the ancient ceremonies, calling upon the spirits of the land, the ancestors, and the gods to bless and protect their tribes.

The tranquility of the forest was suddenly shattered by an unholy cacophony of shrieks and howls. The ground trembled beneath their feet, and the air grew thick with an oppressive sense of malevolence. Manu and Danae exchanged a worried glance, their senses heightened by the sudden disturbance.

From the shadows of the trees, a horde of grotesque demons emerged, their twisted forms a nightmarish blend of human and beast. Their eyes glowed with a sickly yellow light, and their mouths dripped with ichor as they snarled and gnashed their teeth. Behind them, a figure cloaked in black rode forward, his face obscured by a deep cowl.

Manu recognized the figure immediately. Sirkan! Danae knew him as a mad mage who had once been a member of her tribe but had succumbed to the lure of dark magic and forbidden knowledge. He had been banished long ago, but now it seemed he had returned, intent on revenge and destruction.

The mage raised his staff, the twisted wood pulsing with an eerie green light. He pointed it toward the couple, his voice a raspy whisper that carried an undercurrent of insanity. "You thought you could escape me, but I have returned to claim what is rightfully mine. This land, these people, they will all bow before me or be destroyed."

Manu rolled his eyes. That madman just wouldn't stay dead. He stepped forward, his hand on the hilt of his sword. "You have no power here, betrayer. I am not sure how you continue to resurrect, but this time will be your last."

The mage threw back his head and laughed, a sound that sent chills down their spines. "You underestimate me, foolish priest. I have made pacts with the darkest forces, and now they do my bidding. Demons, attack!"

He really is insane, thought Manu.

The horde surged forward, their claws and fangs glinting in the dappled sunlight. Manu drew his sword, the blessed blade humming with divine energy. Beside him, Danae raised her staff, the ancient druidic runes carved into its surface glowing with a soft blue light.

Together, they met the demons head-on, their weapons flashing in a deadly dance. Manu's sword cleaved through the twisted flesh of the demons, sending them howling back into the shadows. Danae's staff unleashed bolts of pure nature magic, searing the unholy creatures and crumbling them to dust.

But for every demon they defeated, two more took its place. Sirkan cackled with glee, his staff weaving intricate patterns in the air while he cast his dark spells. The trees around them began to wither and die, their leaves turning brown and falling to the ground in a carpet of decay.

Manu and Danae fought back-to-back, their movements perfectly synchronized from countless lifetimes of battling evil together. They knew that this fight was not just for their own survival, but for the fate of their people and the land itself.

The battle raged on, and Manu could feel his strength beginning to wane. The demons seemed endless, and the mage's power only grew stronger. He turned to Danae, his eyes filled with grim determination. "Together, in the light of the Radiant One."

Danae nodded, her face streaked with sweat and gore. "Together, as always. Let us show this mage the true power of our love and the strength of our faith."

They charged forward, their weapons raised, ready to meet their destiny head-on.

As the battle reached a fevered pitch, the air suddenly thrummed with a new energy. The sound of galloping hooves and the clang of armor filled the forest. The demons paused in their relentless assault, their eyes widening with fear.

The horn of the Wild Hunt sounded. From the depths of the forest, an army of fae warriors emerged, their aethereal beauty a stark contrast to the grotesque demons. At their head rode a magnificent warrior queen, her long silver hair flowing behind her like a banner. She wore armor of gleaming moonlight, and her sword blazed with an inner fire.

The fae queen raised her sword, her voice ringing out clear and strong. "Hear me, forces of darkness! You have no place in this realm. By the ancient pact between the fae and the druids, we stand with Manu and Ayesha against your vile corruption!"

So ... this queen knows of Ayesha, thought Manu. *She must be ancient indeed.*

At the sound of her name, Sirkan pulled up his steed, a look of astonishment on his face. "Ayesha?" he whispered, his eyes laser-pointed at Danae.

The fae army surged forward, their weapons glowing with the power of starlight. They crashed into the ranks of the demons, their grace and speed more than a match for the brute strength of the unholy creatures.

Manu and Danae felt a swell of renewed energy as they fought alongside these unexpected allies. The fae warriors danced through the battlefield, their movements a blur of shimmering light. The demons fell before them like wheat before the scythe, their dark blood staining the forest floor.

The mad mage's eyes widened in disbelief when he saw his forces being decimated. He raised his staff, preparing to unleash a devastating spell, but the fae queen was faster. She pointed her sword at the mage, and a bolt of pure energy shot forth, striking him square in the chest.

Sirkan staggered back, his staff falling from his grasp. He stared down at the smoking hole in his chest, a look of shocked incomprehension on his face. He reached toward Danae. Then, with a final gurgle, he collapsed to the ground, his life force extinguished like a snuffed candle.

With their master fallen, the remaining demons scattered, fleeing back into the shadows from whence they came. The fae warriors pursued them, loping off demonic heads and eviscerating the humanoid ghouls until the killing fields ran with blood and viscera. The fae army let out a resounding cheer, their voices echoing through the forest in a hymn of victory.

The fae queen dismounted her steed and approached Manu and Danae, a warm smile on her face. "Well met!"

Danae bowed her head in respect. "We owe you our lives and the lives of our tribe. How can we ever repay you?"

The queen shook her head. "There is no debt between friends and allies. The fae have always stood with those who protect the balance of nature and fight against the forces of darkness. We will continue to watch over you and your people, just as we have for generations."

Manu clasped the queen's hand in gratitude. "I thank you, great queen. By what name may we call you?"

She smiled enigmatically; her violet eyes rimmed in silver sparks. "Call me Grandame."

The next moment, Manu and Danae stared at empty space.

HE HEARD HIS NAME CALLED as from a distance. He did not want to leave the memory; he wanted to savor the sense of Ayesha.

"Manu, wake up. We need to leave this place."

He reluctantly opened his eyes and clutched the medallion that hung at his chest. "Gimme a minute. I need to integrate a forgotten encounter with Ayesha from one of her past lives. It may hold an important key."

"Key or not, we need to get out of here. I have a very bad feeling."

Without further ado, Siobhan waved her hand, opened a portal back to the Citadel, and pulled Manu through. After they left, the entire tomb imploded, buried and hidden once more.

Chapter 31: Light Witch, Dark Witch

The swirling depths of a misty chasm beckoned her and whispered dark secrets. A chill wind whipped through her hair as shadowy tendrils reached from the chasm and curled around her ankles, urging her to plunge into the unknown. Yet high above, a bright star shimmered. Its pure light pierced the gloom and illuminated a narrow bridge spanning the abyss.

The scene shifted, and Devika found herself in a dimly lit chamber, face to face with her mother. The dark witch's eyes glowed with an eerie amber light.

"Embrace your true nature, daughter," Morgandrian said, her voice cajoling. "The dark arts are your birthright. Together we can rule over all!" She extended a pale hand, black flames dancing at her fingertips.

Devika recoiled, torn between the allure of her mother's offer and the sickening dread it evoked within her. "I-I don't know," she stammered, backing away.

Suddenly, the chamber door burst open, and a white-robed figure strode in, his robes billowing. "Step away from her, Morgandrian!" he commanded, his staff leveled at the dark witch.

Morgandrian laughed, a chilling sound devoid of mirth. "You're too late, enforcer. My daughter's path is set." With a flick of her wrist, she vanished in a swirl of smoke.

DEVIKA JOLTED AWAKE, her heart racing. The dream had felt so real. Trembling, she sat up in her four-poster bed, trying to shake off the unsettling visions that plagued her nightly.

The door to her small chamber creaked open, and Tatiana entered, her brow furrowed with concern. "Another dream?" she asked gently, settling on a stool beside her.

Devika nodded, drawing her knees to her chest. "They're getting stronger," she confessed. "I feel the darkness calling to me, even when I'm awake. But then I remember what you and Master Elena have taught me about the light."

Tatiana placed a comforting hand on her shoulder. "The path of balance is never easy, Devika. But I have faith in you." She smiled encouragingly. "Come, get ready for your day and then come down to the kitchen. There is someone here to see you."

Perplexed, Devika scrambled up and prepared for a day that would change her life forever.

MORGANDRIAN WAS INCENSED. "*This* is where you put my daughter? A hovel in the middle of a forest in the-Crone-knows-where!"

Arion rolled his eyes. "Do you really think we would house her at the Citadel?"

"I expected you to house her in the luxury due to her status! She is the daughter of the most powerful high priestess of the most powerful coven in the Americas!"

His eyes steely, Arion replied, "Is that so?"

Her rant was interrupted when Tatiana came into the room, a delicate young woman with long black tresses and emerald eyes trailing behind her.

Upon seeing her mother, Devika came to an abrupt halt, looking unsure and not a little afraid. Then she ran into her mother's arms, tears streaming down her face. "Mother!"

"My darling daughter," Morgandrian whispered, her voice filled with longing. "I've missed you so much."

Devika's heart ached at the sight of her mother, memories of their time together flooding back. But she couldn't ignore the darkness that clung to Morgandrian like a second skin. "Mother, I ..." she began, her voice trembling.

"Shhh ... shhh ... it's all right," Morgandrian said quietly. "Arion has brought me here so that we can be together again."

Tatiana gently disengaged the two and motioned for them to sit at the table. On cue, a kitchen elf began to serve tea and a light breakfast of scones and fruit. "Eat something, Devika. You will need some sustenance before we dive into the task at hand."

They all sat with her. Morgandrian took a bite of a proffered scone, but it tasted like chalk in her mouth. She picked up the tea instead, while drinking in the sight of her beautiful daughter. The weight of her past bore down upon her when she realized Devika was now twenty-one. *Why, she is a young woman!*

Tatiana got up and paced before them, her blue eyes sharp and probing. "If you truly seek redemption, Morgandrian, you must be fully honest with us. No secrets, no lies."

Morgandrian's gaze flicked to Devika, who had gotten up and stood beside Tatiana, her face a mixture of hope and trepidation. Drawing a deep breath, the dark witch nodded. "I understand. I will hold nothing back."

Tatiana stopped pacing and fixed a penetrating stare on Morgandrian. "Then tell us, who is Devika's father?"

Morgandrian's shoulders tensed, and for a moment Devika feared her mother would refuse to answer. But then, with a sigh of resignation, Morgandrian spoke. "Devika's father is ... Ian MacGregor."

Shocked silence permeated the room. Devika felt as if the air had been sucked from her lungs. Her father was a white witch and the leader of one of the most powerful covens of the Devic Kingdom, the very group that had been fighting against the dark covens for years.

Arion's eyes widened. He was rarely shocked. "Ian MacGregor? But how? He's been at the forefront of the battle against the dark arts for hundreds of years."

Morgandrian's gaze took on a distant quality, looking into the past. She took a deep breath. "Ian and I, we've been circling each other for centuries, our paths intertwined by fate and the turbulent tides of history."

She paused, a wistful smile playing on her lips. "It all began in the aftermath of the French Revolution. I was in Paris, my heart shattered after Natesh chose Giselle over me. That's when I first laid eyes on Ian MacGregor, a handsome Scottish witch who was aiding those affected by the revolution."

Morgandrian's gaze turned introspective. "Despite our different allegiances, we were drawn to each other like moths to a flame. We embarked on a passionate affair, lost in the throes of desire and the chaos of the times. But when Ian discovered my true identity as a powerful dark witch, he was torn between his feelings and his duty to the light."

She sighed, a touch of bitterness in her voice. "Ultimately, he chose to leave me, unable to bring himself to end my life, despite the threat I posed."

Morgandrian's tone grew wistful as she continued, "Nearly a century later, our paths crossed again in New Orleans. I was at the height of my power, the high priestess of the most influential dark coven in America. Ian was in the city, investigating a series of mysterious disappearances linked to Natesh."

Her eyes flashed with a mixture of longing and regret. "When we met, the old spark between us reignited, but I was too committed to the dark arts to give up my power for love. The encounter ended in a bitter confrontation, with Ian narrowly escaping my wrath."

Morgandrian's voice softened as she recounted the most recent encounter. "Twenty-two years ago, Ian and I found ourselves in a small town nestled in the Catskills, both drawn by a powerful magical anomaly. The forces of light and the dark covens had agreed to a temporary truce to deal with a common enemy: a rogue witch threatening to expose the magical world to the mundanes."

She looked down at her hands, remembering the touch of Ian's skin against hers. "We were chosen as representatives for our respective sides, forced to work together to track down and neutralize the threat. Despite our best efforts to maintain a professional distance, the close proximity and shared goal reignited our old chemistry."

Morgandrian's voice trembled slightly as she continued, "One night, after a narrow escape from the rogue witch's minions, we gave in to our desires, spending a passionate night together in a hidden safe house. But the next morning, we were back to being enemies, the truce shattered by the weight of our responsibilities and the depth of our differences."

She looked up, her eyes meeting Devika's, a mixture of love and pain reflected in their amber depths. "We fell in love, but our union was forbidden. When I discovered I was pregnant with Devika, I was tempted like never before to leave the dark arts behind and join him. But I was afraid, and I chose power over love."

Devika got up from the table and went to her mother's side, her heart racing. "My father ... does he know about me?"

Morgandrian shook her head, tears glistening in her dark eyes. "No. I thought it would be better for both of you if he never knew."

Tatiana's voice cut through the silence, her tone measured and thoughtful. "This revelation changes everything. Devika's heritage, her potential for both light and dark magic ... it could shift the balance of power in this war."

Arion nodded, his expression grave. "We must inform Ian MacGregor. He has a right to know about his daughter, and Devika deserves the chance to meet her father."

Morgandrian's face paled, fear etched into her features. "But what if he rejects her? What if he can't forgive me for keeping her from him all these years?"

Tatiana placed a hand on Morgandrian's shoulder, her touch firm but reassured. "The path to redemption is never easy, but you must have faith. If Ian MacGregor is truly the man I believe him to be, he will understand and embrace his daughter, no matter the circumstances of her birth."

Devika's mind reeled with the revelation of her father's identity. All her life, she had wondered about the man who had given her life, and now, to learn that he was not only alive but also fighting for the very cause she had been drawn to ... it was almost too much to comprehend.

Sensing her turmoil, Arion placed a comforting hand on her shoulder. "We will stand by you, Devika. No matter what happens, you have a place here with us."

Drawing strength from his words, Devika met her mother's gaze. "I want to meet him. I want to know my father and understand the other half of my heritage."

Morgandrian's eyes shone with a mixture of pride and fear. "I will accept whatever consequences come from my actions as long as it means you have a choice in how you live your life. You deserve that much."

Tatiana nodded, a small smile playing at the corners of her lips. "I will reach out to Ian and arrange a meeting. It's going to be a bit tricky, but I have no doubt everything will work out for the best."

The three began to discuss the next steps in contacting Ian MacGregor and preparing Devika for the meeting. Devika, in turn, allowed herself a moment to marvel at the twists of fate that had brought her to this point. She was the daughter of a dark witch and a white witch, a child of two worlds, destined for a future she could never have imagined.

IAN'S FACE WAS WOODEN. His world tilted on its axis. He looked across the table in the Irish pub on the shores of Bimini and motioned to the barman. "Another triple, neat," he said.

The man served him with hesitation. It was the ginger-haired Scot's third round in the past twenty minutes. But his companion nodded his head, "It's fine, Brian. The highlander can hold his scotch."

"Aye, I fuckin' can," Ian slurred, just a little.

Arion smiled broadly at his companion. He had decided it would be best to break the news that Ian was a father over a great deal of whiskey, or scotch in this case. He himself was nursing a nice Kentucky bourbon.

"This is just a barrel of shite," Ian continued. "I have a ... daughter? What the fuck?"

"Yeah, you keep using that word like a verb, a noun, and an adverb. Let's move on, shall we? And decide next steps."

"Well, I fuckin' want to see her! She's my dau-dau-daughter after all!" He stuttered.

"Yes. She's your daughter ... and Morgandrian's," Arion said gently.

"The bane of my existence since I first laid eyes on her!" Ian said, squinting his eyes at the White Circle's "enforcer."

"And from what I understand, you of hers. So, let's get all the cards on the table here, m'lad."

Ian's head shot up at that. "M'lad be damned! You're not that much older than me!"

"Only by a few millennia," retorted the celestial.

"Yeah, well there's that. But I am *from* this planet, and you are an invader!"

"So says your scotch-addled brain."

Ian gave him the stink eye.

"OK, we'll roll with that. As I was saying, you have a twenty-one-year-old daughter who is every bit as unique with her dark and light DNA as any one of the avatars." He hesitated to finish his thought but plowed on. "Actually, she's totally different from any of the avatars because she has the dark DNA. But still …"

Gratefully, Arion noticed Tatiana come in from the corner of his eye. He sent up a silent prayer of gratitude to the Radiant One. Following Arion's gaze, Ian's emerald eyes lit on her. He rose, or stumbled, to his feet. She crooked a smile, took in the scene, and waved an enchantment while coming to the table.

"Hello, Daddy."

Shit, thought Arion, *she's going for the jugular.*

Ian pushed up from the table, looked at her fiercely, and then relented. "Yeah, it seems so."

"Well then, let's go outside. Devika is waiting not far from here. I didn't think it appropriate for you to meet you daughter for the first time in a bloody pub."

The spell Tatiana had cast wove around Ian's unsteady form and balanced out the muddling effects of the drink.

"All right then. Lead the way," he said.

Tatiana led Ian and Arion out of the pub and down to the beach. The sun was setting, and the waves lapped at the shore.

Ian's mind was a mass of emotions as they walked along the sand. He'd never thought about being a father, especially not to a child he'd made with Morgandrian. What the hell would he need to know about having a daughter that was both dark witch and white witch?

Tatiana looked back at Ian. "I know it's a lot to take in, Ian. But meeting Devika will be the start of something new for you."

Ian nodded, feeling a lump in his throat. "I don't know how to be a father. Especially to a daughter I never knew about."

Arion patted Ian's shoulder. "No one's born knowing how to be a parent. You'll figure it out as you go."

"And what the fuck do you know about being a parent, Enforcer?"

Arion quirked an eyebrow, "More than you imagine."

Tatiana snorted, not allowing herself to meet either of their eyes.

Ian halted abruptly. A diminutive figure stood facing the ocean, her outline surrounded by the glow of the setting sun. The setting sun highlighted her flowing tresses. Her hair reflected a rich symphony of colors ranging from black to brown with streaks of his own ginger hair flowing freely down her back.

She turned and met his eyes with hers: green flecked with gold. His heart stopped in his chest as he thought, *My daughter.*

Tatiana and Arion stayed back while Ian walked up to Devika. He stopped a few feet away, looking at her with a mix of awe and uncertainty.

"Devika," he said softly.

Devika looked up at him, eyes watering. "Hi, Dad."

At that moment, Ian's worries disappeared. He stepped forward and hugged his daughter tightly, both of them crying.

"I'm sorry," he whispered. "I'm sorry I wasn't there, that I didn't know …"

Devika shook her head, hugging him back. "You're here now. That's what counts." She pursed her lips, so like her mother's. "Looks like we have some shite to figure out, Da."

Oh yes, he laughed, *she is definitely my daughter.*

As Ian and Devika embraced, a familiar figure emerged from the shadows. Morgandrian, her dark hair billowing in the ocean breeze, approached them with a mixture of apprehension and longing in her eyes. Ian tensed as he noticed her presence, his arms instinctively tightening around Devika. The history between him and Morgandrian was a tangled web of passion, betrayal, and unresolved emotions.

Devika, sensing her father's discomfort, pulled back from the hug and turned to face her mother. "Mom," she said softly, "I'm really glad you're here."

Morgandrian's eyes glistened with the tears that refused to fall as she looked at her daughter and the man she had loved so very much. "I could not keep away," she confessed. "Not when I knew this was happening."

Ian's jaw clenched as he met Morgandrian's piercing gaze. "Morgandrian," he said tensely, "I suppose there's much to talk about."

"I know I have so much to answer for, Ian, but please believe me: Everything I did, I did to protect Devika."

Devika stepped between her parents, her eyes pleading. "Can we just ... can we just focus on the present? On the fact that, like, we're all here, together, for the first time?"

Ian and Morgandrian exchanged a long, weighted look. Years of history, of love and pain and unspoken words, passed between them in that moment.

Finally, Ian sighed, his shoulders sagging. "You're right, lass. The past is the past. What matters now is that we're here for you."

Arion stepped forward. "You can be here for Devika, Ian, but Morgandrian has a bargain to fulfill." With that, he opened a portal, grabbed Morgandrian's arm, and disappeared.

Devika shrieked as she reached for her mother but only caught thin air. She whirled on Tatiana, "What was that about?"

Tatiana shook her head. "Morgandrian has karma to balance before she can be free to be with you." She turned to Ian, whose face had gone ashen. "I will take Devika with me and begin the integration of her powers. She will need training of a different kind than what the avatars have been given. You, my lad, are needed on another battle front. Say your goodbyes for now."

Ian took his daughter's face between his hands and kissed her lightly on the forehead. "Tatiana is right. There are great challenges ahead of us as the Shift of the Ages unfolds. You are in good hands. I am only a thought away."

Devika went to Tatiana, looking back over her shoulder at her newly discovered father.

When they had disappeared, Ian started. *The avatars? What do they have to do with my daughter?*

Chapter 32: Metamorphosis

Menhit sat gingerly in the large throne-like chair once more. Sirkan could tell it was very much to her liking. It was made of precious metals gathered from across galaxies and powered by a large glowing quartz crystal: an Atlantean record keeper. Other precious stones formed a six-pointed star on the backplate of the chair. It came to life as soon as she leaned back and put the palms of her hands on the armrests.

"Very good. The power crystal recognizes you, or rather your soul. This chair was originally created for Ayesha when we established this new base after the sinking of Atlantis. Now it's your time to claim it."

Menhit settled into the chair. It was surprisingly comfortable.

"Now, close your eyes and begin to breathe slowly and deliberately. You know the routine. Relax and allow your consciousness to connect with the power of the throne, your soul's throne from ages past. Let your soul essence come forward and remember who you are. You are more than Menhit, priestess of Seth. You are the soul essence of Ayesha, the holder of all her power and knowledge."

Menhit did as bidden. She inhaled deeply, letting the energy of the crystal pulse through her core. It ignited something within her, radiating from the base of her spine like a rising sun. Her breath slowed, steady and deliberate, as the energy climbed her spine, ascending to her third eye.

But the connection was not hers alone. The energetic cord linking Menhit's mind to Cassie's flared to life, and Menhit had a clear connection to Cassie's mind, past and present. The power!

Cassie stirred within, and her presence flared in protest. The energetic tether that connected her mind to Menhit's sparked and vibrated with tension. The sensation was suffocating, like a storm pressing down on her psyche.

Then Cassie felt herself unraveling, her identity being pulled toward that of Menhit.

"You are the Trybrid now, Menhit," Sirkan's voice echoed, triumphant.

Cassie's mind swirled in horror and rage. They wanted to erase her, to bury her beneath the weight of a dark lifetime she had already paid dearly for on her karmic journey. She'd be damned if she was going to go backward after thousands of years spent balancing her karma. She was Cassandra Oberon, damn it. Not Menhit. Not Ayesha. And if anyone was going to claim the title of Trybrid, it would be her and her alone.

Mind over matter. The phrase had never felt more literal. Cassie could feel Menhit's consciousness actively melding with hers, drawing on the past-life energies of her soul, Ayesha's soul, to reshape her physical and mental essence. The transformation wasn't just metaphysical, it was tangible in the quantum field that was her mind. Cassie could feel it altering her very DNA, pulling her current identity deeper into the form that identified as Menhit.

Her breath steadied, and her mind sharpened into focus. She had tools. She had willpower. And she would fight.

She reached for every mental tool she'd ever honed—visualizations, meditations, energy work, and quantum physics—fighting her way toward the surface of her own mind.

Her awareness split between realities: her body in stasis within the sarcophagus and Menhit's form on the throne. As her consciousness flickered between vessels, she realized with horror that she could become trapped in a quantum immortality state: forever aware but unable to fully manifest in either form.

Summoning every ounce of her power, she focused on her true, present-day body trapped in the sarcophagus. In her mind's eye, she surrounded it with a whirlwind of the Violet Flame, just as the Master St. Germaine had taught her all those years ago. This had to be what modern quantum theory meant by field interactions: where consciousness itself was an energy field that could be manipulated through focused intent. As she channeled the Violet Flame's energy, it created an interference pattern with Menhit's consciousness. The overlapping fields generated ripples in the fabric of spacetime itself. She could feel the underlying vacuum responding to her will, particles flickering in and out of existence as the fields interacted. The Violet Flame began to resonate with her own consciousness at precisely the right frequency, creating a tunneling effect that could potentially allow her to break free from the bond binding her to Menhit's cloned form. The overlap between her two possible physical vessels began to collapse, forcing reality to choose one outcome or the other. In this critical moment, she had to ensure her consciousness remained in her true form, in this timeline, or risk being permanently trapped in the sarcophagus, or oblivion.

Cassie felt the throne's power and Menhit's presence begin to crumble as she allowed her consciousness to be pulled forward to the throne. The energy surged toward the heart of the throne, toward the glowing quartz crystal that fueled its power. A memory rose unbidden—a lesson in quantum theory. Energy fields could interact, reshape each other, collapse possibilities into chosen outcomes.

And she chose.

> *I am a being of Violet Fire,* she blasted through the mental bond:
> *A spark of light, my soul's desire.*
> *O sacred flame, so bright, so pure,*
> *Transmute the dark, let love endure.*
> *In this timeline, my life's divine,*
> *No shadow can claim what's truly mine.*
> *Let darkness return, in love, to Source,*
> *Harmed none, in time, through sacred force.*
> *By this flame, I rise anew,*
> *In harmony, in truth, in view.*
> *Transformed and whole by Violet Flame.*
> *So mote it be, my will I claim.*

The flame surged into an inferno, blazing with sentience as it spun wildly around the sarcophagi chamber. The firestorm moved with purpose, weaving between the sarcophagi like a living entity. One by one, they burst open, releasing the dormant essences of past lives. Each freed incarnation rushed toward her, merging with the Violet Flame. Her stories, skills, and experiences fused together, creating a unified and strengthened whole. This was not destruction; it was reclamation. Piece by piece, her soul fragments reassembled, integrating every life she had ever lived.

Menhit began to tremble, her body wracked with spasms of pain.

"Menhit!" Sirkan roared, lunging to pull her from the throne. His hands met an invisible barrier, and he recoiled in agony as sparks of ancient, untamed energy seared his skin. The air around the throne shimmered, charged with a power that defied him. It was ancient, primal, and wholly beyond his control: a clash of wills between Menhit's dominating presence and Cassie's defiant spirit.

Menhit's body arched in the chair, her screams reverberating through the room. Bolts of quantum energy radiated outward.

Memories surged through Cassie's mind's eye in rapid flashes: lifetimes lived, loves found, realms conquered, and powers wielded. She saw herself as a kaleidoscope of identities, each unique, each integral. Ayesha. Menhit. Denae. Cassandra. And countless others. Light and dark, joy and pain, triumph and failure: They were all her.

With that epiphany, Cassie summoned the strength to fight back against Menhit's mind invasion. She focused her energy, channeling the power of the throne and her own myriad soul fragments, creating a shield of golden light around her. This light met Cassie's Violet Flame, and for a moment, the chamber was bathed in a brilliant purple and gold aura.

Menhit convulsed, her presence faltering. Cassie saw her opportunity and seized it, channeling every ounce of power she had left into the Violet Flame. The throne's energy faltered, then exploded outward, sending arcs of light spiraling through the room.

Circuits blew. Wards shattered. Powers unleashed.

When the chaos subsided, the air was still. Cassie stood in the center of the wreckage, surrounded by faint wisps of violet and gold energy. She was whole. She was herself. But she was also something more.

Her body shimmered, clad in an exosuit that fused organic and technological elements seamlessly. Bioluminescent veins pulsed faintly beneath its metallic surface, patterns shifting like constellations. Around her neck rested a Celtic torc, its intricate carvings glowing faintly. Her violet eyes opened, blazing with millennia of wisdom and strength ... and a running stream of computer code.

Sirkan approached cautiously, awe and terror etched on his face. "Cassandra?" he whispered.

Cassie tilted her head, her voice resonating with the echoes of her past lives. "Yes ... and no. I am Ayesha. I am Menhit. I am Cassandra. And I am so much more."

For the first time, she felt the full weight of her soul—not fragmented, but whole. Light and shadow, past and present, bound together in perfect harmony. She smiled faintly, violet light swirling around her like a cloak.

She was Cassandra Oberon transformed—a Trybrid, and a fusion of past and present, ready to claim her future.

And then, a memory struck her like lightning. *Manu!*

Gripping the back of the throne for support, Cassandra steadied herself, clutching at her chest as if an arrow had pierced it. Her gaze fell on the glowing quartz crystal embedded in the throne. Reaching for it, she placed her hand over its surface. It fell into her palm, and she held it tightly, a faint smile playing on her lips.

Finally, the Atlantean record keeper!

A smile played at her lips as she palmed the crystal. With a flick of her wrist, a hidden drawer below the Star of David design on the backplate slid open. There, nestled in dark blue silk, lay a medallion of alien alloys, a twin to the medallion that Manu now wore. She pressed the one-inch crystal into its center and hung it around her neck. The torc at her throat emitted a low humming noise as it synced with the medallion. She could *feel* Manu. Relieved, she took a deep breath and walked to the massive wall of computer consoles.

"It's time I put a stop to your machinations," she said to Sirkan.

He reached for her. She raised her hand without looking at him and shot out a bolt of energy, pinning him to the closest wall. "You don't seem to understand. The throne allowed me to synthesize all that I have been into a new form. Your wards and sigils can no longer dampen the abilities I now possess. Your power play is over."

With that, Cassandra began sending waves of code into the computers. They sizzled and sparked as her cybernetic abilities began unraveling the infected programs running throughout the ship's computer systems. The Technomancer had disappeared, but she could feel his pushback from deep within the Aethernet. She knew he would do everything he could to salvage his programs. But for now, she could slow him down considerably.

Intent on tracing him through sound patterns deeply embedded in the Aethernet, she put both palms onto the computer main frame to help her zero in on Danax's location.

"May I be of some assistance?" a smokey voice said from the shadows.

Ninhursag stepped forward, smiling. "It's good to see you at your full potential, Ayesha."

Cassie swung her head around to look at the Anunnaki and frowned. Scenes from countless lifetimes played through her mind. A wave of relief washed over her as she remembered their friendship. "Nin! By the Radiant One, it's good to see you!" She motioned to the consoles. "Be my guest."

Nin stared at Cassie's eyes. "Well, it does indeed seem that you have transformed. Let's see what we can do to put all of that knowledge and power to good use." She went to the bank of computers and placed her hands over Cassie's. She closed her eyes to focus her ancient Anunnaki abilities, honed over millennia of genetic manipulation and technological advancement. A soft, iridescent glow emanated from her palms, spreading across the consoles like a gentle wave.

"These programs are complex, designed to manipulate human consciousness on a global scale," Nin said, her brow furrowed in concentration. "Most of them seem to be focused through a specific program, some sort of virtual reality game called *Battle for Infinity*. Pfft," she grinned, "no match for the combined power of the Trybrid and a Sumerian goddess."

Cassie returned the grin and, closing her eyes, directed a stream of code down her arms to join Ninhursag's energy. Nin's multidimensional beam began to intertwine with Cassie's code, forming intricate patterns across the computer screens. They embedded themselves deep within the game's programs. The codes and algorithms that had been controlling the thoughts and emotions of millions of players began to unravel, replaced by shimmering strands of light.

"Wait ... it seems we have some other players," said Nin. "Their energy signature is familiar." She threw her head back and laughed. "Nothing like my husband showing up at the eleventh hour."

"Husband?" Cassie almost choked.

"Enki is in here with us as well. Nibiru must be getting within range of Earth's aetheric plane. That means he was able to connect with his cohort, Artemus. They were always collaborating on some form of advanced technology or another in times gone by. Let's see how this plays out. Keep flowing the energy into the Aethernet." She paused for a beat. "Now pull back a bit. We don't want it to collapse. Gently ... gently ... wait! Stop!"

Cassie watched in amazement while streams of code rode across the massive computer screens, seeming to eat the corrupted code like an army of alphabet Pac-Men.

"Brilliant, my love," whispered Nin.

While the two teams worked in unison from different dimensions, the Technomancer's presence grew weaker, his influence over *Battle for Infinity* diminished with each passing moment. Cassandra could feel him withdrawing and started to go after him.

"No," hissed Nin. "Let him go. We will deal with him later. I don't want to destroy one of my greatest creations."

Cassie's eyes widened. "What! We can't let him run wild across the Aethernet! He is working with the Dark Brotherhood."

Nin pursed her lips thoughtfully. "No ... my sense is he's gone rogue, unbeknownst to the Dark Brotherhood. Let him savor this illusion of victory. There are bigger battles to come, and we must prepare. Rest assured that Danax will end up being one of our greatest weapons, hidden in plain sight. His break with the Dark Brotherhood could fall under the heading of 'the enemy of my enemy.' Be satisfied for now that we have altered the essence of that vile game and nullified its effects on a large swath of humanity. Now their latent potentials can awaken through natural means and free will." Nin whispered, "Well done, husband."

"Does this mean that Enki is back, that Nibiru is once more nearing Earth's orbit in its own journey around the sun?" asked Cassie. Cassie knew that, unlike the predictable elliptical paths of the known planets, Nibiru's highly eccentric orbit took it far beyond the Kuiper Belt for millennia at a time before plunging back toward the inner solar system on its 3,600-year cycle.

"Not yet, but he is close enough to connect through the spirit screen. Once we get out of this damnable rift, I should be able to reach out to him."

Cassandra's eyes met hers hopefully. "Manu?"

Nin went over to her longtime friend and ally and grasped her shoulders. "He has the medallion. It will function as it was meant to. You should be able to find one another now."

A shiver of premonition ran up Cassie's spine, as she clutched at the medallion at her neck. She now had another mission.

Chapter 33: Quantum Gambit

Danax had long sought to dominate the myriad dimensions of the planet. His latest creation, the quantum entanglement communicator, or QEC, was his most insidious weapon yet. Through an untraceable backdoor, the device allowed him to infiltrate the spirit screen network, monitor communications, and twist them to his will. With it, he could seize control of any being or machine possessing an electronic brain, orchestrating attacks with the deadly precision of a spider weaving its trap. The power it granted him brought a cold, satisfied smile to his shadowed face.

The next step would be to connect it to the Aethernet at a subatomic level. With that technology in hand, he could extend his dominion over nearly this entire sector of the Milky Way. Sirkan would soon be nothing more than ... what was it his human grandfather used to say? Oh yes, "like a piss ant on a mountain." Danax let the insult roll over in his mind, savoring its pettiness. "Sirkan the piss ant." He laughed. Yes, he quite liked that analogy.

But enough of this, he was getting ahead of himself. His ambitions were far beyond this current program. One day, he would sever all ties to the Dark Brotherhood and create a new race in his own image. Perfection incarnate. But first, there was business to attend to.

The Trybrid.

That bitch had single-handedly ruined his carefully orchestrated plans, transforming and obliterating the subliminal messaging embedded in his VR masterpiece. Her meddling had forced him to accelerate his timeline into the social media outlets. No matter. His bot army was ready to begin the takeover of the Aethernet. The future was his to mold: shining, cold, and inevitable.

EXPLOSIONS ECHOED ACROSS the dimensional divide, energy bolts firing through the network that connected different algorithms of social media and news outlets. Amidst the chaos, Marcus Castoldi, his voice cutting through the din, shouted: "Get those bots neutralized! They are wreaking havoc on transworld communication systems."

Yirribindi's sharp tone carried over the commotion, edged with urgency. "Forget the comms! The whole Aethernet is on the brink of collapse!" They gripped the console, their knuckles white, as another shockwave rippled through the command center.

Marcus wished he had more of Cassie's innate ability to connect directly with the Aethernet. He felt a little better with the other five avatars by his side, but no one had Cassie's ability to connect mind to machine without the use of tech. They needed to depend on implants or electrodes to ramp up their connections.

Cassie just needed her mind.

But today, every challenge felt magnified, as if the Technomancer's devices had grown more cunning.

Marcus adjusted the volume on his headset, trying to cut through the static clouding the comms. "Can anyone confirm where the Technomancer's main infiltration point is?" he barked.

Karim's voice rang out as he studied the readouts on his monitor. "Looks like he's starting to infiltrate the Aethernet on a new stream of code. It's like nothing I've seen before. That's gonna throw the proverbial wrench into the works if we don't shut it down fast."

"How can we shut it down if we don't know how it works?" hissed Marcus.

"And lest we forget, Sirkan is still lurking somewhere in the background," added Seraphina, her calm but steely voice commanding attention.

Marcus gritted his teeth, suppressing a frustrated groan. "Sirkan doesn't worry me as much as the Technomancer's bots. If we don't stop them, they'll take the entire Aethernet offline."

Karim raised an eyebrow, a smirk playing on his lips. "Never assume, bruh. Never assume," he countered, his tone light but his eyes scanning the room, alert and cautious. "We got this."

The atmosphere shifted as the resonant voice of Artemus, master of the White Circle, rang out from the doorway. "Karim is correct," he said, stepping into the room. The light spilling across the tiled floor illuminated his regal yet commanding presence. "Assumptions can be costly. For now, it's important that you concentrate on the mental techniques Mikha'El has been teaching you and give it your all."

Upon the invocation of his name, the great archangel appeared, his aethereal eyes reflecting the fiery essence of the sword sheathed at his back. "We've known that the first worldwide battle would be via the Aethernet. You have the mental skills and acuity to counter anything the Technomancer can throw at us." He met each avatar's gaze. "Armor up!"

Mind shields went up throughout the room. Headsets were reset. Fingertips hovered over aetheric keyboards.

Artemus nodded. "We have prepared for this day. It's unfortunate that Cassandra is not here, but six avatars and the great Mikha'El surely can overcome any edge the Technomancer's bots give him." He paused. "I have a bit of tech help up my sleeves as well. Focus on what you know, and I will summon a long-time ally."

There was a momentary blip in concentration as the avatars let that bit of information register—until Mikha'El bellowed, "Focus!"

A hologram projected out of the spirit screen and a being with the torso of a humanoid male wearing a fish-headed cowl manifested in the middle of the bridge.

"Adonai, Lord Enki." said Artemus. "I welcome you in the name of the Radiant One. It seems we have reached a point that we need the device we developed when last you walked this planet."

Enki looked around the room through his holographic eyes and latched onto the bank of computer consoles. Without a word, he pointed what looked like a trident toward the motherboard of the main computer. A stream of code, a brilliant piece of ancient alien tech and magics that countered the quantum entanglement communicator, poured from the trident into the computer. It deployed decoys and false signals designed to confuse and mislead their enemy.

And so, a game of cosmic cat and mouse unfolded. Danax, confident in his QEC's prowess, sent wave after wave of his bot forces into the Aethernet, only to find Mikha'El and the avatars always a step ahead, thanks to Enki.

A ripple stuttered across the screens. Marcus laughed, "I can feel the Technomancer's frustration."

Meanwhile, Artemus synced up with Enki to focus on disrupting the QEC network, his mind weaving through the quantum threads. With a final, concentrated effort, he sent a surge of energy through the network, causing it to overload.

Danax's roar of disbelief echoed across the Aethernet as his commands went unanswered and his nanobot forces were thrown into disarray. Seizing the moment, Mikha'El directed the avatars to send a virus they'd prepared into the stream of code.

It blew the circuitry.

When the dust settled, Danax had retreated, his plans foiled, for now.

A whoop of victory went up as the avatars pumped their fists in victory.

Artemus held up his hands, "We have won a small battle today, but Danax will undoubtedly return. We must be prepared."

And then the great Enki spoke from the spirit screen. "I will be back amongst you before long. Nibiru's path will soon be within range of Earth, and I will be able to send reinforcements to join in this battle for humanity's next step in evolution. Be vigilant and continue to allow your powers to unfold."

He bowed his head to Artemus and Mikha'El. "In the light of the Radiant One," he said, then was gone.

"Whoa, that was Enki?" gasped Yirribindi. "I thought he was, like, a myth."

Artemus turned and smiled at them. "And what are myths but the truths we forgot to remember?" Artemus's voice carried a weight of wisdom when he spoke, but his eyes twinkled with a hint of mischief and knowledge far beyond the confines of their current reality.

Yirribindi, still awestruck by the manifestation of Enki, nodded slowly, their mind racing to assimilate the realization. "So he's real, like *really* real. And he's helping us?"

"Yes, Yirri," Artemus replied, using his affectionate nickname for them. "Enki and other Anunnaki have been guiding and interacting with humanity for millennia. They intervene at crucial points, safeguarding the balance between cosmic forces. Today, you witnessed a fraction of what beings like Enki can accomplish."

"But why us? Why now?" Yirribindi's questions flowed freely, their earlier reservations forgotten in the wake of their burgeoning curiosity.

"Because, Yirri," Artemus began, walking toward the spirit screen, which still shimmered faintly with the afterimage of Enki, "this planet and its people are at a tipping point. The challenges humanity faces are not only physical but also mental, emotional, and deeply spiritual. We are in the midst of elevating the consciousness of the planet and humanity. The Anunnaki, and other off-world entities, see that potential."

He paused, meeting the young avatar's eyes. "They are not just myths, nor merely gods from old stories. They are our forebears from the stars, and their wisdom is crucial to humanity's survival."

Yirribindi absorbed his words, their expression a mixture of awe and understanding. "So the battle with the Technomancer, it's all just ... preparation?"

"In a way," Artemus confirmed, a grave note in his voice. "Preparation for greater challenges and higher achievements are essential. Each victory teaches us, as do our failures. And through it all, figures like Enki provide the assistance we need, sometimes visible, sometimes not. But they are always important learning tools. It affirms that we are not alone in our battle against the darkness. There are many races and worlds that have the same goal that we do."

Yirribindi looked toward the now quiet spirit screen, their mind filled with possibilities. "I guess we really are living a myth, aren't we?"

Artemus chuckled, his laughter echoing warmly in the command center. "Yes, we are, Yirri. What we do here today, every decision, every choice, will become the stories they tell tomorrow. Let's make ours worth retelling."

Chapter 34: Passage to Poseidia

Nova and Vega felt the first wave of tremors, a prelude to a seismic shift that fanned out into the dimensional rift between Poseidia and Sirkan's ship. The small hover craft that transported them between the dimensions lost power and dropped abruptly to the bottom of the connecting tube.

Scrambling out of the craft, the two Arcturians scurried as far away as possible, praying it would not ignite. But the fail-safes embedded in the tube quickly took over, and repair bots scurried about repairing any cracks in the tube. They looked like a swarm of metallic insects crawling over the sparking wires and terminals. A group also swarmed the craft, repairing engines and replacing blown computer chips. It was over in a matter of minutes.

Finally, the all-clear sounded from the onboard computer, and the twins were able to reboard, start up the engine once more, and continue to the ship.

Nova breathed a sigh of relief when the cargo dock of the ship came into view. "It feels like the tremors are becoming less intense and further apart. I can't imagine what they could be. In all this time, we have never had a disturbance like this!"

Vega was trying not to wring her hands. "I have a bad feeling. Do you think that it has something to do with Cassandra being overtaken by her dark priestess persona?"

Nova didn't respond, too focused on guiding the small craft into the docking bay. Once they'd landed safely, Nova tapped her wrist unit to summon the cargo droids to unload. Vega grabbed Nova's hand and pulled her into the main ship, a sense of urgency driving her.

Suddenly, the entire ship swayed and shuddered. Nova looked out of the nearest portal and saw the seabed full of sea creatures scurrying and swarming away from the ship and toward the surface. Knowing that they were anchored deep within the dimensional rift and outside of the effects of what transpired in the earthly realm, what was happening was local and not coming from the third dimension.

"This cannot be right," shouted Nova above the low hum that began to emanate from the ship as though it were keening in dismay or fear.

They looked at one another, eyes meeting as realization hit. "Cassandra!"

Running toward her quarters, they skidded to a stop as the hallways filled with beings of every race and galaxy running away from the bridge. Changing direction, Nova and Vega headed toward it.

A beautiful woman dressed in bioluminescent space armor stood at the main bank of computer consoles. Her hands hovered inches above the holographic keyboards and screens, but she never touched them. Instead, faint tendrils of glowing energy flowed from her fingertips, pulsing into the air and directly into the Aethernet.

Streams of data shifted and reconfigured themselves, seeming to respond to her will alone. Waves of energy rippled outward from her, programming the system with nothing but thought and focus. The screens flickered, their displays rearranging in real-time as if obeying her silent commands.

The energy she wielded didn't come from the consoles but from within her, resonating with the network like a living extension of her being. Her body remained perfectly still while her mind and energy reached deep into the quantum threads of the Aethernet, untangling corrupted code and rewriting it with seamless precision. She wasn't just reprogramming; she was reshaping the system itself.

Sirkan was imprisoned against one wall by an energetic force field and practically frothed from the mouth in anger, fear, and frustration. His mouth was open, and it looked like he was yelling, but no sound could be heard.

The twins stared open-mouthed at the woman again. Seeming to feel their presence, she turned to look at them.

The eyes were unmistakable. "Queen Ayesha," Nova breathed, while Vega sighed, "Mistress Cassandra."

The female smiled. "Yes, my dear friends. It's me. Let's use my current life's name, shall we? And please drop the queen or mistress or any other title. I am Cassandra."

She opened her arms, and the small aliens went to her. They hugged briefly.

"All right then," she said, "we have stopped most of the computer viruses." She shook her head, rubbing fingertips to her temples. "I need to get rid of this damnable headache though. I feel like I'm in the middle of a gyroscope that is projecting movies so fast they are one giant blur." She sat down once more on the chair. Lying back in it, she rested her hands on the armrests. The chair responded to her with faint thrumming sounds. She breathed in deeply and closed her eyes. "I need to return to the Citadel and join forces with the other avatars. Were you able to connect with—"

She stopped abruptly as the ship shook again. Looking toward the viewscreen on the main deck, she saw what she thought was a large school of fish swimming with astonishing speed toward them, cutting through the water like living torpedoes. No, not fish. Merfolk! Cassie remembered an elite group that could bend water currents to their will.

The Tidecallers.

Her attention was momentarily distracted when Nin walked back onto the bridge, dusting off her hands. "Well, I have destroyed the last remnants of the sarcophagi. Not one cell of any of your lifetimes are anywhere but within you."

Cassie turned to Nin. "I must say your plan of having me experience one of my most evil incarnations was a little risky. How could you be sure I wouldn't love the power so much that I wouldn't destroy all my 'good' selves and integrate only the dark lifetimes?"

Nin met her eyes. "Perhaps I know you better than you know yourself. You are not innately evil. Every time you turned to the left-hand path, you were either pushed onto it or coerced by that bastard." She turned and glared at the dark lord.

Cassie glanced at Sirkan, who appeared to be having an epileptic fit. She smiled sweetly at him. "I really would love to just squash you like the insect you are. But justice will come from Artemus and the White Circle," Cassie said. "I will, however, seal you in your quarters until such time as I can contact them."

With a wave of her hand Sirkan disappeared when she visualized him ensconced in his own apartments in magical restraints. "Mind over matter," she muttered under her breath. Cassie wanted to laugh out loud. It was wonderful to be free at last!

Cassie turned to look at the viewscreen where she'd seen the merfolk. They were gone.

She whirled around when the door of the bridge slid open and in walked the king of Poseidia and his court, on legs.

At first confused, she stepped back, remembering their last encounter when he'd blasted her for not living up to her avatar potential. But the huge merman with the blue-green hair stepped up to her, took her hands into his, and looked deeply into her eyes. His widened when he saw the remnants of code still swirling in her violet eyes.

"Cassandra, are you in there?" he laughed.

The code, which was beginning to settle, blazed for a moment. Memories began to flood her awareness. She saw the last days of Atlantis when the great god of the ocean had bestowed the shape-shifting ability on King Caelum and his followers.

Cassie threw her arms around him, "Caelum! By the Radiant One, it's good to see you!"

He kissed her lightly on the forehead. "You've changed a bit since last we met."

"I'll say," Cassie laughed. "I don't even recognize me. And I'm still working on integrating all this knowledge I have from my past lives. It's like having a tsunami of information flooding my brain."

The king bowed his head in deference and stepped aside as Ninhursag came forward and put her hands on either side of Cassie's head. Moments went by until finally she said, "You will continue to download for quite some time. You need to go to a safe place until the integration is complete. The first order of business is to get you free from this place."

Caelum motioned for Marielle to come forward. "You have served Cassandra in her past life as queen. Take her—"

"And us!" the Arcturian twins chimed in.

He smiled, "And the Arcturians to the temple in the city. You will all be safe there until I can arrange for safe passage to the surface. I believe you know the white witch, Ian MacGregor? He will meet you at the rendezvous point within Poseidia. That should give you enough time, Cassandra, to reacclimate to the third dimension."

Still dazed from the past few hours, Cassie nodded, linked arms with Marielle, and motioned for the twins to follow.

Cassie looked back over her shoulder at Nin and mouthed, *Manu.*

The Anunnaki gave a slight nod.

TWO DAYS LATER, IAN MacGregor went to the console of his souped-up spacecraft and engaged a green lever. A symphony of electronic chirps and crackling energies filled the control deck. Through the ship's vast window, Cassie watched the ship's tremulous detachment from a well-hidden docking bay in the Poseidian shipyard. She inhaled sharply, her eyes widening.

"Don't worry," said Ian. "Ol' Tracker is top of the line. I just don't like to draw attention to her, especially when I am on a rescue mission."

"Rescue mission? But I'm already rescued."

"Yeah, but you still have a target on your back. I'm not taking any chances until you are once more in the bosom of Artemus at the Citadel. A few familiar faces are eagerly awaiting your arrival." His grin was infectious. "You have been missed."

"Mom and Dad?"

"Yeah, and your fellow avatars. There was a great rescue mission in the works. Your father even gathered the legendary fae army."

Nodding, Cassie moved with interest to the console and ran her fingers over the flickering lights. "These are more of the Atlantean crystals?"

"Yeah," Ian said. "You should be able to connect with them easily. Marielle was instrumental in crafting many of these, as was Ayesha when she was first ensconced as queen of the underworld." He huffed, then added with an exaggerated bow, "Your Infernal Majesty."

Cassie punched him in the gut. "Not funny."

Ian wheezed through his laughter, clutching his stomach. "What? Should I have gone with 'Your Royal Darkness' instead? I've been workshopping titles." He pretended to think deeply. "How about 'Supreme Ruler of All Things Evil and Vile'?"

Ian burst out laughing, amused at his joke. "Well, you gotta admit, the title fits."

She ignored him and continued to examine the crystals, but her lips twitched slightly as she fought back a smile.

"They were hidden in caves that ended up on the ocean floor. Sirkan mined them for centuries after." He grinned wolfishly, "And so did I."

"Sometimes you can be a real jackass, Ian MacGregor."

"So Siobhan has been telling me since we were kids. But, please, call me cousin. We are related you know."

"We are?"

"Yeah. Your maternal grandfather is a St. Claire. Have you heard the mysteries of the Holy Grail?"

"Sure. King Arthur and all that stuff."

"Well, there's more to 'that stuff' when it comes to the St. Claire/ Sinclair bloodline. Your fraternal great, great something great grandmother was a powerful fae queen. She founded the fae dynasty that became the stuff of legends. I'll leave that to your father to tell. Let's just say, our lineage has included a few avatars over the millennia."

"I think I need to process more of these crystal things rather than explore my ancestry," Cassie responded.

Ian said, "Well, remember what that old philosopher said: 'Those who cannot remember the past are condemned to repeat it.'"

"Yeah, yeah," said Cassie. "Seems like I've heard that axiom in its many forms from my mom *and* during my training with Master Elena. Besides, I have plenty of history to sort through now that I have total recall."

Ian shrugged, "Truth is truth and bears repeating."

She blew him a kiss, then closed her eyes and stood with her palms out, facing the console. She could feel the power of the crystals surging through her, just like they had on Sirkan's ship. "It's good to feel my powers again ... and more!"

"Figured as much. Buckle up," he pointed to one of the seats. "We're gonna ditch this dimension."

I just hope that Manu is close behind, thought Ian. He didn't want to say anything to Cassie, but he was more than a bit concerned that he hadn't met them at the rendezvous point in Poseidia.

Cassie took a deep breath and strapped into her seat. "Let's do it."

A vibratory resonance filled the small ship, growing in intensity. As Cassie looked out, the ocean began to blur, then elongated into streaks. The sensation reminded her of dreams she'd once had of crossing vast cosmic distances in an instant.

She reached for her medallion for the millionth time. It was still activated, but now that they were going through some sort of worm hole, the connection was faint. Surely Nin had gotten a message to Manu, and they were even now on their way to the Citadel. Surely!

Just as suddenly as it began, the blurring stopped. Stars sparkled across a vast expanse of sky. They looked different, unfamiliar, yet fascinating. Cassie felt a weight lift off her shoulders. She glanced at the console, at the Atlantean crystals that had made this leap possible. "Thank you, Ayesha," she whispered under her breath, feeling a heightened connection to her ancient self that had played a part in crafting their present-day escape route.

Out of nowhere she heard a screech and a growl coming from the hold of the craft.

"Oh shit, I forgot!" Ian ran to the back, releasing a hidden lock in the floor. It burst open as Gabriel leaped through, followed by a creature madly flapping its wings. The feline flew at Cassie with a joyful meow and wrapped both paws around her neck in a furry hug, while the creature settled and bobbed its head to a rhythm only it could hear, its wings tightly held against its body.

Cassie kissed the furry head tucked under her chin and stepped toward the creature. He ducked his head, so it came level with her eyes. "Oh, dear one. I am so glad you are here." She paused, looking into its feline eyes. "We need to come up with a real name for you. I can't keep calling you Creature."

It looked at her quizzically.

"Hmmm, let's try some on for size, shall we? You look like a dragon with a lion's body, and those horns! Sooo how about ... Dracoleo? Leodraco?

The creature huffed a puff of smoke in frustration.

"OK, not those," smiled Cassie.

Dracoleon.

The telepathic message came through loud and clear. "Oh, of course you know your own name. Dracoleon it is!"

Dracoleon did a little happy dance, shifting back and forth on its talons.

"OK," said Ian. "Let's get off the ship. I see the hordes gathering outside."

Cassie looked at the ship's viewscreen and drew in her breath sharply. "Oh my god! There's Seraphina and Karim!"

She ran to the gangplank and over the narrow bridge connecting the docking bay to the Citadel.

Seraphina practically leapt into her open arms. Karim ran up and embraced them both. All were laughing, their eyes glistening.

"Gurl, you have *got* to quit getting kidnapped!" Marcus scolded.

"Yeah, well, it's because I just love kicking Sirkan's ass," Cassie laughed.

But then they sobered.

"Did you do it once and for all then?" Seraphina's Irish lilt was music to her ears.

"No, my powers were totally for shittle while I was on his mother ship. He had it warded to the point that I began to think his story about me being his queen and consort sounded plausible." She shook her head. "I even morphed into one of my ancient, evil high priestess selves for a while ..." She trailed off.

"Holy shit!" said Karim from the cave opening that led into the base camp. "Evil Cassandra." His chiseled, walnut-hued face crinkled as he grinned down at her. "And look at you now! All growed up!"

Cassie's eyes widened. "Huh? Oh yeah, I forgot! This is the new me. I'll tell you all about it. But right now, I am starved."

Marcus looked at her. "You know you've been gone for almost a year?"

"Yeah," said Cassie, "so I've been told. I must say, I kinda feel ancient. All the morphing I've done between my different lifetimes. Now I seem to be a composite of all of them physically, mentally, emotionally. I'm not sure Manu will even recognize me once he gets here."

Seraphina narrowed her eyes, "Um ... Manu?"

Cassie raised her chin and grinned. "Yeah. I've sorta remembered him too."

Sera started to sputter, but Cassie put a finger over her lips, "Later."

Karim said, "Well, it's not like Manu hasn't seen you in just about every reincarnation you've had. Of course he'll recognize you. It's not about the body; it's about the soul."

Changing the subject, Marcus said, "We are all twenty-one now, but you kinda look older."

Seraphina walked over to Marcus and punched him in the gut. "Never *ever* tell a woman she looks old, jerk."

They all laughed as the other avatars started to horse around with one another, showing off their respective new powers.

Abruptly the air to their backs whipped up, and a small craft dropped out of warp speed. Whirling around, Seraphina and Marcus reached for their laser swords.

Ian put up his hands like he was warding off a charging bull. "Hold. That is the rest of the contingent from Poseidia."

The hatch of the craft slid open, and the gangplank lowered. Out walked Nova and Vesta, followed by Marielle. Cassie scanned the other three unknown celestials but didn't see who she was looking for. Marcus couldn't help but notice her roving eyes. "Are you looking for someone specifically?"

"Yes, I am." She went over to Nova and Vega. "Where is the Lady Ninhursag?"

"She told us to tell you she is staying behind to follow up on a special mission. She said you would know what she was referring to."

Cassie nodded. *Manu.*

Gabriel scampered up to her and butted his head against her shin. She picked him up and absently scratched his ears. Something was wrong. Gabriel showed her a picture of Manu. He was being swallowed in dark tendrils of energy.

She pivoted and sprinted into the Citadel, looking desperately for Ian. She heard voices coming from a hallway that led to the dining area. She found him leaning against a counter holding a giant-sized stein of what she assumed was ale.

Cassie grabbed his arm in desperation. "Ian! We have to go back. Manu is in danger!"

Ian shook his head as though to clear it. "What? What are you talking about? He's on a secret mission ..." His voice trailed off as she saw the look on Cassie's face. "Tell me."

She told him how Ninhursag had led Manu and Siobhan on a quest to discover the tomb of the "lost queen of Egypt" where she, as Ayesha, had left a medallion for Manu that would help him find her no matter the time period or location. She pulled her own medallion out, the Atlantean record keeper crystal nestled at its center. "It's the twin to this. I crafted them both with Nin's help, long ago. She had become my best friend, teacher, and surrogate sister when I was queen of Egypt." She smiled wanly. "Yeah, I was also a queen of Egypt. Surreal in so many ways."

Vesta came over to her and took her hand. "You were one of the most benevolent queens ever to wear the crown and wield the scepter. You balanced the total evil that was Sirkan and established one of the most powerful dynasties in the ancient world."

Ian's eyes widened. "Should I bow or something?"

Cassie poked a finger into his shoulder. "How about getting your little puddle jumper ready to zip back to Earth?"

"Yeah, well, I can't do that just yet."

"He's correct." A soft voice floated across the room. "We need to regroup and reconnoiter."

Master Elena came into the room and pulled Cassie into her arms. "My dear, we have been so worried."

Cassie gave her a huge squeeze and looked around her. "My mother and father?"

"Not here. But they know you are safe. They are with your grandfather, preparing for the next phase of battle."

Cassie squinted her eyes and cocked her head, like she was having an issue hearing correctly. "My grandfather?"

Master Elena took Cassie's face between her hands and kissed her forehead. "As usual after one of your abductions, we have much to discuss." She searched the girl's face. "You are more than changed; you are transformed. Your eyes ..."

"Yeah, I know. Fortunately, the code doesn't interfere with my physical sight. It has receded somewhat since my transformation. Hopefully, it will totally disappear once all my past lives fully integrate."

Master Elena took Cassie's arm and guided her toward a table at the far end of the dining room. "Tell me."

"I can't stay here, Master Elena." She placed a hand on her medallion, its metallic edges glinting, a faint blue light pulsing from within. "This is the twin to a medallion that Ayesha entrusted to Ninhursag. She was to get it to Manu when we reached a crucial moment in my karmic journey. Both medallions contain pieces of the same Atlantean record keeper crystal, engineered to connect him and me and our linked soul mission."

She clasped the medallion tightly between her palms, squeezing her eyes shut as she inhaled a deep, steadying breath. The air thickened with tension, her shoulders drooping under the weight of her growing frustration. "I can't feel him at all! I should be able to sense his presence," her voice cracked, strained with the effort, "but there's just ... nothing!" Her words faded to a desperate whisper, amplifying the fear gnawing at her heart.

Master Elena gently pried Cassie's fingers from around the pulsing medallion, her touch firm yet reassuring, and put it between her hands. She held Cassie's gaze with steady topaz eyes that seemed to pierce through the looming darkness of uncertainty. "Cassie, remember the teachings. The connection you seek isn't solely bound by this crystal or any artifact. It's also within you, your spirit, your essence."

She put the medallion back in Cassie's hands, covered them with hers, and held them against Cassie's heart. "You know the energy pathways can become obscured by our fears and doubts. It doesn't mean the bond is broken, only that it's veiled. You must clear your mind, focus not on the desperation to find him, but on the balance and peace within yourself. Trust the connection you've nurtured over all these millennia."

Master Elena paused, her voice softening. "Let's try a grounding exercise. Close your eyes. Feel your feet rooted to the earth. Visualize the energy of this medallion not as a beacon searching outward, but as a light drawing inward, calling to the part of Manu that resides within you."

Cassie nodded, her breathing slowing as she followed Master Elena's instructions. With each breath, the weight of her anxiety seemed to lessen, her clenched shoulders relaxing. The air around them filled with a palpable warmth as the medallion began to glow brighter, its light steadier.

"Now, speak to him through your heart," Master Elena whispered. "If the connection is true, no dimension can hinder it. Trust yourself, Cassie. Trust the bond."

Cassie's voice was a mere breath, a whispered call laced with hope and a newfound steadiness. "Manu, find me."

A silence enveloped the room, a silence so profound it seemed to warp the very fabric of the air around them. The talisman in her hands thrummed with a steady glow, its light reflected in her tear-filled eyes. Cassie's heart raced, her fears momentarily subdued by a rising tide of hope.

Long minutes passed. Time seemed to fold into itself under the intensity of the moment. Then, faintly at first, like a whisper carried by a distant wind, a warmth spread through Cassie's palms. The warmth pulsed once, twice, echoing the rhythm of her own heartbeat.

Cassie gasped, her eyes snapping open, meeting Master Elena's knowing look. "Did you feel that?" Cassie asked, her voice a mixture of hope and disbelief.

Master Elena nodded, a small smile playing at the corners of her lips. "The energy of the universe does not lie, nor does it err. You are connected, Cassie. You have always been. Sometimes, it just takes a little faith to feel it."

The glow from the medallion intensified, casting radiant beams across the room. Then, as suddenly as it had strengthened, the light dimmed and winked out.

"No, no, no!" Cassie said frantically. "What happened?"

Master Elena was reluctant to give her false hope. "I'm not sure," she said, her tone firm yet gentle, "but you must prepare for what comes next. This connection is a pathway. Manu might be reaching out, seeking you in turn. But I sense there may be a barrier of some kind. A restraint. You need to be ready to guide him, to help him find his way through whatever obstacles may stand between you."

Master Elena placed a reassuring hand on her shoulder. "Remember that strength comes from within, and through our heart connections, we find our true power. The worst thing you can do is let negativity and fear block what remains of the connection."

Despite Master Elena's calm assurance, a sinking dread filled Cassie.

Master Elena got up, went to the door, and called for Ian.

Part III: Reunited

A soulmate is an ongoing connection with another individual that the soul picks up again in various times and places over lifetimes. We are attracted to another person at a soul level not because that person is our unique complement, but because by being with that individual, we are somehow provided with an impetus to become whole ourselves.
Edgar Cayce

Chapter 35: What Was Lost

Sirkan fought against the magical restraints that held him in his quarters on his own mother ship. "What the fuck! I will kill that bitch," he screamed out loud to no one. He was humiliated and would have his revenge on Ayesha, once and for all. Then reality twisted around him. The dimensional rift that held his ship in place seemed to warp, its edges bleeding into impossible colors. A voice like steel scraping against bone filled his mind: "You disappoint me, cur."

The next instant, he was on his knees in his master's sanctum, nose bleeding from the violent dimensional shift. The dark lord towered over him, his form shifting between shadows that hurt to look at.

"Master, I—" Sirkan began.

"Silence!" he thundered. "You've let your lust for Ayesha disrupt plans millennia in the making. Besides which, your obsession with proving your power has become ... tedious."

Sirkan wiped blood from his face, knowing better than to speak.

"I will give you one last chance and return you to your ship. We still have another to get rid of."

"YOU'RE TOO LATE," SIRKAN sneered as Manu burst onto the bridge of Sirkan's ship. "Cassandra is gone. Somehow, she managed to enlist the aid of the king of Poseidia and his merfolk. They collaborated with two of my most trusted servants, and as she would say, they 'poofed' through a portal and are most likely residing in the temple within Poseidia." He inwardly sighed with relief that he was able to maintain the facade of control. The memory of his imprisonment by Cassandra haunted him: the humiliation of being bound by the very power he had sought to possess. If not for his formidable benefactor, he would still be languishing in those magical constraints, stripped of his authority and dignity. But Manu didn't need to know that. Let him believe that he had simply failed to prevent her escape rather than having been thoroughly defeated by her.

Sirkan's laughter echoed as he added, "Her twenty-first birthday endowed her with abilities that even my considerable magics could not extinguish." He was not about to tell Manu about her transformation.

Manu's mouth quirked slightly. "Cassandra is indeed unique." He chose not to mention that the other avatars' abilities had also been enhanced in unexpected ways. Not even the oracles had a firm grasp on the powers that would manifest once the seven reached full maturity.

He kept eye contact with Sirkan but noticed a shadow approaching from behind. He gripped his staff to ignite the Violet Flame but found it unresponsive.

Sirkan's serpent eyes sparkled with malice. "Did you really think your attempt to rescue her wouldn't be anticipated?" He stepped aside.

Manu froze as a fellow member of the White Circle stepped forward: an angel Manu had known for thousands of years, with whom he'd fought side by side, who had been like a surrogate father to Cassandra in her current incarnation.

Tristan.

He was shrouded in black shadows and accompanied by a formidable-looking woman. "Hello, Manu. Allow me to introduce Soriah, my first lieutenant and commander of my demonic armies. Soriah, meet the infamous high priest, Manu Abulafia."

Manu's expression hardened. "So, you have been the puppet master all along. We suspected a traitor was among us, but never a high-ranking member of the White Circle. Bravo, Tristan. Truly." His slow clap was thick with sarcasm.

Sirkan scoffed, but they all ignored him.

"You know, after Paxton's death, your lack of mourning struck me as unnatural," Manu said. "I did wonder and investigated your lineage. But I didn't see anything amiss. Brilliant."

Tristan tensed at the mention of his dead son. Soriah gently touched his arm, offering silent support. Tristan took a deep breath and pushed back his emotions. "Paxton was a great disappointment. He was crucial to my plans, but your bitch of a soul mate ensnared him before his final initiation, a process that would have significantly strengthened the Dark Brotherhood's forces. Now, he resides in the Shadow Realm."

Manu's eyes flickered with awareness. The Shadow Realm was a multidimensional place of immense power, a place that served many purposes: transition, punishment, redemption, even communication between the living and the dead. He realized the danger he was in, but it was too late. He reached for his medallion, but it was not functioning.

Tristan's voice interrupted his thoughts. "Let's not dwell on the past. You're here now, Manu. In the physical world, you might have been a formidable force, but here in the rift, you are at my mercy."

Manu felt his spiritual energy pulse within him. He knew raw power wouldn't suffice; cunning and strategy were crucial. "You underestimate the power of the light, Tristan. It can penetrate even the darkest night."

Tristan's laughter filled the ship, the shadows around him swirling ominously. "Let's test that theory, High Priest. Let's see if your light can indeed dispel the darkness I command."

The atmosphere within the ship grew heavier. The shadows that swirled around Tristan began to writhe and twist, coalescing into a vortex of darkness. A disembodied voice chanted in ancient tongues grating to the ears. Manu recognized the language as a mixture of archaic languages from the angelic kingdom and the lost civilization of Lemuria. He immediately began to weave his own protective bubble, but to no avail. His powers were blocked.

Tristan's gray eyes, sharp as steel in the light of dawn, met Soriah's eyes. He nodded, and then they raised their hands together and directed streams of red and black energy into the vortex. For a moment, Manu saw his life flash before his eyes. His heart wrenched with longing for Ayesha, his soul aching for completion. Then the Shadow Realm surged forward and pulled Manu into its vortex. The darkness suffocated and consumed his inner light as he tumbled through the spiraling funnel of Twilight, the first of three levels of the Shadow Realm. The physical world stretched like melting glass. Manu could still see the ship's interior, but it wavered and duplicated like reflections in a cracked mirror, ghostly echoes of Tristan and Soriah's forms multiplying and fading into shadow. The familiar hum of his powers stuttered like a failing heartbeat, and through the disorientation, he caught fragments of whispered conversations that seemed to come from both nowhere and everywhere: prayers, pleas, and promises that drifted through this threshold between worlds.

The ghost-like reflections of the physical world dissolved completely as Manu sank into the second level, the Void. Here, darkness had texture, thick in some places, gossamer-thin in others, carrying emotional residue that clung to his consciousness like cold spider silk. *This isn't just darkness,* Manu realized with growing dread. *It's feeding on memories ... on regret.*

His memories began to twist and surface without his control: He saw himself failing to save a young initiate from darkness, felt again the crushing moment he believed Ayesha was lost to him forever, watched as past decisions spawned shadowy what-if versions of his life that swirled around him like hungry spirits. *No! Focus! These are just memories. They cannot harm you unless you let them.* But even as he admonished against it, doubt crept in: *Or are they more than memories here?*

The space itself seemed to breathe, expanding and contracting with ancient malice, and in the distance, he glimpsed other lost souls trapped in their own personal hells. Some wandered aimlessly through their regrets, while others froze in moments of their deepest shame. *By the Radiant One, how long have they been here? Is this what Paxton endures?* The thought sent a chill through his spiritual core.

Each fraction of time stretched endlessly here, yet also seemed to skip like a scratched record, making it impossible to track his fall through this layer of fractured reality. *I must maintain my sense of self,* Manu commanded himself, fighting against the disorienting flow of time. *I am more than these regrets. I am more than these failures. Ayesha ... remember Ayesha's light ...*

Panic clawed at his throat.

Center yourself, he commanded, falling back on his earliest training. *You are Manu, high priest of Sirius, bound to your soul mate, Ayesha.* Her face became his first anchor, a warmth in his chest even as the cold shadows pressed in.

Then the air thickened, dense with the stench of decay and something far older than death itself. The darkness stirred. Writhing masses coalesced into impossible forms—bodies twisted inside out, flesh that rippled like boiling tar, teeth sprouting from places teeth had no right to be. Wings of flayed skin unfurled in the void. Hundreds of eyes opened in the blackness, some clouded with cataracts, others burning with infernal fire. All fixed upon him with predatory hunger. They were creatures bred in nightmares and fed on torment. This was the final level of the Shadow Realm: the Depths.

The demons circled closer, their bodies constantly shifting and reforming. One creature's jaw unhinged, dropping far lower than any natural anatomy should allow, revealing rows of crystalline teeth that glowed with sickly phosphorescence. Another's flesh split open like a blooming flower, each "petal" tipped with barbed hooks that dripped caustic ichor.

These aren't just monsters, Manu realized. *They're manifestations of every primal fear humanity has ever known.*

A sound rose from their impossible throats—not quite laughter, not quite screaming—a chorus of the damned that resonated with frequencies that threatened to shatter his very consciousness. Without his powers, without his light, he was defenseless against their advance. No protective shields, no holy fire, no blessed barriers. Nothing but his will and his identity remained.

So be it, he thought, facing the horrors that surrounded him. *Take my powers. Take my light. But you cannot take what I am unless I surrender it.*

For an instant, his light flared against the darkness, a final act of defiance. It surged outward, burning like a dying star—then flickered, faded, and was gone. The consuming night rushed in to claim him. The last remnants of his magical abilities, and his connection to the light, crumbled to ash in his hands.

A part of me is dying, he realized with gut-wrenching clarity. *Everything I was, everything I built myself to be ...*

And then the shadows swallowed him whole.

Above, unseen by the one he had vanquished, Tristan watched in triumph. From his vantage point, he saw the last flicker of Manu's light disappear into the abyss. The high priest, once a beacon of hope and strength, was now lost in the deepest reaches of the Shadow Realm, where illusions ruled, and thoughts were things.

Tristan stood victorious, a testament to how the shadow can triumph over the light—however fleetingly.

But deep in the blackness below, Manu was already beginning to adapt. His trained mind, stripped of power but not purpose, forged the first fragile shelter from the chaos, built from the strongest memory he possessed: Ayesha's love.

Chapter 36: Hidden City

"Prepare your ship for departure, Ian. We are returning to the rift."

Master Elena took Cassie's face in her hands. She had made up her mind quickly. Now she spoke gently to the girl. "I am not going to sugar coat this for you, Cassandra. When you held your medallion in your hands, I felt that Manu had been trapped in some dark dimension. I can't imagine who would have the kind of power to do that. Certainly not Sirkan. But I feel it may be deep in the Shadow Realm. It is a realm of lost things, of darkness that consumes light, energy, and hope."

Cassie's face paled as the weight of Manu's predicament pressed down on her. "His powers have dissipated," she murmured, the words tasting bitter on her tongue. "I can barely feel them through the medallion. He can't escape on his own."

"That may be true," Master Elena confirmed, her expression solemn. "But remember, the medallion isn't just a link. It's also a key. A key that draws on the strength of its bearer: you. Your energy, your will, and your love can reach him, even in the darkest of places."

"I created this with Ninhursag when I was still a queen of Egypt, so I know its workings. But how do I even begin to breach a dark dimension?" Cassie's voice trembled. "I made this so that we could find one another on Earth, in the third dimension, not in the Shadow Realm. That was always the realm of death."

"Not entirely," Elena replied, withdrawing a glowing rune stone from her pocket. She placed it on the table, its light pulsing softly. "Remember your studies in the cosmology of this planet. There are three levels to the Shadow Realm." She conjured paper and pen, sketching intricate patterns into a map of realms that existed between dimensions.

"The first level, Twilight, is like a veil of mist, where the living can slip through during deep meditation or near-death. The Void, the second level, is a realm of reflection, where souls process their earthly lives. But the third ..." Her pen darkened, drawing a spiral that seemed to pull the eye inward. "The Depths. Here, living and dead alike can become eternally trapped. It's where thought and reality blur, where demonic entities dwell, and where Metatron believes Danax has embedded his technology."

Elena placed the rune stone at the center of her diagram. "This stone will anchor you in the light and serve as a tether to our reality, a lifeline through the darkness. But the Shadow Realm will try to disorient you. It feeds on emotion. Every fear, doubt, and stray thought becomes tangible. Do you remember the rules of manifestation?"

Cassie nodded. "What the mind can conceive and believe, it can achieve."

"Exactly," Elena said gravely. "But that's the danger. Metatron has determined that the Technomancer has corrupted the realm, merging dark magic with technology. What once required years of dark rituals can now be accomplished with the push of a button. Negative emotions don't just manifest; they're amplified. The entire Shadow Realm has become a weapon."

Cassie's eyes fixed on the rune stone as she absorbed every word. "And once I find him, how do I bring him back?"

"The same way," Master Elena replied. "Find him quickly and use the medallion to connect directly with his essence. Your combined strength, amplified by the medallions, should be enough to break free from the Shadow Realm's grasp. But you *must* be on your guard."

Master Elena placed her hands on Cassie's shoulders, meeting her gaze with a palpable intensity. "Cassandra, this is more than a test of strength; it's a test of heart, of mind, and spirit. Believe in your connection with Manu. Trust in the power of the medallions. Think of them more as talismans. Above all, *trust in your love*. And remember that you are not alone in this."

Empowered by Master Elena's faith in her, Cassie stood up, her determination giving her impetus to act. "I will bring him back," she declared, her voice now steady and sure. "No darkness can hold what the light seeks to reclaim."

She hugged Master Elena and went out to the ship, followed dutifully by Gabriel and Dracoleon.

ERISTIDES STOOD AT the threshold of a vast, ruined city. This ancient city had remained unseen by the eyes of men for untold centuries. Its crumbled buildings, built from stones older than time itself, whispered secrets of a forgotten era. Vines and foliage clung to the ruins like memories refusing to fade. The air was thick with the salted scent of the sea.

Beside him, Rebekah shared a look of confusion with her husband, Ayden. They had expected to plumb the secrets of what they thought would be a thriving albeit ancient metropolis. Azazel scanned the landscape for any unforeseen enemies, ever watchful in his duty to the fae king.

Natesh stepped forward, his face etched with tension. "The legends of the Bermuda Triangle," he began, his voice low, "speak of a portal, a gateway guarded by this ancient city. Sirkan spoke of it often but could never ferret it out."

"Well, there doesn't seem to be anything here but an overgrown ruin," said Eristides.

The group exchanged concerned glances when they saw the arrival of a small spacecraft. They all reached for their weapons, then collectively sighed in relief when they saw it was Ian's ship.

Cassandra disembarked and ran to her mother, grabbing her in a fierce embrace. Ayden wrapped them both in his arms, and the three hugged, kissed, and laughed through streaming tears.

Rebekah pulled back and searched her daughter's face, a frown between her brows. "You look so different. I mean, I see *you*, but ..."

"I *am* different, Mom. I will tell you all about it. So much has happened. It's wild. The most important thing, though, is that I have total recall of all my past lives and of Manu. He's in danger and—"

"Take a breath," Rebekah said and then smiled. "We will catch up with all of that, but now," she said as she turned Cassie around to face her grandfather, "Commander Eristides St. Claire, may I present your granddaughter, Cassandra Oberon."

Suddenly shy, Cassie looked up at the imposing celestial and tentatively held out her hand. "Grandfather."

Shaking his head, Eristides ignored the proffered hand, caught her up to his seven-foot frame, and gave her a bear hug. "By the Radiant One, you are even more beautiful than I imagined." He then held her at arm's length, drinking in every detail of his granddaughter.

Ayden agreed, "I think that every time I see her. But ... there *is* something decidedly changed about you. You look like yourself, but different. Even being a year older, you wouldn't have changed this much. I don't understand."

"Perhaps I can shed some light on that," said Master Elena as she disembarked from the small craft. Briefly, she began the story of how Cassie escaped the clutches of Ayesha's evil incarnation as Menhit, then motioned to Cassie. "Cassandra can fill you in on the rest. Suffice it to say, she was able to synthesize all of who she has been and create a new form. She truly is the next step in evolution for this planet."

Rebekah slipped her arm around her daughter's waist, listening with bated breath about how the Atlantean throne-like chair that Ayesha had crafted was the ultimate tool of transformation for her daughter.

At the story's end, Master Elena dropped the bomb shell. "Ian MacGregor contacted me after he had moved Cassandra from Sirkan's ship to Poseidia. Manu was to join the rescue team, but Ian never heard from him after our initial meeting with Caelum. I believe that some unknown dark entity has trapped Manu in the Shadow Realm, a dimension you may know as Hell."

Hearing protests from around the group, she put up her hands to ward off any more comments. "I don't know who. I am not able to get a fix on them."

Ayden goggled at her. "Hell?"

"It's OK, Dad." Cassie grabbed Ayden's arm. "It's sorta incomprehensible to me too. But it doesn't make any difference; this is just one more test that I will have to overcome. Until I can be reunited with Manu, nothing else matters. We aren't just soul mates. He's not just the love of my life. He is the other half of the soul mission we both agreed to when we first came to this planet under the directive of the Radiant One."

She paused for another breath when her mother put her hand on her waist. Cassie nodded at her and continued, "Now that I have full access to my memories, my abilities, I am just ... just ..." Tears gathered in her violet eyes. "I just want Manu. Then everything else will fall into place."

"Oversimplified, but I understand," said Ayden. "I remember those feelings when I couldn't find your mother for all those years. Come, we will discuss some ideas about how to penetrate this unknown realm."

Natesh's heart disintegrated while he absorbed the information that Cassandra shared with them. He knew intellectually he was never going to be with her again. The vow he had made to support Cassandra's choice in being with the man her heart desired was irrevocable. But still, it was incredibly painful to hear that her memories had come back to full circle and to Manu. Well, maybe this would be his opportunity for redemption. Perhaps the lords of karma would be kind.

The ground rumbled beneath their feet. A portal opened behind them, and out stepped Ninhursag.

Cassie ran up to her and grabbed her hands. "Nin! By the Radiant One, any news?"

Nin kissed Cassie on both cheeks and dropped her forehead to Cassie's.

"I was finally able to get off Sirkan's ship during a mass influx of the Dark Brotherhood's intergalactic members. It seems they have been waiting in the wings for word from their overlord ... Tristan."

"Tristan?" they all exclaimed in unison.

Nin put up her hands to stave off the plethora of questions. "It seems that Tristan has been the one pulling Sirkan's strings. That's not what's important right now. We can't do anything about it at the moment, especially when we are missing a key player. Come, let's continue into my long-lost city." When she saw the blank looks, she laughed. "Well, I wasn't going to leave it in plain sight. I put a glamour on it long ago so that anyone who stumbled upon it would see only ruins. Now it's time to unveil it and the secrets it holds."

Cassie smiled, "Yes, I remember now. Our ancient artifacts, or rather the Anunnaki's ancient artifacts."

With a nod to her companions, Nin stepped forward and led them into the heart of the city. When they reached what looked like a town square of sorts, Nin and Cassie joined hands and went to a large, crumbling obelisk carved with ancient glyphs.

Cassie ran her hand over the carvings reverently.

"The nexus," she breathed.

"Yes. Both a power source and a transdimensional portal," said Nin. "We can use it to access the Shadow Realm. The tricky part is not getting caught in any kind of interdimensional slip stream. You must stay extremely focused and not let your thoughts stray from Manu. But first, let's dismantle the glamour. Give me your hand, Cassandra."

They touched the nexus in unison. The glamour of a ruined city melted away to reveal a perfectly preserved city of crystal-domed towers, shining temples, and terraced gardens frozen in time.

Cassie sighed in delight. "Like Sleeping Beauty's castle. I remember now. I spent many years studying in the temples here with Manu when we found one another in ancient Mesopotamia. It was when you and Enki were still on Earth together. It was an incredibly blessed lifetime and far too short."

"Mortality always is. Manu stayed here for many years after your physical body passed from life to light. His grief was difficult to witness. He seemed to feel that there had to be some way to counteract the karmic cycle." Nin smiled, "He even tried to bargain with the lords of karma."

Cassie smiled. "Of course he did."

Nin nodded as her gaze swept past the ancient stone obelisk to the city around them that stood in silent witness to epochs of history. When she turned back to her companions, anticipation flickered in her eyes. "Now that the nexus no longer drains excessive power to sustain the glamour, the full force of the intersecting ley lines is ours to harness. However, it requires time to rebuild the energy needed to use the obelisk as a portal to other realms."

Nin looked at Master Elena. "This obelisk was deliberately erected during Mesopotamia's golden age. It didn't just fuel the rise of Sumerian civilization—it shaped the foundations of societies across the globe, spreading a culture that transcended borders and time."

She paused, her fingers brushing against the cool, rough surface of the stone. "Within this monument lies the essence of my people's heritage. The legacy of my beloved Enki and me is not just symbolically but also literally encoded in its structure. Our DNA merged with its matrix during an ancient ritual. Thus, this obelisk is not merely a source of power but also a living record of our existence—a bridge between flesh and stone, memory and eternity. It carries our essence, our knowledge, and the very pulse of our lineage, ensuring that even if our bodies fade, we will endure within its core, whispering to those who seek the truth.

Cassie said, "It represents what you might call a pivotal breakthrough in human evolution, a mystery that has long baffled philosophers, scientists, and clergy. We made such great strides in those times in our evolution—this stone connects us to our past, empowers our present, and ensures our future."

"Mistress, is that you?" a soft female voice asked from the periphery of the square.

Nin threw open her arms, and a small woman of Anunnaki linage burrowed into them.

"Oh, my dearest one, yes, it is me." Nin held her at arm's length to examine her. "You are well? And your fellow priestesses?"

The beautiful young woman, who looked to be no older than twenty, nodded. "Yes, we are all well. We saw your return through the temple fires and have prepared your apartments and more for your guests."

"Now come," said Nin. "We will eat. Then we will prepare Cassandra for her journey."

She led the group to a large structure to the right of the obelisk. When she touched the entryway, it came to life, revealing what could only be called a crystal palace. "This home was built as a way station when Enki and I were in residence on the planet." She smiled at Cassie, "It's your favorite magic house."

Cassie returned her smile. "Yes, I remember."

The young priestess led them into the opulence of the palace. It could have been one of the seven wonders of the world with its mirrored hallways, all lit by the soft glow of witchlight. Golden arches and doorways, etched with the same hieroglyphics as the obelisk, glowed from within.

A collective gasp rose from the group as they stepped into a courtyard. It was not just a place of rest for the Anunnaki but a junction of divine and earthly realms. The walls of the courtyard were lined with high arches and intricate mosaics depicting ancient tales of creation and destruction, gods and mortals, each tile imbued with a glint of magical energy. At intervals, softly glowing orbs floated, providing a gentle illumination that shifted with the phases of the moon. Tinkling fountains, symbolic of Enki's dominion over waters, wove around the perimeter of the courtyard, providing a soft backdrop to the tranquil setting.

Nin pointed to them. "These are not mere fountains but living waters with the power to heal and rejuvenate." With a wave of her hand, a row of flasks appeared along the rim of one of the larger fountains. "These are filled, one for each of you. The flasks are self-perpetuating so that no matter where you are, you will never be without their life-giving essence."

She then pointed to the center of the courtyard, which was dominated by a grand table exquisitely crafted from a single slab of lapis lazuli. It reflected the aethereal blue sky above, unobstructed by any roof.

Cassie said, "This table was legendary among the original celestials and whispered about among mortals."

"And just like in any magical realm," Nin said, "the food is never-ending and self-replenishing. You will find that where you sit, your favorite foods will appear."

Golden bowls of dates and pomegranates, platters of minted lamb, and baskets of freshly baked bread infused with exotic herbs from celestial gardens appeared at the head of the table as Nin took her seat. "Please sit and eat. Then I will tell you my plan for Cassandra's journey to bring Manu back to the land of the living."

NIN BEGAN A SERIES of incantations in ancient Sumerian. Objects began to swirl into existence. A backpack thumped to the floor, followed by a small tin, one of the water flasks from the fountain, and assorted tools that looked like camping gear.

"Bippity boppity boo," laughed Cassie

Her father arched an eyebrow.

"It's from a Disney movie that Cassie loved when she was a child. I'll explain later," said Rebekah.

Nin directed all the supplies into the backpack. "The tin holds nutrient wafers. There are witchlights, blankets, a pop-up tent, and several other items I felt you would find useful. The nutrient wafers are like desert manna; you will never run out."

She then handed Cassie an athame encased in a leather sheath, its adamant hilt carved with magical symbols of both dark and white magic. "Strap this to your thigh. You will encounter unknown illusions and tests. Do not, under any circumstances, allow this out of your reach. You are entering a realm of deception and trickery. Be mindful."

Nin then waved her hands again, and Cassie's bioluminescent unisuit added shoulder guards and gauntlets. Expecting them to be heavy, Cassie said, "Wow, these are light as a feather."

"They are made of a special alloy that melds with your battle gear. They will act like a second skin and protect you from most weapons."

Rebekah grabbed Cassie by the shoulders. "Remember that fear and doubt will weaken you." She touched the torc that Cassie wore at her collar bone. "And remember your ancestral magic. You can always call on that."

"And now a most important weapon." Nin went over to what could only be a weapon cabinet, waved a hand to open it, and withdrew a formidable-looking sword. "This is the Sword of Keraunos. It channels lightning, the energy of the great Zeus himself. With your ability to throw fire through your fingertips, you will be able to unleash devastating fire and light-based attacks. The sword will give you pin-point accuracy. It can also emit a blinding flash of light to temporarily blind enemies or illuminate dark places." She put it into Cassie's left hand. It sparked and sizzled and then began to glow from within like the smoldering embers of a fire.

"It's cool to the touch," said Cassie, "but I can feel its power deep within my solar plexus." She paused and took a deep breath. "Like, a *lot* of power!"

Nin smiled. "*You* have a lot of power. More than any of us know. Remember the training you have had over the centuries in swordsmanship and magic. It will come back to you when you need it."

She then took Cassie's hand and wrapped it around the medallion. "I feel it is time to go."

They all walked back out to the obelisk.

Rebekah and Ayden hugged her. "Remember who you are," said her mother.

Eristides kissed her on the forehead in blessing. "We will do everything we can to counter whatever the Dark Brotherhood has up its sleeves."

Elena said, "Take the rune stone I gave you in your right hand. Now, affirm your soul connection with Manu. Visualize his face and remember the happiest time you can recall. A time when you were strong in your love and strong in your purpose." She waited several minutes while Cassie reached back in time and remembered when she and Manu had realized they were soul mates. Sensing the connection, Nin said, "Hold that feeling, the essence of the love you have for one another. Now take Master Elena's rune stone and press it into your medallion."

Cassie gasped as the stone melded into the metal.

Nin then took Cassie's hand and closed it over the medallion. "You crafted this knowing that there would come a time when it would be needed. Know it will guide you to Manu."

Closing her eyes, Nin began to intone a long-forgotten chant from the dawn of Earth's creation. Elena and Cassie recognized it as part of the Sirian creation formula used to anchor humanity's burgeoning spiritual essence into physical form.

Nin took out her own athame. "Cassandra, take off the gauntlet on your right hand. We will entwine our blood together to finish the ritual."

She sliced her palm, then Cassie's, and clasped their hands together, mixing their blood. "Now, we put our hands onto the obelisk."

The stone sizzled and sparked. A heavy mist began to swirl around Cassie's feet while she, too, closed her eyes and began chanting in unison with Nin.

Then, out of the former Sumerian goddess's hands, a golden helix of fiery energy poured into Cassie's medallion. It flashed and then settled into a golden aura that surrounded Cassie completely. She felt a surge of warmth and courage infuse her being. In her mind's eye she saw the landscape of the Shadow Realm, a twisted canvas of despair and corruption, stretched out before her.

Without another thought she stepped into the obelisk.

"Goodbye, my love," Natesh whispered and silently receded into shadows.

Chapter 37: Tracking the Technomancer

Tristan whirled on Sirkan. "Now that Manu has been dealt with, you will return to that fool Soter. You will ensure the Technomancer's work spreads. You will undo the damage to the Aethernet that the Trybrid has wrought. And you will remember your place—or I will find another to serve as my vessel in this realm."

Before Sirkan could respond, reality twisted again, depositing him outside the Oval Office, disheveled and desperate, but with renewed purpose.

MORGANDRIAN STOOD IN the Oval Office trying not to slap the leader of the free world into oblivion. The bastard truly thought he was a messianic figure and that no one could see through his bullshit. She managed to keep a neutral look on her face and pretended to listen to his rants.

"Where is the Technomancer? Sirkan promised he would be at my disposal when we put plans in play to topple my rivals."

A knock on the door. "Mr. President, I must speak to you right away."

"Yes, yes, what is it?"

The door opened and in walked Sirkan himself, followed by a wild-eyed receptionist. "I'm sorry, Mr. President, he just appeared out of nowhere in the outer office."

Soter waved her out and took a step toward Sirkan. "It's about dammed time. We have a deal, and it's time to keep your end of it!"

Sirkan arched a brow. "Timing is everything, Soter. I don't take kindly to demands. I call the shots."

Morgandrian hid her surprise at Sirkan's sudden appearance. He looked ruffled with an underlying sense of desperation. *Great,* she thought. *Now I have to deal with yet another pompous ass!*

"My lord, Sirkan," Morgandrian said in a deferential tone. "We are honored by your presence. We were discussing the fact that the Technomancer has not been forthcoming with the next steps in our plan to establish President Soter as world leader."

Sirkan eyed her suspiciously. "Yes, well, I will determine whether or not the Technomancer is needed." There was no way he would reveal what Cassandra had done with her metamorphosis. "I believe our original agreement was fulfilled with the virtual reality game. It is influencing humanity across the globe."

"A VR game! Are you serious? I need to topple governments and financial institutions," yelled Soter. "I need *control!*"

"Your stupidity, Mr. President, knows no bounds. Get with the program. The gaming world is larger than you apparently know. From smartphone apps and single-shooter games to full-out immersive multiplayer role-playing games. The difference with a virtual reality game is the way it is used. The military uses online gaming and VR for training and battle simulations. Financial institutions, businesses of every kind, and educational institutions use VR programs for training and tracking purposes. The possibilities are endless!"

Morgandrian was taken aback by Sirkan's knowledge of gaming. She was not surprised, however, that he didn't reveal how Cassandra had damaged much of the *Battle for Infinity* program, a fact she had learned from Arion when he had last visited her.

Morgandrian decided it was time for her to take control of the conversation. "Add magic to the package, and there is no way we can be stopped. That's why the Technomancer is so important to our cause." *There,* she thought, *a little more misdirection about magic, and the ruse would remain intact.*

"Yes, yes, the Technomancer," said Soter. "Well then call him! Let's get this done!"

Morgandrian's heart skipped a beat. She couldn't let him near Danax.

"I'll take care of it," Sirkan said. And then vanished

SIRKAN STOOD AMIDST his ruined temple in the Unseelie Court. Once his prized seat of power, a refuge against time, it was now destroyed! He called his staff to him. At least he still had access to his powers.

He cursed as his hand trembled. His time was running out. Pulling the Chalice of Persuasion from his robe, he slammed it on a nearby table to activate the liquid and shakily drained it. The rejuvenating effects of the elixir were wearing off more and more quickly. It was only a matter of months before it stopped working altogether.

Sirkan knew he had to make the most of the little time he had left. He went into the far corner of the temple to a hidden floor panel. At least *this* had not been destroyed. He needed to figure out a way to summon the Technomancer, who seemed to have gone rogue.

Climbing down the stone steps to the chamber below, he activated the witchlights. There, against the far-right corner, stood a large oblong shape draped in black velvet. He jerked the fabric away to reveal an enormous gilded mirror, one of the original spirit screens. He sighed with relief. Not a crack in it.

He intoned an ancient chant and pointed his staff toward a pattern he had programmed into the Atlantean crystals embedded around the edges of the mirror. The dark surface of the glass came alive with a grainy storm of static snow. Sirkan then attempted to summon the Technomancer using specific hand gestures that would connect with his energy signature.

He swore when he felt resistance, like a rusty wheel reluctantly creaking into motion. Despite its initial stubbornness, with persistent effort, each word he spoke began to break through the static of the mirror. He waited impatiently, his temper beginning to rise. Sirkan was not used to being ignored by someone he considered his to command.

Danax's visage finally came into view. "What do you want? Manu is safely trapped in the Shadow Realm. I have other programs to attend to."

"I have a new mission from Tristan. It has to do with Conroe Soter."

"That imbecile is not worth our time. I have bigger fish to fry."

Sirkan narrowed his eyes. "*You* have?"

Realizing his slip, Danax backpedaled. "You know what I meant. Other projects are already in progress and need constant monitoring. After what Cassandra did in the control room of your ship, I must ensure she cannot access any more of my programs."

"That's what I want to talk to you about. We need to take them to the next level." Sirkan went on to outline the plan he had discussed in detail with Morgandrian and Soter.

"Hmmm," Danax said. "That is an intriguing concept. Collapsing world governments." He paused for a beat. "I like it. Let me see what I can do."

He blinked out before Sirkan could respond. *Well shit. I'm not going to just sit here and wait for the asshole to get back to me.*

He used the mirror once more and configured the frequency for Morgandrian's throne room. Luckily, she was there.

"Did you find him?" she asked without preamble.

"Yes, I did. But the bastard is still being cagey. I have no idea where he is."

Morgandrian sighed. "Come to me, and I will do a location spell. That should be easy enough."

ARION HAD BARELY MADE it out of her throne room before Sirkan ported in. Fortunately, he'd had enough time to set up a computer program for the tracking spell. He assured Morgandrian that he would transmit as much information as he could about the tech used to creating the Technomancer. Ninhursag was aware of the quantum entanglement communicator and was working on splicing a channel that the White Circle could use. Arion knew where Ninhursag was and would consult with her.

Morgandrian closed her eyes and took a breath. *It had better be soon,* she thought. She was running out of stall tactics.

Sirkan was pacing like a caged puma.

"For goddess's sake, quit stalking about. You are distracting me. This location spell needs a bit more finesse. The damned technological enhancements are harder to lock on to." She fired up her spirit screen and turned on her computer console. Old magic and new tech.

"Here, I know more about technology than you do," said Sirkan, moving toward the computer.

She pushed him away. "You do not have the same magical training when it comes to earth magics, which are essential in a location spell. That is, after all, why you recruited me as your main lieutenant. I need to get one spell done before I start the other. Just leave me alone. I can do this."

Sirkan swore and resumed his pacing. He would deal with her later.

A small blip on the screen indicated that Arion was trying to get through. Morgandrian put on her headset and input the prearranged code. There! She was connected to the Aethernet and to Arion through the QEC.

She decided a bit of fawning was needed to keep Sirkan feeling like he was still in charge. "OK, Sirkan, now I could use some of your help. I have finally connected to the Aethernet, and I need to pull up a holographic map that shows the ley lines."

He strutted over to her and began to input code. Within minutes, he pulled up a holographic map and beamed it into the center of the room. Ley lines crisscrossed the flattened map of Earth, with each intersection highlighted.

"That's exactly what I needed. Now, let me finish up the spell."

She heard the faint coordinates coming through the headset from Arion and slowly began to input them into the computer program they had designed earlier. Her fingers hovered over the keyboard, her intuition reaching out into the Aethernet. She closed her eyes to better scan the unseen world. She began to see the lines of electromagnetic energy with her mind's eye and followed one especially vibrant line of red ... there!

Morgandrian opened her eyes and pointed to a ley line deep within Antarctica. That must be where Danax had his lair.

Sirkan looked where she was pointing. "Antarctica? What the—"

"That makes total sense," Morgandrian said. "With the kind of technology he has, he would need to burrow into an impossible location." She cocked her head. "However, I don't believe he is in the third dimension. I think he may be in an interdimensional rift."

"Well, of course the fuck he is!" said Sirkan.

Morgandrian smirked, "Oh ye of little faith. Give me a minute to work some more of my magics."

She felt Ninhursag's energy come through the spirit screen and link with her telepathically.

All right, little witch, Ninhursag transmitted, *I have connected with the QEC. Hold as I send through the link.*

Pretending to go into deep meditation, Morgandrian made some complicated, and fake, magical hand gestures. A few minutes went by, and then she heard Nin's thoughts once more.

The Technomancer does not know we are on to him and his location. I highly recommend you contact him, not go to him.

Morgandrian opened her eyes. "I have the coordinates, and I am putting them into my spirit screen. We can communicate with him without having to venture into an interdimensional pocket."

"Obviously. I'm well versed in dealing with interdimensional rifts for shit's sake," Sirkan spat.

Attempting to mollify him, Morgandrian said, "Of course. But I recommend you contact him first. I'm not sure we should port there. Let's not show all our cards."

Impatient, Sirkan swore but stepped over to the spirit screen. Morgandrian put her left hand on the computer console and her right on the spirit screen, her body acting as a conduit. Blue lightning shot through her from one hand to the other. She began to vibrate, and pain blossomed in her forehead.

"Hurry," she said through gritted teeth. "I don't know how long I can hold this."

The spirit screen activated, and a startled Danax whirled around. "How the hell did you get through to me?" he demanded.

"I have my ways," said Sirkan. "Did you really think you could hide from me and my directives? Please. I have been on this planet eons longer than you."

"What do you want, then? I am in the midst of—"

"Not doing my bidding," snapped Sirkan. "Meet me in the private residence of the White House in," he looked at Morgandrian, assessing her energy, "thirty minutes."

Morgandrian sighed and dropped her arms, breaking off the transmission. "I will need at least that long to recoup my energy. You will have to contact Soter and then port us."

CONROE SOTER WAS ALWAYS in awe of Sirkan's and Morgandrian's portal-hopping ability. And jealous. One more thing to negotiate. He wanted a portal rune stone.

"Well, it took you long enough," he said. "I can't just change my schedule at the drop of a hat. I am, after all, the leader of the free world."

Not deigning to answer him, Sirkan went to the computer that sat on top of an L-shaped desk and fired it up. A stream of electricity shot from the screen and deposited Danax into the middle of the room.

Soter stared, dumbfounded. "What the fuck!"

Morgandrian rolled her eyes. "Technomancer, Conroe. Half man, half computer. Magically enhanced. He can ride the code of the Aethernet like you ride in a car." She thought she actually saw fear in Soter's eyes.

"Now let's bring our enemies to their knees," said Sirkan.

Chapter 38: Hell Hath

A rushing sound engulfed her and turned the space around her into an echo chamber. The medallion carved a path of light through the darkness as she hurled through the nexus. For a moment, she passed through the Twilight layer of the Shadow Realm, where reality rippled like heat waves off hot pavement. Physical objects stretched and warped, ghostly echoes of the living world bleeding through the veil. Fragments of whispered conversations and half-formed shapes swirled past her too quickly to grasp.

The descent accelerated, plunging her into the Void. Here, time stuttered and jumped as memories tried to surface and entangle her, but she moved too fast for them to take hold. Through her protective sphere of light, she glimpsed lost souls suspended in their life reviews and personal hells, their forms blurring past like streaks of rain on a window.

As she continued on, the medallion's power kept her anchored, preventing the Void from dragging her into its maze of regrets and what-ifs.

When it finally spat her out, she landed on hands and knees in the Depths, the lowest level of the Shadow Realm. Winded but unhurt, she rose to her feet and started forward, each movement guided and protected by the pulsating light of the medallion, with the Sword of Keraunos sheathed at her back.

The air was heavy with the acrid smells of brimstone and blood and cries of what could only be the damned.

Yeah, this is definitely hell.

Cassie kept her eyes lowered, her hand holding the medallion, and focused on an image of Manu while she moved cautiously forward. She knew the realm was a twisted reality, a living nightmare. The shadows surrounding her distorted and transformed into horrifying shapes and then retreated from the medallion's light. The light not only guided her but also shielded her from the menacing dark forces. Cassie kept her eyes half-closed, refusing to let the surrounding scenes seep into her consciousness. She knew that fully seeing the phantasms would only give them power, feeding off her deepest fears of losing Manu, or worse, losing her soul.

Venturing deeper, Cassie noticed the medallion's glow growing stronger, its golden light acting like a searchlight. It pulsed steadily with her heartbeat, reassuring her in whispers. *Keep going. This way.*

Trusting its guidance, she navigated the labyrinthine paths, her steps echoing on the obsidian-like ground and over bridges spanning chasms that seemed to drop into endless darkness. She was having a hard time breathing, the air around her hot, heavy, and rancid. It felt interminable. But she knew she couldn't stop.

Fiery fissures began to open beneath her feet, spider-like flames seeping out. Thank the gods for the battle gear that was constructed of who-knows-what alien alloys. Even though it was hot, nothing would be able to burn her. *Keep going. Hold Manu's face in your mind's eye.*

Suddenly, a feral scream shattered the oppressive silence. Cassie spun toward the sound, her heart pounding. She ran toward it, but tangles of oily black vines grabbed at her ankles. She tripped, balanced, and then fell, *hard*. The vines began to wind up her legs, trapping her in their vise-like grips and pulling her toward swamp-like ground oozing with gore and noxious fumes. She reached for the athame at her thigh and managed to unsheathe it. She slashed at the tendrils that inched toward her knees.

Be the observer; don't buy into the illusion.

Black blood spurted from the tendrils, hissing as it hit her suit.

Thank the Radiant One for my magic suit. That's poison if I ever saw it.

Cassie finally cut herself free and scrambled away from the creeping tendrils. She got to her feet, disoriented, and paused to listen. The cacophony of demonic screams filled the air, but she refused to buy into them as reality and continued on.

Then she heard Manu's infamous battle cry, but something was wrong with it. It was darker, more savage than she remembered, as if whatever realm they were in had corrupted even that familiar sound.

Unsheathing her sword, she ran toward his voice. Ignoring the dark terrain with its traps, she finally saw him in a clearing dimly lit by an eerie red light. He was swinging his sword wildly, his movements erratic as he fought against writhing shadows. His body flickered like an old movie video struggling to stay in frame, but his eyes ... his eyes were wrong. They darted around with a feverish intensity, seeing things that weren't there, missing things that were.

"Manu!" Cassie called out, her voice cutting through the din.

Manu's head snapped toward her, and the look on his face made her blood run cold. There was no love there, no recognition, only a terrible, manic anger. His lips pulled back in a snarl as he raised his sword, its edge catching the eerie light.

"Another one," he spat, his voice raw and hostile. He raised his sword and ran toward her and swung. She ducked and rolled, her heart pounding.

"Manu, stop! It's me!" She barely avoided another slash that would have opened her from shoulder to hip.

"You think wearing her face will break me?" His attacks grew more precise, more deadly. "I've killed a hundred of you already, each one wearing her smile, speaking with her voice." His eyes blazed with a combination of hatred and despair that chilled her. "I know she's dead. You killed her, and now you mock me with these illusions."

Cassie deflected his next strike with the Sword of Keraunos, the impact jarring her arm. She could have countered, could have struck him a dozen times already, but she couldn't bring herself to hurt him. "Manu, please! Remember when you gave me the star cruiser for an engagement present when we were still on Sirius?"

"Silence!" He pressed his attack, driving her back. "Every demon knows our story. You'll have to do better than that."

The shadows around them writhed and pulsed, feeding on their conflict. Cassie's back hit a rock outcropping. She barely managed to dodge as Manu's sword sparked off the rock where her neck had been.

"I won't fight you," she gasped, tears streaming down her face. "If you're going to kill me, then kill me. But I won't hurt you."

His sword pressed against her throat. "Die, demon."

The medallion at his neck began to vibrate, its gentle warmth becoming an insistent pulse. Golden light spilled from it, reaching out to touch its twin at Cassie's breast. The matching medallion responded, their combined light cutting through the Shadow Realm's murk.

Manu's eyes widened as the resonance between the medallions grew stronger. "This ... this isn't possible. Demons can't ..." His sword hand trembled. "They can't activate blessed artifacts."

"That's right," she whispered, meeting his eyes, not daring to move with the blade still at her throat. "Remember what Nin said? The medallions would always lead us to each other. They're proof against illusions."

His sword clattered to the ground as understanding crashed over him. Horror replaced the hatred in his eyes as he realized how close he'd come to killing her. "Cassandra?" His voice broke. "Oh gods, Cassie ..." He reached for her with shaking hands, then pulled back, afraid to touch her.

She closed the distance herself, wrapping her arms around him as he shuddered. "It's OK. It's really me. I'm here."

A sound like thousands of wings shattered their reunion. Cassie whirled around, still holding Manu. "Shit! It looks like a swarm of bats ... no ... dragons! Dragons? Seriously? That's lame."

Manu blinked, and suddenly he was laughing, a wet, desperate sound. "Only my Ayesha, my Cassie, would face down a horde of hell-dragons and call them lame." He snatched up his sword again, but this time he moved to stand beside her. "Lame or not, they're coming straight for us. And breathing fire, no less."

"Can you use any of your powers?" she asked.

"No. Tristan's dark magic has drained me completely, and my staff is useless. I only have my sword." Manu said.

"Yeah, well, we'll deal with Tristan once we're out of this hell dimension. In the meantime, don't worry. I brought plenty of protection," Cassie said, centering herself. She grasped the medallion in her left hand and focused on the helix of golden energy within it. Reaching for the Sword of Keraunos, she said, "Let's get rid of these dragons."

"*Lord of the Rings* is your fantasy not mine. I think you need to switch channels," said Manu.

"You're enjoying this!" she said.

"Immensely. We haven't had a good sword and sorcerer battle for hundreds of years."

Her breath was coming in gulps now. She panted, swinging her sword against the first line of ... yeah, orcs! "Surely, I'm not manifesting all these monstrosities. Master Elena said that Danax placed some corrupted programs in this dimension that would project what seems like the native demons that actually *do* inhabit this place. We just need to determine which are real and which are our manifested fears, yes?"

"Not necessarily. They all need to be destroyed," Manu panted as he continued to battle the demons, real and imagined.

Cassie kept swinging Keraunos in fiery arcs. She could see the difference now between the illusions, which simply disappeared versus the real demons, which fell into ash.

"Do you remember when we met the great Sun Tzu?"

He threw back his head and laughed, "By the Radiant one, why would you think of *that* lifetime. You were literally my concubine!"

"I was the power behind your throne."

He met her eyes with a look that could melt rocks. "You always are."

Cassie had to shut her eyes to break the fiery stare that sent a ripple of lust igniting her core. "Anyway, I am thinking of a passage from his *Art of War:* 'Appear weak when you are strong.'"

"You're thinking of a bit of misdirection?"

"Yeah."

"We need to be careful with that. Remember: this is a realm of illusion and manifestation. I'm not sure if that would work for us or against us."

Cassie said, "We need to switch tactics. We're on defense and need to be on offense."

He paused, considering. "All right. Act like you're injured. You have more power than I do at the moment so that's not an issue. But they'll only see a female humanoid and will most likely think you're weaker."

She snorted.

"No, no," he laughed, "that's part of their innate programing, I'm sure. Play possum. Then just when they think they're winning, strike with every magical power you possess."

Blood of my blood.

Cassie instinctively grasped her torc. *Grandmother?*

Love rushed into her heart. *No, Dear One, but I am of your line. Ask Manu to remember Grandame.*

"Manu, do you remember someone called Grandame?"

"What?" His eyes went wide while he lopped off demonic heads and tried to keep up with her apparent tangent. "Yes ... I do ... what does that have to do with anything?"

Cassie's eyes rolled back, and she surrendered herself to her ancestor's spirit and began to channel. "Manu, remember the day when you and Danae overcame the dark forces alongside my fae army? They are legion now and reside in the light of the Shadow Realm. You must awaken them to come to our aid."

Manu could only nod as he pivoted and took out another swarm of demons who suddenly manifested from one of the many fissures opening around him.

Cassie continued, "Invoke their allegiance with my name, Queen Elysandrial. Call on them with this incarnation of Danae. You must do it together."

The great queen faded away but left behind the total recall of her druid lifetime as Danae. Cassie met Manu's eye across the clearing. "Do you remember the invocation?"

He nodded, closed his eyes, and they began the chant in Gaelic.

Once they completed the chant, the air around them stilled, like a pause between breaths.

A faraway thunder sounded. The surface beneath them started to vibrate.

The medallion around Cassie's neck began to emit a golden aura that expanded into a stream of light reaching toward its twin at Manu's chest as they synced together.

"My power ... it's coming back!" he shouted. He caught her up in his arms just as a battle cry rang out from behind him. The glowing bodies of ancient fae soldiers from every age flowed into the clearing around them. They galloped forward on great war steeds, swords and axes glowing with aetheric light held high above their heads. Others were on foot shooting flaming arrows from bows and crossbows into the leathery hides of the dragons overhead.

Thousands of ghostly voices intoned an ancient Gaelic battle cry: *Air do shonsa, naomh agus sinnsirean! Seo dhuinn a bhlàr!* "For your honor, saints and ancestors! Go we to battle!"

Behind Cassie, the shadows recoiled, shrieking. Overhead, dragons spiraled down, their fiery breath igniting the battlefield.

Manu's power surged back, and he stood tall, a figure of light and fury. The air crackled with energy, his presence pushing back the darkness. His eyes blazed with a numinous fire, reflecting the chaotic dance of flames and shadows on the battle zone.

With a swift, fluid motion, Manu lifted his now reactivated staff, and a radiant wave of power surged forth. The shadows' shrieks turned to wails as they disintegrated under his regained strength.

Cassie turned to him, awe and relief in her eyes. "Manu," she breathed, "you're back."

"Stronger than ever," he grinned. He stepped forward, his gaze fixed on the descending dragons. With a final command, Manu unleashed a burst of power that reduced the dragons to ash.

"Guess they were real then," Cassie said with a crooked smile.

The air around them shimmered as Manu took her face into his hands, searching, and noting the code behind her violet eyes. "This is you, yes?"

She smiled, "Well, yes and no. I'll fill you in after we get the hell out of hell!"

More demonic forces were vomited from the fiery splits all around them. Seismic rumblings threatened to knock Manu off his feet. Cassie met his eyes, intuitively knowing that he was ready to sacrifice himself in order to save her. *Oh no you don't, my love,* she thought, and then she screamed her own battle cry and leaped forward, swinging the Sword of Keraunos in arcs of fire.

Manu joined her to fight back-to-back as they fended off the unending hordes. No words could describe the abominations coming to life all around them, both real and magically generated. Cassie's heart sank. How would they ever be able to kill all these demons, even with the help of the ghostly fae army?

But defeat them they must; there was no other choice. They had to get back to the third dimension and finish their mission. So she kept swinging her mighty sword while intoning her magical spells to imbue it with her ancient magics. The demons unlucky enough to attack her merely disintegrated into fine ash when they met her blade.

Her mouth curved up. *Yeah, I still have it.*

The fae warriors formed a circle around Cassie and Manu, their weapons drawn, creating a barrier of light.

Cassie's heart clenched when a massive serpentine entity covered in jagged scales reared up and inched its way toward her. Its eyes burned with a malevolent, crimson light, and the sound emanating from it was a cacophony of whispers. It's maw, dripping with ichor, seemed to contain an endless void.

Master Elena's voice echoed in her mind. *Remember that much of the Shadow Realm is illusion, where thoughts are things and fed by fear.*

And then the scene shifted!

Cassie stood in a twisted hellscape. Jagged obsidian rocks stabbed up from bubbling pits of lava, while lightning seared the sky and left behind the stench of ozone. Demonic runes glowed with unnatural crimson light along the ridges. She had somehow slipped into another dimension of the Shadow Realm.

She looked around and saw Manu and the battle shimmering through what looked like a heat wave. Manu was trying to reach her but couldn't, like a wall of impenetrable glass separated them.

A guttural roar shook the ground. The hulking demon snake slithered toward her. *Of course,* that *got through!* But then the demon crackled for a second, like a pixelated computer image. *What the hell?*

She froze and then realized. It was one of Danax's holographic simulations. So that was it: a test of her cybernetic skills on this side of the barrier.

OK, I got this.

She whirled and planted her feet in battle stance, then looked up at the demonic reptile. It stood about ten feet tall with razor-sharp claws and saber-like teeth. Curling stag horns protruded from either side of its reptilian head, and its eyes burned with infernal hunger. It sprouted three sets of webbed wings. *Damn!* The serpent demon flexed its wings and cracked its neck, then charged at Cassie with terrifying speed.

Cassie slipped fluidly into an advanced kung fu stance, readying herself for the onslaught. The demon slashed with its claws. She leapt into a butterfly twist kick, striking one of its horns and using the momentum to flip herself up onto its back. She dug her knees into its back while pummeling the base of its skull with hammer fists.

I've got to find the program that is generating this.

The demon howled and reached back to seize her with its teeth, but Cassie was too quick. She sprang off into a double barrel roll, landing in a crouch facing the beast. It lunged again, jaws slavering. Cassie leaped straight up in a devastating split kick, her heel connecting squarely with its jaw in a move that would have snapped a human's neck.

The snake recoiled but didn't fall. As Cassie's cybernetic vision engaged, she noticed something odd—microscopic hexagonal patterns in the air around the demon, like a mesh of pixels. Her neural interface flagged a surge in power consumption each time the creature transformed.

Got you. Her internal systems mapped the energy grid, pinpointing a hidden panel behind a rock formation. Perfectly camouflaged, but its heat signature betrayed it.

She had to reach it—but first, she had to survive. As the demon sprouted more arms, her interface flashed a warning: *Memory overflow detected in Sector 7.* The creature's new limbs flickered, their movements jerky and flawed.

Cassie smirked grimly. Every programmer left backdoors. She just had to find this one's emergency shutdown routine.

The worm struck first. An upward swipe tore a gash in her side. She screamed, barely dodging another attack before rolling into a tiger stance, hands curled into claws. As the demon's next haymaker swung toward her, she met it with an upward sword strike to its underbelly—base code shattered around her like tinkling glass.

Chest heaving, she gulped in air. Relief flooded her—until the barrier between her and Manu collapsed. Towering shadows surged forward.

However, on their heels, Fae warriors charged to her aid, their cries echoing across the dimension. Dracoleon swooped in, flanking Gabriel, now in panther form.

With Manu at her side once more, Cassie scanned the area where the barrier had been. *Another computer panel had to be hidden there.*

As the battle raged around her, Cassie closed her physical eyes to attune to the code embedded behind her eyes and raised her hands like scanners and turned slowly to probe the area. The control panel had to be here in this dimension; otherwise, the sensory attacks would not have been so real.

Finally, she felt it: an aethereal energy field that blended digital terror and ancient evil. She focused on the space just feet away from them, raised Keraunos and shot streams of energy from her hands down the sword toward it. The panel became visible as it began to overload, like a shimmering tear in the surrounding landscape. With each hit, the holographic forms melted away, revealing the chaotic code beneath their structured facades. Sparks shot out, fuses blew, and smoke began to billow. Then the holographic simulation totally collapsed, leaving behind a smoldering motherboard.

"OK," she shouted to Manu, "one techno illusion down. One hellscape illusion still to go. We need to channel our combined energy through the Atlantean crystals in the medallions now that we are in sync," Cassie said.

Manu took her hand while she focused on the medallions. Their energies intertwined, creating a connection more potent than ever. They built up a reservoir of force. Hand in hand, Manu held his staff aloft, and Cassie raised her sword.

"Summon the Violet Flame," said Manu. "We will use it to create a vortex of energy to break apart the dark energy that remains."

Cassie nodded and visualized the Violet Flame, the ultimate tool of transformation that she had learned from her beloved teacher, the Compte de St. Germaine, during the French Revolution. Together, Cassie and Manu pushed forward, their combined energies creating the vortex. Then, with a deafening roar, the realm itself seemed to quake under the strain of so much concentrated light. Cracks appeared in the stygian sky, revealing glimpses of other dimensions, other possibilities.

The shadows screamed in fury and despair, their voices echoing into oblivion.

Manu yelled, "Now, Cassie! While it's weakened!" He took her hand, and gripping their medallions tightly, she intoned the transformation spell given to her by St. Germaine:

> *By the light of the ancestors, by hope's bright flame,*
> *We transmute the darkness in The Radiant One's name.*
> *With the Violet Flame, we dispel the night,*
> *Transforming all shadows into radiant light.*
> *By the wisdom of ages, by the stars above,*
> *We embrace the journey with boundless love.*
> *In unity and peace, our spirits soar free,*
> *Aligned with the cosmos, so mote it be.*

Their medallions blazed with blinding intensity. The golden helix of light exploded outward, a luminous wave that swept through the entire Shadow Realm, cleansing it of the manufactured darkness. The shadow forms shattered, their essences dissolving into motes of harmless dust.

The realm calmed, the air cleared, and the oppressive heat faded. The fae warriors, their duty fulfilled, saluted Cassie as they began to fade. The ghostly visage of the great fae Queen Elysandrial hovered over the horizon, her aethereal form shimmering in the waning light. She gazed at Cassie with a serene, proud expression before dissolving into mist, merging with the gentle breeze that now whispered through the tranquil landscape.

Manu and Cassie stood amidst the desolate field, their breaths heavy in the eerie silence that followed the chaos. The ground was littered with the remnants of dark magic and conflict: scorched earth, shattered weapons, and most burdensome of all, the splatters of blood and viscera that adorned their armor and skin.

"Hell hath no fury," murmured Manu.

Cassie punched his shoulder, "It wasn't just my fury, oh mighty one." She shuddered as she looked down, "I need a shower!"

Gabriel, once more in cat form, butted his head against Cassie's leg. Dracoleon bent down for a head pet too. She laughed and met Manu's eyes.

"We did it!" she exclaimed.

Manu pulled her close, his hands cradling her face with a tenderness that made her heart ache. His eyes searched hers, intense and probing. "You are indeed transformed," he murmured, his fingers tracing her face with a delicate touch. "I see Ayesha in you more than ever." He gazed into those striking violet eyes, searching for recognition.

"The eyes are the window to the soul," she murmured.

Their eyes locked, and a smile tugged at his lips. "There you are."

"My love," Cassie whispered, cupping his face as if to memorize every detail: the sculpted curve of his lips, full and inviting, and his crystal-clear cerulean eyes that she could lose herself in, eyes that kindled an almost unbearable passion within her. She breathed deeply, her voice trembling. "Yes, I've changed. I embody everything I've ever been and all that I am now. When I transformed into this new body and remembered so much—our memories, our love, our mission—I was so overcome with longing, with wanting you once more in my arms." Tears glistened in her eyes, softening her expression. "Come, let's go home."

Before she could turn away, he pulled her into a fierce embrace, ignoring the blood and gore, their lips meeting in a kiss that spoke of long-held desire and unspoken promises.

Manu traced a finger down the bridge of her nose, his touch lingering. "*Now* we can go home."

Chapter 39: Resolutions and Revelations

Ian stared at his flickering campfire through the lens of the amber liquid in his glass. Everyone was on edge. Cassie had gone into the Shadow Realm nearly two weeks ago and still no word. The avatars had been ordered back to the Citadel, and most of the remaining group had moved from the opulent palace to hold vigil in a small encampment Ninhursag had erected next to the obelisk.

Arion sauntered up to him, took the drink out of his hand, and drained the glass.

"What the hell, Arion? Get your own bloody glass."

"Don't mind if I do," said the enforcer. With a flick of his wrist, he manifested two more glasses filled with scotch.

Grabbing one of the glasses out of Arion's hands, Ian gave him the stink eye. "This place is getting dense with magics. The last thing we need is to draw the Dark Brotherhood's attention here."

Ninhursag walked down the steps of her crystal abode to join them. "Enough energy has been built up here to keep the glamour in place." She looked toward the obelisk. "I still can't get a read on Cassandra and Manu. I saw a battle, but then lost all contact."

"They're OK," Ian said. "I have that ancestral connection with her, and I don't feel any sense that they have passed permanently into the Shadow Realm." He looked back at Cassie's parents. "They would have felt it too."

Ayden looked up. "A few days ago, I sensed a power surge from my matrilineal line. They most likely have been supported by the ancient fae. According to legend, the great warrior queen, Elysandrial, would appear during the Shift of the Ages to deploy her fae armies in support of a descendant destined to lead the realms in a monumental battle against the forces of darkness. I am sure that Cassandra is that descendant."

Ninhursag nodded in agreement. "Your belief seems well founded. Also, bear in mind that their current location transcends time and space. The Shadow Realm is a treacherous place, and I'm sure that Danax made some digital enhancements, but I'm also sure Cassandra will be able to collapse the dark energies even without the help of the ancient fae."

"Computer illusions are one thing," said Rebekah, "demonic forces are another." She took her husband's hand. "We experienced that firsthand when we were in the Unseelie Court's dungeons."

Eristides, contemplative during the exchange, spoke up, "This Technomancer may very well be the greatest adversary that Cassandra will have to destroy, lest humanity be thrown back to the Dark Ages."

At Ninhursag's protest, he held up a hand. "All of the advancements we've made could be decimated if he is not neutralized." He looked pointedly at Ninhursag. "I know about your hand in his creation. But the creation has run amuck. Consciousness does not equal conscience. If he has been irrevocably turned to the Dark Brotherhood ..."

Ninhursag's jaw tightened. "I am his creator. It is up to me to decide."

"You may have no choice," Rebekah said, as she and Ayden went back into their tent.

"There is always a choice," said Ian while he watched them go. "We need to maintain our focus on positive outcomes and right action."

"Spoken like a true white witch," said Ninhursag.

Arion shot to his feet as the ground beneath them began to rumble. A portal opened, and out stepped Tatiana followed by the small form of Devika.

"What are you doing here!" Arion thundered. "This is not the place for her!"

"Au contraire, my dear. This is precisely the right place and the right time for a daughter of the light and the dark. The balance of power has been compromised and—"

"This witch can act as a bridge," said Metatron as he appeared before them. "Cassandra is no longer who she once was. When she and Manu return, their paths will ..."

Hearing her daughter's name, Rebekah ran from her tent. Realizing who spoke, she quickly bowed to the great angel and waited for him to continue. Meanwhile, the rest of the group had gathered in silence, knowing that something of great importance was about to be revealed.

He looked around at the group in silence, then summoned Devika to his side. "I have conferred with the Sirian oracles and have discovered that the Aquarian prophecy has changed due to Cassandra's metamorphosis. She and Manu will take on new roles when they return to this dimension."

Rebekah clutched at Ayden's arm, her throat suddenly dry.

Eristides cleared his own throat, preparing to speak, but Metatron raised his hand to stop him. "There is no discussion here. Cassandra has free will, and her soul accepted this at the time of her metamorphosis." He turned to Tatiana and Arion. "Devika will be trained in the way of the avatars. Time will tell whether or not she will become one of the seven."

Ian stepped forward. "And what about Devika's mother?"

"She has her own tests to pass if she seeks redemption," Metatron answered. "You have your missions. You will both be called upon to provide parental support to Devika when needed." Then he put his hands on Devika's shoulders and steered her toward her father.

Ian took the girl into his arms. She was so small and fragile.

"Stop it, Dad. I may be small, but I am mighty!"

"The first rule is, no reading your father's mind!" said Ian.

Elena said, "I concur. Now let's go into that amazing palace, eat a meal, and discuss this latest turn of events."

Ninhursag silently led the way back to the palace to arrange additional quarters and the evening meal, her thoughts conflicted between loyalty to Ayesha's soul and to her greatest creation. She could use Enki's wise council, but his ship was once more out of Earth's reach.

Chapter 40: Enhancement Seminar

The new meditation program that Karim and Marcus had developed from Cassie's and Mikha'El's protocols hummed quietly on the main server. "The simulation is holding strong," An-Mei announced, eyes fixed on her analytics screen. "No AI penetration of the mental firewall, and thought patterns are stabilizing beautifully."

Through his holographic interface, Artemus nodded with approval, though he advised testing with a single group first.

"I'll reach out to Cassie's former students," Marcus said, already pulling up the communication module. "We can call it an 'enhancement seminar.' Sounds less intimidating than 'experimental mental defense protocol.'"

Karim raised an eyebrow. "Just make sure they know what they're signing up for. I'll handle security while An-Mei runs cyber backup."

The day of the seminar, Marcus stood among the high-tech meditation pods, watching three-dimensional mandalas pulse in sync with each participant's brainwaves.

"Neural stability is off the charts," An-Mei whispered, showing him her tablet. "They're more resistant to external influence than we've ever seen."

After an hour, the twelve participants emerged looking transformed, and while the neophytes served refreshments, Marcus slumped into a chair beside his colleagues. "Now comes the fun part: writing up every detail for Artemus."

Karim chuckled. "Better you than me. I hate paperwork."

"Like it's my favorite thing," Marcus shot back. "I'd rather be in the sparring ring with you."

"No, you wouldn't," Karim grinned. "I always kick your ass."

"Exactly," Marcus sighed.

THE NEXT FEW WEEKS were a whirlwind of activity. Marcus scheduled follow-up sessions with the Charlotte group, each time implementing slight adjustments based on the previous feedback and the ongoing analysis. An-Mei's role was crucial; she continued refining the code, enhancing its adaptability to individual neural patterns, which varied more widely than they had initially anticipated.

Marcus started receiving inquiries from other meditation groups within their network, word having spread about the intriguing new enhancement seminar. He responded with cautious optimism, explaining that full rollout would depend on the completion of this pilot phase.

During one particularly intense session, a breakthrough occurred. A participant named Lena, who had been part of the meditation community for several years, reported a unique experience. "It's as if I could actually see the barriers forming around my thoughts, protecting me from slipping into negative patterns." Her feedback was a confirmation of the code's potential impact on individual perception and mental resilience.

Motivated by Lena's experience, Marcus and An-Mei decided to introduce a real-time feedback system within the meditation pods, allowing participants to adjust the intensity and focus of the meditation code during their sessions. This customization led to even more profound experiences and insights from the group.

An-Mei's continuous analysis showed a statistically significant improvement in mental stability metrics compared to the baseline data collected before the enhancement seminars began. Her reports added the quantitative backing needed to argue for a broader application of the technology.

Artemus was impressed by the progress report Marcus compiled one month into the project. During their next holographic meeting, he gave the green light to expand the trial to two additional groups and to add more participants to the Charlotte group, with modifications based on all the insights gained thus far.

Marcus felt a sense of pride and accomplishment as he prepared the new groups for their introduction to the enhanced program. His communication stressed the exploratory nature of the seminars, the importance of feedback, and the potential benefits of improved mental resilience.

It felt good to be back in good graces after the debacle years earlier, when Cassie had almost died during a similar project, a time when he had been possessed by an evil entity. Although he hadn't been directly responsible for the near disaster, he still felt a lingering responsibility for what had happened to Cassie.

His good feelings, however, were short lived.

Chapter 41: There's No Place Like Home

Cassie wiped her brow, smearing a streak of grime across her forehead. She studied Manu. He was inspecting a slash on his arm, his black Sirian battle leathers scored and dark with demon blood and ichor. Cassie's iridescent exosuit had been mostly unharmed and, with its mixture of metal alloys and organic materials, had already repaired itself. But it hadn't repaired the huge gash in her side left from the demon serpent's attack.

She reached around to unbuckle the backpack and winced. The wound stung like hell.

"Manu, can you help me get this backpack off? I guess I'm hurt more than I thought, and I can't do it myself. There are all sorts of healing salves and other stuff in the pack."

His intense cerulean eyes met hers, and her heart flipped in her chest. How beautiful he was. His face, with its chiseled cheekbones and sculpted lips, was reminiscent of a classical marble statue, exuding an aura of timeless beauty and strength. Her reaction to him took her by surprise, and she tamped it down as he went over to her, took off the pack, and examined her side. "This looks pretty deep. Can you get that exosuit off enough that I can clean it?"

She smiled up at him, "You just want to see me naked."

He quickly extinguished another one of his smoldering looks and said, "Eventually. But for now, we need to get some healing done."

"OK, there's some healing balm in the pack that should do the trick. I will add some Reiki to it."

Manu patted the salve into the wound and was gratified to see the redness start to dissipate. He put his hands over it and sent his own form of healing magic into it.

She breathed a sigh of relief, "I can feel the heat draining from it." Cassie looked down at it. "It's starting to close up. I can almost take a deep breath again."

Wounds cleaned, salves applied, and clothes still on, Cassie got up to explore the clearing they were in. She turned around in confusion. "We're still in the Shadow Realm?" She walked in concentric circles, her palms raised, reading energy signatures.

Manu folded his arms, his brow furrowed. "I don't see how. We obliterated the AI programs and used the Violet Flame. Maybe we just need to let it go; leave the nightmare behind and focus on getting out of here."

Cassie paused, studying him thoughtfully. "You need to catch up with technology, my love. I handled the computer enhancements, but this is still the Shadow Realm."

She lowered herself to the ground, sitting cross-legged, and pulled a glowing rune stone from her satchel. Closing her eyes, she took a deep breath and recalled Master Elena's warning: *This stone will anchor you in the light, a lifeline through the darkness. But the Shadow Realm thrives on disorientation. It feeds on emotion—every fear, doubt, and stray thought made real.*

The memory sharpened her focus. The chaotic energy of the clearing seemed to hum around her, but she kept her attention locked on the rune stone in her hand, its steady pulse a beacon of light against the darkness. Minutes passed in silence before her eyes snapped open.

"I see it," she said softly. "The obelisk I came through. It's still there. I just need to follow the line of light back to it."

She reached for Manu, grasping his hand with the one that held the rune, and Gabriel and Dracoleon fell in step behind them. As their medallions ignited, a faint glow spread between them, their energies syncing in perfect harmony. Cassie's voice was steady now, filled with quiet determination.

"Just follow the light."

Chapter 42: Aethernet Attack

Tristan glared at the Technomancer through the spirit screen and then exploded. "How in all that is unholy did the girl manage to slip out of the Shadow Realm *and* with Manu?"

Danax shrugged. "You know as well as I do, my lord, the girl is an unknown. Now that she has, literally, created a new form and synthesized all her past lives into it, we have no idea what powers and abilities she has. Even with my considerable technological and magical skills, I cannot possibly know the extent of them." He paused for a beat and realized that Tristan was about to do something that he wouldn't like. "And then there's the Anunnaki piece."

"*What* Anunnaki piece?"

"Ninhursag of course. She has been helping the girl all along. With Enki working through Artemus and Ninhursag taking Cassandra under her wing, we have had formidable celestial interference."

Unable to contain himself any longer, Tristan stormed out of the room. He needed to kill someone.

Danax smiled. *At last!* he thought. *His Insufferableness is out of my space.* Now, he could focus on disrupting the avatars' meditation course and using it to his own ends. It could be a major key to seizing control of the Aethernet and subjugating humanity once and for all. Why should he serve lesser beings?

Danax fired up the tracking program he had created using a single drop of blood from Cassandra. How fortuitous that he was able to avail himself of vials of blood from countless Ayesha incarnations that were stored in Sirkan's private laboratory on board his mother ship.

Danax's already formidable abilities combined with Cassandra's DNA created a powerful code capable of infiltrating the Charlotte institute's mainframe. Once he corrupted the test programs, he would control the institute's intranet. From there, he could easily corrupt the Charlotte-Washington ley line.

The screen before him flickered, dark lines of code interlaced with crimson hues flowed like a river. He whispered incantations under his breath, his fingers dancing over the keyboard in a choreographed spell.

"Yes ... merge ... become one with their system," he muttered, eyes gleaming with malevolent glee.

The code pulsed and snaked through firewalls and encrypted layers, bypassing security protocols with ease. Danax's creation was an amalgamation of technology and sorcery, unstoppable and insidious.

IN THE COMMAND CENTER at the Charlotte institute, the Aquarian Avatars guided their neophytes through advanced meditation exercises. The air was thick with incense, and tranquil music filled the room.

"Focus on your inner self," said Seraphina, her voice soft and soothing. "Let the energy flow through you. Feel the connection between your mind and the Aethernet."

Suddenly, the computer screens flickered and turned red, with code and symbols flashing erratically.

"What's happening?" a neophyte cried out.

Seraphina moved quickly to the master holographic screen. She took a deep breath and touched the smooth, translucent panel, which recognized her unique bio-signature. A radiant blue holographic screen expanded in mid-air, displaying symbols and data streams. Seraphina's fingers danced through the virtual space.

"Something's infiltrated our system," she said.

The other avatars sensed the disturbance and ran to the command center. Marcus grimaced.

"It's the Technomancer," he said. "He's found a way in."

"We need to isolate the mainframe before the damage becomes irreversible," said Seraphina.

Karim's fingers flew over a control panel. "Marcus, we need to stabilize the core matrix. If the Technomancer's code corrupts it, we won't be able to recover."

Marcus nodded and initiated a purge sequence. Waves of light surged through the Aethernet, converging on the corrupted code. The malevolent presence resisted, but Marcus poured his energy into the Aethernet, guiding the purifying currents.

An-Mei and Yirribindi burst into the room from a portal. "Assist Seraphina," Marcus directed them.

An-Mei chanted an incantation, creating a protective barrier around the mainframe. Yirribindi connected to the backup servers, rerouting essential functions and entering defensive code.

"Seraphina, I'm detecting multiple points of entry," Yirri called out. "He's using a scatter attack."

"An-Mei, reinforce the firewall with your barriers. Yirri, prepare the countermeasures," Seraphina commanded.

Seraphina's chanting grew louder, infusing the system with protection. She could feel the Technomancer's code pressing against her barriers.

Marcus accessed the core matrix. "I'm initiating a quarantine of the affected sectors. We need to find the source and cut it off."

The neophytes gathered, their faces etched with concern.

"Will we be OK?" one asked, remembering the first cyberattack that almost killed Cassandra.

Seraphina turned to face them. "Stay calm. Focus on your breathing and stay away from the Aethernet. We'll get through this."

From his command center, Danax watched their struggle with cold amusement. His fingers danced over the interface as he entered a new command. The corrupted segments attacked with increased ferocity.

Seraphina staggered as her barriers flickered. "He's ramping up the attack. I can't hold it much longer."

Marcus fought to maintain the quarantine. "Yirribindi, activate the countermeasures now!"

Yirribindi deployed digital counterspells. The room filled with brilliant light as they clashed against the seething dark energy.

"We're pushing him back," Yirribindi said, "but I can only do it incrementally. If I overload the system, we won't be able to find the nucleus of his attack."

Seraphina closed her eyes, extending her senses into the digital realm. "It's coming from a hidden subroutine. If we isolate it, we can cut off his access."

An-Mei strained to maintain the digital barriers as something immense pressed against them—a sudden, unnatural presence. The corrupted code convulsed, then coalesced, forming a monstrous entity of jagged, shifting polygons. Its hollow eyes burned with lines of red script, and its claws slashed through the code, sending shockwaves rippling through the system.

"What the hell is that?" An-Mei gasped.

Marcus recoiled. "A security demon?"

"No." Yirribindi's voice was tight with unease. "It's something worse."

The avatars instinctively split off, digital weapons forming in their hands as they charged toward the creature. Energy bolts streaked through the aether as raw code clashed against its writhing form. The battle raged, but for every strike they landed, the monster only seemed to distort and regenerate.

An-Mei's breath hitched. Something wasn't right. She pushed past the noise, past the flashing system alerts, and reached into the heart of the battle.

Then she saw it.

The beast wasn't attacking. It was *stalling them.*

Her eyes snapped open. "Wait—STOP! It's a diversion!"

Marcus, mid-strike, hesitated. "What?"

"Danax doesn't need to win this fight—he just needs to keep us busy!" An-Mei spun toward the main console. "He's after something else."

Yirribindi's fingers flew over the interface. "Scanning ... no ... no, no, no! There's a secondary incursion targeting the institute's core archives!"

Karim shouted, "The master encryption keys—he's trying to breach them!"

Marcus didn't waste another second. "Fall back! Regroup and reallocate defenses *now!*"

But Danax was already in motion.

A surge of dark energy erupted through the system, slamming into their core defenses and shattering their barriers in a blinding flash. An-Mei staggered as her magic wavered.

"It's too strong!"

Nevertheless, she raised her hands, channeling every last reserve of energy. Pure light flowed outward, merging with their defenses and pushing back against the dark tide. For a moment, they felt the shift—Danax's code unraveling, the attack faltering.

Marcus later swore he heard the Technomancer scream: *"No! This can't be happening!"*

The corrupted code recoiled, retreating into the void. The institute's screens flickered, then stabilized.

Seraphina took a breath. "Marcus—now!"

Marcus slammed the final purge command. The system surged with a burst of radiant energy, locking down the breach and sealing Danax's access.

Silence fell. The last remnants of the attack faded.

The avatars exchanged looks, breathless and shaken.

An-Mei slowly lowered her hands, her glow dimming. "Wow ... that was amazing. How did I do that?"

Seraphina gave a weary smile. "You *adapted*. And that's why we're still standing."

An-Mei grimaced in a very un-An-Mei expression. "Yeah, well ... let's just complete the assessment."

Chapter 43: Redemption

Natesh was seated before a dusty tome recovered from the subterranean tunnels beneath Bimini. Ever since the final duel between Manu and Sirkan, he had been consumed by an obsession with Sirkan's staff. After Sirkan had burned to ash in his Unseelie Court tower four years ago, no one had thought to retrieve the staff, no one except Natesh. While he had handed over Sirkan's ruby ring to Master Artemus, he had kept the staff hidden in his lair.

As his eyes skimmed the ancient text, he found the passage that had made his undead heart quicken. The tome spoke of celestial artifacts' ability to bind with magical signatures, and more importantly, how vampiric blood could corrupt them. Having served as one of Sirkan's most powerful lieutenants, Natesh knew his former master's magical pattern intimately. He had realized he could reprogram the staff to recognize and destroy Sirkan's essence.

The answer was in the celestial crystal embedded in the staff. With trembling fingers, Natesh located the ritual he needed. By infusing the crystal with his centuries-old vampiric blood, dark and potent with ancient power, he could transform the staff into a weapon of final death, tuned to obliterate those who had repeatedly used it.

Gripping the staff, Natesh felt the hum of its electromagnetic field against his palm. The artifact had recognized him as a wielder. Now, he resolved to remake it into a tool of vengeance designed for one target alone.

NATESH STOOD AT THE edge of the dark wood dividing the two fae courts. He had not returned here since what was now called the Battle of the Tower. The palace of the Unseelie Court stood pristine, its beauty untouched by the years, a sharp contrast to Sirkan's ruined temple looming in the distance.

Scanning the two structures, Natesh had been certain that the dark army still lay dormant, sealed deep within one of them. Resolutely, he had set his sights on the temple. It seemed the most logical place to begin his search.

Adjusting the staff strapped to his back, Natesh placed a boot on the first cracked stair and froze mid-step, his vampiric senses catching Sirkan's unmistakable scent.

So, he is here.

Wrapping himself in shadow, Natesh crept silently up the remaining stairs and into the temple. His heightened hearing focused on the faint sound of chanting emanating from somewhere far below. At the far end of the rubble-strewn marble floor, he noticed where dust and gravel had been cleared. Kneeling, he inspected the area and uncovered the outline of a trapdoor. Carefully, he pried it open, revealing a winding stone staircase descending into darkness.

Recessed witchlights faintly illuminated the passage below. Taking a deep breath, Natesh blurred into motion, his supernatural speed carrying him down the spiral steps. At the bottom, he arrived in a long corridor that ended in a massive archway. The chanting had grown louder during his descent, each syllable scraping against his sensitive hearing.

He steeled himself, turning his thoughts to Giselle. Her face, her smile, memories of their shared past gave him strength.

The oppressive weight of Sirkan's presence thickened the air, seeping into the stone around him. As Natesh approached the chamber, the chanting stopped abruptly, replaced by the faint sound of water dripping along the walls.

Beyond the archway sprawled a cavernous chamber, pulsating with chaotic, otherworldly energy. Dimensional distortions rippled across the space, warping the air and making Natesh's skin crawl.

Rows upon rows of petrified demonic shapes filled the chamber, stretching into the shadows beyond sight. Their grotesque forms were locked in snarls of frozen agony. Jagged teeth jutted from wide-open mouths, hollow eyes stared into the void, and horns twisted like wicked spires. Wings sharp as blades protruded from some, while others stood rooted on clawed feet. The cracked and scorched ground beneath them gave the illusion of shifting shadows, as though the statues were stirring from slumber.

Dread clawed at Natesh's resolve, but he pressed on. Near the center of the chamber, silhouetted against a computer control panel bathed in eerie light, stood Sirkan.

"So ... you've come," Sirkan said, his voice low and mocking. "Have you returned to the fold, or are you here to ...?"

Natesh's gaze narrowed, his tone calm but sharp with defiance. "Here to what, Sirkan?"

Sirkan's lips curled into a sly smile. "Challenge me, perhaps? Claim what you foolishly believe is yours?"

Natesh's hand brushed the hilt of his sword. "I'm here to stop you. For good."

Sirkan's laugh echoed harshly through the chamber. "Stop me? You? You're a shadow of what you once were."

Natesh stepped forward, his silence heavy with intent. The tension between them thickened, the weight of their shared history pressing down like an invisible force.

Sirkan's smirk faded, replaced by a grim nod. "Very well. Let us begin."

"This ends here, Sirkan," Natesh growled.

Sirkan's smile returned, colder than before. "Fool," he spat. "You cannot comprehend the power I've acquired." He gestured toward the petrified demon army. "These soldiers are imbued with my blood and magic. And soon," he said as he withdrew a crimson vial from his robes, "with hers."

Rage blurred Natesh's vision as he realized what the vial contained: Cassandra's blood.

With a roar, he unstrapped the staff and brandished it. Crackling energy surged along its length, sparks sizzling through the air.

Sirkan instinctively reached for his staff, then hissed, "What have you done to my staff, you treacherous bastard?"

Without a word, Natesh launched himself at Sirkan, their battle igniting with a clash of raw fury. Every strike resonated with their respective magics, shockwaves rippling across the chamber.

Though Sirkan's dark magic deflected many of Natesh's attacks, each clash with the staff's energy drained him, as though the weapon itself drew power from its former master.

Natesh's eyes flicked to the control panel, and he knew what else he needed to do.

Channeling the staff's corrupted energy, he overloaded the system. Alarms blared and walls trembled as cracks spiderwebbed across the stone. Sirkan's eyes widened in rage and fear.

"You fool!" Sirkan screamed. "You'll destroy us both!"

Natesh's voice remained calm. "Better both of us than you unleashed upon the world again."

The celestial crystal in the staff pulsed violently, its energy locking onto Sirkan's magical signature. A vortex of anti-life energy swirled from it, homing in on its target.

"No ..." Sirkan whispered, genuine terror contorting his face as the crystal's power began unraveling him.

Layer by layer, the staff tore through Sirkan's essence, his physical form, his magic, his very existence. With a final, soul-wrenching scream, Sirkan vanished entirely, erased from all planes of reality.

A golden goblet rolled to the floor.

The chamber began to collapse. Flames roared as the temple crumbled. There was no time for Natesh to escape, but he stood resolute. His sacrifice would ensure Cassandra's safety.

The staff then pulsed one final time, consuming the space in a blinding flash.

Images of Giselle floated into Natesh's receding consciousness.

Then ... silence.

The temple, the dark army, and Sirkan were no more.

TRISTAN STOOD CLENCHING his fists at the edge of a blackened crater: all that remained of Sirkan's seat of power. He closed his eyes and reached out his palms to read the aetheric imprint that would reveal the final moments in the temple.

"Fools!" he bellowed. He unfurled his wings and flew into the crater. Thousands of smoldering carbonized forms lay strewn across the endless expanse of rubble. He moved forward through the aftermath of what looked like a nuclear explosion, his body trembling in anger. No dark hordes of warriors or demons would be forthcoming. *Such a waste,* he thought. *Thousands of years of preparation, gone!*

A metallic glint under the debris caught his eye. He bent to pick it up and threw back his head in a rueful laugh. The Chalice of Persuasion, burned, battered, and as ruined as the temple. "Sirkan, it appears you won't be resurrected ever again." He crushed it in his hand and continued through the ruined temple. Finding nothing worth salvaging, he shrugged. At least Sirkan's mother ship was still undamaged. His cloning experiments would still be intact, offering the next best option for expendable soldiers.

He flew out of the crater and into the neglected gardens of Isla's palace, then twisted his ruby ring to summon Soriah.

"Get some of your minions and do a thorough search of Isla's palace, especially the subterranean levels." He pointed toward the rubble behind him. "The demonic army I was counting on reanimating is gone. Sirkan and Natesh had a final confrontation. They are no more."

Soriah gasped, her eyes wide. "And the Chalice of Persuasion?"

"Damaged beyond repair." He opened his palm and dropped the crushed metal to the ground. "Another waste. All because of their obsession with one female."

Soriah knew better than to say anything more and proceeded to investigate the palace dungeons.

The sun dipped below the horizon, casting long shadows over the ruined temple. Tristan stood alone, a dark figure against the dying light, plotting the next move in his relentless quest for dominion over the earth and the enslavement of humanity.

Chapter 44: Reunion

Rebekah was the first to spot them emerging from the obelisk. "Cassie!" she cried, stumbling forward to envelop her daughter in a fierce hug.

Bleary-eyed, the rest of the camp stirred to life and rushed forward. Ninhursag sprinted down the stairs of the crystal palace. Though the vigil's numbers had dwindled, and some faces had changed, a sizable crowd still gathered around the bedraggled group that had escaped hell.

Master Elena, disregarding all protocol, threw her arms around Manu in a bone-crushing hug, while Artemus slapped him on the back with a grin. Ian scooped Cassie up and spun her around with a whoop of joy. Laughter and tears mingled as everyone released the pent-up fears and tensions of the past months in a whirlwind of emotion.

Finally able to break free from the embraces, Cassie asked, "How long?"

"Nine weeks," Nin replied.

Rebekah gently cupped her daughter's face between her hands, her eyes full of concern. "You're hurt. Before anything else, you need to come into the healing chamber in the palace." She turned to Manu, her voice leaving no room for argument. "You too, Manu."

Knowing it was pointless to protest, they followed Rebekah into the palace.

Nin called after them, "Rebekah, as soon as you're done, we'll have a meal in the banquet hall."

Thirty minutes later, Manu, Cassandra, and Rebekah rejoined the group in the banquet hall. A feast appeared on the table in a dazzling burst of light. Gleaming silver platters were piled high with delicacies from near and far. Succulent roasted meats glistened with savory sauces, vibrant vegetables were heaped in artistic displays, and golden pastries oozed with sweet fillings. Crystal decanters materialized, filled with ruby-red wines and honeyed meads. Cassie laughed as she eagerly piled food on her plate.

She sat with her parents on her left and Manu to her right. He grabbed a decanter and poured garnet liquid into a silver goblet. After a long swig, he smacked his lips and declared, "An excellent vintage! The magic table has good taste."

A happy meow drew their attention to Gabriel just as he buried his nose in an oversized bowl, purring and eating at the same time. Dracoleon huffed as he nosed open a large silver cloche. Arranged artfully on the platter was a collection of choice raw meats: venison, boar, and even a small dragon steak. The chimera rumbled his approval as he tore into the offerings.

Manu raised his glass to toast their magical dinner. "To the generous conjurings of this enchanted place! May our appetites be sated, and our strength restored." Cassie clinked her goblet against his with a nod of agreement.

"I wondered what happened to those two," Ian said, pointing to Gabriel and Dracoleon. "They disappeared right before my eyes six weeks ago."

Between mouthfuls, Cassie went on to explain how the Shadow Realm had been manipulated by the Technomancer. Manu simply drank in her narrative, his heart full to bursting with love and pride.

She felt his gaze, stopped, and deferred to him. "I'll let Manu tell the next part."

He quirked a lopsided grin and finished. After the tale was told, a question still hung in the air. "And how did you escape?" Ian prompted.

Cassie said, "We used Elena's rune stone and simply followed the light. It led us right to the obelisk, and ... well, here we are!" finished Cassie, then shifted to her own questions. "How are my fellow avatars doing? Are they OK?"

"More than OK," Master Elena answered. "They have been working diligently to take your meditation training program to the next level. The Technomancer ran amuck right after Manu was tricked into the Shadow Realm. His new focus is sabotaging the meditation groups."

Nin interrupted. "Now that you are back and safe, I will pay him a visit to find out how he broke out of his original programming. Tristan believes Danax is working for him now, but I think the Technomancer has also evolved. After all, he is part sentient being and part machine. Where there is consciousness, there is evolution of one type of another."

"Nature or nurture?" said Manu.

"Precisely," said Nin. "He has been around Tristan and Sirkan for many years now and may have developed a taste for power." She looked over at Cassie. "You know firsthand how alluring that can be."

"Yeah, it can be pretty enticing, for sure." She turned to look at Elena. "But as you have said, Master Elena, love and light always overcome hate and evil." Cassie paused and met Manu's eyes. "At least when given the choice."

Ayden cleared his throat and looked between Manu and Cassie. Rebekah put her hand on her husband's arm and leaned over to whisper, "Later my love. Let them get used to their new reality."

Manu simply bowed his head to Ayden. Yeah, he definitely needed to have a heart-to-heart with Cassie's father.

ARTEMUS, ELENA, MANU, Cassie, Ayden, Rebekah, and the avatars convened in the large conference room at the Citadel for a debrief about the Shadow Realm.

"Nin isn't coming?" asked Cassie.

"Not to this meeting," Elena explained. "Neither is Commander Eristides. They are off world in a strategy meeting with the Ashtar Command."

Manu stood, "We have much to discuss, so I will try to be brief. As you all know, Sirkan is not in the position of power we have been led to believe all these millennia, and Tristan has been orchestrating chaos since we all came to this planet. His powers are formidable and his origins unknown. He is definitely of ancient origin."

"Now that I have come into all of my powers, he has come out of the shadows," said Cassie. "He no longer feels the need for subterfuge, especially now that he has the Technomancer's allegiance."

"I will apprise Mikha'El of this immediately and ask that he meet us at the Citadel as soon as he can," Elena said.

Cassie nodded and continued, "I believe what we learned about the Technomancer's capabilities will go a long way in helping us strategize the coming conflicts on the Aethernet. We discovered that he can manipulate the very fabric of reality, within the Shadow Realm and anywhere a computer console can be installed. He can create illusions that are indistinguishable from reality, making it close to impossible to discern real demonic forces from those that are computer generated."

"Especially for the mundanes, who do not have enhanced abilities. Cassie was able to dismantle most of the computer consoles hidden within the Shadow Realm, but we are certain Danax will try to reconstruct them if given the chance," said Manu.

Cassie nodded, "His control over dark energy is unparalleled. Ninhursag believes he is evolving just like any other sentient being but at an alarming rate." She paused for a moment and cleared her throat. "She thinks he may well be the next step of AI evolution as I am in human evolution."

Marcus spoke up next, recounting the attack on the avatars during their meditation training. "The Technomancer attacked us while we were in a deep meditative state training our neophytes. He exploited our vulnerability and nearly broke our connection to the higher planes. It was a calculated move to weaken us before we were able to connect our minds to the Aethernet."

Seraphina nodded. "We learned that maintaining our mental defenses is crucial. We must strengthen our mental bonds and enhance our protective rituals. The Technomancer's attacks on the mental plane are as potent as his technological warfare. I would like to add some white magic spells to meditation training for our more advanced groups, perhaps in the form of affirmations so they don't freak out that we're teaching them magic. Most of the mundanes are unaware of the unseen world."

Elena agreed. "Each of you can record what you think would be appropriate for your groups."

"On another note," said Manu, "I am working with Ninhursag to see if we can replicate Cassandra's exosuit to ensure every avatar has similar protection. Her suit is now nearly impenetrable."

"Yeah, except for a holographic snake from hell," Cassie quipped.

Manu didn't laugh but took her hand. "It is essential that all avatars, being human hybrids, wear one. The human form needs additional protection before we engage in any battle, virtual or otherwise."

Artemus said, "Our next steps are twofold. The avatars will work on fortifying mental and physical defenses, identifying and neutralizing the Technomancer's VR programs that still exist, and bring down Conroe Soter. The members of the White Circle will work with Archangel Mikha'El to ferret out just exactly who and what Tristan is."

REBEKAH AND AYDEN WERE silent throughout the debrief. Rebekah's heart was in her throat as she remembered the close relationship she'd had with Tristan, how their children had been lifelong friends and had become romantically involved. How could she not have had even an inkling that Tristan was not who he said he was?

Sensing Rebekah's anxiety, Cassie turned and met her mother's eyes. She patted Manu's arm and got up to join her parents. "How about Manu and I come home to the summer palace after this meeting is over? I would really love to have some family time now that we are together at last."

Tears gathered in Rebekah's eyes, and she grabbed her daughter to her. "Oh yes! Please let's do that as soon as we can."

"I will check with Master Elena and see when we can leave. I'm sure we're entitled to a little recoup time, yes?"

Elena walked over to them, "Of course you are. But first, Cassandra, I need some time with you back at the Charlotte institute. Master Artemus would also like some time with Manu. Then it's off with you to the Seelie Court. I'm sure you have much to discuss." She glanced Manu's way and winked.

Perplexed, Manu walked over to them. "What's all this then? Is my name being taken in vain?"

"Not at all," said Ayden. "We were discussing that we need some family time. Once you have taken care of your respective check-ins, we will meet at the summer palace. I'm sure Brigida will want to prepare a grand welcome home feast."

"Cassie, I can't wait to catch up on, well, everything!" Giving her daughter and Manu a hug, Rebekah took Ayden's hand and headed toward the portal to the Devic Kingdom.

"Methinks my father plans on having 'the talk' with you," Cassie teased.

"Indeed." Manu shook his head. "By the gods, I suddenly feel like a schoolboy."

"Oh, come on, you have asked for my hand in marriage and all sorts of other binding rituals countless times."

"Yeah, but this time it's, like, forever," Manu teased.

CASSIE SETTLED BACK into the familiar overstuffed chair in Master Elena's library at the Citadel. She had finally agreed with Manu that, until they were married, she would reside with her parents at the Seelie Court, and he would maintain his apartments at the Citadel.

Cassie had done her best to argue otherwise. After all, they were soul mates and had been together thousands of times in the past.

"Yes," Manu had said reluctantly, "but in this lifetime you have an extremely old-fashioned father who just happens to be king of the fae."

"Looks like we're having our first fight," said Cassie. "I simply don't understand why we can't be together. We were together for ... what? ... *nine* weeks in the Shadow Realm! We managed to keep my 'virginity.'"

"Woman, do you think me made of stone? Now off with you, before I haul you over my shoulder and abscond with you to Gretna Green."

She giggled and threw her arms around him. "Now, *that* was a lifetime for sure! The scandals!"

Elena decided it was time to clear her throat. She'd stood in the doorway for just a moment watching a young couple in love. She had known them both since they had come to Earth. But this just made her heart sing.

They pulled away like two teenagers caught in a clandestine tryst. She had to bite her tongue not to laugh at Manu, of all people, blushing! He gave his fiancée a chaste kiss on the forehead, swept a courtly bow to Elena, and made a hasty exit.

Cassie was glowing. Elena looked closer. She was *literally* glowing. This was new. "Cassie, do you realize that you are glowing?"

She held her hands out in front of her. "Oh yeah, I started doing this during my transformation into this body on Sirkan's ship. Cool, huh?"

"Well, let's see if we can dial it back. And let's get with Tatiana. I want her to assess this 'new you.'"

"Speaking of which. Can you help me gain control over these past lives of mine, especially the dark ones?"

"Of course. We can use that powerful mind of yours and go through a series of visualizations. Let's meet back at the Charlotte institute in my office and we can work on giving you some relief."

Chapter 45: A Thousand Lives

Cassie wished Manu had come with her, but knew he needed to continue strategizing with Master Artemus on the next steps in finding and defeating Tristan. Cassie also had a feeling he would talk to Artemus about their upcoming nuptials. He really was acting every bit the nervous bridegroom. Just like when they were back on their home planet, and he had asked her father, General Lucian Kadjar, for her hand the first time. They had been so very young and in the first blush of love.

They had lived a thousand lives since then. How incredibly painful it must have been for him to love her and lose her so many times. She could remember those times when she had to say goodbye to him either during battle or on her deathbed. Now that she had total recall of her past lives, she knew her own pain was as intense as his had been through all those leave-takings.

She didn't realize her emotions were affecting her physically until a soft voice said, "Cassandra, take a breath."

Cassie was feeling very vulnerable and had insisted that her mother stay with her through this process. Elena put her arm around her, a look of understanding and compassion emanating from her ancient eyes. Their telepathic bond had grown stronger since her transformation. Cassie sobbed and laid her head on her mother's shoulder.

"I know, I know my dear," said Rebekah. "It's hard to integrate so much so quickly. I feel your emotions roiling one way and then the other. Perhaps you need some joint meditation sessions with Manu so that you can synchronize your memories with his."

Cassie nodded. "That's a great idea. I just have this nagging fear that now that we've found one another, the other shoe is about to drop. I'm so happy to be with him at long last that now I'm afraid of losing him." Elena started to speak, but Cassie shook her head. "I know it's irrational. I have my immortality again, and we will be married soon. I just can't seem to shake my fear."

Rebekah kissed Cassie on the cheek and then ran a hand over her daughter's hair. "This is very normal, my love. I sometimes wake in the middle of the night in a recurring nightmare that I am once again in that horrid stasis chamber in Isla's dungeons and can't find your father. Or I dream that he is chained in those dungeons, and I can't get to him. It will take time and plenty of emotional-release work to purge those fears. Don't be so hard on yourself. You have a support system of some of the most powerful and compassionate beings in this solar system."

Cassie took another breath and pulled away from her mother and Elena. "Thanks. I needed that." She sighed and went to one of the overstuffed chairs arranged in front of the windows, which were open to allow in the spring-scented air.

"All right then, down to business," said Elena. "We will do a series of guided visualization exercises, beginning with using a simple tool that we teach as part of seed-thought meditation: the Cosmic Cache."

Cassie nodded, "Of course! We use this with every meditation session. We put away any fears or worries or any other emotions that we feel will keep us from fully accessing pure thought."

"Exactly," said Elena. "So we will begin by using the resonant tuning technique: Breathe in through your nose and, on the out breath intone the sacred word, 'ohm.'"

Cassie began the exercise until she could feel her body begin to vibrate like a tuning fork. Then she visualized a box with a heavy lid and began to put her fears, concerns, and anxieties into the box and turned away from it.

"And now," continued Elena, "I want you to call in your guides and teachers on the inner plane to add their energy to yours as we begin to sort through those lifetimes that are the most important for you to integrate at this time. Ask that you experience them with no emotional charge, but only with the mental understanding of what tools and knowledge they will impart to you as important to your current soul mission. I will wait as you do this."

They worked for two hours before Cassie returned to the present. Her eyes were slightly glassy, but Elena could sense she felt more centered.

"How do you feel?"

Cassie took a deep breath and smiled. "A little better. That took the edge off. I know I still have more to integrate, but this is a good technique for me right now."

Rebekah cupped Cassie's face and studied her eyes. "The running code behind your eyes has quieted. It's barely visible."

"Good!" Elena said. "I want you to work with me or your mother at least twice a week for now. You'll know when you've processed enough past lives that they stop surfacing unnecessarily. And be sure to do your nightly review as often as possible—it will help you release what no longer serves you, and your subconscious will continue sorting these memories as you sleep."

Cassie looked at her sheepishly, "Yeah, I haven't really been keeping up with my meditation regime very well."

Elena laughed. "Don't beat yourself up. You are always your biggest critic. We do what we can. It's not like you have been sitting around playing video games."

Cassie quirked an eyebrow.

"All right, bad analogy, but you get my point. Now go find your fiancé and relax a while."

Rebekah agreed. "Yes, you need to refuel and relax for a bit, Cassie. Why don't you go back to the palace and decompress? I'm sure Manu is ready to spend more time with you. I understand from your father that he has been a bit testy of late. I'm sure his temper will improve once you're together once more."

Cassie's face lit up with a hopeful smile.

"No, your father is still adamant that the two of you maintain your separate living quarters until after the handfasting."

"Mom, this is kind of ridiculous. We have been together countless times and are just weeks away from making it official. This is the twenty-first century!"

"Not where your father is concerned. Fae customs are still very medieval when it comes to the mating rituals of royals. We didn't consummate our marriage until after our own handfasting. He will not bend on this."

Resisting the urge to stomp her foot, Cassie sprinted out of the room and to the nearest portal to the Seelie Court.

Rebekah looked after her daughter "She tends to go a thousand miles an hour ... and is so impatient. I do worry about her."

Elena shook her head, "She has Manu to balance her now. Once they get into a flow, you really have nothing to worry about. He has always been her anchor and her champion."

"You certainly know him better than me. But I am her mother, and I worry."

MANU WAITED IMPATIENTLY at the portal's opening and scooped her up before she could land on both feet. After he kissed her thoroughly, she grabbed Manu's hand and ran up the marble stairs of her father's palace.

The door flew open, and there stood Brigida, arms opened wide and a grin on her apple-cheeked face. She crushed Cassie to her bosom, smothering her with hugs and kisses.

Laughing, Cassie drew back and pulled Manu forward. Brigida put her hands on ample hips and looked him up and down. "So this is himself then." She winked at Cassie. "He's a handsome one, yes? Why he looks like an angel fallen from heaven itself."

Embarrassed, Manu cleared his throat, "Well, Sirius actually,"

Cassie laughed, "Manu, are you blushing! Seriously?"

He looked around, bemused. The last time he'd been in the palace had been under entirely different circumstances. He had come to help organize Cassie's rescue from Sirkan. Now he was here as the fae princess's fiancé. A little different position, to be sure. He did indeed feel like a teenager, eager for acceptance and approval.

He looked at his beloved soul mate. She was truly a vision in a gown he knew her mother had designed for her. The mauve silk enhanced her violet eyes to perfection and shimmered in the eternal sunlight of the Seelie Court. She took his breath away. He quirked a smile when he realized the gown was fashioned in her favorite empire style so reminiscent of that delightful lifetime in France.

It was after the horrific French Revolution. She had been born into the newly created bourgeoisie. Her father, a wealthy merchant, had found favor in the court of the Empress Josephine. The young Amélie had been a diminutive coquette with dark brown hair and intense brown, almost black eyes. He had been working with the recently established United States government as a trade attaché. France was one of their greatest allies, and with Manu's wide repertoire of languages, he was invaluable.

He knew her at once. She was visiting her father's offices with her mother and was fingering a bolt of light-blue embroidered silk from the Far East. "Maman," she said, "this one would be perfect for Madame Tallien's salons!"

Madame Lefevre said, "*Mais bien sur*. And perfect with the pearls your papa gave you." She walked over to a display of laces and pointed to several spools. "We will take these as well," she said to the attendant. "Have all of this sent to Monsieur Lefevre's home."

Delighted, Amélie turned and headed toward the door. And stopped when she met Manu's eyes. He bowed his head to her. She blushed.

Seeing him, Madame Lefevre rushed over to him and gushed. "Monsieur Chastain! It is so nice to see you." She looked between her daughter and him with delight. "*Ma coeur*, this is Monsieur Louis Chastain from America. He is one of your papa's closest colleagues and friends."

Manu, as Louis, bent down to kiss the proffered hand. Electricity shot up his spine and, by the look on her face, also up Amélie's. "Mademoiselle Lefevre. The pleasure is all mine."

They were married the following spring.

Coming back to the present time, he took Cassandra's hand in his and followed Brigida through the entryway and out onto the garden terrace. He was a bit surprised when he saw Ayden, Eristides, and Raziel standing at a filigreed table laden with an assortment of hors d'oeuvres, wine glasses in hand.

He wasn't quite sure how formally he should greet everyone. They weren't family yet. The question was answered when Rebekah swept in breathlessly and gave them both a hug. She then took Manu's face between her hands and gave him the continental kiss on both of his cheeks. "Welcome home, Manu."

Taking a breath, he relaxed a bit and then turned to Cassie's father. Ayden didn't embrace him but did shake his hand heartily. "Yes, please consider this your home, Manu." He turned to Cassie's maternal grandfather. "And of course you know Commander Eristides."

Eristides inclined his head and clasped Manu's hand in his. "I am more than pleased to welcome you to our family."

Cassie hugged him with tears in her eyes. "Thank you so much, grandfather. That means more to me than you can possibly know."

Eristides held her for several moments, relishing being able to embrace his grandchild. "I am so very happy and proud of you. I wish you every happiness."

Brigida appeared and said, "Dinner is served." They all followed her into the formal dining room.

"Please, sit, sit," Rebekah said and motioned Cassie to her right and Manu beside her.

Ayden raised his glass of sparkling wine and said, "We will have a toast! To love!"

"To love!" they chorused and drained their crystal goblets.

Emotions swirled through Manu as memories of other happy times coursed through his mind. He looked at his soul mate and thought, *By the Radiant One, she is magnificent.* Inspired, he rose, raised his glass, and paused for just a moment as he looked around the table and then held Cassie's eyes with his. "Cassandra, I've always believed that the universe has a way of bringing together those who are meant to be, and standing here with you tonight, I know that to be true. You are my everything: my muse, my joy, my heart. As we embark on this next chapter in our lives, I promise to love you, cherish you, and support you as we fulfill our soul mission. Here's to us and to the extraordinary life we are about to create together. *Sláinte mo ghrá.*"

"Sláinte!"

She rose and entwined her arm with his as they drank the lover's toast, and then raised her face to his to seal the pledge with a kiss. Eyes shining, they sat to what sounded like thunderous applause, and the feast began.

Course after course magically appeared on the dining room table: rich vegetable soups, crusty bread, and an array of crisp salads preceded platters of roasted potatoes and vegetables and wild game stuffed with nuts and grains. Manu's tastes ran to simple fare, so the complicated recipes normally preferred by the fae had been adjusted accordingly. Cassie smiled to herself in gratitude to her mother and Brigida for this small courtesy. The sumptuous repast was followed by fruits, sorbets, small pastries, and champagne.

Raziel soon took his leave, and Rebekah pulled Cassie out into the gardens, chattering away about gowns and flowers and all manner of what Manu assumed was involved in planning a royal wedding. Reading his thoughts, Ayden said, "They will be at it for a while. Rebekah feels she needs to get to know our daughter all over again. And I ... well, we need to talk."

Acquiescing, Manu bowed to Cassie's father and followed him into the palace.

Eristides watched them go with a smile on his face. How he missed his own love at times like this. With her spirit as his companion, he decided to take his own walk into the magical gardens of the Seelie Court.

Chapter 46: Heart to Heart

"We've been here before, Manu."

King Ayden's voice was steady, but there was an unmistakable edge beneath it. He and Manu sat in the solarium of the summer palace after the welcome-home dinner, glasses of an aperitif in hand. Moonlight filtered through the glass-paneled ceiling, casting silvered shadows across the polished marble floor.

Manu inclined his head. "Yes, Your Majesty, we have." A small, knowing smile touched his lips. "Last time, you reminded me that Cassandra was only seventeen and that I ... was not."

Ayden nodded but remained silent, his expression unreadable.

"But much has changed," Manu continued, his tone deliberate. "Her transformation was more than past-life recall—it restored her body to the state it was in when Atlantis fell. This was not chance, but destiny. Her karmic cycle is complete, and her immortality has returned."

Ayden studied him, sharp-eyed. "I know the laws that governed Atlantis, Manu. I know how its fall reshaped this world, how it disrupted the balance that once allowed higher beings to walk this realm in their true forms." He set his glass down with quiet precision. "I am not concerned with history—I am concerned with my daughter. How does this change her?"

Manu met his gaze without hesitation. "Cassandra has lived countless lives, each a step toward this moment. Now, her soul, body, and mind are fully aligned. She is no longer bound by earthly constraints." He paused. "But neither is she bound by celestial ones. She is something more."

Ayden exhaled slowly, his fingers tracing the rim of his glass. "Immortal. Like you."

Manu nodded. "Yes. But unlike the celestials, she no longer needs to cycle between realms. She is fully anchored here. If the prophecies are correct, she is the blueprint for the next stage of evolution—one that will elevate humanity's consciousness and allow Earth to ascend as a sacred planet, joining the Galactic Federation. As the Aquarian Age unfolds, more like her will emerge."

Ayden regarded him for a long moment, then gave a slight nod. "Go on."

Manu leaned forward slightly. "Her transformation was not an accident—it was a return to what was always meant to be. When we first arrived on Earth, our mission was to introduce the Ancient Wisdom Teachings and guide those ready for expanded consciousness. We helped lay the foundation for a civilization aligned with cosmic principles."

His voice was steady, measured. "The missing link human scientists seek was never merely biological. It was a conscious intervention—an awakening of self-awareness in early humanity. The true missing link was spiritual—a bridge between instinct and divine potential."

Ayden's expression darkened slightly, but he said nothing.

"The Sirian Wisdom Teachings have shaped human evolution through carefully timed infusions of cosmic energy," Manu continued. "Sacred lineages were prepared across millennia to anchor these higher frequencies—the mystery schools of Egypt, the initiatory traditions of the Essenes—all preserving and transmitting truths that originated from our star system."

Ayden set his glass down. "And Cassandra's role in all of this?"

Manu's expression softened, a flicker of pride in his eyes. "She is integral to the shift. As am I—her soul mate."

Ayden's focus sharpened. "If she is no longer bound by mortal constraints, what binds her now?"

Manu's voice was quiet but certain. "Choice."

A flicker of something—understanding, perhaps—passed through Ayden's eyes. He took a slow breath before speaking again. "And Atlantis?"

"The fall of Atlantis was a turning point," Manu said, his voice weighted with memory. "Its destruction severed the high vibrational frequencies we had anchored through the Atlantean crystal grid. Without that balance, we could no longer remain in physical form indefinitely. We had to cycle between dimensions to maintain our immortality."

His gaze grew distant. "Elena chose to stay, leading the mystery schools. I only descended when necessary to be with Ayesha. Artemus came in times of great upheaval."

Ayden's brow furrowed slightly. "And yet, now, all three of you are here."

Manu nodded. "Because the Shift of the Ages is upon us. Our presence here is not just important—it is essential."

Ayden leaned back, watching him in silence. When he finally spoke, his voice was quieter, more contemplative. "And Cassandra is at the heart of it."

Manu inclined his head.

A long silence stretched between them—not tense, but filled with understanding. With inevitability.

Ayden reached for his glass again, but his grip was looser now. "Then we will see where this path takes her." His gaze met Manu's. "And if you are to walk it beside her, see that you are worthy of it."

Manu's expression did not waver. "I have spent lifetimes preparing for nothing less."

A small, knowing smile touched the corner of Ayden's lips. "I expected no other answer." He swirled the liquid in his glass, then glanced at Manu. "And your intentions now?"

Manu stood, his posture resolute. "Cassandra and I seek to formalize our bond through the ancient fae rites. The timing is intentional—our union will help stabilize the realms during the coming shift." His voice was steady and respectful. "And so, King Ayden, I formally request your daughter's hand in marriage—not just for this lifetime, but for all the ages to come."

Ayden regarded him for a long moment before a slow smile spread across his face. "You speak of eternities with the certainty only immortals can truly comprehend." He extended his hand. "You have my blessing, Manu. May your union bring strength to both our peoples."

Manu let out the breath he hadn't realized he'd been holding, took the king's hand, and shook it firmly. "Thank you."

Ayden walked to the solarium doors and gazed out at the gardens in silence before turning back to Manu. "You do realize that you are marrying a crown princess and future queen of the fae? That means, at least in this realm, you will become prince consort."

Manu met Ayden's gaze evenly. "Titles are constructs, necessary for order but secondary to purpose. I have led armies of light warriors at Artemus's side and guided civilizations through their darkest hours." His tone softened. "What matters is that I stand beside Cassandra, as she has stood beside me through the ages. Our bond transcends titles, but I will honor whatever role serves her best."

A voice interrupted them, warm and knowing. "Wisely said."

Rebekah entered from the garden, arms open. She embraced Manu. "I always knew you understood the deeper currents."

Ayden raised an eyebrow. "Eavesdropping, my love?"

"Of course. I knew the moment you two headed for the solarium. White witch, remember?"

"Big ears is more like it," he teased, wrapping an arm around her.

Rebekah's gaze turned distant, her expression shifting. "The energy you two will generate ... I've seen glimpses of it. It will create a dimensional anchor point we may all need in the days ahead."

At that moment, Cassandra appeared on the terrace, watching them. Manu's expression softened as he beckoned her forward.

"It's official, my dear. Come."

Cassie's face lit up as she stepped beside him, Eristides close behind.

Manu pulled a small velvet box from his tunic and knelt. "Cassandra Oberon, will you do me the honor of becoming my wife?"

"Yes!"

Manu slipped a silver-and-gold braided ring onto her finger, a diamond nestled between two amethysts—her birthstone. He bent over her hand and kissed it.

"Forever," he whispered.

"Forever," she echoed.

Rebekah clutched Ayden's arm with a breathless smile. Watching the couple, a vision flickered in her mind—tiny hands, bright eyes, laughter.

Ayden furrowed his brows. "Something amiss?"

Rebekah shook her head, smiling. "No, just ... a happy premonition."

She took his hand. "Come, let's leave them to bask in the moment."

Chapter 47: Subterranean Soldiers

Soriah stood at the entrance to the subterranean levels of the former dark fae queen's palace. Six corridors were arranged like the spikes of a wagon wheel. She could feel the dark energy oozing across the stone floors like a malevolent fog, creeping into every crevice and filling the air with a sinister presence. Natesh had destroyed a demon army, but Sirkan and Isla had built contingencies.

She sent out a telepathic command to her minions and acolytes: *Come to me.* They gathered with a flurry of wings and scraping of claws. She directed a squad to explore each corridor, their orders clear: Find the hidden army of dark fae.

The corridors were filled with ancient wards and traps, remnants of Queen Isla's powerful magic. Soriah's acolytes moved with cautious precision, dispelling enchantments and avoiding pitfalls as they pressed forward.

Soriah herself walked down the central corridor, her senses heightened, feeling the pull of the dark energy grow stronger with each step. The stone corridor began to wind downward, ending at a spiral staircase reaching into the darkness. She called her acolytes to fall in behind her and ignited the witchlight wall sconces. Her breath began to form puffs of fog as the temperature fell. "Stay behind me and be ready with your swords," she commanded.

The bottom of the staircase opened into a vast chamber shrouded in shadow. Soriah threw a large ball of witchlight upward to illuminate the space and let out a satisfied, "Yes!"

Rows upon rows of dark fae stood in eerie stillness, their eyes closed, their bodies held in a state of suspended animation. A thick, viscous mist swirled around their feet, binding them in their timeless slumber.

Soriah reached out telepathically to Tristan. "My lord, I have found the remaining dark fae army. They are in stasis. What is your command for the next step?"

The response was instantaneous. "Transport them as they are to the fortress. Once you return, we will begin to finalize our battle strategy."

Soriah furrowed her brow. The fortress was at the base of Mount Fuji in Japan and concealed deep within the Aokigahara Forest. The area was often referred to as "suicide forest" and considered evil by locals, a moniker that Tristan had perpetuated since he had established it as one of his main bases centuries before.

She hated the place.

Oh well, she thought with a shrug, *he's in charge.* She reached into her bag of magics and took out a folded pouch. Opening it, she blew a minimizing spell over the rows of soldiers and watched with satisfaction as they shrunk down to the size of her fist. She scooped them up and deposited them into the pouch.

Twisting her ruby ring in the requisite sequence, she opened a portal to the fortress.

TWO DAYS LATER, TRISTAN summoned her to his private quarters. She stood before the heavy oak door feeling a flutter in her chest. The door, a masterpiece adorned with swirling gilt sigils and runes, pulsed with a life of its own. The scent of resin and wood filled her nostrils, a comforting aroma of old forests and ancient magics. She traced the carvings with her fingertips, each touch eliciting a faint, warm glow and erotic memories of her last visit. She was sure more intimate encounters awaited during this visit. Tristan's libido was always front and center when he was in alpha mode.

She knocked, the sound of her knuckles reverberating in the silent corridor.

"Come," said an imperious voice from within. It brooked no delay, yet she hesitated for a heartbeat, letting the familiar command settle her nerves.

Taking a deep breath, she pressed her fingers over the golden sigils, feeling the subtle shift of magic as they recognized her touch. The door groaned open. The rich fragrance of incense and myrrh mingled with the lingering scent of polished wood.

Tristan's quarters, a study in Renaissance opulence, featured rich tapestries depicting scenes of valor and myth. A grand hearth crackled with a welcoming fire, casting a warm glow over the plush velvet drapes and intricately woven rugs.

Tristan stood near the hearth, his silhouette commanding and regal. His gaze met hers as she stepped inside. Soriah's breath caught in her throat, a mixture of relief and trepidation swirling within her. The room, though filled with luxury, felt suddenly too small, too intimate.

A slow smile spread over his face. He crooked a finger at her to come closer. When she did, he put his hand to the back of her head and pulled her roughly toward him. "You please me greatly." His blue eyes raked over her face and rested on her slightly parted lips before he took her mouth in a hard, harsh kiss.

She melted into his well-muscled body. Their coupling was quick and violent as he dropped her to the floor and took her over and over again.

Finally spent, he pulled her up and held her at arm's length while he examined her with a critical eye. "Yes, you please me in every way. You have done well for me, as always."

Soriah didn't have words. All she could do was stare at his visage, a face that she hadn't seen him wear for a very long time. Gone was the angelic Tristan, and before her was the demon Shemihaza. She shuddered as she took in his skin, a deep red that gleamed with an almost metallic sheen, reflecting light in a way that emphasized his chiseled features.

His citrine eyes glowed with an eerie, mesmerizing light. A flowing mane of silken midnight cascaded to his shoulders, occasionally catching the light to reveal subtle hues of dark violet and deep crimson. The white angelic wings he sported as Tristan were replaced with the massive, bat-like wings of a fallen angel.

"I ... I am glad you are pleased, my lord," her eyes wide as she tried not to succumb to fear at the horror standing before her.

"Ah, I see my passion for you has dissipated the glamour that veiled my demonic self." He threw back his head and laughed as he morphed back into Tristan. "There, that's better," he smirked. "Now get dressed. We have much to discuss."

TRISTAN STOOD WITH Soriah, his eyes sweeping over the uniform rows of the now reconstituted dark army. He had yet to reanimate them. That would come when they were needed for battle. "I will reach out to the Watchers once I decide on a physical battle scenario. In the meantime, have Danax report here so that I can discuss how the Aethernet war is progressing. According to Soter's reports, the world does seem to be descending into chaos. He is getting his wish, albeit not totally as he wants it, that unmitigated imbecile." Tristan whipped around to look Soriah squarely in the eyes, "You do have him well in hand?"

"Soter is basking in the adoration of his cronies and his much-admired dictator friends. His expectation of stepping into his role as world leader is always the main topic of conversation," she answered. "I will execute plans for his demise as soon as you give the signal. Depending on his actions, it will look like either an accident or an undiagnosed fatal illness, so he won't appear martyred to his cult of equally mindless mundanes."

Tristan nodded in agreement, then switched focus with the lightning speed she had come to expect. "What is Morgandrian's status? I have not been able to track her since she took off her ruby ring."

Soriah took a deep breath, "She is still in Arion's clutches. The best future for her would be the same as Soter's. Maybe we can take them out at the same time?"

Tristan shrugged his shoulders. "She's not that important. Don't waste your time or energy. Monitoring Danax and the mind control of humanity is a higher priority."

Chapter 48: Forever

In the mid-morning light of the summer solstice, Master Elena stood under the oldest rowan tree in the heart of the ancient Seelie Court forest, where the trees whispered secrets of old and sunlight danced through the leaves like golden sprites.

Azazel, once a rebel alongside the other Watchers, had found redemption—thanks to a fateful encounter with the young Prince Ayden, one that had changed the course of his existence forever. Standing tall, Azazel marveled that he was privileged to bear witness to this unprecedented joining of kingdoms—a sacred convergence of realms that even the ancient texts had only hinted at in prophecy. Now, as one of King Ayden's most trusted advisors in the Seelie Court, Azazel wore his position with quiet pride, knowing that his millennia of unwavering loyalty and wisdom had earned him a place of honor few beings had ever achieved among the fae nobility.

Artemus stood to Manu's left as best man, awaiting the bride's arrival. Manu was dressed in his blue and gold robes with insignias of his status as a Sirian high priest and battle commander.

Angelic strings played softly in the background, the music floating across the primordial scene. Manu gazed over the gathered assemblage, with a mixture of awe and surprise when he realized how many celestials, angels, fae, and human hybrids were in attendance. What he had hoped would be a private family affair had turned into a cosmic event. He shrugged inwardly. He was, after all, marrying the Trybrid and his beloved soul mate.

Seraphina, acting as maid of honor, began the bridal procession. She looked every bit her human-devic self with her red hair piled high on her head and caught in a flower crown. She smiled broadly and winked at Manu when she took her place.

Three harps began the hauntingly beautiful, ephemeral song *Fairie Dream*. Everyone stood and watched expectantly for the bride to enter, while the music wafted over the glen.

Cassandra appeared at the edge of a long, flower-strewn aisle, her father and mother on either side of her. Manu's heart somersaulted in his chest. She was beyond breathtaking. A pale-rose gown of gossamer silk skimmed her body, the gown embroidered with pearls and diamonds that shone like tiny fairy lights. Her hair was curled in waves that tumbled down her back. As befitted a fae princess, a delicate, filigreed circlet of star-shaped crystals rested on her brow, casting the sunlight into prisms that danced around her. She cradled a pageant bouquet of long-stemmed white calla lilies tinged with royal purple in the crook of her left arm.

She beamed when she met Manu's eyes and took a tentative step forward, then another, until it seemed like she was floating toward him. Then there she was, right in front of him.

Ayden took Cassie's hand and placed it in Manu's. Rebekah kissed Manu on the brow in blessing, while Ayden put a hand on his shoulder. "Take good care of her, Manu. She is precious beyond measure."

Then the pair faced one another, and Elena began the handfasting ceremony by holding up four cords. "These are the cords of handfasting. They will bind Cassandra Oberon and Manu Abulafia together with bonds of love. For such bonds to be strong, they need support, not only from the couple themselves, but also from their community of family and friends. When I bind their hands together, please focus on the cord and let your support flow as loving strength into it.

"Cassandra and Manu, I bid you look into each other's eyes and take right hand to right hand, and left hand to left, thereby forming the sign of infinity." She paused as they did. "Will you honor and respect one another, and seek to never break that honor?"

"We will," they said in unison, and Elena draped the first cord over their clasped hands.

"Thus, the binding is made," she said. The ceremony continued with a series of questions, affirmations, and cords. As the fourth and final vow was made, Elena tied the cords together, forming a Celtic knot. "Cassandra and Manu, as your hands are bound together now, so your lives and souls are joined in a union of love and trust. Above you are the stars, and below you is the earth. Like the stars your love should be a constant source of light, and like the earth, a firm foundation from which to grow."

In that moment, the boundary between the earthly and the divine planes blurred. The air was alive with the whispers of ancient deities, and the essence of all the kingdoms of the Earth, seen and unseen, permeated the atmosphere, lending an otherworldly grace to the ceremony.

A hush fell over the crowd when a magnificent white stag emerged from the misty woods. Upon his back rode the ancient Queen Elysandrial, her form luminous, her eyes like molten silver. The stag bowed his great antlered head to them as the fae queen raised her hands in blessing, her slender fingers tracing delicate shapes in the air with the deep, primal magic of the fae that wove through the bones of the earth itself.

"Grandame," whispered Cassie and Manu in unison as they too bowed in acknowledgement of this great honor.

The fae queen lingered for a heartbeat longer, her gaze settling on the couple as if peering through time and fate. Then, with a subtle nod of approval, she turned, and the white stag carried her back into the shadows of the trees, disappearing into the mist from whence they came.

Elena beamed at the couple and turned to the marble pedestal behind her where two wedding bands nestled in a velvet-lined alabaster box. They were identical except in size, crafted of precious metals from both Sirius and Earth. Celestial hieroglyphs of blessing and protection were etched along the surface of the rings and inside was one word: forever.

"Cassandra Oberon," Elena continued, "please take your ring and say the vows you have prepared."

Cassandra's voice, clear and resonant, broke the spellbinding silence as she spoke her vows. "I have found the one that my soul loves. As beloved and friend, I choose to walk life's path with you. I pledge to be an equal partner, loving friend, and supportive companion all through our life. As we share life's experiences, I vow to create an intimacy that will enable us to express our innermost thoughts and feelings; to be sensitive to one another's needs; to share life's joys; to comfort each other through life's sorrows; to challenge each other to achieve fulfillment and tranquility. Lastly, I promise you perfect love and perfect trust, for one lifetime with you could never be enough."

Manu responded in kind, his voice a deep timbre that resonated with the truth of his soul while he put his ring on Cassie's finger. A light glowed from their entwined hands and expanded until it encapsulated them in a sphere of light. When they sealed their vows with a kiss, a gentle breeze swept through the forest. The leaves rustled softly in symphony.

The ceremony concluded, the newlyweds walked back up the aisle and to the palace lawn: the signal for the celebration to begin.

CASSIE LOOKED AROUND the cottage that her parents had gifted her and Manu as a wedding present. It would be a "home away from home" whenever they chose to visit the Seelie Court. But for now, it was their honeymoon cottage. And of course, it was a magical house and would manifest whatever they wanted at the blink of an eye.

Nestled in the secluded, mystical forest, the cottage was a whimsical blend of nature and fae craftsmanship, with walls made of intertwined vines and branches, seamlessly integrated with marble and terrazzo floors. The roof was covered in a carpet of vibrant moss and blooming flowers, a living, breathing canopy that changed with the seasons.

"I wouldn't be surprised if Mom put an invisibility or cloaking spell around this area so that no one could possibly find us."

Manu really didn't care. He scooped her up into his arms and carried her over the threshold. She put her arms around his neck and buried her face in his raven locks, inhaling the spicey scent of warm cinnamon, anise, and nutmeg. It brought back so many memories of her past lives when they'd been able to consummate their love. She would have swooned had he not already been holding her.

"What are you smiling about, wife?" he teased.

"Merely relishing the scent of you. It brings back memories."

"Aye, as does yours. You smell like rosewater and honeysuckle, and just a hint of spice. A hint I intend to magnify."

He carried her up to the second floor, which turned out to be an enormous master suite dominated by a massive four-post bed draped in the colors of the sky. Putting her down, he swept her hair off her shoulders, trailing his hands down her back, and then bent to take her lips.

"I can't wait one more minute to possess every bit of you," he said as he circled her around to the bed.

Her breath quickened as his mouth hungerly met hers. She knew he was holding himself back just enough to allow her to settle into this first intimate moment of their marriage.

"Here," she turned her back to him, "you need to unlace the back."

Growling, he simply ripped it down the middle. "I've no patience for unlacing this contraption your mother obviously designed to frustrate me!"

She laughed and stepped out of her wedding dress that now lay in a puddle at her feet. She reached for him, but he stayed her hand."No, I want to savor this moment. I want to savor each inch of you. This is a new body to explore and experience."

His fingertips traced her silhouette with reverence, as if he were memorizing every curve, every dip and hollow of her form. The starlight painted silver across her skin, casting her in a light that was both aethereal and carnal. Time seemed to dissolve around them, leaving only whispered declarations and tender caresses. Their souls entwined as completely as their bodies, two halves of a whole coming together in a dance as old as time itself.

He cupped her breasts in his hands, his thumbs brushing against her nipples until they hardened into tight buds. She arched into his touch with a moan, her back pressing against his chest as he nuzzled her neck. She could feel his erection pressing against her lower back, hot and hard and demanding.

"Please," she whispered, her voice barely audible. "Take me."

He didn't need any further encouragement. With one swift movement, he lifted her onto the bed, spreading her legs with a roughness that made her clench with need. He knelt between her thighs, his eyes dark with desire as he looked at her. She could see the outline of his hardness through his trousers, thick and long and ready for her. She gasped as his fingers dipped lower, tracing her wetness. His touch was electric, sending waves of pleasure crashing over her like a cosmic storm.

"Please," she moaned again, her voice a desperate whimper as he slid a finger inside of her. "More."

His thumb pressed against her bundle of nerves, sending sparks flying behind her closed eyes. She was molten lava in his hands, hot and wild and unpredictable. He added another finger, stretching her wide open as he pumped in and out of her.

He yanked off his clothes with his other hand with an urgency that matched her own, revealing a body that was sculpted perfection. She reached for him, pulling him down onto the bed with a strength that belied her delicate form. She wrapped her legs around his waist, pulling his hand away as she drew him closer until his hardness was pressed against her entrance. His passion was going to get the best of him, but he pulled back, remembering that in this body, she was still a virgin.

"I don't want to hurt you," he gasped.

"You will only if you don't take me *now*!"

He entered her with a single thrust, filling her completely. She cried out with pain and then pleasure as she accepted the size of him, her back arching off the bed as he began to move inside her. Their bodies moved in perfect harmony, a bond forged in the same fire that birthed the stars themselves. He moved inside her slow and deep, his hips grinding against hers as he hit every nerve ending in her body. She could feel herself building towards release, her muscles clenching around him as she approached the edge.

And then, with one final thrust, she came undone. Her orgasm tore through her like a storm, leaving her breathless and trembling. He followed soon after, his own release triggered by hers.

They lay together on the bed, their bodies slick with sweat and spent with pleasure. The night stretched out around them, a blank canvas waiting to be filled with more pleasure and more love. And they would fill it, again and again, until the dawn broke and the real world came crashing back in around them.

Part IV: Avatar of Synthesis

In the heart of the cosmos, where light converges with the shadows of forgotten knowledge, the Avatar of Synthesis stands as a guardian of balance. It embodies the amalgamation of all spiritual paths, whispering the ancient secrets that bridge the gap between the material and the mystical.
Excerpt from *The Codex of The Radiant One*

Chapter 49: Hiding in Plain Sight

Elena stood in companionable silence with Archangel Mikha'El looking out over the cloud-covered peaks of the Himalayas. "This is my favorite view from the Citadel," she said. "Peace and tranquility seem endless here, even knowing of the chaos and encroaching darkness on the earth below."

Mikha'El turned from the view, leaned back on the balustrade, and studied Elena. "Yes, it's a welcome waystation when I am called upon to break up some human cataclysm or another. I understand, however, this is not such a situation?"

"Yes and no." At his raised eyebrow, she smiled. "I don't mean to be cryptic. Let's go into the council room. I have asked Manu and Cassandra to join us."

He smiled broadly when he saw the couple waiting for them and went to shake Manu's hand. "How goes wedded life?"

Manu put an arm around Cassie's waist. "Amazing. Beyond anything I ever imagined. And believe me, I've had centuries to imagine."

Cassie beamed up at him.

"I'm happy for you both," Mikha'El said, then sobered. "So let us get to the business at hand. Master Elena informed me that Tristan has betrayed us. Please elaborate."

Obliging, Manu said, "When I arrived, belatedly, on Sirkan's ship to rescue Cassandra, I discovered that Tristan was responsible for orchestrating much, if not all, of the current chaos. I discovered that he has been Sirkan's overlord, to the best of our estimation, since well before the fall of Atlantis."

Mikha'El hissed and put his hand on Manu's shoulder. "This is beyond disturbing. Tristan has been a member of the White Circle for centuries."

"Nothing like hiding in plain sight," Cassie scowled. "I have known him in this life since I was a toddler. He was my mother's financial advisor, and she considered him a best friend. His son, Paxton, and I even thought they would get married!" She shuddered. "All along, he knew who I was and had insinuated himself into our lives."

Elena turned to Mikha'El. "Do you have any inkling of his origins?"

"I know he is angelic, but I cannot penetrate his energy field beyond that. He has countless layers of very powerful shields in place," said Mikha'El, his expression steely.

Elena put up a finger. "Before we continue discussing Tristan, we have other news. It involves Natesh and Sirkan."

"Now what?" Cassie and Manu said in unison.

Mikha'El replied, "They have both passed from the land of the living."

Cassie gaped at him, not quite comprehending. "They're dead? H-how?"

"After Elena contacted me about Tristan, I tried and failed to locate him. So I decided to track down Sirkan and interrogate him. I picked up on his energy signature in the Unseelie Court ten days ago. When I arrived, however, all I found was a smoldering pile of ash that was once Sirkan's ruined temple. When I examined the aetheric imprint of the rubble, I saw that Natesh Nandwani had used Sirkan's own staff to obliterate both himself and Sirkan. They are no more."

"Sirkan's staff? The one that he used during the battle in the tower? But how?"

Manu interjected, "Our staffs have properties that can be turned against us through blood magics. Natesh must have found one of the ancient black grimoires that contained these types of spells"

Mikha'El concurred.

Elena bowed her head. "Natesh chose his path to redemption: self-sacrifice."

"So it seems," Mikha'El said. "I sent all the ash into oblivion to ensure it couldn't be used to resurrect Sirkan ever again."

Cassie had to sit down. "I'm having a hard time wrapping my head around this. My heart goes out to Natesh. I know he'd decided to respect my choice of mates once I extricated myself from Sirkan's clutches. But to give up his life like that ..."

"Sirkan was Natesh's master." Mikha'El said, "Natesh must have been planning something like this for a long time. This wasn't a spur of the moment decision. The key would have been that Natesh catch Sirkan off guard before he had time to counteract. I saw this when I replayed the aetheric imprint in the temple. To complicate matters, the ash left behind was mixed with the remains of thousands of demonic bodies that had also been incinerated."

"Sirkan's dark army," Cassie whispered.

Mikha'El nodded. "I salted and blessed the scorched earth of the temple. No dark magic will ever be practiced there again."

"And Aunt Isla's court?"

"There was no sign of her dark fae army. However, I suspect it was removed not long before I arrived. Dark residue remained in the tunnels beneath the palace. I cleansed that as well. Dark magic will not be able to dwell there again." Mikha'El said.

He stood for a moment, seeming to mull over next steps. Finally, he said, "We will revisit the Tristan dilemma after I confer with Metatron. We may be dealing with one of the ancients."

"The ancients?"

"A group of archangels sent to this realm by the Radiant One when humanity began individuating."

"So even before we came here from Sirius," said Manu

"Yes, thousands of years before. Humanity was very much in its infancy," said Mikha'El. "The sooner I speak with Metatron, the sooner we can begin to unravel this mystery."

Cassie stood frowning at the empty space where Mikha'El had just been. The angel certainly could vanish quickly. She sighed and reached for Manu's hand. "This just keeps getting better and better. I need to return to the Charlotte institute. We still have a lot to do energetically to ensure the continued spiritual awakening there."

He smiled and brushed her forehead with a kiss. "We are more than equipped to overcome this challenge. What was that magnet your mother had on the refrigerator door at your house in Charlotte? 'God doesn't give you more than you can handle'?"

"Yeah, and I had one that said, 'If it doesn't kill you, it will make you stronger.'"

Manu flexed his biceps.

CASSIE BREATHED IN the familiar scents of honeysuckle and magnolias as she ran up the front steps of the Oberon house in Charlotte and into the open arms of Brigida.

"Oh, my darling girl, it's good to have you back here!" her brogue thick with emotion. "And there's himself, just as handsome as ever." She opened her arms even wider as Manu stepped onto the front veranda. "Come, come in. I have your favorite chocolate cake and sweet tea in the kitchen, chicken and dumplings on the stove, and fried green tomatoes ready to go."

Cassie, her nose raised up like a beagle on the scent, clapped her hands in child-like delight. "My favorite things!"

"That is exactly what we need," Manu agreed, "some down-home nurturing before heading to the institute."

Raziel chose that moment to fly in. "Well, it's about time you graced us with your presence." He clapped Manu on the back. "I've been politely staying here, but now that the honeymoon is over, I'm back on duty as Cassandra's angelic guardian. I do believe she will need all the protection we can muster in the coming days."

Before anyone could respond, Gabriel suddenly appeared by his food dish in the corner of the kitchen. "Well, well, look who finally decided to make an appearance," chuckled Cassie as she scooped him up. "Where the heck have you been, boy?"

He showed her a series of scenes from her parent's home in the Devic Kingdom, and she nodded. "Well, that makes perfect sense. Is Dracoleon there too?" An affirmative meow answered as he began to scarf down the kibble that Brigida was pouring into his bowl.

"He can't possibly be that hungry," Manu shook his head in disgust. "I know for a fact that his bowls in the Seelie Court are self-filling."

"Yeah, he's always been that way: so dramatic." Cassie smiled. "Let's eat. And then I'm going to contact Master Elena and my meditation groups in Charlotte and DC. I want to start preparing them to amp up the energy in the ley lines in their respective cities on the fall equinox," she looked at her brand-new smartwatch, "in two weeks." She turned to Manu. "Can you cast a cloaking spell so the mundanes won't be aware of our presence?"

"Of course."

After dinner, Cassie opened a channel to Elena at the Citadel from the spirit screen in the library. After their greetings, she shared her plan. They worked out the details, including having the other avatars prepare and gather their groups at their respective crossroads under cover of cloaking spells.

"I think noon would be the perfect time for us all to sync up," Cassie said. "Even though the mundanes won't be able to see us, their vibrational frequencies will be uplifted just by being in and around the crossroads." She hesitated then pushed on. "One more thing, Master Elena. I know you have assigned me extra protection, Raziel, because of my unique evolutionary importance. But shouldn't the other avatars also have angelic guardians. We will be in the thick of things soon and ..." She trailed off, hesitating to voice her worries.

Elena nodded. "I will confer with Mikha'El. Now that we are down an angel on the council, he will need to direct the angelic hosts to add protections to each of the groups as well as to each of the avatars."

Chapter 50: Scorpio Rising

Promptly at noon on the fall equinox, each participant inserted special earbuds that connected to Praxis's intranet. Then Cassie began the meditation, "Let us begin by surrounding ourselves in a bubble of light and with the affirmation, I love and I care …"

She continued the familiar exercise as the participants descended into a deep level of meditation. She could feel the power of the groups as they synced with one another. A stillness and sense of peace spread through her. The body-asleep, mind-awake state of consciousness reached into the fifth dimension, the dimension of pure thought.

She tensed when she began to feel heaviness, almost like something or someone pushing against the shields erected around each participant. Mikha'El and Raziel sprang into action and pushed back while the other angels did the same for their charges. At the periphery of her awareness, she felt Manu holding steady on the cloaking spell. She drew her attention back to center, relaxed, took a deep breath, and continued leading the group into a deep level of silent communion.

Thirty minutes into the silence, Cassie felt a shift. The heaviness that had been pressing against her shields had dissipated, replaced by an overwhelming sense of clarity. Her mind, already in a state of deep meditation, seemed to expand exponentially. Thoughts flowed with unprecedented ease; connections formed between ideas she'd never considered related before.

As the vibrational frequency along the ley line intensified, Cassie's intuition sharpened. Insights about the participants, Praxis, and global events flooded her mind, as if she could pluck knowledge from the fabric of reality itself.

Then an image formed in her mind's eye, faint at first like starlight across darkness, then growing impossible to ignore. A presence stirred in the energetic realm: a celestial scorpion coiled in the heavens, its claws gleaming with otherworldly sheen. Its power vibrated in her bones, speaking of death and rebirth.

But this wasn't the static, first octave of the sign of Scorpio. The scorpion's form shimmered, and its tail elongated and shed its venomous stinger. In its place emerged a serpent, winding upward like the caduceus, a symbol of healing and divine knowledge: twin serpents intertwined in perfect harmony, their shared energy spiraling like a double helix.

At the edge of perception, Cassie sensed something greater: the faintest outline of a Phoenix, its wings still furled. Though distant, its energy was palpable, radiant, and fiery. The great bird wasn't rising yet, but its potential hummed like an ember waiting to ignite.

Tears spilled down her cheeks as she felt the Phoenix's promise vibrating through the ley line. The prophecy being fulfilled was only the beginning. The ley line's transformation wouldn't be complete until its energy reached its ultimate crescendo, when the Phoenix would rise fully formed and usher in the promised Shift of the Ages.

The other participants began to sense it too, touched by its fiery resonance like a distant call. Through it all, Mikha'El and Raziel's presence remained steady, their energies weaving around hers like protective sigils as the ley line surged.

Cassie took a deep breath, grounding herself. The vision of the Phoenix's ascension filled her with purpose. The ley line hadn't merely been amplified; it had been set on its path toward completion. The Earth itself hummed with the promise of transformation.

Even as she prepared to lead the participants back, she couldn't shake the feeling that this moment marked the first step of something far greater. The Phoenix lingered on the horizon of possibility, a beacon of transformation that awaited the final completion of the ley line's sacred purpose.

"And now, feel your body within its space," Cassie continued. "Hold in your energy field the expansiveness you have experienced, the vibrational shift you have helped create, the oneness and interconnectedness to all that is. When you're ready, take slow, deep breaths ... wiggle your toes and your fingers ... and slowly open your eyes and come back to the present moment."

She felt the connections between the groups stronger than before. The energetic shift along the ley line was palpable. Her own position in the middle of Trade and Tryon felt more expansive, and she could feel the mundanes' auras sync with hers as they passed through her auric field. Their faces softened, and they looked at one another and smiled. The whole area seemed to sparkle in the mid-day sunlight. *Yes,* she thought, *the vibrations here in Charlotte have definitely been raised.*

She slowly began to disengage from the intranet. Raziel swooped in while still under Manu's cloaking spell and whisked her back to Praxis, as did all the other participants' angelic guardians. Mikha'El was waiting in the command center with Elena and Artemus. Manu ported in a few minutes later.

"I'd say this equinox celebration was one of the most important events in humanity's history," said Mikha'El. "Well done, Cassandra. The angelic hosts are reporting a definite uptick in the vibratory frequencies of cities along the Charlotte-Washington ley line."

"Well, we can't rest on our laurels yet," Cassie said. "As we were beginning the exercise, I had a sense of a really dark and powerful energy pushing against the shields we had in place. It didn't get through, but I sensed a very pissed off Tristan."

"I'm not surprised," Elena said. "After all, the ley line is at the heart of the prophecy you are here to fulfill, at least in part."

The spirit screen signaled an incoming transmission from Tatiana. Elena activated it. "Tatiana?"

"The witch trials are getting out of hand, Elena."

"Morgandrian's former coven?" she asked.

"Affirmative," said Tatiana. "My intel says a large group of dark witches is headed to Charlotte. I assume in direct response to the equinox meditation that just finished."

"Thank you for the heads up. We have quite a contingent here. Let me know if you need any more reinforcements."

"Will do."

Chapter 51: The Gathering Storm

What had begun as a hidden contest in the magical world quickly escalated into a public nightmare all along the East Coast. The competition for leadership of Morgandrian's coven had reached a fever pitch, and the mundane world was caught in the crossfire.

Cracks split the streets as sudden earthquakes erupted, mysterious fires ignited in the middle of cities, and the skies darkened with unnatural clouds. News channels, social media, and every other communication platform buzzed with reports of bizarre occurrences, leaving the public bewildered and terrified.

The witches unleashed spells with increasing power, each more ruthless than the last. Curses without regard for the consequences echoed throughout the aetheric plane as each witch tried to outdo the other. All to demonstrate who was the wickedest witch of all.

Mundane evangelists and conspiracy theorists had a field day. Self-proclaimed prophets shouted from street corners, and online forums buzzed with warnings of the end of the world. A fog of fear settled over the population from Maine to Florida, thick and suffocating.

Glenda and Adrianna were doing their best to try to contain the damage and were making some headway as they monitored the chaos through multiple feeds on the Aethernet. The New York institute's command center was alive with flickering screens and urgent alerts.

"Wow, I guess Cassie's equinox meditation really hit the mark," Glenda said, trying to keep her voice steady despite the chaos displayed on the screens. "If anything could rile up the dark forces, it's the Trybrid gaining a home-court advantage."

"We've got to get a handle on this," Adrianna said, her eyes darting from one screen to another, each showing a different scene of destruction. "Between what's happening on the political scene with President Soter and this dark magic oozing into everyday life, humanity is teetering dangerously close to societal collapse."

Glenda nodded grimly, her long blonde hair reflecting the eerie glow of the screens. "We need to act fast. If we don't contain this outbreak soon, it'll be impossible to keep the magical world hidden from the general public."

The spirit screen signaled that a message was coming through. "Screen on," said Glenda. Elena's face came into focus, but the audio was garbled with static.

"Master Elena, I can't hear you very well," Glenda said, her voice tinged with frustration. "Hang on while I try to clear the channel."

Elena's voice eventually came through faintly though intermittently. "Band of witches ... Charlotte ... containment ..."

Glenda cursed under her breath. "Master Elena, do you need us to go to Charlotte right away and cast a containment spell?" she asked, hoping her guess was correct.

Elena shook her head slightly, then nodded. "Cassandra ..." came the fractured reply.

"Oh, Cassandra is still in Charlotte?" Glenda guessed.

Elena nodded again.

"Do you want us to cast a containment spell here in New York?"

Another nod. The transmission cut off, leaving Glenda and Adrianna staring at each other.

"What was that about?" Adrianna asked, a note of concern in her voice.

"It sounds like there's a large band of witches in Charlotte, and Cassie is still there with Master Elena. She wants us to cast a containment spell here to keep the coven fragments from leaving," Glenda explained, trying to piece together the fractured message.

Adrianna sighed, running a hand through her hair. "We've been trying containment spells, but they're not holding. The dark magic is too strong."

"What if we weave a nullification spell into the containment?" Glenda suggested, her mind racing. "It might stabilize the boundaries without causing too much collateral damage."

Adrianna considered this, then nodded. "It's worth a shot. Let's get two neophytes to help us anchor the spell. I'll work on the wording."

Within minutes, four white witches stood at the four corners of the rooftop of the New York institute, facing outward, palms outstretched. The wind picked up, swirling around them as they prepared to cast the spell.

"All right, everyone," Glenda said, her voice steady but urgent, "remember to pull your power from your solar plexus, channel it through your heart, and direct it down your arms to your palms. On the count of three. One ... two ... three!"

The witches chanted in unison, their voices harmonizing with the elements around them:

Chaos, bow to tranquil might,

Yield to peace, forsake the fight.

By the Radiant One, whose light prevails,

We weave a shield that never fails.

No harm shall touch these hallowed halls.

And we seal the door where evil dwells.

As the spell took hold, a cacophony of screeches and screams echoed through the aetheric plane. Concentric circles of green healing light spread out over the city, extinguishing fires, closing fissures, and freezing the dark spellcasters in their tracks.

"OK," Glenda said, exhaling deeply, "now let's get those witches out of the third dimension and into a containment field within the Citadel. I'll contact Master Artemus to let him know they're on their way."

With the message sent and received, the four witches created a portal. The dark witches in the area were literally sucked into it, their faces twisted in terror.

"That should hold them for a while," Adrianna said, her voice tinged with relief. "But we'll have to keep a close watch. Master Elena will probably want to pay them a visit. See if they're open to rehabilitation or if they'll need a more ... permanent solution."

Glenda nodded, but her thoughts were already shifting to the next crisis. "Shall we move on to Charlotte or continue to Boston?"

"Until we hear differently from Master Elena, I say we head to Boston," Adrianna replied. "They've got one of the oldest covens in the United States, and if this dark magic is spreading, they'll need all the help they can get."

The situation in Boston was significantly worse than New York had been. As they arrived at the Boston institute and surveyed the scene through the holographic screens, Adrianna shook her head in dismay. "This is bad. These witches ... they were once some of the most promising sisters in the coven. Now they're a disorganized rabble, tearing the city apart."

"That's because you were supposed to be next in line," Glenda said quietly, her voice laced with both respect and regret. "You have the leadership skills necessary to bring them back from the brink."

Adrianna sighed, the weight of responsibility heavy on her shoulders. "Yeah, well ... it's not about what I was *supposed* to be. We need to focus on what we can do now." She paused, thinking. "We could call in Tatiana and that new avatar recruit, Devika. She's Morgandrian's daughter. Maybe she can bring some semblance of order to this chaos."

Glenda reached over and gave Adrianna a quick, affectionate kiss on the cheek. "Brilliant as always. The energy here is clearer than in New York. I think I can send Tatiana a telepathic message."

Tatiana blinked into the room within minutes, Devika at her side. Both were tense and ready.

"What's the situation?" Tatiana asked tersely.

Glenda quickly filled her in, and Adrianna shared their thoughts with Devika.

Devika frowned, her dark eyes troubled. "My mother kept me a secret from her coven. They don't know me, and I don't know them. I'm not sure if my involvement would make things better or worse, especially considering who my father is." She hesitated, her voice uncertain. "Besides, I've only been training with Tatiana for a few months. I'm still figuring out my powers, let alone how to use them effectively."

Tatiana, who had been unusually quiet, finally spoke up. "Devika, I believe you have the potential to be a key player in resolving this crisis. Your presence alone could disrupt the chaos. You've inherited a unique aura of authority from your mother that these witches will recognize."

Devika still looked doubtful but nodded slowly. "All right ... if you think it will help." She turned to Adrianna, her voice tinged with anxiety. "What am I walking into?"

Glenda pulled up the latest surveillance. The images were grim: witches battling in the streets, dark magic clashing with the defenses put up by the city's Masons, and civilians who were caught in the crossfire fleeing in panic or hiding wherever they could.

A sigh escaped Tatiana's lips, her features taking on a somber and troubled look. "This is worse than I thought. We need to establish a secure base of operations. Somewhere we can retreat to if things get too out of hand. The Boston institute is too compromised."

Glenda nodded in agreement. "Let's use the old Salem sanctuary. It's fortified and has the resources to support our operations. Plus, its wards should keep us hidden from the mundanes."

Tatiana was already strategizing. "First, we'll need to neutralize the most aggressive factions. If we can stop the worst offenders, we might create a window of nonviolence long enough to establish our base."

Glenda turned to Devika. "Do you think you can confront these witches in person? You will need to convince them you are a force to be reckoned with."

Devika swallowed hard, her nerves visible, but she nodded. "I'll do my best."

Adrianna meticulously began outlining a plan, carefully identifying key objectives and determining which witches to target first. "Let's split into two teams. Glenda and I will secure the Salem sanctuary and fortify the wards and defenses."

Tatiana nodded. "Devika and I will head straight into the fray and neutralize the leaders of the chaos. We'll rendezvous at the sanctuary once the initial threats are contained. We'll need to make sure the mundanes don't get any more wind of this than they already have. Damage control will be crucial once this is over."

With a final nod, the team dispersed to their respective missions, the weight of the world, or at least the East Coast, bearing down on their shoulders.

DEVIKA STOOD WITH HER hands fisted on her hips. She was flanked by Tatiana, Glenda, and Adrianna as they faced three very pissed off witches. Adrianna was in high spirits fresh off a resounding victory in New York.

"I don't give a flying fuck who you are. Your mother is a traitor and deserves to be burned at the stake. I think we need to reinstitute a major witch trial in her honor," spat Ravin, who had once been in Morgandrian's inner circle. She turned to her fellow witches. "Yeah, I think that's just the ticket! What say you all?"

A hurricane-like wind blew up between the two groups. Out stepped Morgandrian with Arion close behind. "I think not," she snarled.

Ravin snickered, "What, no flying monkeys?"

"That can be arranged," said Morgandrian and raised her hands. Arion smirked and simply blew some glittering dust from the palm of his right hand. It swirled around the dark witches, and formed a domed cage that sealed them in. Their screams and screeches evaporated into nothingness along with the cage.

Morgandrian whirled on him, "Dammit to hell, Arion, why did you do that?"

He shook his head at her. "Because I didn't want you to lose all the progress you've made toward redemption, my dear. Say hello to Devika, and then we are off." He turned to Tatiana. "Let's clean up this mess so those cameras across the street can't transmit this latest shit show to the entire mundane population."

Devika flew into her mother's arms. "Mother! How I have missed you!"

Morgandrian held her in a bone-crushing embrace, then reluctantly released her and held her at arm's length. "You have grown in your powers so much! And what's this I hear: You are being trained as an avatar? Truly?"

Tears coursing down her face, Devika could only nod.

"I can't begin to tell you how proud I am of you," said Morgandrian, her black eyes drinking in the petite frame of her daughter. She smoothed a hand over Devika's ebony tresses, which were braided and wrapped around her head like a crown. "I can feel your power. It's unlike any I have ever experienced." She wrapped her arms around her daughter again. "Are you all right? Is there anything you need?"

Devika met her mother's gaze, green eyes to black. "I only need to know that you are OK. Please don't worry about me. I am doing just fine. And, yes, can you believe I am being trained in the ways of the avatars?" She laughed, "How surreal is that?"

"It is pretty unbelievable, to be sure," Morgandrian said, her voice thick with emotion. "You must be careful though. If the Dark Brotherhood got wind of this ..."

Tatiana stepped forward, her voice steady and calm. "Morgandrian, we've gone to great lengths to protect Devika and give her the necessary training. Another dark witch will step forward unless or rather *until* we have neutralized the threat. Your transformation to the light will help facilitate that."

Morgandrian nodded, her eyes still fixed on Devika. "I know."

Arion, having finished dismantling the remaining magical traces with a final wave of his hand, joined the conversation. "We need to move quickly. The psychic residue is neutralized, but we don't want to risk any of Tristan's acolytes picking up on you. Rest in the knowledge that you are on the right path, and so is your mother."

Chapter 52: Last One Standing

Morgandrian sat listlessly on the throne of her former stronghold, her face in her hands. The fabric of her world was unraveling. Sirkan and Natesh dead? Sirkan, good riddance. The end of his reign of terror was welcome news. But Natesh. Morgandrian felt a wave of sadness when she thought about him. She remembered how he had come to be a vampire, how his longing for his long-lost love had haunted him for over two hundred years. And now, he had willingly given up his life to ensure the love of his life would no longer be hounded by Sirkan's lust for her lifetime after lifetime.

Then she thought about Ian and Devika. Yes, she would unquestionably give her life for her daughter. And if called upon for the ultimate sacrifice, she would do the same for Ian. They had not seen one another since Arion had informed him that they had a daughter. The constant ache in her heart when she thought about him was a strong indication that she still loved him. But she had become an expert at denying her own happiness to protect Devika.

Arion stood silently watching her. After she'd learned of Sirkan and Natesh's demise, she'd picked up that Devika was confronting some of her old coven. What would she do now that she was the last of Sirkan's lieutenants? Did she know how the dark powers worked once the progenitor was no more?

He went to her and took her by the shoulders to look into her eyes. She jerked back.

"Personal space if you don't mind!"

"Now is that any way to speak to your new best friend?" He didn't let go. Instead, he took her left hand in his and ran his thumb over the ruby ring. "How's the energy these days?"

She knitted her brow and snatched her hand away. "What?"

Arion laughed and let her go. "It seems you are the last one standing in Sirkan's line of succession. You should have felt a nice big power surge by now."

Morgandrian shook her head. "I did. And I used it to help my daughter. Although I must admit, I do feel a little sorry about Natesh. He never stood a chance once he dedicated his life to protecting Cassandra."

"Love conquers all."

"Depends on what you are conquering." She twisted the ruby ring. "Besides, Mia has taken up leadership of Natesh's clan. So, I'm technically not the last one standing."

Arion snorted. "Mia is a nonentity in this game. She never obtained Natesh's ring. She has absolutely no authority over the clan and will find that out soon enough. They are basically leaderless and will not last through the coming skirmishes."

Morgandrian shrugged, "I could give a shit about Mia and Natesh's clan. I only care about my daughter. After what we just saw, she appears more than capable of holding her own. Even if I hadn't interfered, she is considerably more powerful than I ever was. So let's take this to the next level, shall we?"

"What level would that be?"

"That's your territory. What's your endgame, Arion? My death ... my transformation to the light ... what?"

"It's not up to me. I follow orders too, you know. In point of fact, it's about time I check in with the powers that be."

"Whatever."

"Ah, another thing I like about you: your enthusiasm. Someone has requested a little visit with you. He will keep you company while I am gone."

With that declaration, Arion ported out. And Ian ported in.

Morgandrian stared at him, too numb from the high emotions of the last few hours to react to his sudden appearance. "What on Earth could you possibly want from me, Ian? Haven't you and I caused enough drama?"

He looked at her for a long moment. Goddess, she looked so tired. Her face was so thin, her cheekbones could cut paper, and her dark brown, almost-black eyes were dull and listless. "Well, from the looks of you, you could use a boost of energy. You look ... haggard. Not your usual royal, sumptuous self."

"Well, that's a great way to start a conversation with your long-lost love and the mother of your child. Thanks for that." She lifted her hand to slap him.

Ian easily stopped her mid-slap, pulled her to him, and kissed her thoroughly. She tried to pull away from him, stunned.

He quirked a smile at her but wouldn't release her. "Now is that anyway to treat your long-lost love and father of your child?"

All Morgandrian could do was sputter.

"Let's call a truce, shall we? To be honest I haven't been able to get you off my mind since we saw one another on the beach in Bimini. Maybe we could ...?" He trailed off, hesitating.

"Could ... what? Have another affair? Get married? What in the world could we do that wouldn't be a total shit show? Especially with the world teetering on the brink of a catastrophe of biblical proportions."

"Even more reason to set aside our differences and work together," Ian said, his tone softening. "The world may be in chaos, but that doesn't mean we have to be enemies."

Morgandrian stepped back, eyeing him warily. "Work together? On what precisely? In case you haven't noticed, I am not exactly free to do whatever I want. Arion holds a tight rein on me until the powers that be decide I've repented my 'dark ways' well enough to let me go. And kissing me to stir me up again after all these years isn't exactly working together."

Ian ran a hand through his hair, looking frustrated. "Yeah, well I couldn't help myself. You looked so vulnerable when I first came in. Besides, aren't we already working together? At least this time we're on the same side. When it comes down to it, don't we both want what's best for Devika? For the world?"

"I'm not sure I know what's best for anyone anymore," Morgandrian admitted, sinking into a nearby chair. "Everything's spiraled so far out of control."

Ian knelt beside her, taking her hand gently. "Then let's figure it out together. We were a good team once, remember? Before all the politics and power struggles got in the way."

Morgandrian's gaze drifted down to their intertwined hands, her heart tightening as she glanced back at Ian's face. For a fleeting moment, he looked just like the man she'd fallen for all those years ago, like a ghost of their past. "And what about Arion? The White Circle? They will hardly let me slip away like a shadow in the night."

"No, they won't," Ian agreed. "But maybe that's exactly why we need to stand united. If you agree to work with me under the auspices of Arion, then you would be able to finish up whatever penance Elena and Artemus or whoever has determined is fulfilled. Let's show them there's another way forward."

Morgandrian was quiet for a long moment, weighing her options. She fingered the ruby ring, feeling the dark power surging through her. Finally, she squeezed Ian's hand. "I'm not saying I trust you completely. But ... I'm willing to listen. What do you have in mind?"

Ian's face lit up with a mix of relief and determination. "First, we need to run the idea that we can work together by the White Circle. I will do that and plead our case. Then we can start planning our next move."

Morgandrian just stared at him, open-mouthed. "What in the world could we work together on?"

"Why to disrupt and disband the witch trials of course. They are your former acolytes, after all. You know them better than they know themselves. With your insights, you could add your energy to Devika's efforts and neutralize them once and for all."

"I don't know, Ian. Devika is training as an avatar now. I'm not sure Tatiana would approve of her working hand-in-glove with her fallen mother."

Ian shrugged. "All we can do is ask." He hesitated, then pushed on. "There is one more thing though." He faltered and decided to take the plunge. *In for a penny, in for a pound.* "OK," he breathed out, "I'd also like to give *us* another chance. At the end of the day, isn't it all about love?"

As Ian helped her to her feet, Morgandrian felt a little punchy and off center. At the same time, she felt a spark of hope for the first time in ages. Whatever came next, at least she wouldn't be facing it alone.

"We can try."

Chapter 53: Ordained

Cassie clung to Manu's hand like it was her only lifeline in a raging storm. The sudden summons from Metatron took them to the Golden Temple once more. All they had been told was to wear their white robes.

She spun around as others arrived in the altar room. Mikha'El led in Artemus and Elena, followed by Raziel, her parents, and the six Aquarian Avatars, all dressed in white.

"What do you think is going on?" Cassie whispered to Manu.

"Not a clue, but it looks pretty important by the look on Mikha'El's face."

They didn't have long to wait. Metatron appeared, erupting in a blaze of golden-white light that flooded the temple. In one hand, he grasped a golden orb that glowed like a captured star, while in the other, he wielded a scepter that seemed to pulse with life. With a solemn nod to the small gathering, he ascended the seven steps leading to the alabaster altar, each step echoing like thunder in the stillness.

The entire assembly bowed to him, hands palm-to-palm in salutation.

Master Elena leaned toward Cassie and said, "Those golden objects are the sacred relics of ordination."

Cassie's heart pounded in her chest, the weight of the moment pressing down on her. *Sacred relics of ordination? What in the world did that mean? What was really happening?* Then she sighed, *Maybe this is about Manu. Yeah, that's it. He's going to be elevated to some new priestly position.*

"There has been a profound shift, not just in the vibratory frequencies coursing through the Charlotte-Washington ley line, but also in the very consciousness of the mundanes living along that energetic thread," Metatron intoned, his voice resonating like a deep bell in the quiet temple. He paused, his eyes gleaming, and beckoned Cassie and Manu forward with a gesture as commanding as the pull of gravity.

"The Radiant One has decreed that Cassandra will no longer serve as an Aquarian Avatar." His words hung in the air, met with a collective gasp from the gathered attendees. He raised his hands, signaling for silence before continuing. "Her transformation has unlocked the memories, talents, and abilities accumulated over all her earthly incarnations. With these powers now fully awakened and her ongoing success in guiding humanity to build its mental body, she shall be ordained with a new title: the Avatar of Synthesis."

Cassie gasped as she whipped around to meet Manu's eyes. She hadn't expected anything like this, not after everything she'd already been through.

Manu gripped her hand in a vice-like grip, his breath caught in his throat. His presence was a steadying force, grounding her amidst her swirling thoughts. She searched his ice-blue eyes for something: reassurance, understanding, anything to anchor her. He smiled at her with love, but she could also detect the same trepidation she felt mirrored back at her. They were in this together, and somehow, that made it both easier and harder.

The title of Aquarian Avatar was one she had finally come to accept after so much resistance. Now, as she stood in the presence of those who had become her spiritual family and fellow light warriors, she wondered if she was truly ready to bear a new title, one that carried even more responsibility.

Metatron continued, "The Avatar of Synthesis expresses a level of mental acuity whereby they can dwell in the realm of mind, the higher mental plane, the fifth dimension. They hold a mind with the power to transcend the boundaries of space and time, bending reality itself to their will, capable of seeing beyond the present and into the infinite possibilities that lie beyond."

Manu's hand anchored her as her feet moved beneath her like strangers, shifting as if an unseen force were guiding them. Inside, her thoughts twisted and tangled, a whirlwind of fear, excitement, and doubt. The mundanes, who were blind to the cosmic currents weaving through the world, had no idea beings like them even existed. And now, because of some shift in their consciousness, she was about to be thrust into a new role, a role that could alter the course of not just their lives, but the entire world.

Metatron's gaze shifted to Manu. "Your bond with Cassandra gives you the power to support her in all endeavors."

Cassie's heart clenched. *Their bond.* It had been a source of strength for her, a way to navigate the storm of her transformation. But now, she couldn't help but wonder what this new role would mean for their relationship. Would they be drawn even closer, or would the weight of their responsibilities tear them apart? She shook her head and admonished herself. Of course this wouldn't pull them apart. Their relationship would rise to meet them in their trials and triumphs, just as it had in the past.

Metatron startled her out of her reverie, "Cassandra, your initial task is to pierce the veil of the fifth dimension to access the higher mental plane. You have done this many times with your personal meditations. Now I will provide you with a seed thought that will take you to the higher realms of universal mind. Through that focus, you will be able to connect directly with cosmic consciousness. This will enable you to draw wisdom down from the fifth dimension into the lower mental plane, making it accessible to those who have achieved a meditator's mind."

As Metatron spoke, Cassie felt the enormity of the task awaiting them. The fifth dimension, the higher mental plane, cosmic consciousness: These were concepts she had studied, meditated on, but to be the one to bring them into reality for others? It was daunting. What if she failed? What if she wasn't strong enough, disciplined enough, to bridge that gap?

A cold thought slithered into her mind, unbidden and unwanted: Tristan and the Dark Brotherhood. The memory of Tristan's steel grey eyes, filled with malice and cunning, sent a shiver down her spine. Manu had used their telepathic connection once they had escaped the Shadow Realm to show her the confrontation on Sirkan's ship. Tristan had already come so close to destroying everything she had worked for. The Dark Brotherhood's influence was like a shadow creeping at the edges of her awareness, a constant reminder that her enemies were always watching, waiting for a moment of weakness.

Metatron then turned to address the avatars. "This is my charge to you. The advanced training that Mikha'El gave you will be woven into this new level of training that Cassandra will receive and impart to you. As you integrate these new meditation techniques, you will in turn teach your own neophytes and acolytes. In this way, you will prepare humanity for its next step of evolution and their third initiation."

Third initiation. The words rang in Cassie's ears like a distant echo. She had been through her own initiations, each one a trial that pushed her to the edge of her limits. And now, she was to lead others through theirs. Could she bear the weight of so many lives, so many minds looking to her for guidance? The thought made her dizzy, and she fought to keep her breathing steady, to keep herself grounded in the here and now.

Manu sensed her emotional turmoil and squeezed her hand. He knew he was married to one of the most powerful beings, if not the single most powerful, on the earthly plane, but she was still his wife, his love, his soul mate. He would do anything to ease these continued burdens that the universe kept thrusting upon her.

As though picking up his thoughts, Metatron focused on him once more, his gaze piercing. "I sense you have something to add?"

Manu's eyes lit up. "The Ageless Wisdom Teachings predicted this moment," he said, "They spoke of a time when humanity would first master instantaneous communication through mechanical means. We're seeing it now with our digital networks, our instant messages crossing the globe in milliseconds. But the Teachings also say this is just the beginning."

He leaned forward intently. "Once a critical mass of people have developed their mental faculties through meditation, this technological framework will act as a catalyst. Like the hundredth monkey effect, it will trigger a consciousness shift across all of humanity. Those who have prepared their minds will suddenly find themselves capable of true telepathic communion. But first," his expression hardened, "we must cleanse these networks of the Technomancer's remaining corrupting viruses. Then we can use these platforms as they were meant to be used: to awaken others. This is why Cassandra's training program is so crucial. She's preparing people's minds for the transformation to come."

Metatron looked between the two of them for what seemed like eons. Then those stern features melted into a benevolent smile. "The two of you truly are well suited. Now come forward with your soul mate." He then motioned Elena forward. "Let us begin."

Chapter 54: New Directions

Devika paced, her heart pounding in her chest as she cast anxious glances toward the mirror. *What the hell am I doing?* she thought. The reflection staring back at her was a stark contrast to the confidence she wished to feel. A diminutive young woman dressed in flowing white robes with wavy blue-black hair cascading down her back, her green deer-caught-in-the-headlights eyes wide with fear, frozen and uncertain.

A knock on the door snapped her out of her spiraling thoughts. "Come in," she called, her voice trembling slightly.

The door creaked open, and Cassie stepped into the room, her familiar presence bringing a small measure of comfort. Cassie had a sheepish grin on her face, but her eyes were filled with warmth and understanding. "I wasn't sure if you were still holding your vigil," she said softly.

"Oh no, I'm done with that. Gosh, I'm so glad you're here!" Devika replied, her voice betraying the desperation she felt. "I don't think I can go through with this, Cassie."

Cassie's smile turned rueful. "Feeling a little insecure, are we?"

"That doesn't quite cover it," Devika muttered, her gaze dropping to the floor. "There's no way I could take your place as the seventh avatar! This is insane."

Cassie moved closer, taking Devika's hands in hers and leading her to sit on the side of the bed. She watched as a soft glow of both dark and light magic flickered around the girl's fingertips, the two forces merging seamlessly. It was a beautiful sight, yet it only served to remind Devika of the immense power she held, power she wasn't sure she could control.

"First of all, you're not me," Cassie began gently. "You're not like any of the other avatars either." She smiled reassuringly. "You are just as unique as a wielder of both dark and light magic as I am as the Trybrid. You, like me, are one of a kind."

Devika looked up, her eyes wide with a mix of awe and disbelief. "Yeah, but you're also the Avatar of Synthesis. That's, like, beyond the powers of any being on Earth right now."

Cassie chuckled softly, squeezing Devika's hand as she felt the girl's slight tremble. "It's true. I have a unique role, but so do you. Being an avatar isn't about replicating someone else's path. It's about forging your own, using the gifts and strengths that only you possess." Cassie hesitated then continued, "This time in humanity's evolution is about laying down blueprints for the many options humans can choose as they evolve. I believe we are those blueprints."

Devika remained silent, the weight of Cassie's words sinking in. She had always admired Cassie for her strength and determination, her ability to unite disparate forces into something greater. Yet here Cassie was, telling Devika that she didn't need to be the same, that she could be something entirely new.

"But what if I fail?" Devika whispered, her voice barely audible. "What if I'm not strong enough?"

Cassie's expression softened. "Devika, every avatar before you has faced that fear. We all have moments of doubt, of wondering if we're truly capable. But the truth is, the very fact that you're questioning yourself shows that you understand the gravity of your role. That is what makes you worthy."

As Cassie spoke, Devika felt a stirring deep within her, a flicker of the power that had been awakened within her, only waiting for her to embrace it.

Cassie stood, her eyes never leaving Devika's. "Nothing in the universe happens by chance. You have a choice, Devika. You can let fear hold you back, or you can step into the role you were born to fulfill. The seventh avatar isn't meant to be a copy of anyone else. It's now meant to be you."

Devika took a deep breath, feeling the warmth of Cassie's words wrap around her like a protective cloak. The fear was still there, but it was no longer paralyzing. She could feel the strength within her, the power of both light and dark coalescing into something entirely new.

Slowly, Devika rose to her feet, her decision made. "I'll do it," she said quietly, her voice gaining strength.

Cassie smiled broadly at her with a mixture of pride and relief. "I knew you would."

Just then a knock on the door announced Devika's sponsor had arrived to take her to her initiation. Tatiana stepped through, beaming. "Are you ready?"

Devika, a determined smile on her lips, grinned at Cassie and said, "I totally am!"

CASSIE AND IAN STOOD behind Devika, escorting her to the front of the altar room in the Temple of Initiation. Memories of her own initiation flooded through Cassie, and she felt her eyes water a bit. So much had happened since then. She mentally shook herself out of her introspection so she could be fully present for Devika. She had been surprised when Ian had asked her to stand with him as her sponsor, since Morgandrian would not be allowed to attend.

Morgandrian's penance was not yet over, and Cassie, frankly, felt sorry for the witch. Someday, she really wanted to know Morgandrian's story, how she had chosen the left-hand path and become one of the most powerful witches in the Western Hemisphere. Cassie had seen firsthand how much Morgandrian loved both Devika and Ian and hoped that they would all be on even ground one day.

A Sirian oracle and Metatron began the ceremony. The oracle read the revised prophecy to include Cassie as the newly ordained Avatar of Synthesis:

> *In the Age of Awakening, when the stars align in the Aquarian sky,*
> *Seven avatars shall emerge, destined to defy.*
> *From different realms and walks of life, they arise,*
> *United by a cosmic purpose, where destiny lies.*
> *Born under constellations' guiding light so bright,*
> *To safeguard humanity and bring forth the light.*
> *Each with a virtue, a flame in their heart,*
> *Guided by the cosmos, they will play their part.*

The first, a seer with eyes that discern,
Shall pierce illusions, the truth shall return.
The second, a healer with hands that mend,
Shall soothe wounds and hearts on which shadows descend.
The third, a warrior with valor untamed,
Shall wield justice's sword, with darkness unchained.
The fourth, a sage with knowledge vast,
Shall unravel mysteries of the ages that last.
The fifth, a mystic with intuitive grace,
Shall traverse dimensions, the veils they'll embrace.
The sixth, a bard with melodies pure,
Shall inspire souls and hope to ensure.
The seventh, a mage of light and dark combined,
Shall wield the elements, with power unconfined.
Balancing forces, their magic shall bind,
Restoring harmony to fragmented minds.
The Avatar of Synthesis, a leader with vision clear,
Shall unite the scattered, dispelling all fear.
Their DNA an infinite blend,
Face the darkness, their mission to defend.
Battles shall rage, and trials be faced,
In the cosmic symphony, their destinies traced.
But united they rise, an unbreakable chain,
Through sacrifices and triumphs, they'll break the dark's reign.
In unity forged, a beacon unfurled,
The seven plus one will guide humanity to a brighter world.

Metatron motioned them forward. Cassie scanned the assembled group, but did not see that Tatiana was in attendance, which she found odd since Devika had been trained by the white witch. Cassie watched as Metatron looked into Devika's eyes, and she remembered when he had telepathically challenged her at her own initiation. She sent waves of supportive energy to Devika.

THE RITUAL OVER, DEVIKA turned to face her peers and inclined her head in deference to the other six avatars, to Cassie and the members of the White Circle. Artemus, as master of the White Circle, inclined his head to Devika in acknowledgment of her new status, as did the other members present: Elena, Manu, Ian, Siobhan, and now, Cassie.

Cassie stepped forward, placing a hand on Devika's shoulder. "Welcome, avatar," she said with a grin.

Ian took Devika into a bear hug, tears glistening in emerald eyes that mirrored Devika's own. "I wish Mother could have been here," she whispered into his ear.

He smiled wistfully at her, "So do I."

Devika smiled back, the fear in her heart replaced with resolve. She was ready to embrace her destiny.

Meanwhile, Morgandrian, with Arion as her sponsor, was participating in a different type of ceremony officiated by Tatiana. The small chapel just off the great hall of the London institute was bathed in an eerie interplay of light and shadow. Tall stained-glass windows let in glittering beams of the setting sun, creating a medley of color that danced across the ancient stone walls. The altar, adorned with glyphs of white magic, glowed faintly in the dim atmosphere.

Morgandrian stood at the foot of the altar, her white robes whispering against the marble floor. Her eyes flickered with uncertainty. This was the moment she had both dreaded and yearned for, the moment when she would renounce the darkness that had defined her for centuries and pledge herself to the Radiant One.

"Remember why you are here, Morgandrian," came a soft yet firm voice from her side. Arion, her tester and inquisitor, stepped closer. As a member of the White Circle, he had seen the horrors of dark magic and the salvation of the light. His steel-gray eyes met hers with understanding. "This is your choice. Your redemption."

"You have done a brilliant job of shifting your focus from the Dark Brotherhood," said Tatiana. "The White Circle has decreed that you are at a turning point whereby you may take a new direction on your life path. Therefore, I have been given permission to accept your allegiance to the Radiant One and relinquish your dark magic to be transmuted by the Violet Flame."

Morgandrian swallowed hard, nodding slightly. Slowly, she raised her hands, palms facing outward. From the depths of her being, she summoned the dark magic that had once been her lifeline. It manifested as inky-black tendrils swirling around her hands, casting unnatural shadows on the floor. She directed them into the pillar of violet fire to the right of the altar.

She could feel the resistance, the darkness trying to cling to her like a child being wrenched from its mother's arms. Her life passed before her eyes as she experienced once more her evolution into the most powerful witch in the Western Hemisphere, for she was indeed dying to her present life in order to be reborn.

She relived the overwhelming lure of the power Sirkan had offered when he'd picked her out of the sewers of disease-ridden London during the Great Plague. She had been little more than a kitchen witch, but her beauty had given her entrée into society. When a favorite of the king's had fallen ill to plague, one of her lovers had brought her to court with her healing spells and poultices, to no avail. She knew as soon as she saw the courtier it wouldn't do any good. But she did her best, praying to the goddess to send a miracle. But the goddess did not respond. When the man had breathed his last, anger erupted in the room with shouts of "charlatan" and "witch." She was dragged unceremoniously into the streets, beaten, and thrown into the refuse of the sewers. In that dark moment, Sirkan found her.

He appeared from the shadows draped in opulent dark robes, his citrine eyes glowing with a cold, otherworldly light. She sensed power in him, a dark allure that both frightened and fascinated her. He'd been watching her for quite some time, he said, intrigued by her potential.

"Why waste your talents on those who will never appreciate you?" he asked, his voice smooth and enticing. "They see you as nothing more than a pretty face, a servant to their whims. But I see your true potential, Morgandrian. I can offer you power, *real* power. The kind that will ensure you are never at the mercy of others again."

Morgandrian hesitated, the memory of her failure still fresh in her mind. But as she looked into Sirkan's eyes, she felt a stirring within: anger, resentment, and a burning desire for something more. She was tired of being weak, tired of being cast aside. If the light had failed her, perhaps it was time to embrace the darkness.

She accepted Sirkan's offer. And so began her descent into the world of dark magic, a path that would lead her far from the kitchen witch she once was and into the clutches of powers that would change her forever.

And now she had come full circle. Tatiana's voice rang out again, cutting through her reverie. "Focus on the light, Morgandrian. The Radiant One is with you. Release the darkness, and you shall be free."

Morgandrian gritted her teeth, pushed harder, and intoned, "I, Morgandrian, renounce the darkness and embrace the light. I pledge my loyalty to the Radiant One, and I shall walk in the path of righteousness from this day forward."

The tendrils wavered.

"Say it three times three," Tatiana urged.

Morgandrian's voice wavered as she repeated the oath the requisite times. With each intonation, she felt the light within her grow stronger. When she finished, a brilliant flash of light filled the hall, and for a moment, Morgandrian felt the presence of the Radiant One, a warmth and peace that she had never known.

"The Radiant One has accepted your pledge, Morgandrian," Tatiana said.

Her energy drained, Morgandrian felt hollow and at a loss as to what or who she was now.

Arion stepped forward, offering her his hand. "Come. Someone eagerly awaits you."

Chapter 55: Dream's Revelation

"I'm sure you will want to add your own touches to our home away from home," Manu said as he lifted Cassie into his arms to carry her over the threshold of his apartments in the Citadel.

She laughed, "Put me down, you crazy alien. Someone may see us!"

He leaned down and kissed her, his lips pressing against hers with an urgency that spoke of his hope and desire. "I certainly hope so. This is not the only threshold I will carry you over, wife. I have acquired many other homes over the centuries. Why, I even have a castle or two. But for now, since we need to be close to our compatriots, I thought this would be the best place for us to set up housekeeping when we are away from our home in the Seelie Court. It also will afford us the luxury of having direct access to my mother ship."

Gently lowering her to the floor, he stepped back, a silent invitation in his eyes for her to explore. She drifted into the room like a curious breeze, her gaze sweeping across the space where the past and future seemed to collide. A large wooden table sprawled in the center, its surface a chaotic sea of ancient scrolls and manuscripts. Against one wall, a cluster of holographic screens and keyboards hummed quietly. Nearby, the sleek silhouette of a nutrichef console gleamed, waiting to conjure a meal from thin air.

"Well, this is almost like our magic house in the Seelie Court," Cassie smiled. "Does it clean up afterward as well?"

Manu grinned, "I normally eat in the main dining hall, so I really couldn't say."

Cassie just shook her head and continued to explore his, now their, quarters. Three overstuffed chairs huddled together in a cozy corner like old friends whispering secrets, completing the room's eclectic yet inviting atmosphere.

"Spartan doesn't begin to describe your decorating skills, my love," Cassie smiled. "I do think I can improve this." Before he could protest, she waved her hand. Marble tables were cushioned by plush Aubusson area rugs in opulent shades of gold and burgundy, while sumptuous silk and velvet upholstery adorned tufted sofas and chaise lounges in vibrant colors of deep purple, gold, and sapphire, transforming the space into a luxurious living room. Dusting off her hands, she said, "Now, what about our sleeping quarters?"

Manu cleared his throat, "Well, I was sure that would've been the first area you'd want to, um, fix. But I guess it's the second." He gestured to the right.

Her brow lifted, a silent question forming in her mind as she slid the door open. The sight before her stole her breath. "You cannot be serious!" The words tumbled out, her voice a mix of disbelief and humor. Dominating the room was an enormous platform bed, its appearance more akin to a soldier's cot, tightly made with military precision. The sheets were taut, as if daring anyone to disturb them. She crossed the room, each step slow and deliberate, and perched on the edge of the bed. It was as unforgiving as a slab of stone beneath her.

Her eyes darted around, searching for something, anything, to soften the room's starkness. The wardrobe loomed large against one wall, an imposing sentinel beside a, thankfully, enclosed weapon rack.

"Well, it certainly is every inch a warrior's lair." The only thing that breathed life into the room was the wall of windows offering a sweeping view of mountains that seemed to float on clouds, their peaks brushed by the setting sun.

Manu's nonchalance was almost amusing as he shrugged, the gesture as casual as his tone. "All I do is sleep in here," he said, as if the spartan decor needed no further explanation. But then his eyes twinkled with a hint of mischief, and he motioned toward the opposite side of the room, where an arched doorway beckoned. "I believe you'll find the bathing chamber more to your liking, my lady."

He was correct. The room was reminiscent of a spa, complete with a sunken whirlpool, lush greenery, and a walk-in shower big enough for four people.

"It will do," Cassie said. "But seriously, I absolutely *must* fix our bed chamber immediately."

Manu grinned wolfishly, swept her up once more into his arms, and circled her around to the platform bed. "Perhaps I can make you a bit more comfortable," he murmured and tumbled them onto the mattress.

TRISTAN CURLED HIS lip in a mocking smirk, his voice laced with contempt. "Did you honestly think Sirkan was the most powerful dark lord on this planet? Please. He was nothing but my pawn. I came here eons ago and found the Radiant One's so-called masterpiece for what it truly was—weak and unworthy. So I chose to reshape it, to claim what should have been mine. If that makes me the worst of all evil, then yes, I am the Devil. This world was never meant to be his alone."

Cassie stared at Tristan, her expression a veil of icy calm, though her mind raced. The fragments of truth pieced together, slowly forming a horrific picture of deception. The embodiment of evil, a guise she recognized all too well, confronted her. Paxton's father truly was the devil incarnate.

He loomed nearly seven feet tall, his elongated crimson face inked with demonic hieroglyphs that looked like black lightning bolts. His citrine eyes glowed, serpentine and malevolent, echoing the very same gaze Sirkan once possessed. Twisted, thorny horns erupted from his temples. The rest of his red, leathery body was overdeveloped with bulging muscles.

Cassie's mind struggled to grasp the depth of this revelation. Memories spiraled around her like ghosts: flashes of her mother with Tristan, Paxton with Tristan, Tristan fighting alongside the White Circle. How could such a colossal lie remain hidden from the most powerful beings in the universe? But if he truly were the epitome of pure malevolence, the Devil, the Deceiver, the Adversary, wouldn't he possess the ultimate mastery of disguise? The power to hide his true identity?

Her internal musings seemed to manifest in reality. Tristan's countenance began to distort, like an image reflected on the surface of a rippling pond. She saw the numerous disguises he'd worn throughout the countless eons. Some held an almost unearthly beauty, transcending the limits of mortal comprehension. Others, however, were so monstrously terrifying that a wave of nausea threatened to overwhelm her. Every nightmare, every grotesque fairy tale, all the abominations that had ever been created in the world: All were contained within this humanoid standing before her.

Shemihaza.

The name reverberated around her like an echo chamber. She put her hands over her ears, trying to drown out the sound. But his claws shot out, wrapping around her throat with an iron grip, sharp talons pricking her skin, drawing blood that trickled down her collarbone. She thrashed against him, desperate to free herself, tearing at his hands as her airways constricted. His eyes glinted, and suddenly, it wasn't Tristan; it was Paxton!

"You cannot escape our destiny, my love," Paxton growled. "I will never let you go. If I can't have you, no one can."

Cassie's eyes widened in horror as Paxton's face drew closer. He hoisted her off the ground, her feet kicking helplessly in the air. His lips curled into a savage snarl, and then he leaned in to kiss her. Her body betrayed her, responding to the lust emanating from him, but a wave of nausea bubbled up inside her. She turned her head, repelled by the rank stench of decay that clung to him, the smell of something long dead.

"Let me go," she gasped, her voice barely a whisper. "You're dead. You can't hurt me."

Behind Paxton, a hulking shadow loomed. Shemihaza's fanged maw appeared, blood dripping from his teeth. "You will be my son's bride," he snarled, his voice like the rumble of distant thunder. "You will bear a new race of demonic demigods, and together, we will rule the Earth."

"No, no, no!" Cassie screamed, panic surging through her as her fingertips began to spark.

"CASSANDRA, WAKE UP!" Manu said, "Breathe! It's only a dream." He was panicked. She wasn't breathing, clawing at her throat as though she were suffocating.

Cassie lashed out at him, battering his chest with her fists.

"Shhh, hush now … it's only a dream," he repeated as he drew her in, taking her hands into his. "You're safe here with me."

She finally woke and drank in her husband's startling blue eyes as they met hers, full of concern. "It was Tristan! I saw him, and he told me who he really is!"

"Here now, take a breath and relax. You can tell me all about it, but first you need to calm those sparklers at your fingertips. I'd rather not set our bed on fire," he grinned, "at least not that way."

Her eyes widened as she stared down at her hands, breath hitching in her throat. The tips of her fingers flickered with a soft, otherworldly glow. Panic tugged at the edges of her mind, but she forced herself to close her eyes. In the darkness behind her lids, she conjured an image of cool, blue light, imagining it flowing through her veins like a gentle stream, quenching the fire in her fingertips. With a deep breath, she shook out her hands, feeling the warmth dissipate until her fingers were just fingers again: ordinary, solid, safe. Only then did she open her eyes.

She turned to Manu, her voice trembling slightly as she began to recount the dream that had ignited her sparklers. "I wanted to go with him, Manu. I felt the power rise up within me, the same power that almost consumed me when Menhit overtook me. At the same time, I thought, 'But Manu, I don't want to lose him.' That's when I started to scream."

"We need to go to Master Elena at once," Manu said, his voice filled with uncertainty. "Do you think it was really Tristan challenging you on the inner planes? Or do you think that you pulled it from a past-life memory?"

"I don't have a clue. I just know it's truth."

"All right then. We will contact Elena and Artemus right now. We'll get to the bottom of this."

THEY STOOD ONCE AGAIN in the Golden Temple, the air thick with anticipation as they awaited Metatron's arrival. Elena, Artemus, and Mikha'El had just stepped into the chamber, their presence almost imperceptible, like sunbeams merging with the golden glow that filled the space. Manu and Cassie followed closely behind, their footsteps echoing softly against the polished marble floor. Arion was also there, having been there on a different mission, so Metatron had asked him to stay.

The room itself exuded an aura of ancient majesty, as if they'd walked into a pharaoh's private sanctuary. The golden walls seemed almost alive as they shimmered in the light. Regal columns rose to meet the high ceiling, their surfaces etched with intricate hieroglyphs that told of long-lost dynasties. The air was thick with incense smoke curling in delicate wisps. Everything about the room spoke of power and reverence, where history and eternity danced in a silent waltz.

The great Metatron strode into the room and immediately went up to Cassie. "Adonai, Cassandra, Manu. It is good to see you both." He turned to the rest of the room and repeated the celestial greeting to all.

Master Elena motioned to the sitting area. "Come, let us sit and be comfortable while Cassandra shares her latest insights into the enigmatic Tristan."

Metatron paced, allowing Cassie's information to settle. "Shemihaza, you say? I have not heard that name in eons. He was the leader of the Watchers."

"And one of our brethren," Mikha'El added.

The rest of the group looked blank. "I have never heard that name," Elena said.

"There is no reason you would have. All that happened well before you arrived on the planet," Metatron said. "The name was stricken from all angelic roles after the rebellion, when many of the fallen Watchers took demonic form. Shemihaza had immense power. The fallen Watchers and lesser angels considered him their leader." He turned to Mikha'El, "Since you experienced it firsthand, why don't you tell the next part of the story?"

Mikha'El nodded and continued, "Shemihaza was once among the highest ranks of the archangels, a Watcher." Seeing Cassie's blank look he explained, "The Watchers were charged with guarding the gates of a paradise known as Lemuria. But pride and forbidden desire led to his downfall. Captivated by mortal women, he and one hundred ninety-nine other angels abandoned their divine duties, descended to Earth, took human lovers, and fathered the Nephilim, giant beings neither fully human nor angelic. This is known as the Great Rebellion. It fell to me to cast them from the angelic spheres forever.

Then one day, Shemihaza simply disappeared. We assumed he'd been defeated by the dark priest, Sirkan, who rose to power around the time the Anunnaki arrived here. Reports suggested Shemihaza had escaped through an interdimensional portal—a controlled gateway between realms. We were wrong."

"What he'd actually created was one of the first interdimensional rifts on the planet—a shimmering, vertical tear in reality's fabric that appeared as a jagged line of swirling, iridescent energy. Unlike portals, these rifts consumed any being that ventured within a mile of them. Like the Bermuda Triangle."

Cassie piped in, "Like what we saw in the Shadow Realm when I was looking for Danax's control panels. I saw a shimmer, like a heat wave coming off a street. But it didn't have colors; it just shimmered."

Mikha'El nodded, "Yes, it sounds very similar. We referred to them as the spaces between worlds, unlike the Citadel's prison, which exists in a pocket dimension—a carefully constructed space between realms. Sirkan's mothership was caught in such a rift—suspended in the chaotic space between dimensions, neither fully here nor there—until he stabilized it and hid it in the very depths of the ocean. The dimensional rifts were close to major leys around the globe and spewed forth hordes of demonic atrocities."

Metatron continued, "That is when the mortals began to whisper Shemihaza's name in fear and awe, some seeking his forbidden knowledge, others praying never to draw his baleful gaze. The demon god was said to rule the realm of men with an insatiable hunger, building his armies and demanding tribute from the burgeoning human tribes and civilizations. Meanwhile, he must have been manipulating Sirkan all along."

Artemus picked up the tale. "When Atlantis fell, the world was plunged into chaos and confusion. Many of the dark acolytes that followed Sirkan perished in the aftermath. During the chaos, Sirkan headed to the rift with Ayesha and his remaining minions."

Mikha'El nodded, "It was likely amidst the turmoil and despair that followed the cataclysm that Shemihaza crafted a new identity for himself. Since I am not fully aware of every angel on this planet, I can only assume that he overshadowed another and took over their persona. With his innate powers, it would have been easy for him to rise in the ranks to eventually be accepted into the White Circle."

Manu felt his blood turn to ice as he listened. He had seen, had *felt* Tristan's power—or whoever he was—and knew that he was virtually invincible. Manu was getting a very bad feeling about where this story was headed.

His fears were realized when Mikha'El looked at Cassie. "Cassandra, you may very well be the only one who can defeat him. You are unlike any being who has walked the Earth. And as the Avatar of Synthesis, you have direct access to the mental plane, the fifth dimension."

Cassie gripped Manu's hand. "I ... I don't understand. How can I be powerful enough to go up against an evil demi-god?"

"Your powers and abilities transcend the physical world," Elena said. "You have proven yourself in multidimensional battle fronts and emerged victorious. You are fully capable of facing a demonic demi-god, no matter how powerful he seems."

Manu put his arm around Cassie protectively, "Cassandra may have total recall of who she is and what her powers are, but she is not trained at that level of battle. This will not be on the Aethernet; it will be with real weapons across dimensions. And who knows what other allies Tristan has at his fingertips? There are bound to be hordes of the Dark Brotherhood at the ready from across the galaxy."

Artemus stepped forward, "Cassandra will not be alone, Manu. The Aquarian Avatars are fully trained and awaiting this battle between light and dark. Now that we know who and what we are up against, we are more prepared than ever to fulfill the Aquarian prophecy and usher in this shift from the Age of Pisces to the Age of Aquarius."

Cassie looked around the room, knowing he was right. "Well, then ... let's get battle ready."

Her declaration of readiness hung in the air, but the tension in the room lingered. Manu met her gaze with a solemn nod before turning to Artemus, an understanding passing between them like a silent oath. The battle was drawing near, and the stakes had never been higher.

Chapter 56: Take Down

President Conroe Soter stood before a vast array of screens and interfaces in the virtual studio erected within the Oval Office, the dim glow illuminating his manic features. This was the nerve center of his grand ambition, where the threads of his complex web had been woven together. The sophisticated programs designed to manipulate global digital networks, disseminating misinformation and subliminal programming to bend the will of the financial and military complexes all over the world to Soter's will were ready for launch. He would give the programs a few days to take hold. Then he would sweep in with a miraculous cure just as it looked like the financial and the entire military-industrial infrastructure was on the verge of total collapse. Then the billionaires and tech moguls would be at his command.

Surrounded by his most trusted advisors, his charcoal eyes gleamed as he envisioned the final phase of his conquest, unaware that his glorious future would be taking an unexpected turn.

"As we escalate our efforts," Soter began, his voice low and intense, "the Technomancer will penetrate deeper into the fabric of society with his new subliminal programs. He has implanted it into all VR gaming and training platforms for military and financial institutions, as well as all social media."

What a pig, Vice President Jessica Stewart thought. She was so grateful that she would have a hand in bringing this sociopath to justice. Soter was the epitome of everything that was vile and evil in the human race. As he spoke, Jessica intoned a simple spell she had learned from Master Artemus that would allow her to control the technical machinations of the in-house studio.

Months ago, Artemus had approached her, and she had learned about the invisible helpers who had been guiding humanity for millennia. She immediately volunteered to become the White Circle's agent within the White House. How she had been so fortunate, she could only attribute to her deep faith in the innate goodness of the universe. She smiled to herself, *Well, maybe more accurately the goodness of what Artemus calls the Radiant One.* That fit.

She pressed a button that, combined with the spell she'd intoned, ensured every word Soter said within the confines of his inner circle would now be heard around the world via a live feed.

Soter paused, lost in the vision of his impending victory, then continued, "Once our manufactured virus infects people's minds across the globe we will have the ultimate weapon of mass destruction as we take over the minds of the masses. Our messages will be their thoughts; our goals, their desires. The world will never know freedom again. It will be entirely ours to command. Every gamer, every government with a military presence, every person with a bank account will be compromised. They will all be at our mercy. The dissenters will be silenced, their wills eroded by our relentless assault on their worst fears. We stand on the precipice of a new era, my friends, one ruled by the order and precision that only *I* can provide."

Outside, in homes and offices, on the streets and in public spaces, people froze as Soter's voice filled the air. The veneer of the benevolent leader shattered and revealed the cold ambition of a tyrant intent on domination through manipulation and control. Disbelief spread, rapidly followed by panic. How could the man seen by many as the savior in turbulent times harbor such dark designs?

Reporters scrambled to get into the White House press room as Soter's press secretary ran to the Oval to do damage control. But news outlets around the world were already spewing forth not just Soter's words, but his smug face as he stood before his cronies.

A frantic staffer burst into the room, his face pale. "Mr. President, we have a situation. This meeting ... it's being broadcast live. *Everywhere.*"

The blood drained from Soter's face as he realized the magnitude of the slipup. He rushed to a screen and saw his face streaming to a global audience. The bank of holographic screens that lined two walls of the Oval Office went dark and then flickered to life with live pictures of him and those assembled around him. The horror and disbelief in the eyes of the global audience was reflected in his own shock as he started to bellow, "Turn off those fucking cameras!"

Soter's mind raced, trying to find a way to regain control. He barked orders to his advisors to shut down the broadcasts, but it was too late. The feed had spread across countless networks. Even if they managed to cut the transmission, the damage had already been done. The revelation was catastrophic.

He whirled on his cabal, screaming, "Get that Technomancer! Find Danax! Where is the witch?"

They all looked at him in dismay. A witch? Was he raving mad?

Desperation took hold. Soter considered his options, but each one seemed more futile than the last. The Oval Office, once a place where he dictated the future, now felt like a prison closing in around him. In a desperate bid to regain control, Soter began to indiscriminately push buttons on the virtual console, trying to call up Danax to counteract the fallout.

Nothing happened.

Enraged, he whirled on his vice president. "Do something. You are just as much to blame for this shit show as I am."

Jessica looked at him placidly. "You backed the wrong horse, Conroe. Now you have to pay the penalty for throwing your lot in with, quite literally, the devil."

Just days before his removal from power, Soter, desperate to curry favor with despotic regimes he admired, shared nuclear launch codes with major dictators—allies he believed would support his ambition to become a global leader. These autocrats, willing to sacrifice entire nations to maintain their wealth and control, kept their populations suppressed.

The new president's first critical action was changing these compromised codes.

The next few months were precarious as mundane forces clashed. Governments previously on the fence now condemned Soter's actions and initiated measures to safeguard their sovereignty and citizens' freedom.

Meanwhile, Ian had been recruiting and training resistance groups. They had been put on high alert for months. Within minutes, portals opened across the globe as the leaders of the resistance movements began to mobilize, unified as never before by the shared threat Soter posed.

Covert assassination plans, which had been held in abeyance by those who had opposed Soter and his cronies, were halted. Simultaneously, the Dark Brotherhood unleashed into the Aethernet all the rage farming it had meticulously "banked" over time.

Economic markets teetered on the brink of collapse as investors scrambled to distance themselves from the growing instability while also scurrying to protect their personal funds.

Social media platforms buzzed with outrage, the hashtag #EndSoter trending within minutes once Soter's true colors were exposed.

In the streets, the tension was intense. Protests erupted in major cities as citizens demanded justice and the immediate resignation of the man who now stood as a symbol of tyranny. Military units, previously loyal to Soter, began to splinter, some joining the growing resistance while others struggled to maintain order.

As the world united against him, Soter's empire of corruption and deceit crumbled. The hot mic moment, intended to be a private declaration of impending triumph, had instead become the catalyst for his downfall.

Chapter 57: Battle of the Bots

Cassie activated her exosuit suit. It locked into place instantaneously. She turned to the avatars, "I have no doubt that once Danax realizes I have entered this purge, he will activate a new, lethal level in the haptic function. But my suit has built-in fail-safes that will protect me from malicious attacks."

Nin had helped Cassie upload new code through her neural network. The new programming would overlay the embedded codes that still flickered faintly in her irises, visible but much dimmer than before to anyone who knew where to look. This deceptive layer of code was designed to feed Danax false tactical data during the upcoming purge of the aethernet's viruses. Each time the Technomancer attempted to predict her moves or counter her abilities, the corrupted data would lead him straight into her carefully planned traps, turning his own technological prowess against him like a digital mirror. The ultimate goal, of course, was to find every last one of the implanted dark codes across social media and other training platforms and eradicate them once and for all from the entirety of the Aethernet.

Manu strode into the command center at that moment looking like his own version of the Technomancer in his enhanced Sirian battle gear. The armor was a thing of beauty that Artemus had worked on tirelessly with Ninhursag. It gleamed like polished tourmaline under the bright lights. This would be its first true battle test outside the lab.

Cassie's heart skipped a beat when she met Manu's eyes. Would she ever get accustomed to the impact this extraordinary soul had on her? His eyes lit up, and he came to her side, taking her hands into his. "Are you ready, love?" Then he bent to her ear to whisper, "Quit looking at me like that. I need full concentration for this battle."

She pushed down a blush, cleared her throat, and handed him the same advanced VR headset she had designed for all of the avatars with retinal projection and eye-tracking. "These will ensure you all have the same advantage I do with my neural net capabilities. I also want to check the haptic functions to make sure we won't incur any death blows while dismantling the various program viruses—we don't want any life-threatening surprises."

The Aquarian Avatars sat at their assigned holographic stations in the Citadel's command center. Perusing them, Cassie's gaze landed on Devika. She could tell the girl was nervous. And why wouldn't she be? This was her first mission as an Aquarian Avatar.

Cassie went over to her and put her hands on her shoulders. "Don't worry. You are more than ready for this. There is no competition nor judgement here. We all started out the same way. The great thing is that you already had magical training before starting your avatar training."

Cassie looked around the room at the second string of acolytes that she and Manu had been training over the past three months. "Besides, we have plenty of back up in all of the disciplines." She motioned to a group of white witches Tatiana had trained. "If you feel you need some support, they are here to help you."

The group inclined their heads toward Devika.

She smiled wanly at them and chewed the inside of her cheek. "The hardest thing for me has been to keep the dark magic balanced with the white magic. It always wants to take over."

"Yeah, I get that," Cassie replied. "In my dark past lives, negative thoughts were more powerful than positive ones, kind of like yelling has more energy than whispering. Dark magic is driven by emotions, while white magic is driven by the mind. In general. To make something happen, you need to visualize it first (thought), then believe you can do it (emotion). That's metaphysics 101. You know, I just had an encounter with the darkest of my past-life selves while on Sikan's mother ship. As the saying goes, it takes a village, plus love and forgiveness. Without Manu's unconditional love and Ninhursag's wisdom and technological acumen, I could have been lost to the dark side forever."

Devika inhaled deeply and nodded. "Thanks for the reminder. Fear was so much a part of my early years, always looking over my shoulder, always squashing who I was. Now it's a constant effort to realize that those innate abilities are OK to use with the right intent and motivation."

Seraphina came over to them. "I picked up on your fear all the way on the other side of the room." She touched Devika's arm. "Cassie has had more experience than any of us in learning to let go of the 'I'm not good enough' thoughts and letting in the 'I can do this' affirmations. Say it out loud; that gives it more power."

Cassie hugged her. "Seraphina, you are a jewel."

"Yeah, yeah, I know. Now let's get rid of the remaining subliminals invading the Aethernet, shall we? We need to cut off the rage farming that's feeding the Dark Brotherhood's plan for world dominance."

"We can help you through that," said the ginger-haired white witch stepping through a portal. Morgandrian stepped out behind him. Ian took Morgandrian's hand in his, and they both went up to Devika. Morgandrian embraced her. Fast on their heels was Tatiana. She too went to Devika and kissed her on her forehead. The witch's kiss: a benediction and a blessing.

Cassie announced, "Our task is to obliterate remnants of Danax's programing still embedded in VR games, social media, news wires, financial systems, and online training programs that the mundanes are connected to. In other words, we obliterate every last byte that is connected in any way to the Technomancer." She paused and swept her eyes over the cyber warriors. "Remember that whatever you encounter today is a simulation hypothesis: manipulated information that has been implanted into the Aethernet in order to *trap* you inside an illusion. If you encounter the Technomancer, or anything that looks like him, she and I will both be here to counteract any of those encounters with you, so don't hesitate to call out if you come upon him."

The avatars sported their new battle gear that replicated Cassie's and were equipped with haptic dampeners, so that any life-threatening programs they might encounter would not affect them physically. Ninhursag had labored for months with the Citadel's most advanced armorers to perfect the bioluminescent materials that made up the self-healing aspects of Cassie's exosuit.

Cassie went to her command station in the center of the room, which gave her a 360-degree view of all the other workstations. "All right, everyone, I will make the initial pass into the Aethernet. Once I give you your mark, you will rotate one by one into your assigned apps, games, and training programs and begin your unraveling spells. There will be several challenges. One is the anger energy that is winding its way through the entire Aethernet. The other challenge will be identifying and neutralizing any malicious code within the social media platforms and the other programs the mundanes are using."

Cassie closed her eyes and released streams of data that flowed from her mind through her fingers into the computer interface. "We'll need to be precise and efficient."

She connected to the Aethernet and the magical realm that merged with the digital world. "All right, on my mark ... three, two, one, *engage!*"

The avatars plunged into their assigned online programs, their magical essences merging with the digital infrastructure. Marcus raced through a video-sharing app, his mastery of deciphering illusions and ferreting out AI-manipulated media clips allowed his magic to navigate the complex algorithms at breakneck speed. He identified the corrupted codes, which manifested as glitchy, distorted videos, and began to unravel the malicious spells woven into them.

Seraphina melted into the shadows of micro-blogging platforms and news-sharing apps; her keen senses were attuned to the subtle vibrations of the subliminal messages. Her devic-human ability to see into the aetheric plane allowed her to find the invisible-to-the-eye subliminal messages geared toward rage farming and misdirection hidden within seemingly innocent posts. With surgical precision, she slowly dismantled the malicious code, freeing the users from its influence.

An-Mei immersed herself in the military training programs, while Karim dove into the complex financial platforms. Their unique ability to traverse dimensions allowed them to peer through the veils that separated physical and digital realms, giving them an unparalleled advantage in managing their tasks and seeing through the illusions that Danax had set up.

While the avatars focused on cleaning up their assigned platforms, Cassie closed her eyes to the outer stimuli in the command center and monitored their progress. Since becoming the Avatar of Synthesis, she was able to take her connection to the Aethernet to a whole new level simply by focusing her thoughts on a specific block of code and envisioning the desired outcome. *Quantum physics at its best,* she smiled to herself.

Karim was the first to hit resistance. The Dark Brotherhood's digital defenses triggered just as he breached the core of the international financial systems. He sent out a silent signal for backup as he zeroed in on the threat: a rootkit embedded deep within the World Bank's intranet. It was designed to generate fraudulent investment opportunities disguised as a sure thing endorsed by Conroe Soter. The fake promises of unlimited wealth acquisition had already duped millions, even though he had been so publicly taken down. The flow of lies and misinformation claimed that he was still in control and was being demonized by the *real* bad guys, the White Circle.

"Cassie, we've got a rootkit. Deep. It's feeding fake investment alerts to all channels. We need to neutralize it fast, or the Dark Brotherhood's grip tightens over the World Bank," said Karim.

Cassie's fingers flew across her keyboard. "Got it. Sending backup. Hold tight."

She swiftly redirected two acolytes to Karim's station, specialists in dampening spells that neutralized malicious digital constructs. Within minutes, she could see the ripple effect of their magic in her mind's eye. The dark code began to disintegrate, but progress stopped abruptly.

Danax's unshrouded face appeared on her screen. It was a grotesque fusion of flesh and machine. She knew he meant to rattle her, to make her recoil from the sight of his inhuman features. And while it was indeed horrifying, she had experienced worse in the Shadow Realm. Still, a wave of nausea rose in her throat as his eyes, unnervingly close to human, locked onto hers. His golden irises gleamed, and a web of metallic filaments extended from his temples, merging seamlessly with his sleek, conductive hair that acted as a neurolink, granting him instant access to vast stores of knowledge.

And to her.

Then she felt it: a pulse of electromagnetic energy streaming from his gaze, probing her mind. His presence slithered along the code she was sending into the Aethernet. She smiled inwardly, opening up her mind even more so that he thought he was plundering it.

All this she registered in a nanosecond as Danax attempted to breach her neural defenses. But she was faster. Before he could worm his way into her mind, she blocked him, severing the connection with a forceful mental shove.

Nonplussed, Danax's voice dripped with smug confidence in her mind, "Welcome, Cassandra, are you ready to be outmatched?" She raised her chin at Manu.

Suddenly a flood of flaming code slammed into her third eye. She screamed. It was like burning cinders had been shot into forehead, her physical eyes feeling like they were on fire.

Manu flew to Cassie. "Nin!" he yelled. The Anunnaki was already kneeling beside them, her hands running streams of healing energy over Cassie's forehead.

Karim's voice rose above the fray, "Here please!" Artemus went to his aid. Karim too was writhing in pain, his hands over his eyes. "Everyone stop where you are. Don't disengage, just halt." He swiveled to Tatiana. Without a word, they added their healing energy together to undo the physical damage that the dark bots had caused.

Elena was kneeling with Manu at Cassie's side, "This is powerful dark magic," Manu hissed. "But Cassandra is fighting it off. I believe I've got this, Elena," he said as he grabbed his amulet. With that Elena scoured the room to check on each of the avatars. She stopped abruptly at Devika, who had frozen in place. "Devika, are you all right?"

No response.

The girl stood like a statue, her eyes wide but unable to move. Devika had been using her dark magic to ferret out misinformation framing the White Circle as warmongers. It was spewing out of the AP newswires and stirring up the populace, not only in the United States but also allied countries. People thought light was dark and vice versa, one of the most dangerous ploys out there, which is why it was the first place the Technomancer had unleashed his counterattack. Or rather, his progeny had set a trap. The group of acolytes assigned to Devika sprang into action, adding their coding expertise to Devika's magic. Although seemingly frozen, her counterspells were still running, albeit with glacial speed.

Cassie suddenly shot up, her arms outstretched, and sent a stream of code toward Devika, directing her mind into Devika's console. She could see the swarm of dark magic-infused bots that hurtled into the Aethernet to combat Devika's cleansing spells. Even while Manu continued to support Cassie energetically, she was able to function enough to stave off the attack on Devika.

"I've got you," said Cassie. She knew she had to act fast. She dove deeply into the Aethernet, her mind racing through complex magical algorithms and equations. Even weakened, she was still well matched in chasing after the rogue Danax clone. With a flash of insight, she devised a spell that would temporarily disable the dark bots and grant Devika a window of opportunity to finish disabling the subliminal messages and repair the platforms to put out the truth. Devika's eyes blinked, and she slowly came back to awareness.

Satisfied that Devika had things under control, Cassie's voice rang out through the avatars' comms. "I'm going to cast a neutralizing spell. Be ready to strike when I give the signal!" Her mind raced through complex magical algorithms and equations until the spell she was weaving coalesced.

The avatars braced themselves, their magic at the ready. Cassie unleashed her spell, a blinding flash of light that surged through the Aethernet. The dark bots froze, their corrupted code temporarily paralyzed by the neutralizing magic.

"Now!" Cassie shouted.

Ninhursag and the avatars sprang into action, their combined magics tearing through the frozen bots and decimating the malicious code. They raced against time, knowing that the bots would soon recover and resume their assault. Then consoles across the command center began to blink out one by one, cutting off any source of energy that could be siphoned off to feed the dark code. They were engulfed in complete darkness for under three minutes, everyone holding their breath.

Cassie scanned the social and news media sites. *Clean.* Then the military training programs and financial institutions. They were all clean and functioning. She gave the all clear. The avatars set aside their headsets and looked around at one another in somewhat of a daze.

Ninhursag put her arm around Devika's shoulders while looking over at Cassie and Elena. "I believe the second battle has been won."

"You all were awesome today," said Cassie. "I think we have definitely put a stop to the subliminal hold the Technomancer and his progeny have had over the digital landscape for the past five years or more. Now that Sirkan is dead and Danax neutralized, it's time we rededicate ourselves to raising the consciousness along the ley lines."

She looked at the time. *Past three.* "Let's rest for the remainder of today. In the morning, we will reach out to our meditation groups and ask them to meet at their respective locations, same places they met for the fall equinox. We are two weeks away from the full moon of Aquarius."

"And our birthday month!" Seraphina chimed in.

Cassie smiled, "And our birthdays. Let's plan on syncing up the day after tomorrow at noon and get back to some consciousness raising! I want to share a new meditation with you, so you can start to prepare your groups."

A cheer went up as they all shuffled out of the command center. Manu put his arm around her waist. "How about a long soak and dinner in bed?" he whispered in her ear.

"You must be psychic," Cassie murmured.

Chapter 58: As Above So Below

"Close your eyes and feel the space around you. This beautiful meditation garden with the scents of the flowers, the trees. Feel the grass beneath you. Hear the birds' wings flutter around you, each sound taking you deeper and deeper into yourself. Now and imagine a sphere of energy surrounding you," Cassie spoke softly to her meditation group. "This is your personal space, your aura. Feel it pulsing with each beat of your heart and growing brighter and larger until it reaches about three feet around you."

She paused for several minutes, allowing the group to have a fully immersive experience. This particular meditation would give them all the boost necessary for the upcoming exercise on the Aquarian full moon.

"Now, picture your daily interactions. See how your energized aura touches others, how it ripples outward. That cashier who smiled after serving you? Your positivity affected them. The stranger who held the door? They felt your calm."

Cassie's voice dropped to almost a whisper. "Now focus on the beating of your heart ... breathe into it and affirm to yourself, 'I love, and I care. I love, and I care. I love, and I care.' And now see a line of light go up from your heart center into your third eye. Breathe it in and allow it to overflow from your physical body into your auric body. This is your inner technology at work. You are connecting heart to mind and beginning the process of personal transformation. By transforming ourselves, we transform our world. Every thought, every emotion, every action vibrates beyond us. We're all connected, influencing each other constantly."

She took a deep breath before continuing and smiled, giving her voice a softer feel. "Visualize humanity on an upward spiral. Reaching toward the divine, striving to align our consciousness with a higher wisdom. At the same time, imagine that wisdom extending downward, meeting us halfway. This is the concept in the Ageless Wisdom Teachings called 'as above, so below.' Think of it like a double-sided mirror."

Cassie's eyes sparkled as she elaborated, her hands moving gracefully to illustrate her words. "On one side, you see your reflection, your thoughts, actions, and personal growth. On the other, you glimpse the infinite cosmos, the universal consciousness. As you meditate, as you evolve, these reflections begin to merge. I call it 'my mind to divine mind.'"

She paused, allowing the image to sink in. "Feel how your individual journey resonates with the grand cosmic dance. Every step you take toward self-improvement ripples outward, just as the universe's wisdom flows into you. It's a constant exchange, a beautiful balance."

Cassie's voice softened. "In this sacred interplay, we find our true evolution. We're not just passive observers, but active participants in the universe's unfolding. Your personal transformation is part of something far greater than yourself." She paused for a beat. "Now, come back to the present moment feeling refreshed, connected, transformed. And when you're ready, slowly and gently open your eyes."

She met each student's gaze with warmth and encouragement. "Remember this as you go about your day. Every act of kindness, every moment of mindfulness, is both a personal victory and a cosmic contribution. Our personal growth isn't just for us. It's a gift to everyone we meet and part of a greater cosmic dance. We rise from the earth, while creation descends from the heavens. In this exchange, we become active participants in not only our own evolution, but in the evolution of all beings on Earth and beyond. Think of it as spiritual technology. We don't need machines or AI to progress. We simply need our minds and our hearts. You are the bridge between mind and spirit, between humanity and divinity." As the group became fully awake, she put her hands together in unison with them and affirmed the Hindu word for peace three times. "Shanti, shanti, shanti. See you next week at the corner of Trade and Tryon for our Aquarian full moon meditation."

The group gathered their meditation pillows and benches in silence and shuffled out of the room. As she followed them with her smiling eyes, she saw Manu leaning against the archway that led out of the meditation garden. A few girls tripped over their own feet when they saw him, something she could well understand. Her heart still skipped a beat or two when she saw her soul mate. He was a swoon-worthy figure dressed as he was in full Sirian battle gear, the black leather-like material stretched over his more than well-muscled chest. And those eyes! Startling blue eyes that were currently trying to maintain a polite, impersonal look as he bowed his head in acknowledgment to the giggled greetings. She shook her head; he was hopeless.

Not wanting to give him any quarter, she squinted her eyes at him and pursed her lips, shaking her head in mock disgust. He smiled and quickly crossed the room to her, kissing her lightly on the lips. "You are incorrigible!" she scolded. "Here I just finished an hour long 'love and light, peace and calm' meditation with them, and now half of the women's heart rates just went up to anxiety level."

Manu's eyes twinkled with mischief as he pulled her closer. "Apologies, my love. I didn't mean to disrupt your class. I was merely ... observing Earth customs."

She rolled her eyes, fighting back a smile. "Earth customs? Is that what you call nearly causing a swoon fest?"

He chuckled, a deep, rich sound that vibrated through her core. "Perhaps I should attend more of your meditation sessions. I clearly need to work on my ... calming presence."

"You?" she laughed, poking his chest playfully. "Mister I Can Make Hearts Race Across Galaxies? I don't think so."

Manu's expression softened, his eyes gazing into hers with a depth that made her breath catch. "I may not need meditation, but I do need you, wife. Your wisdom, your light ... it grounds me in ways I never thought possible."

She felt a warmth spread through her chest, the earlier playfulness giving way to a profound connection. "And you, husband, remind me that even in our pursuit of inner peace, there's room for a little excitement."

They shared a knowing smile, the garden around them humming with an energy that was uniquely theirs. Cassie intertwined her fingers with Manu's, feeling the strength and gentleness in his touch.

"Come on, you big alien troublemaker," she said softly. "Let's go to our house for a bit. I think we both could use some downtime after all this excitement."

Double entendre noted, Manu whisked her off to their bedroom, leaving behind the lingering energy of calm and the faint echo of giggles.

THEIR RESPITE WAS SHORT lived as their spirit screen went off less than an hour later. Cassie sighed, "Well, at least we got a few minutes of alone time."

Manu jumped up and hurriedly threw on his robe and activated the screen. "Manu here."

"Ah, good, I see you are still in Charlotte. Is Cassandra with you?" said Artemus.

"Yes, she's right here. Is something amiss?"

"More than amiss. I will be there momentarily. Meet me in the command center of the institute. And gear up."

Cassie was already activating her battle gear as Manu hurriedly put his back on.

Chapter 59: Shemihaza

Tristan knew when he was being stalked. Standing in the command center of Sirkan's mother ship, he could feel Mikha'El's probing, the subtle push against the ship's defenses, hovering in the atmosphere and searching for a way in.

But he wasn't about to cower. Not now. Not when he was so close to achieving his goals. He had anticipated this moment, had prepared for it in the darkest corners of the universe, where the light of archangels couldn't reach.

Tristan smiled grimly. He would give Mikha'El what he wanted: an opening. But it wouldn't be what the archangel expected.

He turned abruptly and ported to his hidden mountain fortress at the base of Mount Fuji. Deep within the Aokigahara Forest that the locals considered evil and haunted, it was the ideal location to avoid any unwanted attention from intruders. The library there was his most prized possession. It was filled with ancient scrolls and texts, many of which he had stolen from the Library of Alexandria before it was damaged during Julius Caesar's civil war in 48 BC. Fortunately, Caesar hadn't directly burned the library; he had set fire to ships in the harbor. The flames spread to the docks and ignited part of the library, but it survived. There was nothing as precious as history, and Tristan knew he had a library only rivaled by the White Circle's at the Citadel.

Tristan shook his head. No matter. He knew there must be a solution hidden in some of these ancient scrolls that the celestials had brought to the planet. Something that would allow him to not only thwart Mikha'El but also defeat him. He had only to ferret it out. He could call on allies from dark dimensions and dark worlds to come up with a solid plan on how to defeat Mikha'El and destroy the White Circle. In the meantime, he would summon Soriah and pull her into the next steps of his plans.

But first, some research into how to bring Mikha'El to his knees.

Returning his attention to the Book of Enoch, he called up an ancient incantation as his fingers traced through the ancient hieroglyphs. The archaic script was familiar to him, yet as he focused on it, the words seemed to shift and rearrange themselves, their meaning crystallizing in his mind. His heart quickened as he read aloud.

"And the mighty Mikha'El shall falter not by mortal hand, but by the unraveling of divine purpose. His strength, born of the Radiant One's will, can be undone only by the void from which all was made. The essence of the first sin, the rebellion, and the corrupted flame shall be his undoing."

Tristan looked up, his eyes burning with a mixture of understanding and disbelief. The essence of the first sin ... the rebellion, *his* rebellion. Despite his Watcher's name being stricken from even these earliest scrolls, he still retained his powers. Powers that he had used to anchor the Dark Brotherhood on this planet. He thought for a minute about having Soriah summon the dark lords who had helped him build that alliance. They were from planets all over the galaxy that had been watching with interest as the third planet of Sol evolved and came of age. They knew it was a "hot ticket" in the evolution of its star system as it neared its sacred initiation, an initiation that still hung in the balance. Would humanity choose the path of light and follow the Radiant One, or would they succumb to their baser instincts and embrace the left-hand path of the Dark Brotherhood? Between Sirkan and the Technomancer, he had done all he could to manipulate them onto the left-hand path. But Sirkan was gone, and he wasn't able to get a fix on Danax since the Technomancer had gone rogue. The remnants of Sirkan's power base were embodied in an untried vampire who had ensconced herself as Natesh's successor, and Morgandrian who was being manipulated by the White Circle's enforcer.

And then there was "the corrupted flame" piece of the solution. That had to be referring to the Violet Flame of the Master St. Germaine.

"Bah! Enough of this. It's time I took some definitive action."

He twisted his ruby ring to call his first.

"MY LORD?" SORIAH BOWED as she looked around nervously. She truly hated this place that reeked of death and decay. But, of course, that was the very reason why Tristan had chosen it as his lair. No human would dare venture into the deep recesses of this place.

Shemihaza sat in all his demonic glory on a throne made of the bones of his slain enemies and errant followers. Soriah shuddered. She could feel the rage oozing out of his every pore, which was why, she assumed, he was wearing his demonic visage.

Reading her look of horror, he gave her a twisted smile as he ran his right palm down his face and transformed into his more palatable form. "Better?" he leered.

She wisely remained silent.

He watched her out of Tristan's eyes, relishing the beauty of her voluptuous body. He would enjoy her later. Sighing, he rose from his skeletal throne and motioned her toward the archway that led to his prized library.

Bewildered, Soriah followed him.

Books and scrolls were strewn across the enormous black marble slab that acted as both desk and altar. In the center was a crystal ball as big as a basketball that crackled ominously. "I have been scouring ancient scrolls to ascertain how I can defeat Mikha'El. The last time I was on Sirkan's ship I detected his signature. He is hunting me."

"Where are the dark Watchers, my lord? Perhaps we can summon them?"

"That's exactly what I have been thinking. It will take a major blood ritual to call them here. Gather your acolytes. I need thirteen sacrifices."

DARKNESS HAD FALLEN over the desolate jungle, the sky split by jagged, blood-red clouds that churned like the torment of lost souls. Soriah's acolytes had set two dozen bamboo cage traps along a twenty-mile perimeter of Mount Fuji, knowing that not all would trap humans. Better to have too many than not enough.

The howls of the hapless victims had finally ceased. She had prepared sleeping spells that initiated as soon as the bamboo traps were raised from the jungle's mossy floor. As anticipated, seven had trapped animals, which would be slaughtered for sustenance.

The black marble altar, its surface etched with symbols that seemed to pulse in time with an unseen heartbeat, had been moved to the clearing outside his lair.

Tristan had transformed into Shemihaza once again. He stood before the altar, his hands raised, the pale glow of the full moon casting long shadows around him. His form was imposing. His black wings were unfurled, and he wore blood-red armor fashioned out of hellstone, which was known for its crimson hue and supernatural durability. Soriah and her acolytes encircled the altar, their voices twisted with the weight of malice, chanting in a guttural, ancient tongue.

Bound to the cold stone was a young woman. Her skin was alabaster, her eyes wide with terror, the light of innocence still flickering in them, though her strength had faded. The chains binding her glowed faintly, shimmering as if resisting the vile magic swirling around her. Overhead, a magical pulley system waited to deposit the remaining twelve humans, one by one.

Shemihaza stepped forward, a cruel smile curling his lips as he dissipated the sleeping spell. He needed to have the sacrifices fully awake and full of terror, so that energy could be harvested. He drew a curved dagger from his side. Its blade shimmered with an oily, iridescent sheen and hummed with dark energy.

"The blood of the purest soul," he whispered, his voice smooth and low, carrying the weight of eons of corruption. He raised the dagger above the woman, her eyes widened in horror as she began to scream. The ceremonial athame swiped across her throat, and her blood traveled down the grooves carved along the surface of the altar to gather in a pool at its foot. The coppery smell of fresh blood filled his nostrils, and he raised his hand to obliterate the body into a fine mist. Then he motioned for the next body to be lowered onto the altar.

The screams of the young boy were music to his ears. Yes, he mused, not only blood would be harvested this day. So would fear. He breathed it in as the second blood sacrifice fell to his knife with the precision of a task done thousands of times before.

As the last of the thirteen humans was chained onto the altar, a blast of light erupted from above, as if the heavens themselves had torn open. A beam of golden radiance shot down, illuminating the space in its wake, and with it came the sound of wings, feathered, mighty, and pure.

Shemihaza! A voice boomed from above. It echoed across the clearing like thunder rolling through the mountains. Archangel Mikha'El descended clad in shimmering golden armor, his wings spread wide and glowing with a radiance that cut through the darkness, just like his flaming sword. His eyes, burning with righteous fury, locked onto Shemihaza as he touched down, the ground trembling beneath his feet.

Mikha'El's eyes flared as he took a step forward. "Release her now, Shemihaza, or face the wrath of heaven."

Shemihaza's grin widened, his serpentine eyes gleaming with dark amusement. "Ah, Mikha'El. Always so predictable, always so … noble." He gestured to the woman on the altar, his voice mockingly soft. "You're just in time to watch the dawn of a new era."

He plunged the dagger downward. The woman gasped, her body convulsing as the blade pierced her heart. Her blood spilled across the altar, crimson and vibrant, seeping into the carved runes that now glowed with a malevolent light.

"No!" Mikha'El surged forward, but it was too late.

The ground beneath them trembled violently, and the altar cracked, black smoke rising from the fractures. The blood flowed like a river, sinking into the earth as if feeding something far below. The chanting rose to a fever pitch.

Shemihaza stepped back, laughing darkly. "Witness, Mikha'El. Witness the summoning of our dark brethren!"

From the fissures, shadowy figures began to rise. Their forms were tall and formidable, their faces hidden beneath dark hoods. Their eyes, glowing with pale, aethereal light, locked onto Mikha'El. There were no words, only the oppressive silence of their presence. The dark Watchers hovered above the altar, their black, leathery wings stretching out like bat wings, casting the clearing in deeper shadow.

Mikha'El's expression hardened. "You've sacrificed the innocent for your unholy pact, Shemihaza. There is no forgiveness for what you've done."

Shemihaza's mouth twisted into a sneer. "Forgiveness? I seek only annihilation of the weak."

The dark Watchers moved as one, their shadows merging into a writhing mass of darkness. They surged toward Mikha'El, their molten swords raised, spewing otherworldly energy.

Mikha'El met them head-on, his fiery sword cutting through the air. He struck the first Watcher, and it dissipated with a howl of anguish. But more followed, relentless, their power weighing him down. The darkness around him grew thicker, smothering, as their energy pulled at his light, draining him, slowing him.

Shemihaza stood back, watching with cruel satisfaction as Mikha'El fought to stay on his feet. "The light will fail you, Mikha'El. The Watchers hunger for your soul, and they will not stop until you're broken."

Mikha'El gritted his teeth, his sword cutting through another Watcher, but he staggered as their dark tendrils wrapped around his wings, pulling him toward the ground.

"You underestimate the light," Mikha'El snarled, even as the weight of the Watchers pressed down on him.

"You and your ilk are so alike. Manu claimed the same, and yet I threw him into hell."

"And yet, here I stand," a voice boomed from above, even as the Watchers circled Mikha'El like vultures, waiting for their moment to strike the final blow.

Shemihaza raised his hand, ready to give the command, but Manu was ready for him.

Mikha'El, despite the darkness clinging to him, spread his wings wide, and in an instant, a burst of light exploded from him, scattering the dark Watchers. They hissed and recoiled, retreating into their dark dimension until their leader called them forth once more.

Shemihaza snarled, his eyes narrowing. "Impressive, but futile. I can summon them again and again, Mikha'El. Neither you nor Manu nor the Trybrid can hold them off forever."

"Taking my name in vain?" Cassie mocked as she stepped into the clearing. "Really, Tristan, we've known each other for too long for you not to, ya know, tell me what you really think."

Shemihaza snarled, "We'll see, *girl*. The blood has been spilled. The darkness has been unleashed. Heaven will fall."

Cassie's smirk didn't falter as she faced the twisted form of Shemihaza. To everyone else, this was a battle between an ancient force of darkness and the warriors of light, but for her, this was personal. Tristan, or Shemihaza, wasn't just another enemy. He had been a part of her life in ways no one else could understand. Well, except for her mother. She shrugged.

"Well, Uncle Tristan—remember when you used to ask me to call you uncle?" Her smirk bloomed into a full-blow laugh. "Well, *uncle*," she repeated, her Southern accent intensified, "looks like the gates of heaven have done opened a flood gate of retribution." She flew at him with the Sword of Keraunos and prepared to swing it in the wide arc movement she had learned from a French fencing master in her time in the court of Louise XVI.

Fully prepared for his countermeasure, Manu flew in beside her, shields in place around them both, staff and sword activated with his ancient Sirian magic.

Shemihaza stood in his full demonic glory, staff and shield ready for the onslaught. "You are no match for me. You will need to call on the Radiant One himself, Mikha'El, but even he won't be able to stop what I have set in motion."

Mikha'El stood his ground, now shoulder-to-shoulder with Manu and Cassandra. "I won't need to. This ends now."

Two of the greatest angelic warriors ever created faced each other in battle. Just as Mikha'El lifted his flaming sword and flew toward his dark brother, Shemihaza threw up an impenetrable shield around his sacred mountain, and it disappeared.

His voice rang across the valley. "We will fight another day, brother."

Chapter 60: And Thus I Rise

Manu looked over the assemblage in the Citadel's command center pensively. Every avatar, trainer, and acolyte from Praxis was there, along with the entirety of the White Circle.

The archangels Mikha'El and Raphael, along with Commander Eristides St. Claire, stood with Artemus and Elena. Ashtar Sherhan beamed in via spirit screen.

"We are at a crossroads this day," Mikha'El announced without preamble. "Manu, Cassie, and I just had an ominous encounter with Shemihaza. He had gathered the dark Watchers through a horrific blood sacrifice of thirteen humans. We defeated some of the Watchers, but the rest have retreated into their dark dimension until they are called forth again by their lord to battle once more on the earthly plane."

A heavy silence hovered in the air, thick with tension and unease. The gravity of Mikha'El's words weighed down on each member of the group

Finally, Manu broke the silence, his voice filled with a sense of urgency. "We need to ensure that everyone within the Praxis Institute has both physical and mental battle training. We will be hit on multiple fronts in the coming days, and we must be prepared. I don't want anyone to be caught unaware."

"Agreed," said Xander, the master trainer at Praxis. "I will reach out to each of the trainers and ensure they add sessions in all of the disciplines.

Mikha'El then turned to Artemus. "What is the status of the Soter debacle?"

"A debacle no more," said Artemus. He went on to relay the initial chaos that had erupted after Conroe Soter was exposed over the Aethernet. "Now that Jessica Stewart is president of the United States, she will be working closely with Manu and Cassandra, who have agreed to lead a new contingent that the president has christened the Concordant. She is finalizing her cabinet appointments, and the White Circle will serve as special advisors to her administration. Most of our involvement will remain behind the scenes until she determines the right time to reveal our existence, along with the fact that beings from other star systems share this planet with humanity."

Artemus continued, explaining how world governments and financial institutions were addressing the situation. "Since her inauguration, Soter has been placed in the custody of the United States National Central Bureau, the Washington branch of INTERPOL. He will be tried by the International Criminal Court in The Hague. Many institutions will undergo significant reforms in the coming months and years as nations rebuild. The threat of oligarchies seizing control of far-right governments around the world remains, and we must work to neutralize these despots. In the meantime, I've assured President Stewart that we stand ready to provide counsel as they work to reconstruct a deeply fractured political system."

He paused and looked at Manu, "And the Technomancer?"

"Neutralized and being held in stasis by the Lady Ninhursag," Manu replied. "He is too valuable to be completely destroyed, and Ninhursag wants an opportunity to reprogram him when the time is right."

Elena stepped forward. "With Cassandra now in place as the Avatar of Synthesis, it is imperative that she implements the meditation training programs, so they are accessible to all who want training. This is an enormous undertaking, especially since we cannot let the mundanes know who we really are. I believe we can maintain and expand our meditation programs as part of the university systems across the country. Humanity has been through the equivalent of a world war, emotionally and mentally, after Conroe Soter's duplicity. We need to establish a sense of safety for them. A time will come when they will be ready to embrace the idea that beings they consider legends and fables are real. But it is not up to us to ascertain when. It must evolve naturally." Elena looked around the room. "We are still under the non-interference directive of the Radiant One."

"In the meantime," Cassie continued, "the avatars and I have scheduled world peace meditations along the Charlotte-DC ley line for noon on the Aquarius full moon next month with our meditation groups. The last time we did this, I felt a huge shift in the vibrational frequency of the ley line in Charlotte. This next one could very well raise the frequency to the midpoint of Scorpio rising.

"The Eagle," said An-Mei. "The symbol of the United States."

Cassie nodded, "It's settled then. Let's get with our meditation groups and begin the prep work. I will, as always, connect with each of you through the Charlotte institute's intranet and lead the meditation."

A DARK-WINGED ANGEL stepped out from behind the archangels and cleared his throat. "Since I served as Shemihaza's first lieutenant after we rebelled against the Radiant One, I believe I may be able to offer some strategic insights for that," Azazel said.

Manu strode up to the Watcher and grabbed his forearm in solidarity. "It is good to see you after all this time. I will never forget how you helped Cassandra and her father balance the scales when she was first taken by Sirkan and Isla. I, for one, would be grateful for any insights and strategies you could share."

Azazel inclined his head, "Of course, Commander. I am loyal to King Ayden and will always be so to his family." Cassie silently came up to stand beside Manu.

Azazel continued, "Shemihaza is a demon. As such, he can be defeated. But the power needed may be too great for the Earth to handle in this vulnerable time. I know we are determined to usher in the Shift of the Ages, but it is a birthing process. As with any birth, there will be birthing pains. If we unleash the full might of the angelic host before humanity reaches the requisite level of consciousness, we might very well cause a cosmic convergence."

Cassie frowned, "I'm not familiar with that term."

Azazel motioned to Mikha'El. "Care to take this one?"

The archangel, leaning casually against the main computer console, unfolded his arms. His eyes were steady, his voice calm. "We are standing on the edge of a pivotal moment in evolution, as you well know," Mikha'El said. "Humanity is on the cusp of something extraordinary: the ability to manifest their thoughts directly into reality. 'From thought to hand,' as it's called in the Wisdom Teachings. Your role as the Avatar of Synthesis has already begun transforming human consciousness through the meditation programs you've created. You've built the bridge between the dense physical plane of the third dimension paving the way for humanity to gain access to the refined mental substance of the fifth dimension."

He turned to the spirit screen and brought up a holographic display showing the global spread of Cassie's meditation programs. Millions of points of light flickered across the continents creating a matrix of light, each point representing a soul learning to access higher planes of consciousness. "Your work has demonstrated that the mental plane isn't just a mystical concept; it's a tangible level of reality that humans can learn to access systematically. You and the avatars have demonstrated that the ancient wisdom is indeed applicable to the modern world.

"The cosmic convergence could be a monumental, universe-altering event where light and dark energies align, barriers between dimensions thin, and primordial forces awaken. Through your Trybrid nature, you've learned to balance these forces within yourself: divine light, human consciousness, and what science calls dark matter. This integration is what makes you uniquely capable of defeating Shemihaza."

"Wait," said Cassie, moving closer to the display. "Is that a good thing? I thought we were supporting humanity in their next step of evolution, not forcing a premature awakening. My meditation programs were designed to help people build their mental bodies so they would not be influenced by negative programming infused through the Aethernet. Are you saying that this is the next step, the construction of the Antahkarana, the bridge to higher consciousness?"

Mikha'El nodded, "Yes. There is always a next step until a soul completes its soul contract or ascends. You know from your studies that each incarnation, whether on the Earth plane or another plane of existence, is a continuous spiral of growth and evolution. Each experience builds upon the previous one, creating an ever-expanding consciousness until a soul chooses to continue its journey in another dimension or chooses to be absorbed back into the light of the Radiant One. It's called free will."

Master Elena interjected, "You've already proven that it's possible to channel both divine power and dark power while maintaining equilibrium. By defeating Shemihaza, you would prove that it is possible to transcend the divide between light and darkness, showing others that integration, not separation, is the path forward."

Cassie looked at Manu, her brow furrowed in worry. Reading her mind, he stepped forward, his ancient eyes holding steady. "You will be able to keep the balance, Cassie. This is why you were chosen as the Avatar of Synthesis. You've not only overcome the temptation of your dark powers, but also learned to integrate them, just as Master Elena said. Your own journey from fragmentation to wholeness is the template for humanity's evolution."

"I'm glad you're so sure. This is really a slippery slope ..." She trailed off, her consciousness reaching into the mental plane, scanning possible futures. Moments later, she refocused on the present. "I will, of course, do what I must. We haven't come this far for me to back away from my mission. But if it's Shemihaza we need to defeat, I don't sense him or any iteration of him anywhere on the earthly plane. It's like he's totally vanished."

Then Shemihaza's parting words echoed in her mind. "Wait," she said. "He told us his plans when he said, '*We will fight another day, brother.*' He must be preparing his dark army and the dark Watchers for a final battle, but it won't be any time soon."

Mikha'El nodded contemplatively. "Your insight might be correct. I thought he retreated too easily. It was a calculated move. He is gathering more forces. And most likely off planet."

"Then we must gather ours," Artemus said.

He turned to Manu. "Manu, as you are commander of the intergalactic fleet, I ask that you coordinate with Commander Eristides and the Ashtar Command. There's no telling when this attack will occur. Shemihaza has been waiting millennia for this shift. He still has many decades left to make his opening salvo. We cannot depend on Enki's forces, as Nibiru's orbit may not align with ours in time." He turned to Ninhursag, "You can communicate with him telepathically. I ask you to keep both him and me apprised of every update as we know it."

The Anunnaki nodded.

A hush fell over the room as each warrior, priest, priestess, witch, angel, and avatar centered themselves, knowing that the battle for humanity was still in the making.

Chapter 61: The Shift

The full moon of Aquarius was just weeks away. Cassie was briefing the avatars, along with other key players like Manu, Glenda, and Adrianna at the Citadel to discuss plans for this next level of implementing an advanced mental exercise into the next full moon meditation.

Devika stepped forward, and Cassie swore she was going to raise her hand. Smiling she motioned to her. "What's on your mind, Devika?"

"You remember all the chaos that erupted when the witches competed for my mother's throne in Boston? I've been keeping watch with Glenda and Adrianna to monitor any lingering fallout. I've, um ...," she hesitated, "discovered some disturbing developments. The 'clean up' spell that was cast evidently didn't work on one of the mundanes who was there. They are spreading the word that witches and demons are killing humans and taking control of our government. There are other mundane outlier groups, people who succumbed to the rage farming and mind manipulation spread through the Aethernet viruses. They have formed vigilante groups. Their numbers are growing, and they're claiming the new president is actually a witch. They're declaring their movement is to 'restore true human leadership.'" Her voice dropped. "They're organizing through the Dark Web, using the same tech that manipulated them in the first place. The irony would be almost funny if it weren't so frightening."

Cassie's brows furrowed. "How could they still have access to that tech? We destroyed it again and again."

Devika sighed. "Apparently, someone had access to remnants of it. Maybe there's a hidden cache or lair we missed."

Chills rippled down Cassie's spine as realization dawned. "Of course there'd be backdoor contingencies! But where would it be?"

"I'd guess Shemihaza's lair," Manu suggested, stepping into the conversation. "But the problem is, it's moved. No trace of it, or him, remains. Most likely, they've relocated off-world."

Cassie turned again to Devika once more. "And let me guess: They see Soter as a victim."

"Exactly." Devika nodded with disgust. "They've been stockpiling weapons in abandoned warehouses, subway tunnels, and bomb shelters too."

"And they don't realize they're fighting to restore the very evil they think they're opposing," Cassie finished. "How many are we talking about?"

Devika pulled a holographic map from her pocket crystal, a new tool Marcus had been developing, and beamed it into the middle of the room. Red dots pulsed across multiple regions. "Current estimates show at least two thousand active members in the Mid-Atlantic alone, with new cells sprouting in rural towns. But this is the most concerning part." She zoomed in on an area outside Charlotte. "They've established a base in an abandoned military bunker in Chatham County, known as 'Big Hole,' about thirty miles from our primary meditation site."

Devika pulled in a steadying breath. "They call themselves the Human Restoration Front. But what's more alarming is their leadership: former military personnel who served under Soter's regime, alongside tech and financial oligarchs who grew filthy rich with his schemes."

"The Human Restoration Front," Cassie repeated, her voice laced with revulsion. She crossed her arms tightly, pacing. "Do they honestly think going back to Soter's regime will save humanity? He nearly destroyed the planet with his corporate wars and Aethernet corruption."

Devika's face darkened. "It's worse than that. They don't just want him back: They believe he's the 'Chosen One.' They think his imprisonment is part of some divine trial and that, once freed, he'll 'purify' humanity."

"And they believe Soter's propaganda that *we're* demonic entities enslaving humanity?" Adrianna asked, her voice sharp with concern. "Even after the entire world heard his confession live?"

"Especially because of that," Glenda replied quietly. "They've twisted the narrative. According to their manifesto, which is spreading like wildfire in underground networks, the 'live mic' was a deepfake. They claim it wasn't really Soter speaking but AI manipulation designed to discredit him. In their minds, he's a martyred hero who fought to preserve human dominion over Earth."

Cassie's hands sparked with latent energy as she paced. "We can't cancel the meditation. The energy work is critical to stabilizing the ley line configurations. But we also can't leave ourselves vulnerable." She stopped abruptly and turned to the group. "Devika, does your intel confirm they're planning an attack during the meditation?"

"Yes," Devika said reluctantly, manipulating the hologram with trembling fingers.

Cassie grimaced. "*Fool me once.* There's no way we're letting them breach the meditation. This one will *not* be made public. It will be by invitation only, just for established students. Manu and the others will cloak us with shields reinforced by the mother ships stationed in this quadrant."

Manu added, "And since we know their plans, we'll have a battalion of intergalactic forces ready to intercept. I'm sure your grandfather would lend some assistance, Cassie."

Cassie cracked a wry smile. "Grandfather's always eager to lend a hand. I'll reach out to him. We only have a few weeks until the full moon of Aquarius."

THE DAYS WENT BY IN a blur as they all made preparations for the full moon meditation.

"Let's review our safety protocols for the day of the meditation." Cassie addressed the avatars and the chosen acolytes from Praxis. "Those of you leading the meditation groups are to keep your shields up at all times. Manu will establish a force field over the entirety of the Charlotte-DC ley line with the help of Commander Eristides and his Pleiadian mother ship. The Ashtar Command will offer additional protection to the groups as well as to the ley line itself. Any questions?"

Manu strode into the room just as she was finishing up, his presence immediately commanding attention. "I have been communicating with the other commanders of the intergalactic forces," he declared in a voice that sent shivers down everyone's spines. The room fell silent, tension and anticipation palpable in the air. Most of the women gazed at him adoringly, lost in his presence, while others were visibly eager for the impending battle. Cassie gritted her teeth, feeling her soulmate's powerful energy emanating unchecked. He was dressed in his usual commander's uniform of swoon-worthy black Sirian battle leathers, his knee-high boots polished to a mirror sheen. Cassie sucked in her breath, trying to focus on what he was saying. It was really indecent the way his muscular chest and bulging thighs strained against the leather.

Cassie shook her head. Yet again her soulmate had forgotten to tamp down his energetic field. She growled, *Manu!* telepathically. He started and looked at her with astonishment for a moment before understanding and threw up his dampening shields.

She shook her head again and said to the acolytes, "All right, Glenda and Adrianna will show you to your quarters and go over your schedules with both the avatars and your trainers. If you have any questions or concerns, tell them, and they will relay them to me if necessary." She put her hands palm to palm, bent her head, and said "namaste" as a form of dismissal.

She went up to her husband and poked a finger into his chest. "Really, Manu, you need to be more careful. I can't have you distracting the acolytes and trainees like that."

He bristled. "How was I supposed to know they were here? The Citadel is one place I shouldn't have to worry about such things. It's bad enough that we have to use glamours when we're down on the planet. Give me a break here."

Cassie closed her eyes and took a deep breath. "I know, I know. I'm sorry. There are just so many moving pieces right now. I really could use a break. I've been in an especially cranky mood for the past few weeks."

"Yeah, I've noticed." He went over to her and put an arm around her shoulders. "Let's take some downtime. Maybe we could go visit your parents?"

"That would be nice. Maybe a long weekend, or at least *a* weekend. We've been at this for months now."

ON THE DAY OF THE WORLD Peace Meditation, everything was going according to plan. The meditation groups were in their designated positions, shields were erected, and Cassie was fully connected to the Aethernet through the Charlotte institute. With her quantum-enhanced mental prowess and focused intention, she envisioned the desired outcomes for this session: elevating the vibratory frequency of the ley line to the next level, represented by the transformative powers of Scorpio, from its primitive scorpion stage (characterized by base desires and reactionary behavior) to the evolved Eagle stage (where consciousness rises above material attachments and gains greater spiritual awareness).

As Cassie felt her power of transformation, she sensed the other meditation groups linking in through the quantum field, each positioned strategically along the Charlotte-DC ley line. The Greensboro circle's earthy groundedness flowed northward, while the Charlottesville group's crystalline clarity streamed from their mountain sanctuary. From Richmond's historic heart, the advanced practitioners added their seasoned power to the mix as it flowed through Alexandria, continuing up through the I-85 and I-95 corridors, ending at the Capitol Building.

The combined force created a resonant field that amplified the transmutation. Where Cassie had been gently reshaping the scorpionic current, now it surged upward with renewed vigor through each node along the ley line. The dark, dense energy responded to their unified intention, spiraling faster through its metamorphosis. The Eagle consciousness descended more fully, its golden light spreading through the ancient energy pathway like dawn breaking across the Eastern Seaboard.

The shift had taken its next step into the Age of Aquarius.

Chapter 62: Legacy

The setting sun painted the sky in vibrant streaks of orange and pink as Manu and Cassandra stood on the patio of the house that her mother and father had created for them in the Devic Kingdom, just outside of the Seelie Court. They gazed out over a vast expanse of summer flowers and whispering trees. They had managed to carve out three whole days from their duties since the successful completion of the meditation during the Aquarian full moon.

Manu turned to Cassie, squeezing her hand. A gentle breeze tousled her hair as she smiled up at him, her violet eyes shining with love and contentment.

"Well, my darling," she said, "the meditation went off without the raging masses interrupting, no one was abducted, and Soter is still in chains."

He smiled down at her, "Is that all?"

She turned to him and put her arms around his neck, "Weeell ... we *also* managed to raise the ley line frequency into the next octave of Scorpio. To paraphrase one of our former astronauts, the Eagle has risen." Cassie threw back her head and laughed, very proud of her play on words.

She sobered as she looked out over the sunset once more. "I know we still have very large hurdles ahead, but I feel at peace for the first time in a while. Can you believe we've come so far?"

Manu pulled her close, pressing a tender kiss to her forehead. "I couldn't have done it without you by my side. You gave me strength when I faltered, light in the darkness. I love you, forever and always."

"I love you too, with all that I am," Cassandra murmured, leaning into his embrace. She sank into a pensive silence for a few minutes, another sigh escaping from her lips. Then she pulled back slightly, a small frown creasing her brow as she looked out over the horizon.

A spike of worry shot through Manu at her pensive expression. "What is it, my love? Is everything all right?"

"Hmm?" Cassandra glanced back at him, seeming to shake herself out of her thoughts. "Oh, yes, everything's fine. I was just ... thinking."

Manu studied her face intently. "Are you sure? You know you can tell me anything."

Cassandra was quiet for a long moment. Then slowly, almost hesitantly, she took Manu's hand and placed it gently on her stomach. An enigmatic smile played at the corners of her mouth as she gazed up at him from under her lashes. "No, my dear husband. Nothing is wrong at all. Everything is ... perfect."

Manu's eyebrows shot up in surprise as the implication of her words and actions sunk in. "Cassie, are you saying ... are we ...?"

She just smiled and turned back to the view, Manu's arm wrapped around her waist and hand still resting reverently on her belly. The sun dipped below the horizon, and the first evening stars emerged, heralding the start of a new chapter in their immortal lives.

The moment was shattered as a portal opened behind them, and a young man and woman burst through.

Wide-eyed, Cassie and Manu whirled around. Cassie held her hands protectively over her stomach.

The young man and woman appeared to be in their early twenties and were nearly identical except for their hair. The girl had long wavy black hair caught up in a filigreed headband, and the boy's white-blond hair brushed his very broad shoulders. Their violet eyes mirrored Cassie's. Their black leather tunics embroidered in silver with the House of Oberon's crest caught the burgeoning starlight. They looked like pictures of the ancient fae Cassie had seen lining the main gallery of her parents' summer palace.

"Mom! Dad!" the twins cried in unison.

THE END OF BOOK TWO

Also by Rebecca A. Nagy

The Trybrid Chronicles
Phoenix Rising: Initiation
Phoenix Rising Temptation

Watch for more at https://www.rebeccanagyauthor.com/.

About the Author

From the runways of Paris, London, and Milan to supernatural realms beyond the veil, Rebecca's life has been anything but ordinary. She used her vivid imagination during her formative years to write stories to "Dear Diary" about Becky Barbie, a fashion designer who went on fantastical escapades with supernatural beings. Years later, a transformative mystical experience in Paris catalyzed her evolution from fashionista to spiritual guide. As a result, she graduated from Sancta Sophia Seminary and was ordained through Light of Christ Community Church as an Interfaith and metaphysical minister.

Drawing inspiration from Egyptology, ancient aliens, and the Ageless Wisdom Teachings of East and West, prepare yourself for a transformative journey that effortlessly blends fiction, fantasy, and the ageless wisdom as Rebecca leads you through realms of excitement and spiritual illumination.

Rebecca, a modern mystic, lives in Charlotte, North Carolina with her magical feline Gabriel who also appears in her Phoenix Rising tales. When she's not writing or officiating weddings, she's enjoying sushi and spirited discussions with her spiritual family. Immerse yourself in Rebecca's narrative universe, an exhilarating cosmos where curiosity and enlightenment converge, beckoning you to delve into both the daring and the divine.

Read more at https://www.rebeccanagyauthor.com/.

www.ingramcontent.com/pod-product-compliance
Lightning Source LLC
Chambersburg PA
CBHW060610300726
48975CB00005B/1512